TARIA
Forest of Centurion
Kingdom of
Alexandria
Southern Kingdom
of Olderag
THE LAND OF
GRASP

Dear reader,

I am overjoyed to share this world with you, to discover a land of tales thought to be myth, to discover magic governed by barbaric kings. In Grasp, while gladiator-bears duel against one another and witches concoct spells from shimmering brews, some find themselves in a quest for salvation, to be saved from opulent palaces or burnt soil.

The Princess & The Painter is an adaptation of a verbal campfire story I used to tell. And while this story may have fit fine as a children's fairy tale, the world demanded brutality and love with caveats.

I'll cut it short here, and I hope you enjoy this story as much as I did creating it. Thank you for your support!

Caleb J. Gorey

DOGWOOD

THE BLONDE RAPIDS

THE DARK PARTY

FIELD DAY

UNIVERZA

The Princess
& The Painter

CALEB J. GOREY

Table of Contents

Prologue

"How might you see the world now, as I possess your eyes?" A King spat thunder into the hallowed cathedral. "How might you see?" A reverberating tone, one which sat upon silence. A guard could have sworn he saw dust begin to cloud at the foot of the throne. Saliva fell in motes, but all else was still in the vast chamber.

"Holiness…" the stripped man muttered, "Holiness." His plea had no objective, as there was no undoing. His hands fluttered in blood, as if rain found its way through the murals above. Whimpers and crying echoed through the halls, yet the man did so alone. Grand Wizard Joab, standing just behind the King, caught his agitation in the twitch of a raised brow. From the pitch-darkness at one end of the chamber stood one-hundred sword-wielding knights divided to either side of the royally violet carpeted aisle. Then, forty of those who are hidden beneath robes with obscured eyes and are capable of melting stone with the strike of a finger. Ten heavily armored men with nothing but steel-woven gloves over their fists finally stood in the light which cast from the ceiling. A council of those who the folk of this kingdom label the lesser of the *Grand Wizards* and administration, stood behind the King's throne in terraces, and all of whom were entitled to the destruction of this land; they are scarcely seen beyond these walls.

"Sir Zephyr, the King wishes to see, what it is, that you see," Joab instructed. He left his arms out as a storybook would, leaving pale motes shedding from his deep sleeves. In quietness, the man named Zephyr lifted his face, revealing nothing but a garnet-crimson sheen over his face, quivering where his eyes once were.

"Holiness… I see where I once was. A place of beauty and color. Something as…as captivating as the dawn casting on this temple, I cannot recall the hues in which I speak of. So, I repent."

Stillness again, as the King would not even let a hound from the gallows pry his stare from this helpless man.

"In which color, as if mosaic and stained, do I see you?" The King asked but with anger met only by storms. "Boy, tell me!"

"Riverbed," Zephyr interjected the shout. "You see through riverbeds, a color I can no longer describe."

The tension of the King lessened, and he let out steam from his nostrils. The council surrounding the normally ceremonial floor remained silent and awaited a verdict. No light filled the temple but for high glass far above their heads. Though, the overcast day still allowed the blood-pool to glisten. Softly lit, the man Zephyr let himself fall into the shallow red pool.

"Fix him, but taint him, just as he did my impression. Joab, are there any which supersede this man?"

"A boy, and lady Solta. Miss Ambrosia and Leon."

The King did not say a word, and only gestured with his left hand. Joab nodded. It was then that the Grand Wizard then struck up his open palm, casting an iridescent beam lasting but a moment straight at Zephyr. Dust plumed and fell to the blood, and the disgraced man rolled in agony, screaming echoes into the damp halls. Although his eyes were returned, they sat in red swampish pits. Even from a sheen of ruby, Zephyr knew all in which he saw from then on would be tainted. King Olderag had let his eyesight return, after his bout of dismay in response to a gift.

"Granted as such, but your gross expression leads you to a rotten life," spoke Joab as he stalked Zephyr around the blood-pool. "Let it be no mistake that not only am I capable of banishing your eyes from your skull, there is no barrier between the King and your death."

"This painting will be turned to soot and returned to the soil of our busy centers, where thousands will step upon it until the earth is dense, and even the trace of yolk and berry will never dry, never see light," spoke a nobleman named Putrough Salem, a nobleman who stood far taller than any other, with broad shoulders beneath the pelt of a foreign predator. "I stress to you the magnitude of suffering you will live through, that no road will ever be so straight. To have taken the Queen's commission and mistaken the King's tincture can only be declared as invective and blasphemy. Is this not true?"

"Aye," King Olderag grunted. "A *threat* disguised as a gift. Likewise, the coin is not granted." He stopped short and his face fell. The disappointment reigned in his expression. It was evident in his enmity that he there were far more pressing matters. He'd let Zephyr wallow in pain, blind, bleeding, and returned his eyes, but pity fell upon him. Then he spoke low and quiet, "speak then, Sir Solta."

"My King," Zephyr spat out. "Holiness… I shall not make the mistakes I had before. King of the South, Olderag. I give the full spectrum of this world I see once more, as thanks for compassion. " Zephyrs words lessened to a whisper, and he began to pray to hidden gods. Whilst weak, seeing only garnet still, he felt ill as if something else beckoned him.

Following his terror, a low laughter came of the castle. The council watched the red pool expand and thin as it rusted over the stone, drying and staining it. King Olderag flicked his fingers, and his palm rested again. Two black-cloaked knights emerged from the shadow behind the King and lifted Zephyr from his place, whisking him beyond the council to the portcullises just as quickly as this man plead guilty. Then, as the gates sealed themselves again, the council and its jury of civilians turned to the King, awaiting an official verdict for Zephyr's offering.

"Grant your wish for this awful painting, King Olderag," said the Grand Wizard Joab. It only took the King to close his eyelids and his heavy head to nod for the Grand Wizard to act. And, with the separation of Joab's palms, came a white flame which imitated a sudden burst of bright fire that enveloped a framed portrait behind the King. It was paracausal in nature, as only an ordinary flame would just destroy a canvas. Joab caste a condition onto it, one for Zephyr to languish from now, and learn from in time. But the extent of this curse, Zephyr would be unaware.

He would be forced to depart from the barely steaming town of Magberry, a settled community east of the Southern Kingdom of Olderag, though still under his rule. A painter, Zephyr was called for many seasons. The local folk and peasants deemed him worthy of the title, and he'd eventually be asked to paint for the businessmen which surrounded Olderag's castle. It was not Zephyr's original path, for his younger life he would only paint for his wife Ambrosia and son upon request, and they would decorate their walls with his art. In time, the same roots he dug with his fists and traded with, were beaten to pulp and adjusted with sun-bleached petals. It was the dirt, however, which he regularly sorted and traded to grow vegetables and lucky fruit that were less common. The three of him and his wife and child would live off the means of their damp land, and what was traded from their grow. Often, the large shell-roots would be traded for cater meat or sibbers, as the shell-roots were sought after by those herdsmen to feed their stock, less the sibbers as no man owned the brooks.

Zephyr was escorted home with a woolen bag knotted tight over his head, laid over the rump of a horse. It smelt of dung and gravel. He cried knowing Ambrosia would find him in dried blood where townsfolk would see him. Though, he wouldn't need to worry as the velocity and weight of the destrier entering the town could be heard as far as the town's limits, and even the children dreaded hearing those hooves no matter the occasion. They'd all know of his fate in just one tick of the sun. And they learnt to care less of whom was slumped over its' rump, and to just hope it was not of their mothers or children.

Zephyr's boy he named Leon, was stringing up sunfish, one sibber, and a lucky hiddlekin lizard to dry when he felt the ground thump. He looked around, seeing only the smallish hills and surrounding forest north of Magberry. He thought it to be a storm and returned to the fresh-water catch. But he was immediately invalidated as the black horse and its rider appeared through the trees and into the evening light. Then, stopping before the boy and their hut, the white-cloth-masked knight halted the animal, leapt off it, and pulled Zephyr onto the ground. Silent and towering, the knight turned from Zephyr and to the boy. Leon watched the sun split into a thousand pieces against the chain maille. The child's tongue retreated down his throat, and the knights' left arm reached to his side, meeting the resistance of the metal rings. The boy feared to be slaughtered, knowing they could do so without explanation. But there was no sword he saw, for the knight was but a messenger. He instead withdrew a small rope-tied scroll, which he handed to the boy. Still silent, the knight climbed over the horse, taking one last look at Zephyr, and then the boy, and trotted back onto the path in which he came.

"Papa!" the boy cried as he rushed to his father's side, now clear of the messenger's threat. He pulled and pushed his father, getting him onto his side. Leon then pulled off the woolen hood and revealed his father's face. Terror came of the boy as he witnessed the rusted blood rings around his father's eyes. "Mama!"

Then came Ambrosia, nearly stumbling as she ran out of the house. Her brunette curls threw in every which way and her faded blouse danced. She fell to Zephyr's side and saw his arms tied behind his back. "Boy, where is it?" She asked frantically. Leon quickly drew a small stone blade from his pants, which he used to filet the sunfish. She freed Zephyr, letting him freely lay onto his back. He rubbed the dried blood from his face and swiftly embraced his wife and son. "The Kingdom is no place for us; you mustn't dabble with the royals anymore Zephyr!" Ambrosia cried. "*Oh*, my love. Haven't you learned yet of their might? Their *rot*?" She held his face with smallish hands. "Did the King not appreciate it? What happened?"

The man's issue may have not been his dealings with those in the mosaic halls, but that he had been mistakenly guided by the Queen who perhaps knew less details of the King than their love showed in festivals. It was true, and the folk of the villages and inner social communes knew, that Zephyr was a renowned artist. Farmers would frame their lineage in their larger stone houses above live fire, and he'd later be referred to the trading posts. Then taverns, and busier markets. It was an achievement which he'd not fluff up that he was requested to paint the Southern Kingdom's Scribe House's Officer, Mr. Bulpit. The town had gathered for that revealing, which would ultimately find its way from a week's scribe to the Queen's attention.

Ambrosia gathered Zephyr and Leon, shushing Leon to head inside. As Zephyr followed slowly behind the boy, he stopped and faced Ambrosia. Without a word, he shifted his pants until he could retrieve a scroll.

"Olderag's ruling," he said with heavy disappointment. She saw the gloss in his eyes, the pain he was in. Ambrosia took the scroll with a thin, shaking hand and began to read.

8

A PUBLIC DECLARATION FOR KINGDOM BENEFIT

To all who dwell in the Southern Kingdom and its sects and to every eye that looks upon this scroll:

Let it be seen with the seal of King Olderag, true sovereign of the Southern lands and chosen ruler by the grace of the ancient GODS WE INHERIT.

Herein lies the final sentence upon the man known as Zephyr SOLTA of Clope Place, a Man of MAGBERRY, Lady Ambrosia and child, Leon. For grievous acts of defamation.... falsely rendered in both ink and canvas.... against His Majesty, King Olderag, Zephyr's hand has laid upon the image of our sovereign, crafting depictions that twist and tarnish the honorable visage of our beloved King. With colors that mock and strokes that shame, Zephyr has sown deception into the minds of the Kingdom, misrepresenting our ruler in the eyes of both citizen and noble alike.

For this most serious offense, after much counsel and deliberation, it is thus decreed by King Olderag and his Council that Zephyr and his kin be exiled henceforth and in perpetuity. Let no blade of grass, no turn of road, no dwelling, and no face of friend lie within five mils of them in any direction within the bounds of this Kingdom. Their names shall be struck from all records; they are to wander without title, without kin, and without claim to land or belonging.

Should any man, woman, or child offer them aid or allow them sanctuary, they too shall be cast into exile for their defiance of this royal order.

Let this decree be as lasting as the stones of our southern walls, and let all who read or hear of it tremble before the wisdom and wrath of King Olderag. So long as time holds breath, so shall this command endure.

By the will of the Southern Kingdom's council, this scroll bears the solemn mark of the King and the will of the Mor.

Sealed by hand of King Olderag, First of His Name, Sovereign of the Southern Kingdom.

Ambrosia took the scroll and twisted it in one fist, wishing she could force it into a pulp. "They cannot, can they?" She begged in a whisper as to not let the boy hear. "What does this mean? What have you done?" Dirt was dried upon her cheeks, soot fingerprints pressed onto her blouse from cleaning their small hearth.

"Quiet now, my lady. We must be diligent in our leaving. We haven't long."

"Zephyr, you must explain this to me. We abide their laws and we trade within his place, how would he treat his people this way? The Queen commissioned *you*, did you truly disgrace his majesty?"

But the man was silent, unwilling to explain. Her exhaled deeply with his head low, and went on to meet Leon inside their grove-sewn home. Ambrosia grabbed his arm however, and Zephyr fell into a fit and yelled *"They* are earthy!" He spat out. "The Queen's request was faulty! Damn her, for she cursed the painting from the moment I was brought into those walls. The Kings' eyes, I now know, were *not* what she described. Of course he dismissed the gift as insult."

"Zephyr, what must we do?" Her eyes turned glassy and her lip quivered.

"We do what the Council has decided for us," he said sternly, wiping spit from his beard. "We will leave."

"And where to?" Ambrosia tried to unravel the scroll again and flatten it between her palms. "Five mils they say, my lord."

"I will find us a new home. By the serpents' coil, I will build us a better home, one without the rule of that wicked Queen and mad King."

"Zephyr, *oh* Zephyr," she cried once more and embraced him. "Your eyes… what did they do?"

"The Grand Wizard took them from me… as punishment. But…. " he pointed to them, "Joab the wizard took them… and gave them back spoiled. Though, I see your beauty still and for that, I'm so grateful." He spoke almost with humor, but quickly realized she wanted none of it. Then he embraced her. "I was fooled. For no cause…. I was fooled," he spoke softly into her lakebed hair. Zephyr held her off of him. "But as we come from the earth, we will make do with it. Come night, I will consult these lands, and I will find our new place. We've still got the map, yes? Okay… I suspect we have till sun is high and come morrow, pray we are graced with time. We shall leave soon before then, but tonight we must gather ourselves in preparation."

As if forest critters undid their homestead of a river, Ambrosia cried. She went beyond Zephyr and joined their son inside, leaving the man alone. He wiped his face again, flinging broken grass blades and pollen from his cheeks and beard.

Turning towards his home, he saw his ending chapters. The stone and mud he laid many years ago had harbored moss, and steam rolled from the chimney down onto the straw roof. Few wooden frames and stretched poplar leaned against the hut, mocking him. In flashes he saw the only door, wood strung together and sat on a thin stone pillar, become the large heavy gate of castle he was sworn out of. Their home, a dainty creation, then a devilish throne world. Zephyr quickly grew even more angry than before. The King's Hall was burned into his vision. And although he wished for revenge, for the overruling of that governance, he had created a fire but could only find twigs. Thus, he saw it die out. A hoverfly crushed by a wooly boar.

The house of Solta was damp like all the other huts scarcely dotted across the hills surrounding the Southern Kingdom, all slowly sliding back into the earth. Magberry was even more so, in the belly of higher hills where the ground had long ago sunk to mud. Straw was densely packed in bushels over each ceramic-tiled roof. Steam poured and curled from the chute of stone chimneys, often clouding the fields where caters trudged along like sheep.

Each home captured the heat of the day and left the residents wiping salt from their cheeks. Some, such as Zephyr and a decrepit grain harvester named Bolin, would refer to these lands as the Furrow Hills, or the name donned by the Council and recognized by the Empire, Magberry. Purchased from the Kingdom on its' three-hundredth session of governance, Zephyr acquired his own square plot. He only decided to do so once his father had passed. The tailor and his wife birthed him within the densely populated central square, but he yearned for more than the cobblestone streets. Trade between him and Bolin was quite personal and less calculated, though the distance between each house required a horse if it was not war-time and one or the other could obtain one.

This man had a companion, Zephyr did. Not the harvester Bolin, but an equal in stature who would aid Zephyr in finding those to trade with in the inner-towns. Often times, he would also source businesses who might like a portrait to establish their lineage. He was called Jeffrey Flemeth, and much of the Kingdom knew him to be very good at his profession.

"You bargain as if I do not have a choice," a wildly renowned Grand Wizard of Fester once told Jeffrey in a festival, loud enough to spread the word that he, although young and with the mustache of a jester, knew what you wanted, and knew how to get you to buy it. Once Zephyr established himself as a painter, Jeffrey helped earn him commissions. Typical seasons had Zephyr and Jeffrey raising enough coin in a fortnight to last until the following spring, with spare for the alehouse. Though, Zephyr and the rest of the tradesmen of the Furrow Hills, or Magberry, had thrived off their own harvest and each others most years.

Come evening, the heat trapped inside the Solta's home begun to build up. The night brought the sweet notes of vanilla and barley from a neighboring homestead, clouding their tight homely space. But Zephyr did not eat the stew Ambrosia made, and she did not stay out in the firelight out of anger for too long. She and Leon retreated to their cots after an exhausting and irritated dispute. The boy had many questions that his mother refused to answer, and nor could she if she even had the words.

"We will depart before midday," she last told him, pulling a wool cover over him. "Your father has arranged it. You mustn't worry, boy." Ambrosia parted his hair from his forehead and kissed between his eyes. "We don't worry, do we?"

"We don't," Leon said. He turned and faced the cooler air which poured between his body and a framed opening in the wall. The air of the fields could not hold the heat as their hut could, and he found comfort in feeling it the coolness.

"The season is changing soon," Leon whispered. "I can smell it."

His mother smiled, kissing him one last time on his shoulder. A trembling smile came of her, and a sting pierced her eye. Their place would no longer be, and Ambrosia had the hull of her chest collapse as she left Leon to sleep. She went into the only sectioned-off bedroom in the hut, closing a hanging sheet of linen behind her. Zephyr entered shortly after, finally just simmering from his self-loathing feud outside. Leon flinched in his bed once he heard his father's two heavy feet strike the wooden-plank floor. Just two steps. Then two more. Then Zephyrs silhouette eclipsed the firelight blazing in the hearth. He stood for a moment, once looking at the small flames, and then at his son. The floors creaked as Zephyr began to take another step towards his final place beside Ambrosia, but he was immediately halted by the small voice of the boy.

"Papa," he said from his cocoon of blankets.

"Yes, boy." He awaited Leon's concerns, knowing he'd struggle to explain tomorrow's move.

"Could you read a story?"

"Leon, we have a busy morning. You should rest," he groaned, but approached the cot anyways, sitting besides the back of the boy. "I will need your help with the dry-racks. We'll stay along stream, we'll be living off it for…"

"Papa…"

"A story then?"

"Not the one of the sky-garden, or the horned-mutt."

Zephyr got up from the bed and searched beneath it. He pulled a wicker-box out and looked at each leather-bound parcel. He presented one to Leon.

"We've read each one. I thought I'd have many years' worth. This, I believe is the last. *A Mole's Republic.* Good?"

"Good," the boy smiled.

Zephyr opened the small book, separating the waxy pages that may have never been opened before. It was a short story, nearly ancient, and the author was since flattened to the leather from its previous travels. He began to read.

A bustling realm of darkened halls and glittering caverns, where the moles lived in unity and toil. Their land was rich with roots and worms, mushrooms that glowed like candles, and the sweetest tubers, which they called earth apples.

Now the moles, though small and blind to the sunlit world, were clever as foxes and nimble as weasels. They fashioned their burrows with cunning traps and winding mazes, for the predators of the surface... wls, foxes, and snakes... ever hungered for the treasures of the Republic.

The ruler of the moles was not a king but a council of the eldest and wisest among them. The High Burrowers, as they were called, gathered beneath a root-carved arch in the Great Hall to decide the fate of the Republic.

One dark eve, as whispers of danger spread through the tunnels, the High Burrowers met to discuss a troubling matter. A hawk, fierce and golden-eyed, had discovered the entrances to their burrows and had taken to snatching moles as they foraged near the surface.

"We must act swiftly," declared Elder Wormtooth, his whiskers quivering. "If this hawk be not thwarted, we shall starve, for none will dare to gather food!"

"Let us seal the burrows and bar all exits!" cried Elder Rootclaw. "Better to be safe within than to risk the talons above!"

And so, it was decreed. The moles labored night and day to close every tunnel leading to the surface, crafting a fortress of earth to protect their kind.

At first, the moles rejoiced. "We are safe!" they cheered, digging deeper into the earth to uncover hidden stores of food. The Republic grew fat and merry, for no hawk nor fox could reach them now. They held a grand feast, lighting the halls with glowworms and singing songs of their triumph.

But as seasons passed, the moles began to notice strange happenings. The mushrooms withered without the faint light of the sun trickling through the soil. The roots turned bitter, and the worms grew scarce. The air became heavy, and their once-bright caverns grew dim and cold.

One day, a mole named Grimbold, who had wandered far and dared to peek beyond the barricades, returned with a warning. "Elders, hear me!" he cried, his coat matted with dirt. "The land above thrives with life! The rains have softened the earth, and roots and worms abound! If we do not venture out, we shall perish!"

But the High Burrowers, proud of their great wall of safety, dismissed him. "The surface is treacherous," they scoffed. "We shall not risk the hawk's wrath for the whims of a fool!"

Grimbold, disheartened but determined, left the Republic, digging his own secret tunnel to the surface.

Soon, famine gripped the moles. With no fresh food and stale air to breathe, their once-thriving community grew weak. Desperation drove them to dig blindly for food, and their frenzied claws caused the ground above to collapse. The hawk, ever watchful, saw the great mounds of disturbed earth and pounced with fury.

The moles, now exposed, scattered in terror. Their walls, meant to keep the world out, had become their undoing, for they had cut themselves off from life itself.

As the hawk feasted and the Republic fell to ruin, Grimbold watched from afar. Saddened by his kin's fate, he gathered the survivors and spoke thus:

"Safety sought without wisdom leads to folly. In fearing the hawk, the Republic neglected to see that life is a balance of risk and reward. The roots of the earth grow strong only because they stretch toward the sun. We must do the same."

And so, the moles rebuilt their lives, not as a closed Republic, but as a community that dared to tread the surface while honoring the depths below.

The young boy was asleep midway, but Zephyr still read until the end. Once he had, he closed the book and pressed its' leather boundments together, leaving it in the basket beneath Leon's bed He heard just breath in the silence of their home, but not for the periodic ticking of whisperwasps ending their day and sunglints concluding their buzzing songs.

Disgruntled, he sighed and pressed back his long brown hair, then fiddled with his graying beard. Footsteps were heard out of a window, and an aggressive knock rung against the wood. Zephyr quickly ran to the door to shush whoever it may be, but to his surprise Jeffrey stood there panicked.

"*Ambrosia and the boy are sleeping, why are you wailing on our door?* Haven't you any idea what hour it is?" He barked under his breath like a snake would hiss.

"What future is left for *you* is awfully mangled and difficult to envision, my dear friend. Hell, you look like you're in need of a pint!" Jeffrey Flemeth was humorous in the wake of grief.

"We're leaving come dawn; I've no time for ale, less the headache of it." Zephyr joined him outside to prevent Leon from waking up. "They're bastards, the whole of 'em. The Queen *herself* declared every facet, and she didn't know the color of his eyes! And *I* am punished? What have I done to deserve this putrid fate?"

"My friend, eyes are but diamond and bedrock, at least the Mor say in their scribe. They cannot be mistaken; there is no instance you'd have known. You only had her word. But likewise, we're the dirt of the Kingdom, expendable."

"Aye, perhaps we've overstayed our welcome anyhow," Zephyr tried to reason with himself. "Each summer has scorched our harvest, more so than the last. Even Olderag's festivals have come scarce, and famine worse. Maybe we're bound to leave. Jeffrey, would you join at dawn?"

"Leave?" He exclaimed and chuckled. "I can't. Fiona's earned her place as chandler in the Berra."

"The Berra? God, she's quite prestigious then. You'd think the sunglints honeycombs had run dry. Give her my good graces."

It was as if he'd seen his end settled in this place, foraging and growing without issue and glutton with vibrancy. Then, he was fooled by the governance and all of a sudden, the end-place was no longer. Zephyr later left Jeffrey and returned to Leon, lay back across the child's legs and staring tiredly at the bounded straw above. He hadn't a plan, other than to leave as Olderag gave no other option, but he devised to take a last piece of the Southern Kingdom with them on their move. For, it was the least he could do for Leon. For Ambrosia, he could only make thin promises.

The sun hadn't even peaked yet when Zephyr had risen from the arms of Ambrosia. Armed with nothing but degora pelt over his shoulders and his freshly washed trousers she had dealt with two days prior. She did not wake, for not even a crack in the earth could drag her from cratered dreams. He did not bother her yet, and set out to retrieve one last remembrance of home not for him or Ambrosia, but the boy.

It was first Bolin he met, but at a great distance from across their churned fields. Several plots away they caught each others gaze and waved. Zephyr chuckled once he saw the old man kick an escaped cater back towards its' pen. That bug was still a pup, yet as large as a fat pig. It waddled back and the distant yell of

Bolin echoed against the distant valley walls. The old man always struggled these days getting them wrangled.

The bright yellow of the sky nearly lapsed once Zephyr finally reached the place he'd been looking for. Not too far between the Hides and East March of the Kingdom, where the busier farmers' markets met the first general stores and stacked, crumbling homes. There were few folk roaming around, mostly store-owners setting up shop or readying their wooden carts for trade. Others were likely wandering and without a home. They stunk of pruned slug, a product which King Olderag once deemed medicinal to treat aches, and now forbidden as it made folk feel a bit *too* well.

It was the town of Duckwipper in which he stumbled into, but was far more familiar with than he'd tell any decent person. It was the foot of the Kingdom, incredibly dense with no space between brick infrastructure. Years-old banners from prior festivals were beaten to pulp into the mud, and the mud itself had nearly consumed all the road. Down one of the cleaner cobblestone paths between a cathedral and a row of masonry with homes atop, Zephyr made his way through. He glanced upward at exhausted smoke pouring from chimneys onto roofs and settling back onto the streets.

In the quiet of Duckwipper came a muffled disturbance, that of a… fight. Zephyr looked behind himself and then forth. It came from inside one of these storefronts, though he could not decipher which one. Though brutal in appearance, with his ragged beard and tense muscles, he still clutched the pelt over his bare skin as if afraid it would be stolen. He continued on until he found the small center with a dried-up fountain and a decrepit robed woman bathing her feet in its' settled green sludge. Further yelling came from one of the buildings on the leftward corner, which stood-out with its old marbled exterior, tall skinny windows, and bronze piping leading to its metal sign. It was the Library of Bixby, the only archive of books in the East March of this Kingdom, unlike the deeper plazas which harbored three libraries. Before Zephyr could even pass the lady scrubbing her toes in the fountain, the heavy doors of the library burst open.

STOP! STOP WOMAN!

Just as quick as those doors flew apart, a smallish figure draped in a black cloak sprinted away and down the cobbled alley to the left. A pot-bellied man donning a ruby-colored coat and unbuttoned trousers came stumbling out of the library waving his fist.

"You get back here, child!" He yelled to no avail. She was gone through the steam, and the fat man readjusted his glasses and shook his head. "The children of this village are no better than rats, I tell ya."

Zephyr thought first to chase after the girl, but as he took his first steps he realized he would never be quick enough. He joined the fat man to possibly assist him. "What's she done, sir?"

"Well I… I haven't a clue yet," the man scratched his head. He looked back at the library front. "I was just lighting the lamps and there she was! Picking away at the shelves. Surely she'd taken one of my *Codex of Serezona* or… or perhaps a copy of *Field Day Guide*. The children…the rats they are… they've tried taking these for the metal in the bindings you see. They melt 'em down and sell as scrap. *Hah!* If only they knew of the demand for such copies. They could simply purchase the Guide and immediately sell it for more!" He then angled his arm towards Zephyr and clasped his hand to his. "You won't catch her, but I'm glad someone's here to witness this… this gross display."

"Well, Duckwipper is not for the lighthearted, I must say" Zephyr said with a grin. "Zephyr, sir."

"Ron," the librarian said while his eyes drifted upwards. "Ron Bixby."

Zephyr was quick to keep him upright. "Let's get you right again," he told Ron, walking him slowly into the library.

"They know I can't run after them like I used to. I need to consult with the Gerald down the way. I need me a… a grandiose lock and bolt!"

They sat on separate leather settees, ones so packed with down that they may never stand up again. Zephyr had been in this library two times before, and yet he never formally met this man, which he presumed to be the librarian. Though, the first visit was when his father walked him through many years ago to find a scribe for seasonal harvesting, one for beans and other legumes as the whisperwasps seemed to distance themselves from those. His second visit was when Leon was still a small toddler. He wanted to buy his first book, for he hadn't any from his own childhood to provide. But the books were far too expensive, although much cheaper than what libraries in the Center would offer, especially Thillwood the nearest to the castle. *That* library required permission from the State Clerk and a ticket as proof of coin.

"Where did you find that woman?" he asked the librarian, who then pointed over Zephyr's shoulder. He peered back and saw the hundred-shelf bookcase built into the brick wall. At eye-level were black-cloth-bound books with golden embossed titles on their spines. They all were orderly and none seemed out of place. Below them were a series of codex, same with above. Zephyr looked at the other shelves, and the whole assortment did not seem out of place. "You're sure she'd taken anything? It all looks proper."

"I may have caught her before she could. Them children of the March are nothin' but cats when a real threat comes at 'em. Think they can nab whenever they damned please. Then I shout just once and they're gone. Easily spooked, them kids."

Zephyr could only nod as Ron Bixby spiraled into nonsensical stories about how he'd never leave a closed market without goods when he was a boy. His eyes wandered from the librarian at the vast collections he had stored in the walls. Amber lights illuminated a vaulted ceiling with beams running to each pitch.

"I was coming here this dawn, as I am leaving the soon. I wanted to find a story for my child. Would you mind if I looked? I see you haven't even lit your lamps," Zephyr asked, narrowly interjecting Bixby's rambling.

"Children's books? Come on with me," he spoke, but struggled to lift himself from the cushions. Zephyr helped him by the forearm until the man's knees finally locked straight. Bixby then waddled in slow cadence towards the fanciful collection of codex. He pulled a match from the chest pocket of his woolen shirt, struck it against the brick, and lit a lamp mounted in the crevice of two walls. One of the walls to the left of the collection was a smallish shelf which would typically be hidden from plain view. Just a fuss-wide, with pocket-sized books leaning against one another. "We haven't much, I rarely get any with the season's carts. The March-folk love their apothecaries and Invetia. Whatever is easier than school or permits. Gods forbid they read their child a book," he mumbled in a low and reverberating voice. Bixby laid his dense palm on Zephyr's shoulder. "Take a few. They're better with you than to mold at my feet."

"You're a kind man, Mister Bixby. I will only take one."

But the librarian saw Zephyr's heavily stained and otherwise grossly tattered garments, then the glisten of the poor man's eyes as his face could barely muster a genuine smile.

"Take a few," he said with a smile. Then he saw a bit of warmth in Zephyr's face.

Ron Bixby waddled back into the depths of the library, with more lamps coming to life. Zephyr sorted through the small books with his ride shoulder pressed against the codex. He couldn't pick just any story, and most were ordinary and already recited from memory when Leon was younger. He often acquired storybooks from Bolin or other neighbors once their own children and grand children were grown. He found one at the very bottom which was just one thin board above the floor. A red book, skinny. It was of square form and entirely cloth-bound. In white curling letters it read *Bitter Time Lullabies* by Gretchen Terrif. A bit of a hole formed in his stomach, fully realizing that even the oil-lathered and gravel-coated folk of the March understood their place beneath the Kingdom of Olderag. A never-ending period of hollow cheeks and swollen eyes all lived here, yet even his father, Peter Solta, never would explain such customs, but perhaps he never saw it.

Zephyr as a boy would be carried over his fathers shoulders throughout these interconnecting villages, stopping in crowds to catch glimpses of wizards snapping their fingers into flames and pulling out flowers for little girls and elders. Their use of glimmercraft always amused him. He and his father had many great friends among the kingdom's lower sects, like Gered Ziptool of the Hilly Tavern, or Bill Godfrey, the peculiar fellow who seemed to be more alike the mischievous children than the middle-aged smith he was. But it was since Zephyr met Ambrosia and truly grew into his roots just outside the Eastern March that he found less and less time to meet with such friends. Zephyr took the red book underneath his arm and grabbed a second which originally leaned against it. *Codex Univerza* it read in a rosy bronze lettering, and quite strangely without an author. It was of blackened leather and similarly small. He turned the cover and saw no words but for an inky illustration which appeared to be a woman. "This is no child's book," he muttered, but before he could bend to place it back at the bottom, Ron Bixby called to him.

"Sir Zephyr!" The man called from behind a ladder. "Please, oh, please close the doors on your way out. My lamps keep dying."

"Right away Mr. Bixby," he said and rushed towards the entrance. "Mr. Bixby?" Zephyr looked back at the old man, who was holding his pelt pinned to his chest. "My son thanks you." The librarian shot a grin and a nod to Zephyr, and the two had gone their separate ways. However outside the library, Zephyr peered down the steaming alleyway and wondered where the supposed thief had gone. Surely they'd tuck themselves into a nook between storefronts, or climbed atop the roofs. He figured he could wander down there, but found he hadn't much time to return home.

Zephyr returned back to Ambrosia and Leon with two storybooks beneath his arm and nothing else. With the day short and his exile so immediate, he did not need to trade for any additional food for their journey. They'd find it along the way. Even so, Leon could be sent to Bolin for bottled goods before their departure. But the mother and son were already prepared to leave. Smoke plumed from the stone pillar protruding from the huts' side. From the front door came Ambrosia with the boy at her side. Her hair was that of wool, tangled with its millions of tiny rings painted gold of the morning. A densely woven sack hung over each glass shoulder while Leon carried another over his back. They stood quietly against the light which cascaded over the farmlands and onto the neighboring homes. It was all dampened earth, dark, spotted with tiny stones and hilly with rows. A distant stack of smoke came from the neighboring hut which belong to the elderly Miss Pari, who the Solta's never formally met. It was then that Zephyr realized he couldn't speak, just as he couldn't see before. Even a stranger he would miss, the routine of routes he'd follow when trading. Even more so, he'd never pass by one of his paintings framed in different storefronts. They would soon be burned, and he did not want to see it through.

His tongue had not vanished as the Grand Wizard beneath Olderag would have wished, but his mouth and lungs were still paralyzed. He went to his wife and child and planted his gentle palm under the chin of Ambrosia, then the other on top of Leon's head. He took one last glance at the home they'd begun at, then at the distant spears of haze beyond the hills which inevitably stemmed from the Southern Kingdom. Together, they bid their farewell to Magberry.

1. The Fulsie Inn

Jeffrey lingered with the usual drunkards in the Fulsie Inn's underbelly, located in the center-west sect of the Kingdom named the Greater Hillup. It was there in the damp underbelly of the inn that he and others felt safe enough to speak rubbish of King Olderag and his tyrannical wizard council. If they'd spoken this way in the streets, and a guard overheard, every last one of them would be dissected, burned, silenced.

There *were* many such occasions where a starving but otherwise upstanding man or woman did have enough of the rations, enough of the recycled goods, that they'd yell and spit at the guards and officials. Likewise, from outside the spiked and thorny Castle of Deletaria screams could be heard of punished folk, with their teeth turned to shattered glass and skin seared. Then…quietness came, as these offenders' pain would be undone and their punishments reverse. The Grand Wizard Joab simply sought to show them what he and the council were capable of, with centuries-long support of the King, all unchecked.

"Zephyr told of their use of Invetia," Jeffrey said with a growl, sweat darkening the scales of his vest. "Such heinous punishments cannot be just the spells of governing magic. The council continues to abuse the same power they want deem too dangerous for us to wield! *Governing magic,*" he scoffed then. "Order for the many, ordered by full bellies."

"*Ay!* I've heard far too many a tale of their torturous dealings," spoke a bony old rider named George Ada. He still holds medals for his young ventures in the joist, less the sling. "We all mustn't forget the early end they brought to Mr. Gordon and his Mrs. *For we are forever grateful in their trade with Krythia.*"

Some bowed their heads in shared grief, but a younger woman, rough in the teeth and knuckles, yet thin and dainty, chuckled at them. Her name was Sabbath, an orphan who once roamed the streets until the elder Dorian Fulsie who owned the inn gave her shelter and inevitably became her carer until his death a few seasons prior. Now ,she'd grown into her edgy roots and could bark when she threw fists, not one or the other. "I doubt Krythia even exists any longer. That's what the butchers in the Eastern March have been grumblin' about, that no tradesmen or riders have come or return this season. I hear Olderag's sent mercenaries!"

"*Hmf,* enough Sabbath," George ordered. "I suppose that isn't no good if Sir Solta is headed there. He isn't, is he?"

Jeffrey shook his head and leaned back onto the mossy wall. He exhaled deeply and gestured to another shadowed figure, who handed him a wooden pipe. "I haven't a clue. Zephyr did not speak of any destination. I anticipate he'll send letters, but that man is too quaint in his energy. He'll fit just fine on any plot of soil; he'll make do."

"You won't go after him? What about Ambrosia, that *sweet…sweet* Ambrosia?" George questioned with a mischievous tang. In response, the shadowed man whose head was hidden behind smoke threw a pebble at him to shut him up. It struck him in one of his last front teeth and Jeffrey snorted smoke out his nostrils as the dark room erupted in laughter.

"Settle now, settle," Jeffrey declared and quieted the bunch. The smoky haze above the table danced in rhythm with the oil lamp's flicker, the inn's mildew-slick walls seeming to lean closer, listening.

Miss Sabbath spat into the fire grate and crossed her arms. "Still don't see why you sit here preachin' if you've no plans to act."

"Watch yourself, girl," murmured the shadowed man who had thrown the pebble, now leaning forward into the firelight for only a moment…. just enough to see the faded mark on his jaw: a hunter's brand from the Old Vale. His name was Sir Blackmere, and no one in the room dared say it unless drunk or foolish. Although he was the less frequent visitor of the inn, his presence was no less heavy, and none of the others truly knew where he did his business or… really wherever he belonged to. Tonight, no one was drunk enough. He received the pipe back from Jeffrey. "Listen to him very closely."

"I speak for them who can't," Jeffrey said lowly, puffing his pipe with brief, precise pulls. "And I act for those who must never be seen. Zephyr will live on, I assure you all. And their boy will one day be just as celebrated. But the council's actions cannot go on.…" his words stopped abruptly when a heavy door slammed on the floor above them. Then… a series of weighty footsteps came slowly around. They reached the stairwell, which wasn't particularly easy to find through the layers of banners strung across the inn's banisters. But Jeffrey nor the others expected any more guests. A typical Street Guard descended, emerald swatches marking him of the Eastern March.

"Far away from his turf," George muttered. He stood up to face the guard. "You've stumbled into the pit of despair, my friend! What brings you here?" He asked rhetorically. But George was swiftly seated once he'd seen the two tall knights follow behind the guard. Each had drawn their swords and ordered compliance among the underbelly dwellers, yet Jeffrey still puffed smoke from his nostrils. He only choked when a final figure came into the firelight. Sabbath gasped as the Grand Wizard Joab appeared, menace buried beneath his long and pointed white beard.

"I think you are all mistaken," Jeffrey finally nonchalantly said with a grin. "What do you want with old swamp-rags like us? We're just chatting, ain't we?" A knight fixed his sword just inches away from Jeffrey's throat.

The guard approached him beside the blade. "Your 'chatting' is a great play whilst un-taxed pints are served beneath the floors. Likewise, *we* will do the talking."

"Or I," said Joab, who used a force of viridescent lightning to strike the guard, sending him in one shout to the floor. The Grand Wizard walked slowly toward Jeffrey, his feet hidden beneath his long indigo robes. "I care less of what lager has seeped through the floorboards, even less that the curfew of Hillup has come to pass. But what's bothered myself and the interests of Olderag are the ramblings which leave this gods-forsaken cellar. *Insults*," he spat. "*Rebellion*." Joab's nose twitched as he seemed to have smelt Jeffrey's fear, fear of that emerald glow emanating from the Great Wizard's palm. "The council is far more rewarding to… early confessions."

Jeffrey snarled at him. "I only speak poorly; there are no special cases."

Joab struck him down with a cracking bolt of green light. George, Sabbath, and the other shadowed folk scurried away behind chairs or wherever they could. The knights too seemed startled, as both jumped back and then forward to ready their swords for any potential fight.

"Then I am afraid you will face trial," Joab said with a low rasp. "But I promise you, *I'll ensure it is fair.*"

One knight lifted Jeffrey as he grunted in pain, whisking him away up the staircase as Joab followed. The second knight looked to the guard whose wide eyes shared the same terror that George and the others felt. They could only sense that the knight, behind his great helmet, did too. But they scurried up the stairs quickly, knowing they couldn't stray.

A silence followed, this one heavier than the rest. Somewhere behind the walls, a distant dog howled, or perhaps it was the scream of another punished soul wafting from Deletaria's spires. Soon to be Jeffrey's, Sabbath thought. It mattered little.

"Zephyr was last seen near the Weeping Bramble," Sir Blackmere muttered then, cracking the room's hush. "A courier brought word three nights past. They've packed light, he said."

George's gaze lifted, and the weight behind his eyes darkened. "You sure? But what can we do about Joab and his council? We cannot live under this rule. I suggest we leave!"

"As sure as I am that we won't live long if we keep meeting like this. I too suggest our leave."

"But why would they head west? The Bramble is a thieves den. Ambrosia would never let Zephyr drag them there, no matter how convenient," Sabbath said, almost to herself. "The Riven Tree Grotto was bloodbath, and I could never visit the Bramble even in the daytime for just a moment!"

George groaned and leaned back on his stool. "Don't speak of the Riven Tree. Just don't. The roots are still cursed.... I don't care what the crows say."

"The crows warn," Miss Sabbath grinned. "He's no better there, and if he'd known where Jeffrey's headed now, I'm certain he'd return."

"Like all of the Kingdom, we know too well of the conditions of exile. He won't return, even for a second commission from the Queen."

At that, the fire dimmed for a moment, like a lung exhaling its last warmth. And from the rafters above came a single thump. Light. Hollow.

George and Sabbath were on their feet in seconds, weapons half-drawn. Sabbath's a curved dagger, George's a narrow-bladed fang sword he'd hidden in the leg of his trousers. Everyone else froze, even Blackmere. Only the fire moved. Then from above came a low voice… smooth, amused, and unmistakably touched with arrogance. Blackmere stood up then in silence, and left the underbelly just as Joab and his party did, for he wanted no part. Sabbath looked to the old George, nodding as both departed soon after a final pint.

The two later stood in the darkness outside the Fulsie Inn. Sabbath's young head swayed drunkenly. "We must see the council in Taria, I don't see any other way."

"I know, young Sabbath. We can't just sit here and await our turn for the gauntlet. But I fear the highest echelon of wizardry may be just as sick. I can't guarantee they won't torch us upon arrival."

"But surely they hold a greater capacity for reason, *surely*."

2. The Cuepo Landing

The world was not nearly awake yet. The Solta family had traveled on foot beginning northward from Olderag's Southern Kingdom. The foothills were entirely cobalt, as it would rain once the day caught on. Ambrosia raged over their exile, first turning her fury on Zephyr.. Then, just as quickly as she'd erupt, she'd go on silently, extinguished. Though, so were the coals which had just begin to collect dust in the hearth of their old home and their parcel soon to be claimed by Olderag.

"Can I know where we're headed Papa?" Leon asked as he pranced about, not nearly as tired as the father and mother.

"It's a secret," Zephyr told him with confidence. He couldn't admit it, but he hadn't a clue. Though, he *did* know of a nearby settlement northwest of Magberry. Ambrosia's brow furrowed as she realized their destination. A fairly recently formed village, one where wealthier tradesmen stopped for rest between the Kingdom of Alexandria and the Southern Kingdom. Strung at a wooden post was the gold-painted letters which spelled *Cuepo*, a landing for those who were the blood in the veins of the Mor Empire. In any of Cuepo's three inns and two taverns would be fat men, barely taking ten steps from their four steads to reach a glass of mead.

"We're really going to Cuepo?" Ambrosia finally asked as their knees grew sore and sun began its climb. "We haven't the coin for any business there."

"No, but we may find charity. Even if not, I'd rather us sleep in a groomed burrow than the forest."

"What's that?" Leon asked innocently. "Is it a festival?"

"No love, it's a village. A *prestigious* one at that," she said with a disapproving stare at Zephyr. He decided the rile up the child and piss of Ambrosia further.

"The tradesmen aren't so polished, but even more rough are the *hunters*," he said with a grin. "They're great and tall, far bigger than your Papa. But they're scary too… necks stained with blood of their recent kill. And their *kill* are not always wild sheepboars, or any farmed cater. They wear the pelts and scales of beasts so foreign, they'll make you pray you'll never see any alive!"

Ambrosia slapped the back of him, cursing him to stop. And he did, quickly assuring the boy that it was not so dangerous, nor as prestigious as Ambrosia made it out to seem.

"I'm only telling fairy-tale, boy. It's a safe place. The safest place we can be right now."

After a third hour, the weight of their baskets wore them out. The Solta's decided to rest, and it was near midday. The had found a shaded area off the dirt road where a grandiose weeping willow sat in a vast field of bent-over grass. Five carriages had passed them in both directions, some heading onward to Cuepo while others brought beans and fruit to the Southern Kingdom. Zephyr felt the burden of his sentencing then, and he struggled to find anything positive to say. Ambrosia saw his heavy head and decided to tell Leon of Zephyr's great artistry.

"Your father's portraits were so renowned among the villages, I don't doubt we'll see one at some inn in Cuepo. I remember seeing the portrait of Mr. Bulpit at the Scribe House. It was magnificent. We'd walk some days, before you were born, and see each painting meticulously fixed to the innards of each market, office, *even* the eastern Deletaria watchtower. I believe it was the nobleman Zachary Gahhar."

But those days were torn apart now. The folk of all interconnected villages began to recognize the name which stained the posts the Kingdom had strung up. Despite never developing a closeness with Sabbath, George, or any of the others, Jeffrey had made Zephyr known. On occasion they all would drink, but he often kept to Ambrosia, Leon, and their stead. Regardless of his focused life, he was loved by those who commissioned him, and maintained a respected reputation.

Zephyr led them further in the building heat, and they made headway towards the nearest nomadic residents whose tall tents and grazing horses marked the outskirts of the greater village. They then met the slightly flamboyant and busy new village of Cuepo. The lavishly adorned tradesmen had their swords pressed to their hips. They were not simply ambassadors between the various kingdoms, but the greatest at what they did. The Soltas found momentary refuge in a grotto just outside one buzzing inn where they could spread their belongings and allow for Zephyr to go about the Cuepo and concoct a more permanent plan.

Ambrosia tried to keep Leon in the shade with her, but failed once he spotted a group of children passing around a sling and seeing how far each could launch a stone. In her lonesome, she retrieved a drying rack and anticipated Zephyr would find a brook and catch their dinner. In pressing the wooden rods together into form, she stopped to a violent cough, spitting bile onto the dirt. She did not feel ill, and thought the heat and energy spent had boiled her stomach. So she left the unfinished rack and let herself lay back and wait for Zephyr to return.

Zephyr sought out whatever ordinary folk he could find in the single brothel and two of the three inns. But in all his determination, he was surprised to find himself catching donated ales from generous jesters and generals, jokes and stories from heavy-voiced hunters, even a kiss on the cheek from a beautiful, yet elderly, server.

He was able to find calm in the third inn, aptly named the *Third Sister*. Despite much of the settlement being fairly recently constructed, he felt a warmth and liveliness that did not exist in Magberry, even lesser the richest sects of the Southern Kingdom. The Third Sister was slightly smaller than the other two, yet it excelled in its welcome to guests with more luxurious furniture, celebratory banners dating to consecutive seasons of festival game winnings. Zephyr even saw a beautiful young woman who despite her tattered garments, dancing elegantly with coils of her brass hair swinging atop her shoulders. It took the might of his situation to snap him out of the trance.

It was in the corner near a tabletop where a busty server held two full pints foaming onto her knuckles, that Zephyr found a place to sit. A leather-bound stool beneath a portrait *not* of his own claim. It was of an old gentleman whose mustache drooped over a small organized frown. Zephyr looked throughout the place and wondered who may be of good information, a place to reside, perhaps indefinitely. The ceiling was of dark timber with floating oil lamps hovering overhead in scattered formation. The floor was an equal timber, but the walls were of a pale blue and maroon ornate design, and he traced the tiny diamond-shapes and lines until he'd gotten dizzy.

A hearty man who regularly attended the morris table games, coated with a thick smoke in his white beard, sat beside Zephyr. He was grateful he didn't need to search any further, but he was skeptical if this gentleman could offer him anything.

"You don't fit the day here in Cuepo," he said in a hoof of a voice.

The busty server from before approached the two and asked what they'd prefer. But before Zephyr could send her off, as he hadn't any coin to spare, the man only nodded and she went to the barrel.

"Just passing through. Why do you sat that? I haven't even a weapon to look threatening," Zephyr joked, and to his surprise, the man laughed. His big belly quaked beneath a black wool tunic.

His shoulders were padded with even blacker scaly leather. His eyes were deep and all of his face below his nose was buried beneath a dense brown beard. He was a *hunter*, evident by old scars lining his forearms and cheek.

"I see no threat, but you seem out of place. The mrs. felt scared, perhaps you look threatening to her!"

Zephyr looked beyond him at a high-table occupied by three puffy-dressed women with high hair. The server then returned with overfilled glass mugs, and the man quickly began to chug. On his exhale, "I don't often see strangers come here, perhaps the brothel across the way, but not here." His voice turned to a low gurgle. "You're looking for something. Someone?"

"No… no. Not anybody, for there's not a soul more important than my dearests."

"Then was it?" The man whispered. "Treasure? The jewels off our wrists? You're a thief, aren't ya?"

"Not at all! I… I'm in search of a new home. But I haven't much of a clue of where else. You see I…. "

"Save yourself the words, I can barely hear over the barley! A new home then… well our lovely Cuepo is but a station for rest. I don't think you'll find much for hostile here, the inns are always full. Not like you'd like them if you *were* to stay. It's far too rambunctious at night. I can see it in your eyes, you don't need *rambunctious*."

"*Hm*, likewise," said Zephyr. "We aren't looking for an inn anyways. We need a *home*, somewhere far from the Southern Kingdom. You haven't any idea of such a haven, have you?"

The man finished his pint, whereas Zephyr hadn't taken a sip. He burped and glanced slowly around the room. "You might find refuge in the Kingdom of Alexandria, the prettier twin. Their King has welcomed many nomads over the years, so much so that this here Cuepo needed establishing. But these people don't return; they become civilized." The man leaned forward over the table. "You know of it?"

"I know little of it, just murmurs of the heir." He began to elaborate, "she possess great power, yet she's caged in their court. A rabid animal, I hear."

"A man like you cannot be too detailed in your choices. The Southern Kingdom is the grime of the riverbed. Alexandria may be more accepting of you, more than the three others. I haven't too much a say regarding Krythia or Taria.... Alexandria is the oldest, the best governed in their upkeep and tax. A place in which festivals roar each half-season, where even the poorest residents could not see their own rib-cage. It is not, however, any haven of riches nor are any market signs etched in gold. You'd need to travel to Taria for those features. But I suspect you haven't the bite *or* the toes to travel such a distance. A kingdom of austerity nonetheless," he spoke leaning backward and burping once more. "A fabled army of several hundred-thousand, a castle sat above the clouds. Your home beneath the King Olderag is grossly influenced by the magus and wise, and they are the tumor which has consumed that place. But I do warn you, as no governance is so kind as to leave a daring peasant clean of blood in their chamber. But I do assert, you can retreat there."

"And they... follow a similar wizard council?"

"Well yes... they do, but abide by the Great Council in Taria. Their rules are strictly that of the Mor. *The Southern Kingdom,*" he growled. "I've heard the tales of that Joab elder. I promise you a far more lenient arrival."

"I suppose if we keep our heads low, we may be able to get by there. But I've never traveled past here in my life, let alone with my wife and the boy. Is Alexandria far? We may need a carriage, for that boy will outrun our shins," Zephyr joked and finally took a sip from the pint. The hunter's gaze wandered elsewhere.

"I can fetch you a rider heading west, but you mustn't speak of it to any soul."

"Why's that?" Zephyr became restless in his seat, believing the hunter to be fibbing of his promise. But his response was snarky and far smarter than he'd taken the man for.

The hunter stood up from his seat abruptly. "Because you haven't the coin to pay, and I'm in *heaps* of debt. C'mon then, show me the Mrs!"

3. The Dungeons of Deletaria

Sabbath and George had met alone at midday in the gully of a magic-school in Karnithal, a safe distance from the central hub outside Deletaria Castle. Farmers had dragged their keep of vegetables through to the markets while groups of soil-painted children ran about. Sabbath had presented a map to George, who was now sober yet void of the ache which normally plagued her. She unfurled it before the old rider and struck the paper with a finger.

"Here, perhaps forty mil," she declared. "The Great Council will hear our plea and see what tyranny has come of Olderag and Joab."

"But… but what if they strike us down… what if they're no better? I reckon the whole lot are just as iniquitous, young Sabbath. Perhaps we just remain as vermin, but we *keep our mouths shut!*" The frail man turned from her and stood some steps. The young woman was quick to grab his thin tunic and pull him back.

"We've been dormant far too long in the wake of this rule. I may not have lived long enough to see the change, but I know you were just a boy when the first hunts took place. How they captured innocent fathers and mothers and burnt them for

44

their cries. I've read the scriptures, and we've all heard the tales. Time and time again. but *my* hourglass in the matter has run bottom-heavy."

George was moved, unable to speak for himself. His thinning hair and drooping cheeks hung low, almost doubting what he was capable of at his old age.

"Then so be it," Sabbath said in her turn. She left him in the alley, prepared with a dagger concealed to her hip, to confront the very court of wizards who determined the rule of magic. For it was them, bearing names and numbers very few knew, who forged the law which all four kingdoms lived under. Sabbath wanted them to know of Olderag and Joab's corruption, yet even *she* knew little of how odious they were.

Sabbath had made her way to a cart full of redberries and corn where a short, plump man stood idly by. She exchanged a few coin for a wrapped bundle of each. But before she could taste even one berry, a presence came to her peripheral. Her hand already grazing her dagger, then she felt the silhouette lurching toward her.... bent, desperate, determined.

"Sabbath!" he called, winded. "Hold, girl. I'm coming."

She stopped, her face unreadable under the shadow of her cowl. "What's come of you?"

George caught up, bracing his hands on his knees. "You're right," he gasped. "We've waited too long. My bones may be brittle, but they still remember what justice ought to look like.

Damn the council if they've soured.... but I'll not sit idle. Not while Joab's breath still fouls the air. I agree that *this* must be tried."

A slow smile ghosted Sabbath's lips. "Then we ride north."

He nodded. "To the council. May they listen before they condemn us."

The pair shared a stem of sweet berries to their agreement, and set off without further word toward the Outer-Lands adjacent to Magberry. There, George called for his equally-old mare, which came to him in a trot from over one of the smaller foothills. Sabbath adjusted the map rolled and pinned under a leather strap which bound her hips.

"The path north leads beyond Karnithal's high terraces. We'll stop at Zarrhollow along the way for rations."

"I hope you're prepared to traverse frostbitten territory, young Sabbath," George said from the neck of the horse. "Where wild-hexes roam and council spies are known to linger about. Here, take my sword. All the years and I'm still novice wielding it whilst steering.

By the fifth hour, the spring heat had curled away to the highland winds. George's mount needed an extended rest. The black trees around them whispering in tongues neither recognized.

"Do you feel that?" Sabbath said suddenly, leading George to halt along the path which divided steep foothills.

George looked up, squinting into the heavy clouds. "No birds. No sound but the wind." His voice went quiet just then, eyes narrowing to the trees ahead. "We've yet to see any cart, yet I feel a great presence."

Then a shape emerged from the mist…. tall, robed in torn garment, faceless. Not a beast. Not quite man. The thing was entirely white bone, evident from what was revealed from its' sleeves and collar.

"Aye, just a weary laggard. Here," George struck the horse's rib with his heel, and let it continue on toward the wandering skeleton.

Sabbath reached instinctively for her dagger, not having ever met a laggard face-to-face before. She remained at the ready despite George's nonchalance.

The figure spoke without mouth or breath: "*Have ye seen me 'ole mutt? I seen it somewhere, I cannot find it.*"

George was incurious of the being, hinting to Sabbath that he'd dealt with laggards many times in his life. He spoke comically to it, "I seen it out yonder. Continue on, young lad. You haven't far to go!"

The Laggard's skull fell in disappointment, and took steps onward.

"Why've you led him on there, George? Isn't that cruel?" Asked Sabbath, her head fixed backward staring at the skeleton dragging its feet in the dirt.

"He's lucky we even entertained him. Laggards roam all the forest we'll pass through. Just pay them no mind. Even those which bear weaponry. You mustn't forget they haven't the muscle to twitch!"

Sabbath lost sight of the laggard once they'd made ground and her curly bronze hair flew into view. She stared forward, then upward at the sky, pondering what it must feel like to live indefinitely like that. Perhaps she'd lose control of her thoughts, her energy. She *did* know their origin, that laggards were the product of an ancient war five-hundred seasons ago. A Krythian army declared war on the Seplet Coven of the very forest they approached. The laggards were the result of the seven Seplet witch's spell upon the army, which left them as skeletons but alive. Roaming forever, and in Krythia's retreat, left behind and forgotten.

They rode double upon the horse, its coat matted from sweat and wind. The woods curled around them like dead fingers.... gnarled boughs scratching the air, old roots upheaving the earth like forgotten bones. The day was gray, and the light fell in ragged patches through the high, rotting canopy. Sabbath, grown tired, pressed forward against George's back, arms clutched tight around his waist as he guided the horse through the crooked path.

"You ever seen trees bleed, Sabbath?" George said suddenly.

Sabbath blinked awake. "What're you yappin' about?"

He gestured to a nearby trunk, cracked and dripping sap so dark it might've been blood. "There was a time in Krythia, when the harvest moon split the sky open like a wound. I was younger than you then. Maybe seventy seasons. Thought myself immortal."

"Krythia?" Sabbath repeated. "That's so far east. I've never ventured past even the Faebarrows."

"Aye, and colder than a corpse's belly, for it sits at the tail-end of a high peninsula. But beautiful, girl. The snow fell like pearls over the sea, I remember. And their fire-dancers could make flame move like poetry."

She leaned closer, resting her chin against his shoulder. "Why'd you go so far?"

George smirked. "Ah, father 'n I had gone anywhere we could. He'd trade metals. But I went along beside him, always. Call it Adventure. Cowardice. Wanted to find anything but what was given to us. I was a stable lad before all this. But once the first hunts began… once they started dragging folks by the hair and calling it justice… I saddled a horse and rode 'til the wind changed names."

Sabbath was silent for a time. The creak of the saddle and the thud of hoof on mud kept rhythm.

"You came back, though."

"I suppose I did. I guess I was curious about… what would happen to all them folk. Wanted to see something good grow. *Hah!*" He chuckled, "the last good I seen was on my last visit west, eighty-some seasons ago."

"And you made it to Alexandria?" she asked, her dirtied chin sat atop his bony shoulder.

But George's face grew still. "*Aye. Alexandria.*" He spat to the side. "City of marble and columns. They say its spires reach heaven and its rivers sing. Lies, mostly. Aside from the castle nearly touching the stars at night. But one thing was true. The Princess. She was just born at the time."

"What of her?"

"Same name as the kingdom, which dons the name of Jean St. Auclaire's great grandmother," George said. "*Princess Alexandria.* Most folk thought her a gift.... and she was.... but it wasn't just that the St. Auclaire reign would go on. It was *her.* She had the Sixth."

Sabbath straightened once more. "The *sixth?* Persuasion?"

George gave a low grunt. "Indeed so. The rarest magic. No flame or frost. No light or shadow, or poison or levitation. Just *will.* With her eyes and tongue alone, she could make you carve your own throat and thank her for the honor. Her voice could undo armies. I believe her to be caged."

Sabbath shivered, though not from the cold. "But they let her live? Could she not take over Grasp if she wanted?"

George chuckled bitterly. "Let her? They worshiped her at the time. Crowned her in lilies and sat her on a throne of silence.

But they learned to fear her, too after an incident involving her father. I don't know the tale. I'd wager she doesn't walk freely now. Probably buried alive in some marble tomb with a hundred guards who dare not look her in the eye."

Sabbath stared ahead, where the path curved into deeper fog. "You think Joab and Olderag might ever have that kind of power?" she asked.

"No," George muttered. "But I think they *want* it. And I think they're meddling with worse. The hunts were telling, but now they've took Jeffrey." He shuddered. "It can't be invetia, dear Sabbath. Not sanctioned magic. I once thought disquisition, but the screams tell of *miscreancy*. Torture-hexes, rot spells, terror-glyphs.... an evil art. Dark sorcery, yet a force of nature. To melt your legs beneath you."

Sabbath's grip on him tightened. "They'll pay. All abuse is abuse," she said. "*We'll make them.*"

George gave a dry laugh. "We'll *try*. That council's full of snakes in robes. But even snakes die when you burn the grass."

They rode on in silence as the woods thickened, night approaching fast. The path to Taria was still long, and the Great Council farther yet, but between the two, while slouched and sore on a tired horse, they flickered a thread of wild, desperate resolve. And perhaps that would be enough.

4. The Arrival to Alexandria

The world had not yet woken. The Solta family rode in a carriage, courtesy of the hunter from Cuepo. Zephyr informed Ambrosia and Leon of their last fourteen leugas. Just two days, and they would arrive in the home of the King Jean St. Auclaire in the Kingdom of Alexandria. Leon grew restless, begging to be let out more often than the tradesmen warranted. But occasionally he *did* stop and let the child run about in the fields, tire himself out.

As Ambrosia and Leon slept against one another upright within the carriage, he looked outward across the foothills of the flat lands, watching tradesmen head the other way toward the Southern Kingdom. He thought of what remained of him there: canvases and oils burning in small fires, his portraits reduced to soot. That a great sum of his portraits were nothing but soot, now sunk in between the stone of the roads and then earth below.

The Borge knew first, and the heavily crowded roads and homes laughed alongside the flames while smoke settled at the streets with barely any room to escape the terraces and stacked buildings. The children of the East March would create their own portraits of Zephyr and strike them against the towering wall which contained one side of the village. Some businessmen who had commissioned him remained silent and kept their portraits, most being able to avoid the purge. The Center had cared less and quickly dismissed the exile in-turn for the typical stories and tales of the governance. The few folk of Magberry and the Hides understood a bit better… they would, like Bolin, always question Olderag and his council. Jeffrey however, no longer had to question them, for his fate was bound to the cage they dragged him to.

Their last morning, Ambrosia and Leon were in a deep sleep. The wheels of the carriage sang a drowsy rhythm over the flattened sand of the road. Beyond the lantern's dim flame, which swung outside the carriage, mist coiled and lingered atop the earth like low-lying ghosts, rising in slow spirals where hoof met dew. The horses puffed and snorted their breath into clouds, their steady pace unwavering through the hush of dawn.

Zephyr sat near the open slat of the rear, shoulder cloaked in a moth-bitten shawl of Ambrosia's weaving, half-watching his sleeping wife and son. The child's fingers twitched as he dreamt, perhaps of swordplay or plaza sprints, the dreams of those not yet disillusioned.

"Reckon you're far from where you set foot. Further than Cuepo," the rider called without looking back. His voice was gravel carried by a northern wind.

Zephyr did not answer immediately. He watched the tired world pass first. The hills swelled beneath an amaranthine sky, the dark blue of dawn eating away the stars. "Too far to remember what's behind me," Zephyr said at last. "Not far enough to know if what's ahead is worth the ache in my back."

The rider chuckled. "You speak like a man carrying more than a pack."

"I carry a curse," Zephyr murmured, but louder added, "And a family."

Silence again, but not the empty kind. The carriage rocked gently, its hinges creaking like old trees.

"You're Alexandrian, then?" the rider asked.

"No. Southern Kingdom," Zephyr replied. "A village near the Hides."

The man turned just enough for Zephyr to glimpse a beard more ash than black. "Ain't many fleeing north. Most let themselves die and waste before they make such a trip. I suppose most never carry such a weight."

"We're not fleeing," Zephyr said, sharper than he intended. "We're removed."

The rider nodded. "A painter, *hm*? You know, Daysen told me, said the first mayor of Cuepo's face is still hung in the guildhall there. Figured you were a popular figure."

Zephyr blinked, stunned. Then he realized the hunter's identity was this *Daysen*. "That's surprising to hear. I figure on his indefinite leave that they'd tear it down. Or that they'd tear it down now. What do you care of a painter?"

"My brother was a pigmenter," the man said. "There in Alexandria, boiled beetles and berries 'til his knuckles went blue. You've got the shoulders of a man who's brushed too long on uneven canvas. And the eyes… they're painter's eyes. Always watching. Always somewhere else."

Zephyr smiled faintly. "Your brother… still work the trade?"

"No," the rider said. "King Jean had his men throw him in a cater-pen for supplying miscreant dye. An order of tapestries dissolved once they were hung up. They found him lying in the belly of a tavern in his pay. Can't say I don't blame him."

"Well… what's easy isn't always right. Other times the commissioner poisons you before you even ought to think."

"Happen to you?"

Zephyr's face tightened. "The Queen herself. Then… Joab."

"Aye. *Him.*"

They passed through a hollow in the road where trees leaned closely together, their boughs whispering over the roof like gossiping old men.

"The Southern Kingdom has been rotting for a long time. But I think it's finally begun to cave inward," Zephyr said, his voice low. "It is governed by fear painted as order, by men who cast judgments like dice and call it divine."

55

"King Jean may fair only slighter better in the Alexandrian's view."

"I do not know him," Zephyr admitted. "But I know that any court not ruled by Joab's breath is already safer. Still… I fear all thrones share the same foundation. Blood. Just a shame it's their own peoples'."

The rider grunted. "You speak with venom. But measured. Like a man who's seen fire and learned not to touch it twice."

Zephyr looked down at his hands. The nails still held traces of ochre. "I touched it until there was nothing left to burn."

The sky began to warm. Pale gold split the clouds over the far-off line of the Guardant Walls, the magnificent defensive construction of Alexandria. Towers rose like teeth against the light. Faint bells rang in the Kingdom's high steeples…. morning rites.

Zephyr leaned toward Ambrosia and Leon. The boy mumbled something, still asleep. Ambrosia stirred. Her hand reached for Zephyr's knee in her dreaming.

"Will they accept you there?" the rider asked.

"Not a matter of mine. We'll keep to the burrows."

The rider said nothing after that. But he gave a small nod. And in that nod was something beyond words. Sympathy, perhaps. Or the unspoken understanding of men who have watched too many suns rise with guilt in their lungs.

The road narrowed ahead, and the Kingdom of Alexandria came into view beneath the early light.… beautiful, distant, and indifferent. They approached the great monolithic entrance, where the rider spoke to a guard for passage. There was little resistance, though Zephyr couldn't hear. They quickly went on and under a high bridge, and entered the gorgeous world, the Kingdom of Alexandria.

The first village was that of Tuopo. It sat on the kingdom-side of the entrance beyond the Guardant Walls, though it was neither grand or exhausted, but choked with life. It was a breathless clutter, its buildings stacked like books on a forgotten shelf, with plank balconies and sagging canvas awnings casting long shadows over the merchant corridors. Smoke wound from butchered chimneys. The scent of broth and boiled spelt drifted through the claywork alleys. Traders shouted through the sun-slits, hawking wares they barely understood. Zephyr saw archers manned at the great wall.

Fruit, fabric, tinctures. The chorus of haggling rose like liturgy. No one spared a glance for the carriage in which they rode. Zephyr believed many traveled in and out of the walls, that security was lacking. He leaned forward, speaking to the rider. "This is Tuopo?"

"Aye," the man said, tying off the reins to a bar situated beneath a vast overhanging structure. "No richer entrance to the Kingdom. No poorer one, either. You can talk freely here. Tuopo does not care for nobility of its people. For they don't kneel for the King nor whisper of of the Queen unless coin is involved!"

He laughed loudly as Zephyr woke his wife and son, and led them into the burning light. "A place for those between stories.... for sailors turned smith, for widows turned weavers, for men like you."

Once they'd grab their few sacks and inconspicuously began their wandering, the rider departed towards a different sect of the village to retrieve whatever harvest he fancied.

They found lodging through a fletcher's wife named Malvenna, who happened to recognize Ambrosia's weaving draped over Zephyr's shoulders from an older threadwork exhibition once held in the Ringards. Though, Malvenna mistook it, and Ambrosia had no clue who she was. She was not kind, but not cruel either. Her attic was lean and cold, and the Solta family played along. The stairwell inside groaned like an old man's knees. There was no hearth, only a lamp, a cot, and floorboards that remembered every footstep. But it was theirs for the time.

Zephyr offered to paint her husband's storefront signage in exchange for three week's shelter.

"To have such greatness under this roof, *my dear Ms. Seddy,*" she said to Ambrosia, "I'll liken it to four!"

When he told her of his commissions for business she wouldn't recognize; she was falsely impressed and left him a pail of whitewash.

Over the coming weeks, Ambrosia took to weaving small patches, trading them for eggs and boiled grain. Leon, still small, learned the maze of Tuopo's alleys quickly. He helped the lantern-lighter by dusk and ran errands for the man who sold sunroot and boiled snails. They were poor, yes. But unnoticed. Unbothered.

With a few extra coin, Zephyr took Leon to the brim of the greatest region of Alexandria, which he learned was simply the *City*. It was there beyond the knotted streets that they witnessed the castle for the first time. However, the thousands of wide, stone steps were most of what they'd seen, for the castle sat above the clouds. The spires were visible, and levels and terraces at regular intervals leading up. There were *many* more busy sections of Alexandria they had yet to find.

Leon was the one who adapted fastest. He learned the routes between bread-stands and spice-roots and where to avoid fishmongers' slop and where to beg an extra fig from the redberry vendor. Each afternoon, he darted through the twisted marketalleys barefoot, trailed by a mongrel dog he'd named *Parch*.

It was on a Midweek, during the Feast of Stilled that he first saw the local form of glimmercraft. Not all were wizards, but all were licensed. And their fizzing displays and sparks were much more extravagant than what he'd seen in the Southern Kingdom. *There*, the wizards were frail and dirty, old as well, begging for a coin. They would give salamanders wings and watch them fall in their ineptitude. But here, the wizards, both young and middle-aged, would burn stones into a cloud and reveal flowers. It seemed whatever council of Alexandria was far more relaxed in their ruling of magic, so long as though it were harmless.

There was a particular trio of these wizards, clad in red robes embroidered with rusty cords, arrived from the City and took to the center of Tuopo's South Circle. Word spread quickly, and Leon begged his father to go. Ambrosia was pale that day, however insisted they all should. "He ought to see something beautiful," she said to Zephyr in Malvenna's cove, brushing hair from her eyes with a hand that trembled faintly. Leon saw a quiver in her eyelids but thought nothing of it.

The crowd gathered in a soft hush as the wizards performed atop a wood stage. They drew from the air threads of light, stitching illusions with ancient motion. Swans made of glassy fire glided through the air, their wings fanning perfume across the square. A laughing tower unfolded in petals from a child's drawing, and stars…. tiny, perfect stars…. cascaded from a man's open palms like silver rain.

Leon's mouth hung open in wonder. "Papa, it's far better than in Magberry!"

Zephyr crouched beside him. "It appears so."

"Why can they do more?"

Zephyr nodded slowly, his eyes not on the spectacle but on the faces of those casting it. "Less rules here, boy. Look!"

One wizard with a twisted mustache summoned a fiery blaze and out of it came a massive bunch of roses, which he handed off to a little girl watching in awe. Zephyr remained cautious of the display, knowing how easy it would be for the crowd to catch on fire. The way one wizard's lips moved too precisely, muttering to his accomplice, or how another watched the coin dropping before them more than the spell. Glimmercraft was sanctioned magic: visual, harmless, performative. Yet still, it belonged to a branch of dangerous old tongues like all six forms.

That night, Leon slept with his arms above his head, as if trying to catch one of the fiery swan. Zephyr sat by a small window, sketching the illusion of Ambrosia in charcoal while she folded thread into neat spools beside him. But he noticed her fingers missed the thread twice. And again. She blinked, and her eyes watered not from grief but exhaustion.

"You're tired. Why don't you get to sleep?" He asked.

"I might. The dye's been heavier this week." She offered a smile, fleeting and thin.

Zephyr said nothing more. He watched her wrap the thread once again, slower this time. A cough, just once, into her sleeve. She shook her head gently, as if banishing the thought.

It was later that as the boy dreamt of magic and Zephyr of soot portraits, Ambrosia stirred in her sleep. Her breaths came thin and wheezy, like wind pushing through a broken flute. Zephyr sat up but did not wake her. Instead, he turned his eyes to the ceiling, to the low beams that trembled in the wind, sensing that something heavier than spring's pollen was taking hold of her.

5. The Following Harvest

The morning came cobalt and cold, wrapped in an aching haze. The cooler season had set in, one Ambrosia did not live to see. Zephyr stood beyond the rib-cage of a low gate. He faced a freshly stamped tombstone which barred a hallowed name, one he loved. The earth was damp and dark and overturned where a body slept below the surface. Only the caretaker of the graveyard accompanied him, for Leon had not returned since the burial.

Even on this third visit, Zephyr could not summon his face to even twitch, nor could he force his eyes to rest. She was just one stone among fifty in the yard, a short silhouette beneath the blanket of haze. He felt the rot burrowing deep inside him, plaguing his lungs and bones.

From the cloth which bound his waist he unsheathed some silver tool with a wooden handle, bending down to strike it before the stone and into the soil. It pressed deep into the earth. It was a pallet knife, *the* pallet knife in which he scored and spread the oils he would use to paint King Olderag. Once he had admired the tool at the head of the grave, he'd finally depart, only to visit each and every morning and nigh thereafter. Whatever blood still pooled in his veins and lungs would boil from his hatred, and saliva caked the hair crowning his mouth. Zephyr bid farewell to

Ambrosia this morning, and assured her that he would arrive again soon to wish her goodnight

Upon their arrival to the Kingdom of Alexandria nearly one seasons prior to the burying of his wife, Zephyr failed to inform her and Leon that Joab had cursed him further, though he did not know to what extent. The Wizard never told him of what would come, but the lingering thought stirred in Zephyr's head, and he could not just blame the cold air.

Malvenna had relieved him and his son of the shelter once she'd learn the true name of Ambrosia, for she wasn't who she believed her to be. It took but a day, and Zephyr found refuge for them in the same village but within a nook of it. It was beneath an overhanging of stacked homes, incredibly wet from constant settled steam.

While Zephyr took part in many minor hunts with the local folk for degera, they'd determine he was a better fisherman, and then a better farmer. But even with the aid of some of the greater soil-turners who took him in, Zephyr opted for the berry trade which paid far better. But the weight of Ambrosia's loss grew far too heavy for him to carry in the fields, and before long he and Leon were no more than the dark-eyed peasants which roamed the deep pockets of the Kingdom.

Before her death, Ambrosia had aided in the production of clay vessels for the inner city. Although she'd develop great artisanal skills beyond her weaving, loading the carriages with the elders was where her fits worsened. En route to Chanceston beyond the border-walls, she'd find her first fall.... then a second. A local physician was called from the City, along with a high priestess named Shetlan. who in turn brought a horse-drawn carriage with an apothecary.

Dark veins grew from her eyes on their arrival. It was Shetlan who announced the ungodly plague could not be treated. Ambrosia died in the following hours, and Zephyr was quickly taken beyond the village and questioned with the end of a blessed blade at his throat. The priestess, accompanied by Shetlan and four knights, forced him to speak of what he brought into their kingdom. Their people could not be subjected to such a fate, which they believed may spread rapidly. First the bustling inner towns, and eventually the feudal governance. Each fief would seize, after all, the Kingdom of Alexandria had lived it once nearly seven-hundred seasons ago.

The Priestess and Shetlan were greatly displeased by the truth when he spoke. It was not deserving of the man being dragged far over the hills. A knight threw Zephyr off his horses rump and left him pressing down reeds.

"A plague, it is, but it is solely bound to my name. A curse of invetia for my crimes, I believe it to be contained to I and Ambrosia… *our boy*.… "

"Aren't you an unlucky serf? You've traveled here, and for what purpose? How approximate must a person be to reach the same fate as this… Ambrosia?" Shetlan asked. "The Grand Wizards whom find themselves closely tied to Kings grant very unfavorable blessings."

"It is just I," Zephyr barely coughed out. The dust of his face was broken by a mess of tears. Then his fist met the earth in a thumping strike. Then he cried, "I may meet with your might, but it is but a lesser punishment." Zephyr tore at the reeds, eyes locked on the knight's sword. His lip bled under his teeth. "Strike me! Do it! Bastards, end it already!" He pleaded. But Shetlan and the Priestess shared a look of uncertainty.

"This curse you speak of, it is bound only to you, you say?" The Priestess looked down to him. The man nodded with rust. The Priestess then turned away and gestured at the knight with a settled palm. Zephyr took a deep breath and shut his eyes, preparing for darkness. But the knight, with just a greatly shielded fist, lifted Zephyr to his feet.

"Where have you come from?" Shetlan asked Zephyr before joining the Priestess to their horses. The man was shuddering and nearly breathless.

"The Southern Kingdom.. .the Kingdom of Olderag," he said with spit. "The… the Grand Wizard…Joab. They order heinous punishments, and we've been exiled. I thought to find refuge here."

He was shocked, nervously picking at his beard. A quivering smile came, "a bastard of a councilman. Invetia is rarely so ugly, less the summoning of disease."

"We never knew of a *less* gross display. I… I believe this *curse* to not spread. If I can return to my boy…"

"Likewise," said Shetlan. "Our Grand Wizard, Mister Fleschire, will want to document this. I've never heard of such a thing, and I'm certain neither has he. A precarious case you are, Mr. Solta. I apologize for our rudeness. Come Fleschire's determination, I feel you won't be bothered by the state much longer."

He barely recalled that day, yet Shetlan's words remained violently churning inside. He was left then with Leon to make do with their dying days. The boy did not understand the magic branches much, less the law or misuse of it by Olderag and Joab. And Zephyr was uncertain of what still awaited them, if the boy would succumb to the curse as well, and if *he* would too.

In the blue of another late hour, Zephyr returned to the boy at their tightly confined home in-between two expansive buildings which stretched down from one courtyard to another. He had built the shelter with broken carts left for a baker to burn, providing a door, cot, and a half-roof to keep out what secreted from the stone wall this nook was pressed against. A single oil lamp hung by a loose hook, giving some light to the raggedy place. Leon was sat atop a turned-over harvesting basket pressing his left temple. His forehead was folded and his eyes were pierced closed. He coughed relentlessly, but Zephyr knew it was from the mold. He went quickly over to him, tilting the boy's head upward. It was a hallowed sight, that of Leon's pale face.

"My throat hurts, papa."

"Because it is damp. I'll light the kindling," the man told him. "Lie in your bed, and I will make tea." He first lit a small fire in a recovered stone trough that was already left there by flint. "We must keep a fire lit for most of these days, even if it is too hot."

Zephyr boiled water in their only pot until the steam clouded about. A fan of the door relieved the space for some time. From bundles and small baskets Zephyr pulled various medicinal herbs he managed to take that had fallen from carts down the way, and some were remnants of what he and Ambrosia brought to

Tuopo. Dried silverthorn and ashberry dust, wilk-stem too. They would steep in the pot for some time before Zephyr presented Leon with a cracked chalice of it. The boy lay in his cot, dripping from his forehead. The man hadn't given it much thought until he saw the rings around his boys' eyes, a familiar blackness. The boy drank what he could.

"I will have another pot ready. It'll help."

But as he went to grab more herbs, he realized he did not have enough. Zephyr's muscles loosened, his fingers fell limp. He felt hopeless that there was little else to do for him. If the curse *did* go beyond Ambrosia, to Leon and then him, it could be any moment or day, or perhaps longer.

He left Leon to rest, stepping out of their alleyway into the street. His walk grew weak until he stopped. He could barely hold his chest up, wanting to let himself collapse as his world had deteriorated far quicker than he anticipated. It was *infected*. Without consciously deciding to, Zephyr walked slowly in a daze to a local apothecary burrowed into a brick building at the eastern courtyard. He had gone there three occasions prior and never learned the shop's name, nor the decrepit gentleman who sat inside. Though, he was a kindhearted and quiet elder, always sat atop a high stool scrapping seeds from hollow vegetables and pestling dried herbs in a mortar. The elder was quite shrunken than perhaps his younger self, and wore a dense green flannel over his shoulders, highly warped oval spectacles, and his toes were nearly bursting from their leather confinements.

"Good morning sir," Zephyr spoke with a quiver. He barely looked and admired the myriad of beautifully adorned vessels which lined the tall shelves. He went straight to a middle-table to retrieve silverthorn leaves. But to his dismay, there were none. "Sir, you hadn't anymore silverthorn?"

The old man looked toward him and slowly crept down from his stool. "I suppose I've been out for some time," he spoke quietly. "The needles of it, I do not find very useful anyways."

"Well sir, I do. Where might I find more? Shall I go on southward?"

"*Herghh…*" the elder huffed, "silverthorn is no better than common nolipine… and yes it is far more difficult to source, I can say for certain."

Though, Zephyr routinely brought bushels of the plant home with him in the Southern Kingdom. "But sir, it is quite important."

"And for what, its' numbing effects? Well my dearest friend," the elder began to whisper, "there are far more potent concoctions. Now tell me, is this for yourself?"

"Sure, yes. It is for me."

He then went slowly towards his table, opening a drawer behind it. "Give your hand." Zephyr did as he instructed, and the elder pressed a small pinkish flower into his palm. He leaned in, "ferschueska, you only needed a little, brew how you prefer."

Zephyr took the plant but was still greatly disappointed. Leon always preferred the silverthorn because it smelt of their true home. It was a rich scent of the pines and earth, and light. But this ferschueska, if truly as potent as the elder says, may be necessary.

"Thank you sir. Oh, could I write in an order for the silverthorn then?

"I will do so, of course. Ah, and one piece to the puzzle I nearly forgot!" The elder bent over and rummaged around the drawer once again, inevitably giving Zephyr a tiny gray geode. "It must be pestled with it, I promise it is no good any other way."

Zephyr thanked him again, dropping the rock into his trouser pocket, anticipating chucking it into a fire later. He shook the elder's weak grasp, and assured him he'd return the following day for the proper plant. Then, on his walk out, Zephyr made note of a molding sign which hung from a pole, and it read: BILLMON NITANA GROCER.

Once he had arrived back home in-between the sweating flats, Zephyr did as the chemist described. With Leon overwhelmed with a fever, he pressed against the tiny flower with the stone until one of its' four petals turned to a fine dust. Then into the boiling pot, where it'd turn faintly opalescent. He let a portion cool for some time before pouring into the cracked chalice.

"Boy, I've brewed a better tisane," he softly shook Leon awake. The child sat upright, holding his head in one palm. "Here, drink." He did as he was told, leaving it half-full. "More rest may cure your fever. I will leave the fire low, and the windows open." Leon laid back down, turning over. Zephyr stood up, only knowing that he'd sit at the table staring at the boy indefinitely, waiting for the remainder of his life to dissolve.

"Papa?" The boy quietly spoke.

"What is it?"

"Did mother die by the King?"

"She may have, Leon. But even then, your father is… who is at fault."

"But how would you have known the true color of his eyes?"

"I did as the Queen advised, boy."

"So she did not know the color of the King's eyes?"

"She didn't."

"That is not love, then."

"Rulers cannot love," Zephyr assured. "They may promise a love for all their people, but some are more loved than others. A lesser love is no love at all." He felt Leon's forehead and it was cooler than moments before. "But we are not rulers, there are no limits to our care for each other. Rest now."

It was a restless night watching over the boy. Zephyr let him continue his rest through the morning although he was noticeably healthier.

He took the first hours of the day to visiting Ambrosia. Her tombstone was far cleaner than the others, although there weren't many. It sat on the border of the farmlands and Tuopo, with the first trading shacks to the right and a single tavern to the left. He could see the extent of the kingdom from her resting place. A bright and towering dominion set across wide hills, with distant villages hidden beneath morning fog. The castle, a majority of it hidden, struck the white sky like a knife. Some lamplight peered from the even further forests. He still barely knew what this place held for him, but he knew it wouldn't wait for him to experience it. The hunter of Cuepo had only told him of

Alexandria's promises of safety, not of the fertile plots of soil or a place to die peacefully.

The heavy wooden door of *The Crooked Maiden*, which Zephyr had spotted on the large sun-dried sign at its roof, creaked open as Zephyr stepped inside, his garments damp from the morning mist that lingered over the graveyard. The scent of spiced mead, stale ale, and roasted venison filled his nose, a stark contrast to the chill of Ambrosia's resting place. The low murmur of voices halted as heads turned to appraise the newcomer.

Zephyr's appearance did little to inspire ease.... his hollow eyes and unkempt hair spoke of grief, and his presence, unfamiliar to the regulars, carried the weight of suspicion.

At the far corner of the room, Willa Broadmere, a stout woman of twenty winters or eighty seasons, set down a platter of bread and cheese before an older man whose calloused hands betrayed years of toil. When he glimpsed her, something about her struck familiar. A glow softened by the dust-filled air.

Her brother, Tomas, lounged nearby, sharpening a blade with a whetstone. Eldric of Blackmere, a broad-shouldered man with a perpetual bruise beneath his left eye, leaned against the bar-table nursing a tankard. Zephyr approached the counter, his voice quiet but steady as he spoke to the barkeep the barkeep, a wiry man with a sharp eye. "Alike to his, if it pleases." He slid one of his few dirtied silver coins across the counter.

Before the barkeep could respond, a gruff voice broke the momentary silence.

"Hold there!" shouted a man known as Oswin Grith, a corn farmer known more for his temper than his crops. He rose from his seat near the hearth, jabbing a finger toward Zephyr. "You've the look of a man from beyond Alexandria, do you not?"

Zephyr froze, his fingers curling into a fist at his side. "Aye, I may."

Oswin's face contorted in anger. "Then 'tis you who brings ill fortune! *Plague* follows your kind. The fever that claims our kin…. it reeks of curses and sorcery! I seen the burial across the way. How long 'till we see the yard fill up? We've no need of your ilk in Alexandria!" Oswin trudged from his place closer to Zephyr, pointing a thick wilting finger at him. "You ain't gonna turn us to laggards; we don't welcome infections."

Murmurs spread through the room like wildfire, and Zephyr's grip on his composure faltered. He opened his mouth to speak, but before he could utter a word, Willa stepped forward.

"Hold your tongue, Oswin!" she barked, her voice commanding enough to silence the room. "You've no proof of such accusations. The man has yet to sit, let alone speak his piece."

Oswin's eyes narrowed. "And what would you know, Miss Broadmere? Your hands are fit for sowing seed, not judging curses."

Before Willa could respond, her brother Tomas stood, his hand resting on the hilt of his dagger, brandishing it before the old man. "Careful, Oswin. You're far frailer than you think. My sister speaks the truth…. this man is no more a bringer of plague than you are a healer."

Oswin's face flushed red, and he turned toward Eldric. "And what say you, Blackmere? Will you stand idle while this vagabond curses us all?"

Eldric then drained his tankard and set it down with a resounding thud. He stepped forward, his imposing frame dwarfing Oswin's. "I say a man who accuses another without cause is a coward," he growled. "And if you'd like to settle the matter, I'll be happy to oblige you outside."

The room fell silent once more, save for the crackling of the hearth. Oswin glanced around, searching for allies, but found only averted gazes and his farming neighbors returning to their seats. The sheer mass of Eldric would be enough to settle most arguments, let alone whatever ax or hammer he had with him.

Zephyr, his voice steady despite the turmoil, finally spoke. "I bring no plague nor ill will to this place. I seek only solace and a chance, now, to grieve. If that is unwelcome, I shall take my leave." He awaited his first and final sip of the mead.

"Nay, you'll stay," Willa said firmly, placing a hand on Zephyr's shoulder. "The likes of Oswin are far expired, sit."

The barkeep, who had remained silent, slid the tankard of mead toward Zephyr. "Drink, traveler. And know that not all in Greystone are quick to judge."

Oswin, seeing himself outnumbered, grumbled and returned to his seat, though his glare lingered on Zephyr. He raised his own mug to his lips.

"*Good man,*" Willa smiled and returned to Tomas.

Zephyr drank alone for some time, never looking back to Oswin or anyone else. He was no mule to hostility, though it found him like the mudflies back southward. He admired the craftsmanship of the tavern, how horns of oxen were on display above the stacks of barrels, and antlers were fixed to the bar-top. Up until this day, he did not know he had left Tuopo for Greystone. The villages had blended together without signage. Before he could take his final gulp of the mead, a pale auburn-haired child ran up to his side. The girl sported cloth garments and marks of dirt across her arms and cheeks. Her eyes were wide and so was her smile.

"Mister, you aren't from here.... I heard 'em say?"

"Aye, this is true child. Who might you be?" Zephyr's face bled into enthusiasm.

"I'm Pitter," she stuck out a thin arm, awaiting a handshake. He shook her tiny hand. "Where did you come from?"

"A place far from here," he spoke under his breath, still weary of the local folk. The little girl held a warm smile, turning as Willa approached. "Might this be your mother, little Pitter?"

"Hah! It couldn't be, for I would have been a child myself if I'd birthed her." Willa presented her hand to Zephyr, letting him hold it lightly for but a moment. "Willa," she introduced herself. Her hair was short, curled into thousands of bronze rings above her shoulders. Her blouse was old with lace at the neck and tucked beneath a leather vest a man would sport. Zephyr produced a rusty grin before sitting back atop the stool and taking another sip of his mead. "Not even a *thanks*?" She expected him to turn onto his knees, but he knew this tavern was no establishment worthy of such acts.

"I did not recognize you to be so soft, but I do give my apologies before a *thanks*. But… thank you." Zephyr did as she wanted, but reverted to the stein before him. Willa sat beside him and broke him in slower.

"It is true then, that you're from elsewhere?"

"Aren't we all of the Mor Empire? I yield from far. Regardless, I was told I'd arrive in a bastion for nomads. That root-fella assured me otherwise."

"Then, I suppose, you are not a man of this Kingdom. Where might you be from?" She asked once more, and as his mouth pierced a bit of foam, Willa saw him exposed.

"I come from the Kingdom of Olderag," he confessed but with coldness.

"So, you did not come here willingly then," she suggested. "An exiled man, like most are from the south. And so, *man*, what crimes did you commit before you decided to disrupt this…. gritty pit of….angry farmers?" Zephyr brought his palm to her thin shoulder.

"I'll tell you over a pint on any night but this," he concluded, leaving his stein and a coin on the table and leaving her empty of story.

Zephyr made his tired way through the burrows of the Bard residential roads on the cusp of Tuopo until he eventually met where the Market Alleys began. He'd pass Billmon's Grocer, eyeing through the thickly dusted glass to spot any delivery basket. He may have seen a knotted bundle of herbs but alas, nothing silver. Not even the alchemist himself sat at his desk. He wondered what made the flower ease Leon's fever. Still, Zephyr knew better than to trust clerks and grocers, especially in the Bard where most trades came with a secret cost.

6. The Starry Configuration

A week had passed, and Zephyr had paid three more visits to the alchemist, only to find it entirely silent and the door locked. Not even the lamps were lit. Leon desperately needed medicine, but the man was without coin or a clerk to bargain with. He'd journey further into the City away from the Bard and Tuopo, asking the dark-eyed people of the market-square and alleyways whose words all melted together in quick spats, only to be given the sternest stares. Even an elderly woman he suspected of practicing disquisition wouldn't help him. Zephyr understood the scarcity when a second elder woman gripped his forearm firmly and whispered a threatening truth. *The council forbids them grocers in these city parts. And ye won't find no soul who will admit to disquisition. You get on now, ye head to them trench-roads. By the farmland is you're only hope. Get on now.*

It was without luck, this venture and several more. Zephyr felt the pit hollowing beneath his ribs. His boy would soon perish, and the man saw each cloud dissolve above him like a road in life he could never again travel. Eventually it would be just the lonely crescent and its' army to sign a final hymn in condolence.

On his journey home, Zephyr spotted a youngish man dressed in clean trousers, leather sandals, and a proper-fit sleeved-shirt sat on the ground beside the basement window of a towering stone hall. The man's head rested against the pane, with a hand resting on one bent knee. This young man looked familiar in attire. But it was *he* who recognized Zephyr first.

"You there!" The man waved and rose from his nook. "Come here, be quiet." The tone in which he spoke was wildly persuasive, leaving no room for negotiating, and yet it was so friendly. He gestured for Zephyr to peer through the glass. With but a swipe of his palm to clear the mold and dust, he did as he was told. It was a strange sight, looking down below the street into the basement to find a sprawling theater with the stands entirely full of people. They wore uniforms of velvety navy, Zephyr saw the fibers of their vests softly reflect the firelamps above them. The man sat back down. "I know you, from the Maiden. You may not be from these lands, but any man will learn more than he should about the world sat….right….here."

He realized this man was Willa's brother Tomas, who witnessed the entire ordeal with Oswin. Barely willing but without the strength to even clench his fist, Zephyr planted himself on the floor. Though muffled through the glass, he gave himself to listen.

"…. *And so one's eyes with such a genetic configuration, is this ability that cannot be possessed otherwise. Disposition, tendency to persuade, a magic of sorts. Often misused, and you'll see, I am sure you have already, the punishments for such misuse. Their burnings should be noted. The Princess herself is the only body alive within these walls who possess this configuration, and what have you noticed of her? Hm? Yes….you boy.*"

"She dons a mask, sir."

"Yes, the boy is right. Thank you Mister Collettey"

"What is this place?" Zephyr asked Tomas at last. He could not stop staring inward at the elder man draped in a violet cape, adorned in silver calligraphic embellishments.

"The Alchame Astra School," he said. "These kids will better this kingdom someday. I'm a better man just listening to them."

"If she is someday to become Queen, why are they concerned of her eyes? If she were to inevitably rule, would she then remove it? Would she… use her against her people? Us?" A young lady asked the professor.

"Perhaps… perhaps. However, the Princess wears the mask willingly. And with it, no councilmen, grand wizard, no priest will ever do malicious bidding on her behalf. She graciously recognizes it, for the King has asserted Princess Alexandria is not inherently evil as others with Persuasion are often seen. We've gone over the cases of Dougherty Tin and… oh what's their name?"

"Elwood the Jester of Krythia?"

"Yes! That's the one. An old tale."

"The Princess wears a mask? I've heard of such a condition, but I supposed I do not understand that magic. Is her voice not enough?" Zephyr asked, and Tomas only nodded.

"It is pure silver, you will see some day. No soul has seen her eyes but the King and Queen. I suppose they caught her early on.... didn't want to perpetually be handing her sweets each time she demanded."

".... The fibrous strands of the very valleys in which there is an opalescent hue is what appears so special, described by the Great Physician Paul Chanceston. Entirely dictated by....what? Hm?" There was a blistering silence, which happened to wake Zephyr up from boredom. *"We....don't....know. There are hypotheses, and some of you may figure.... no, one of you will in-fact unravel this mystery, and others will unravel others. Whether it be some sort of alignment of the stars or beyond the threshold of the Guardant Walls, just be sure to write it all down and thank your incredible professor."*

Tomas stuck out his hand to Zephyr once the students began to file out of the class below. Uncertain still, he shook it. "Broadmere, and don't you forget it. You'll learn it soon enough."

"You were at the tavern the other day, wasn't ya?"

"The day you were getting the 'ole farmer-special from Oswin, yes sir. Listen, ye ain't got worry about him or the fellows with him. He's just a boar, just feed him leather and he'll turn an eye."

A young man stumbled from an alleyway across the plaza. He laughed and stumbled about loosely, just like how one would prance about in group of comical friends. Though, he was alone, sporting loose maroon university robes and a slanted tyrolean on his head.

"You alright there?" Tomas asked with a sort of authority akin to a broad chieftain.

The student dragged his feet and waved his arms around. He hiccuped, then giggled so hard he nearly toppled backward.

"You got the look of a *cater*, you know that?" he said, pointing a finger at Zephyr's worn tunic and rain-sopped cloak. "A fat one. One of them trench-caters you see in the barley rows. Pork-sized, they are. With skin like yours.... like chewed parchment!"

Zephyr narrowed his eyes. "Are you drunk, kid?"

"Only in spirit and in spirits!" the boy replied, flopping back with a slap of his palm on the stones. "They fed me wine at dinner once. Said it'd calm my *sight*. Said it'd stop me from peering through folks' eyelids." He waved lazily. "Didn't work. Now I see *more*. Like *you*.... I see your guilt, Mister *Cater*."

Tomas smirked, biting off a chuckle. "A bit cracked in the head, ain't ye? I'm itching to finish the job." He approached the boy but stopped in his march when Zephyr stepped in front.

"Wait," Zephyr asked, standing still as stone. "Aren't you a student? Won't learn much waddling in the street while class goes on."

"*Was*," Tomas said, tilting his head and spoke heavy with sarcasm. "You likely used to have a little badge. Gold serpent. Lost it in a bet against a ghost. How's that?"

"And *won!*" The boy added proudly. "Well, more or less." He sniffled, then kicked a pebble with the heel of his boot. "I'm Brigg. Brigg Orlomund. Don't shake my hand unless you want your fate jumbled up like goose eggs in a gypsy's sack. Swear I'll do it!"

Zephyr ignored the invitation. "What'd they expel you for?"

"Nothing!" Brigg said at first. "And *everything.*" He leaned in, lips twisted mischievously. "*Persuasion,*" he whispered. "The real kind. Not your street peddler-hypnosis, not poetry or… or perfume or puppy eyes. The kind that drills right into your ribs and sets your *soul* marching. I wrote a paper on it, third week into lecture. 'Course, they burned it. Twice."

Tomas barked a short laugh. "He described it too well. Gave the Headmasters a fright I reckon?"

Brigg leaned closer still, eyes glinting under the lamplight. "Professor says it's a concentration of stardust in a mother's body before birth, but I know what it *really* is. A curse! I swear it. Imagine someone *thinking for you.* You feel it happen, and you *can't stop it.* Like your spine's been hooked to a marionette string and yanked toward a noose you *smile* to enter. It may be hex-magic, or Miscreancy. I only proposed other ideas. What an idiot *I* am."

Zephyr cleared his throat into his fist. "Have you seen someone with it? What makes you think all this, kid?"

Brigg went still. Then, slowly, he nodded. "There was a girl. Two classes above me. Quiet as a lark, soft as a sheep. But one day she got cornered…. three older boys teasing her for her Krythian accent. She whispered one word. Just one. They stopped. Walked into the lake behind the old chapel. Didn't blink, didn't shiver. Just walked in. One didn't even come out. But… I'm working on furthering it. The Princess, she has it. And I will uncover the origin of it. Mister Zell will eat his own grade!"

He sat back, suddenly far away and exhausted from his rant.

"What're you gonna do, gauge her eyes out and dissect 'em?" Tomas joked.

"What about that child? The girl you suspected?"

"They whisked her off afterward, when Merich of Yippire cleansed the boys. Maybe they *killed* her," he hissed. "Not quite sure. Maybe a dungeon… or a palace with servants wearing… silk-lined gloves offering silver utensils. Can't trust 'em with spoons."

"Why not?" Zephyr asked, started to grow bored of this drunken child. Tomas' eyes were wandering.

Brigg blinked, then grinned with all his crooked teeth. "*They bend* till the soup falls before it reaches their lips."

Tomas shook his head, now rummaging through his satchel. "It's like I told you.… ain't a magic you want. Ain't one to *use,* either. That's why the Princess wears the mask. Not to blind her eyes, but to hide *others* from them."

Zephyr glanced away. "Yet she's the heir still, the only royal child."

Brigg chuckled. "Aye. Imagine that. A whole kingdom led by a girl who could make you love her, fight for her, kill for her... without ever asking."

He scratched his neck, gaze suddenly wary. "Unlike the sitting rule," he joked.

"I sometimes wonder if it's *her* thoughts inside the mask. Or just the King's... humming through her, like a mouthpiece. How would we know?"

They all sat quiet a moment, the dripping from the gargoyle rhythmic and damp.

"I saw her at the last Morgenmete," Brigg said softly to Zephyr. "During the Welcoming Procession. She turned her head, ever so slight, toward me. And though I couldn't see her eyes.... I swear.... I *felt* them. The *heat*. Like hot irons, pressing behind the sockets. I pissed myself and forgot my own name for half a day."

"Pleasant," Tomas muttered.

"Power like that," Brigg whispered, "should be buried. Not *crowned.*"

Zephyr's fingers curled. "So why's the school so concerned with it? Sounds like Alexandria is due for a deconstruction. I could name a *few* governments."

"Because it *exists*," Tomas said, a little more serious now. "And if you don't teach the gifted, they become ghosts. Or worse, *gods.*" Brigg pointed again at Zephyr with a wobbling finger. "You look like a man who's seen too many ghosts."

"I've yet to, perhaps they feel unwelcome." Zephyr replied and his head fell in remembrance, that even if he saw the phantom of Ambrosia, the ache of her fading once more would ruin him.

Then Tomas rose, brushing off his coat. "Come on. Enough of your rambling, boy."

Brigg's eyes had glazed over as his attention turned elsewhere. Some *spirits* must have called to him, and he followed shadows through the streets.

"What of him?" Zephyr asked, nodding to boy as he wandered off.

"I go where the wind don't," Brigg said, lifting an invisible hat. "The drunk are much lighter than us, dear friend."

But Zephyr had enough of Tomas as well, growing weary of the night, giving him a quick nod and a false smile. He felt an absence in his stomach grow, knowing he should get back to Leon. So, he turned away and began his walk, but he could only take a few steps before Tomas ran in front of him. He looked over Zephyr's damp, fraying clothes, his bitten face and matted hair.

"A man your age is primed for battle, or perhaps the fields. What is your ailment again? A curse? Ye don't look cursed."

"It is no ailment," Zephyr signed, letting his back press against the school's exterior. "My son will soon….join his mother. He suffers at my wrongdoing, and my ailment is but a chiseled cliff that I must face each moment. Now excuse me, Mister Broadmere."

"You can spare a moment on this beautiful eve. After all, I've given you a free lesson on the Princess haven't I? Now tell me, have you the plague? Because if that that is true, might I suggest the taverns and lodges are already quite diseased. It may be not be good...."

"This is no disease, Tomas," Zephyr quickly asserted. "I am cursed, and it first took my wife, and it is taking my son." Zephyr looked to his feet. "And I will follow after them. I've slowed my boys' fever on occasion, but it does not grant him more time."

Tomas was frozen in his place. His mouth collapsed and his eyes wandered. The cool of the night set in. Zephyr took a step past him.

"Bring me to him," he called out, but Zephyr had begun walking. "Listen.... listen to me." He grabbed his arm and pulled him back. "I may not be able to help your son, but...." Tomas began to whisper, ".... there is a sorcerer who may. He's is a man of a mysterious magic, haling from Krythia. He's helped me on many occasions.... I think he may be able to help."

Zephyr was not impressed, as he'd about given up entirely. To him, it was no longer a matter of if the winter would be harsh, it was a matter of when the first snow would fall. But....just perhaps....Tomas began a fire for him. He spat out just once.

"I will meet you at the cemetery eastward of the Maiden tavern. If this man is what you claim, if he is no bandit nor troll, you will bring me to him," Zephyr was nearly foaming at the mouth as he spoke. His fist curled into the linen of Tomas' shirt.

"Dawn."

7. The Foothills & Sticks

It was as though the ocean rose and fell over the coastal land, bringing the distant forests, the silent town-square, and all of Alexandria's roads under blue. Not even birds pounced from roof to roof, nor could Zephyr see any deer or degora standing in the vast fields. Lamps which hung from the facades of the storefronts were flickering out from the dampness. In the cemetery, he welcomed Ambrosia's stone in silence, placing one palm over the flat of the stone head. Moss crept from the earth, climbing toward the engraved digits.. He looked across the hills at each stone, then wandered through them. Few had oil lights, and those which did were flickering out. Then, he spotted a figure stood before a grave near a well-kept grove. He approached, standing without a word beside the person who revealed his face as Tomas.

"The Death had gotten him far too soon," the young man spoke. Zephyr read the chipping letters.

"*Frederick Jon Broadmere.* Your father?"

"Yes, it was. A great leader of the West Guardant Walls. I was but an infant when he left."

"Might I ask, what brought the plague to this Kingdom? For, under Olderag's term, we'd suffer only ordinary disease. Most of which was spread about by his leadership. I haven't lived to see a plague wash us." Tomas chuckled, then left into deep thought. "We've fought many battles against rogue Hegane groups. It has been some many cycles, but they'd travel by sea, bringing with them disease and blood. Tartars; the King had yet to send an army on such a voyage. My father fought them from the cliffs. Been a long time since the Hegane have shown themselves here. I doubt they're as much of a threat as they once were."

"Tomas, my son hasn't much longer. This sorcerer you speak of, tell me your faith in him. I can't waste the hour," Zephyr spoke with harshness, still whispering. Tomas swallowed his story, and with a hand on Zephyr's shoulder, he understood.

"Beyond the first bout of forestland, he resides in the hills, still bound to the Kingdom. I will take you there… we'll lose but an evening."

Tomas' did not answer Zephyr's question of faith, but instead made quick work of their talk. It was of no mystery to Zephyr, whose hope was increasingly stark and frantic, that Tomas simply wanted to help. He understood there would be no path which may lead to the curse's resolve, but he could not die knowing he didn't attempt to disrupt the arcane.

The pair traveled northward, initially near the coast where the roads were well-beaten between townships. They were passed by many carts heading from the berry-focused northern farmlands to the Kingdom, evidenced by the dots of blue and red mixed into the dirt. Tomas then led him off the road onto a beaten grass trail which interjected into clear hills. They'd eventually meet the forestland, and Tomas used the time to learn about Zephyr.

"This curse, what've you done to receive such a horrid punishment?"

"I am a painter," he reluctantly told Tomas. Then, he began to smile to himself. "A great one, they'd tell me. They'd hang my portraits in their offices, cathedrals, hell, even farmers would have my paintings hung above their fireplaces. I was a great one. This disease they caste on my family was for that very reason. The Queen commissioned a painting of King Olderag, to which she….falsely informed me of his eye color. The pay would've left me and my family fat until old age. They….they first stripped me of my sight, empty the socket of each eye and let me pool in my own blood before the Olderag. After I pleaded my guilt, I was granted it back. But he assigned the Grand Wizard to leave me with this curse. They voided my years, took Ambrosia, and soon they'll take my boy. If I could just delay his end a bit longer….he'll die knowing I fought." This led to Tomas to stop for a moment and face Zephyr.

"That is very admirable, and I commend you for this effort. Listen, if nothing aligns, my sister and I can help soften the blow the best we can." They continued on. "Unless you've found a proper hostile beyond the Bards or Tuopo."

"Oh, but we live so lavishly in the Bard. We've barely a roof over our heads!" Zephyr's sarcasm made him chuckle at his own misfortune.. "But I will accept offer. It would mean the world for Leon to rest where it's dry."

"We can arrange that, of course."

Zephyr continued to follow Tomas through scarce woodland, fending off the late season's hordes of pests. Sunlight shot through the thin canopies and illuminated each root and grove. The vegetation shimmered as they pressed on.

The forest opened only slightly as the path curved uphill, the mossy ground sloping in subtle rhythm beneath their boots. Zephyr's breath came in labored silence, his legs stinging with fatigue, though he dared not slow. Tomas's stride remained swift, purposeful, his hand occasionally brushing back a low-hanging limb or fallen cobweb. Zephyr broke the quiet.

"Tomas," he called softly, his voice laced with a wary curiosity, "you've known the Princess far longer than I. I know only what the court and the people whisper, but I ask you now… why does she wear it? Her mask."

Tomas slowed but didn't turn at first. The wind whispered through the leaves above them as if echoing the question. When he finally did stop, he looked back at Zephyr, his eyes weary. "She was born with it… no… not the mask. The other thing. The power. Persuasion," Tomas said plainly. "Not simple charm or trickery. With a glance, she could unmake armies. Persuasion… a fabled branch.. It's deeper. A look and word from her, and even the most devout knight might drown his own kin if she whispered it so. You must know the six branches, all bottom-feeders do. Because we can't have *it*."

Zephyr exhaled sharply. He knew magic; he had seen it, studied it distantly in texts and rumor. But *this*… he had felt it in the marrow of his bones when Alexandria first looked upon him with uncovered eyes. It had stirred something he had not dared name. "She hides it. Or they hide it for her?" Zephyr asked.

Tomas gave a humorless smile. "Her mother fashioned the first mask. Gilded in silver. Later ones were forged by smith-priests beneath the Bastion of Candlehall. You've heard of them? They burn their eyes shut before they cast, some say."

Zephyr blinked. By then the two had stopped in the shade of the clearest bend of the path. "Blind?"

"I aren't sure I believe it. But… they say it's the only way to resist her. The Queen had them create bindings to channel her curse. The mask was just the first. Braces, runes, leashes of light you couldn't see unless you *knew* to look. She wasn't raised a girl. She was raised a weapon that they dared not test."

They walked on in silence for a time. The canopy grew denser here, and the sunlight dappled the forest floor with gold and shadow.

"You make it sound as though the Kingdom held her captive."

Tomas scoffed lightly. "The Kingdom *is* her cage. The King her jailer. Her own father. She loved him, perhaps once. But fear twists even love. And when she came of age, they saw not their daughter… but their downfall."

Zephyr mulled over the words, heart heavy with the thought of her eyes… uncovered, unblinking, blazing with truth. Then, Tomas added, voice low.

"Two seasons ago, the Bard Scribe told a story of when she was young, they made her Persuade a deer to walk into a fire. She cried for two weeks after that. She wore the mask every day since. Said she'd rather live unseen than kill."

As they reached a clearing where black thistles clawed at the edge of a mossy stone outcropping, Tomas pointed north.

"A half-mile of rocks and roots. He's a… mischievous fellow… be sure to know what's in your pockets. He isn't much different than you or I, he would never answer to a crown. I don't know if he can undo what curses your family, but there aren't too many *other* wild routes."

Zephyr nodded slowly.

"I am… thankful.

Eventually they stumbled out onto a vast scene of low hills. Without wind, the air was incredibly humid with motes of pollen all suspended. Just a yard from the treeline behind them sat a rotten wood plank against a rock. In a faint red paint it read: STICKS.

"It once was fixed to a post," Tomas explained. "*Sticks Carrey* it used to read."

"Quite an unassuming name," Zephyr laughed.

"Some say he was born long before real names came to be." The two laughed together at the idea, knowing it to be false. The went on through knee-high grass to meet this Sticks man. Across a third hill they finally spotted the cabin at a distance. A decrepit sort of place, appearing abandoned. Once they'd arrive it was apparent that this Sticks fella was huddled up inside, with the clanking of metals and strange mumbling. They heard the man inside seemingly fall from some height onto the floor. Tomas knocked frantically. "Mister Carrey! Mister Carrey, are you all right?"

"What! Who is knocking at my door?" A wobbly voice yelled back.

"You may not remember me, Mister Sticks. But I've brought a friend in dire need of your services. It is incredibly urgent.... " just then, the door flung back into the house and revealed a very short, goblin-like man dressed in a thick green wool and heavily-patched overalls.

"Services? Now that, I do not!" Then he inspected the two men. "*Agh,* if you're here about that the rupplestux beans, I'm fresh out!" Sticks angrily threw the door back, but not before Tomas could extend his fist to it.

"My friend here, Mister Sticks, he's a cursed man. A dark, hallowed curse."

"*Hmm,* have you come with a pouch?"

"The coin will come later, but you must address this."

Then, the door slowly opened again, and Zephyr looked in and saw the mess in which he lived. It was an intensely cramped room with each of the four walls taken up fully by bookcases. Floor to ceiling. The floor itself was riddled with molded papers, and there was no bed but a pile of assorted books with a wool blanket laid across and a sack of grain. Light poured in through an open window in what seemed to be the cooking area, but pots and clay vessels nearly blocked it. Sticks invited the two to sit on top of a half-wall of books, while he sat on the ground. Mister Sticks had pushed his magnified spectacles with one dirt-caked finger.

"Brew?"

"No, thank you sir."

"So be it," Mister Sticks nodded. He assumed a professional posture, and his cheeks relaxed. "A curse then. This is not one of those hiddlekin bites is it? I tell ye before, that is a poison!"

"No-no Mister Sticks, it is not a… hiddlekin bite. My dearest friend here was cursed, a terrible one at that," Tomas explained.

"A terrible… yet dearest friend?"

"No Mister Stix! A terrible curse! He risks losing his very child if you cannot help us." Mister Sticks finally adjusted himself, leaning forward. Zephyr just about had enough, feeling as though this old man was simply that. He thought to leave and waste no more time, but Tomas spoke once more. "It was cast by a Grand Wizard… from the Kingdom of Olderag." Just then, Mister Stick's eyes shut and he inhaled deeply.

"And thus, you bring him here," he began to whisper with a grin, "lawful magic is a blessings, they say." Mister Sticks rose from his pit of books and stared back at where he sat, seemingly searching. "Now, quickly describe this curse."

"It's taken my wife, and it will soon take my son. It is of a….contained disease. My son, he hasn't much time left sir." Zephyr explained. Mister Sticks kicked some books away, threw a couple to the side, and kept digging. He then turned back to Zephyr and Tomas with a small leather-bound journal. The old man read from it's tiny pages.

"Ah, yes… okay." He stood before Zephyr, placing his palm upward and closed his eyes. "*Gates-vox… gates….unbind and unfurl… unlock.*" An emerald flash spewed from the old man's hand, pouring the greenish light through the valleys between his nubby fingers. He slowly clenched his fist as to contain the mess of sparkling light, and in a violet motion he flicked it at Zephyr's face, blinding him. "*Unlock!*" But the cords of light dissipated, and the grossly humid cabin fell quiet.

"Has it worked… Mister Sticks?" Tomas anxiously asked. His eyes wide and troubled. The old man observed Zephyr, seeing what they may not. His face fell.

"Such a legal punishment is bound by many scriptures," he spoke softly. "There are strings which lead to entire archives of literature you and I will never read. I suspect this cannot be unbound…" Sticks scanned the floor. "Your wife and your child, if they were the punishment to a crime you yourself committed, I can only speculate of a vast web of spells.."

The moldy sorcerer sat back onto his pit of books and stared deeply into Zephyr's eyes from across the musty space. If it were true, the sheer maliciousness in King Olderag's ruling was far more heinous than any one man could assume. There was true hatred in his call, and Zephyr felt as though an invasive evilness existed in his influence; the Grand Wizard Joab had cast his arcane magic without a twitch of an eye. And prior, ridding Zephyr's skull of sight and to leave him in a pool of blood led him to wonder how far the root to this curse went. The corruption of it festered in his mind until this day.

"*By the book of the Gods,*" Mister Sticks mumbled and sat upright. "I've a supplemental spell, which you may consider." There was a sincerity in his voice, a tone of reason, one of care.

"Go on then," Zephyr told him.

"It be but a redden spell pulled from the native folk of this land. Greenfolk would grant the spell when their kin would get sick, whether it be….say….a toxin. By ten cycles of the sun the magic would delay. Though, this does not make your child invulnerable to the viciousness of this world, nor any other. An ancient energy comes from another realm from the soul, guarding the heart. But you sir, you must understand," he leaned in closer and whispered, "once its effects dissipate on the tenth evening, the veracity in which the curse returns… the death would be swift."

The silence was incredibly daunting. Zephyr knew there was no other way, though he felt a fire in his heart built around the thought that a true solution was, of course, impossible. Hatred couldn't describe how he felt, and his body was far too exhausted to even twitch in anger. Tomas sat idly by.

"So be it then," he finally spoke with a harsh voice. "If this spell is true, allot my child his final days." Even that was a gift Zephyr couldn't conjure from his own fists. Mister Sticks nodded to him, presenting him with two gemstones he'd retrieved from a large wicker bin full of rocks. Zephyr took one, emerald in color, into one closed fist and a violet one into his other. The sorcerer stood in silence for a moment with his eyes pierced shut and his palms flat together, fingers pointed upwards. His hands parted, revealing an electric red web. He slowly brought individual fingers together and apart, tying loops and knots in the magical web. He continued until the web resembled a complex geometric pattern, then his hands slammed together and released an instantaneous red flash all around, sending pages of books turning in a wind. Mister Sticks' eyes opened.

"And without words, that one! I find the Native folks' redden cradle-use simpler, with a hobbyist-touch to it," he chuckled with pride in his work. "I learned the ties from Greenfolk children…. they always astonish me… how the elders entrust them."

"These Greenfolk, they're peaceful?" Zephyr asked the old man, with concern that, from his experience, most children are careless and could teach a spell riddled with side-effects. "You haven't cursed me further, have you?"

"*Hah!* I wouldn't say so. They are farmers north of here, an incredibly kind people. This spell is of long ago, and I was but a child when they gifted me these books. They hadn't used literature for many… many cycles."

"Might this spell be used again?" Zephyr asked.

"I would not advise overuse," Sticks quickly spoke, "its' affects coordinate the organics of the soul, the dirt of it, and its' health; within a short period it would lose it's potency. Though, beyond the confinement of this curse and some time pestled in, you may see me again." But Zephyr grew irritated, despite having agreed to this spell. He wanted to exhaust all pathways.

"This curse I've brought to you, this cannot be the true end to my family," then Zephyr grabbed the sorcerer's frail arm. "I beg of you, there must be a way. I would give my blood and soul to save him!"

"Thank you, sir," Tomas said sternly, interrupting Zephyr. He quickly presented his hand to shake. Sticks did as such, nodding with a calm smile. "The coins will come once the spells' worn."

"A deposit, kindly," the old man had gripped the linen sleeve of Tomas. His voice did not allow for arrangement. Tomas' head slung backward, then he dug in his pocket for three bronze coins. "I have the brew warm on your return, mister Tomas." Sticks led them to the door but took Zephyr's wrist. It seemed as though he had a change of heart, willingly at that. "I do not advise such a journey, but I can feel the pain you share and I offer nothing else but this, that there is a land not far from this which harbors an ancient site. Many thousands of cycles ago there was a great battle, long before the Mor Empire came to be. I have read legends of entity who remains there, one which may strike a deal with you. This may not be true, but the battle is well ascribed. Should you turn to this land, you may spoil this spell I've granted."

"Keep your childs' tales; I will return come ten days," Tomas turned his head and went onward. Zephyr looked at the paleness in Sticks' eyes. He understood this sorcerer was no more than a kooky elder with access to arcane literature.. They existed in the Southern Kingdom too, but few rarely sought them out for anything other than vittle spore. Tomas wouldn't let Zephyr consider anything Sticks said as truth.

Before they had ventured from the rotted steps of the cabin, Zephyr caught a glimpse of something at his right foot. Something of shimmering silver with weeds and grass strewn over it, consuming it. Tomas went on, but Zephyr pulled the object from its place and found that it was a book. It was small and black, thin. The pages were raw sheets, and the cover was decorated in glistening silver flora. He took it without a word to Tomas, tucking it into the waist of his trousers.

The two journeyed back towards the Guardant Walls. Through the woodlands and hills, the light of day blinded them just as it had that morning. All of the life around them was so heavy, and Zephyr felt not different but for a spasm of hope that he may have a healthy son on his return. He felt grateful for Tomas' favor, but it was all spoiled and guilt-ridden.

"I never heard of these 'Greenfolk', they're farmers who practice the bog?" Zephyr asked while trudging on.

"Froggish folk, they are, and their magic is limited to health and medicine. I'm unsure why, but I hear they're also a cursed people. They bear no army aside from the hundreds of children. A peaceful kind," Tomas told without much breath. "Not much different than the Riverfolk southward of Alexandria."

"Frog-men then. Do they smell as bad?" Zephyr conjured up a laugh.

"Never met a frog that smelt good!"

Nearly out of the forest, the pair took a moment to catch their breath in a shaded grove. Zephyr sat atop a rotten stump an inspected his palms. Dirt was nestled into his fingernails, which were once packed with the pulp of fruit he'd use for paint. His knees were but rusted hinges from kneeling bedside of Leon. Before he could imagine his family's life prior, he first saw a hazy scene of the cemetery near the Greyhound. Though, he did not picture just Ambrosia's stone. No, he saw two on either side of it. Tomas pulled him out of the trance.

"Not much longer to go, Zephyr. Once we're back at the Bard, I'll accompany you to gather your things. Willa will situate the bedding."

"You do not need to do these things; you've done far too much for me. What have I to offer you?"

"Your gratitude is worthwhile. Not many would do so much for a soul, but given your circumstance, we'll allow it," Tomas smiled, patting the aching man on the shoulder. "The peaceful folk are often without community in these lands. We keep to our families until death. We've found ourselves better off than our governance wants, and you'll better our souls and we'll better yours."

Zephyr did as Tomas proposed, finding his damp nook of the Market Alleys. It was a jolt to his system, seeing Leon on his hands and knees attempting to adjust the wood planks, likely to soften to creaking. Zephyr had lost the energy to even hug his son, who was so closely near death. He stood awkwardly beside Tomas, only showing a slight grin.

"You're feeling better?" Zephyr asked without confidence.

"Ye, my fever passed papa! I grew bored and have been trying to get these boards right."

"That's good my boy," Zephyr went to him, looking intently at his eyes and seeing the dark rings had subsided. Leon then looked passed him at Tomas.

"Tomas," he stuck his hand out to the boy. "I met your father at the Bard." The three stared at one another in a moment of silence before Leon shook his hand. "I would like to offer our home to you both."

"We may be a cursed folk, boy, but we needn't count our days fighting the rain in our cots." A slight smile came of Leon. "Pack your books and blankets, Tomas and I will gather the rest."

Though, there was little else to gather. In but two baskets and a wicker-sack, Tomas instructed to leave their few pots and rotting rods for fishing. Once the three were walking back into the alleyway, Zephyr went to blow out four candlelight which illuminated the damp nook. Though, once he leaned over, all four flames died instantly.

"An omen, better to leave it," Tomas joked with a smile. "Come on now."

"Do you live far, young Tomas?" Leon asked while stepping out into the street.

"The village of Kapt, just one avenue of the Ringards. It is not far, but I am sure you haven't seen Alexandria for what its' worth. We'll go the long way," Tomas smiled as he spoke, and he did so with a caring tone. He carried himself as though he was a guardian of Leon, yet less than Zephyr, just as a brother may.

While Tomas and Leon spoke with one another, Zephyr retrieved the dirty book he'd stolen from Sticks yard. He saw its title, *Quire of the Collector*. Like a book he'd seen not long ago, it too did not tell of the author. Before he could open it, Leon called for him.

Beyond the Market Alleys and near the Bard but westward, Tomas led the father and son to a zone of The City's perimeter where the streets had turned to staircases with numerous plateaus. There were specialty markets of what Zephyr saw as luxury, which they once could afford but even then lived less than modestly. One shop sold timepieces and another sold assortments of flowers. The further they went, the more color seemed abundant. There were toy shops with devices Leon had never seen, with children racing around the cobblestone lot.

Up two more wide flights of stairs was a bakery and a vacant amphitheater at their left. Its' stage sat at the western side with appropriately trimmed vegetation acting as a border protecting it from a great drop. Spectators would face the open world and the forestlands far away.

It was apparent to Zephyr that this kingdom was of itself, a mountain. A warmth came of him as he wondered how Leon felt seeing it all. There was an animation of his pupils, a color of his face, a strength in his jolly strides. Zephyr could have bare a tear if his eyes were not so badly abused.

Even staring forward at the vastness of it all, the stairs went on nearly into the clouds to unimaginable heights. The air was unfamiliar, moving freely upward and through the outdoor markets. Whilst the father watched Leon jump across the stone tiles in the amphitheater, Tomas left and returned with powdered pastries to share.

Just before the evening could set in, and with rested legs, Tomas escorted the father and son down some levels of the kingdom's city to a cobble road which led westward. It was seemingly not far from the tavern which sat at ground-level, but in a round-about sort of way. This road, however different than most Zephyr had traveled, was purely residential, with stacking flats scaling the mountainous kingdom-side.

No storefronts sat at the foot of these continuous buildings, just contained gardens and hobbyist contraptions; some elders carved from knots detailed figurines, and some fishing rods. Others plucked bentberries and lemons from low branches, and still, children ran around freely. Beyond this road, the foothills began and met the elevation of the city, and the houses became more scarce. The second cottage on the right from where the cobble ended was where Tomas led them. A thatch roof and pale mud walls, the rest of the homes were all the same.

"Willa must be out for the evening, and you needn't worry; we've moved our cattle to Bitters' fields," he explained, "fella has been buying up the damn lot, but not needing to clean the shit has been a blessing."

The cottage was but three rooms: the hall itself, the buttery, and the second level. Tomas explained Leon would sleep in a repurposed chest filled with straw-packed linen, which was far better than the cot he was accustomed to. Tomas sleeps outside the buttery room, and Willa sleeps on the second level.

"Sir Solta, I've got just the situation for you, and I suspect you won't complain," said Tomas, who led him out of the cottage and around the back of it to a small barn where hay laid in stacks. The livestock was since turned over to the man named Bitters, and what was left was Zephyr's own personal quarters.

"This'll do," he told Tomas with a smile. "For the time being, this is more than enough." Tomas then put his hand on Zephyr's shoulder and spoke.

"I anticipate Willa can relieve you of some duties as well. I hope for you to enjoy these days."

"What you're doing for my boy, I am ashamed I cannot do myself."

"It is not shameful; you'd given the world if it weren't for the rot of it. The fungus it is, nature still thrives in its presence, and will rely on it some. And that, Sir Solta, that is but the world. You repay me in good company, and in another life, riches!" Tomas joked and nudged Zephyr, and the two went on back inside the cottage to assess how Leon fared with unpacking.

8. The Morgenmete Festival

An incredible bout of sugared almonds littered the sky and retreated to the earth. Cheer infested every ear, and the folk of Alexandria were shuffling along in great crowds awaiting the mighty gates of the castle to draw.. Leon sat atop the shoulders of Zephyr and watched anxiously. The day was incredibly bright, and the sun hadn't even met noon.

"Is she coming pa?"

"Oh, I bet she is, boy. Any moment now!"

Festivals were common in Alexandria. Often times, Princess Alexandria appeared at a distance, while King Jean St. Auclaire and Queen Lady Auclaire announced the renewal of laws and trade. Licensed wizards would riddle the city roads and showcase their magic for children, and plays would go on at the amphitheater. Once a cycle a festival would be dedicated to academia, and graduates would be blessed by the Queen herself. On this day, however and overheard from the local folk, celebrated a simple holiday of Morgenmete where a fruitful harvest was on display and feasts were made prior to typical times of eating, which were later in the day.

Just as the people had grown restless, the gates began to lower. Leon stared intently as the gate had bridged the steep mote, revealing the Alexandrian Knights stood inline. Their plates shimmered and the sun illuminated the golden cloth which ribboned from their shoulders. Their swords and shields were parted at their sides, and the forty-some of them split and began to line the new bridge. There, she was finally visible within a litter carried by robed servants. Laid across a bed of velvety red cushion and silver adornments, she was carried with knights on either side, and they stopped at the center of the bridge.

"She's there!" Leon pointed ecstatically, "it's really her!"

Zephyr saw through the heads bobbing to get a better look. In a glimpse he witnessed her face, and immediately understood the gravity of what she possessed, which he'd heard of at the Alcheme Astral School. The sun caught on a glint of metal, a silver mask which covered her eyes and brow, leaving only her mouth, nose, and hair bare. Her nose, mouth, ears, and hair could be seen, yet her eyes, cheeks, and forehead were kept behind the highly detailed mask, entirely silver. With it, the power she wielded was kept at bay, locked indefinitely.

Still, they keep her leashed an old baker murmured to a woman.

Forever, I hope.

God, the Queen's grace is so potent!

The fairest!

"A bloom for the Princess? A daisy for her kindness?" A frail elder woman tapped on Zephyr's belly. She carried with her a basket of flowers, to which Zephyr accepted one and handed it to Leon.

What a sight!

Stop tugging child, I see her. Behave yourself!

Will a suitor be announced?

Though, among the noise Zephyr couldn't refrain from staring at her, and neither could Leon. The servants did not carry Princess Alexandria beyond the bridge, likely to prevent any rebellious folk from climbing up, as they may have in the past. Zephyr attempted to move closer through the crowd with Leon still on his shoulders.

"She's so pretty," the young boy said with a wide smile.

Zephyr couldn't shake the sense that she was no more herself than a statue: masked, muted, and far from the beauty which Leon declared. If she could be trusted without the mask concealing her eyes, the spattering conversations may consider beauty. Instead, most folk saw her as a highly limited in her voice. Many were anxious for the day she be named Queen, with hope of her rule and expression less the appointment of a King who carries Jean St. Auclaire's same grasp over her. For now, the Kingdom flaunts her in the glorious litter at a distance and declare this early morning as a time for feast.

After some hours of devouring fruit, meats, and berries spontaneously thrown about at the castle's perimeter, Zephyr brought Leon back to the Broadmere's home for cleaning up. Tomas had promised the boy that he'd bring him to the brook beyond the farmlands to catch dinner, a great relief to Zephyr who sought to better organize their belongings and ponder the incoming days.

"A fantastic display, yea?" Tomas asked the two once they'd returned. Leon skipped in with his arms flailing.

"It was so great Tomas! There were Bentberries and dried Degora, and so much color! And the Princess, she wore a mask. I heard a woman say she's awfully evil, and that if she took it off she could summon dragons!"

"Take your talk of dragons to fetch supper for us, would ya boy?" Zephyr chuckled as he scuffed up the boy's hair with his palm.

Tomas had the lines and hooks ready by the buttery with a woven basket beside them.

"I'll bring back the biggest warmbelly you'd ever seen!" exclaimed the boy.

"Maybe not such a big fish, perhaps some eels. C'mon now boy," Tomas wrangled him up and the two left the cottage.

In their absence Zephyr fixed up the chest Leon would sleep in, laying flat the pelts he used for warmth. He decided to clean the soot from the smallish fireplace, using a flat stone slab the size of a plate to scrape what had hardened. Once the sap got a hold of it, Zephyr let it be and discarded the stone out the front door. He wasn't one to tidy up their place but had found himself doing so to lessen his anxiety in the recent months. However his linens left him leaving more dirt on top of the dirt which already sprinkled the floor. He figured he'd wander down to the brook come dusk and sort himself out.

After some time of rearranging the haystacks in his humble abode, the hay barrack, Zephyr went to gather Leon's storybooks and hope they hadn't molded through. From a rucksack he poured the small books onto the pelts over Leon's makeshift bed. One was well wasted and the pages out of their stitching. Another had lost its cover. Zephyr had grown weary of the same stories, and thought Leon deserved better, new tales, not these withering books. The coins weren't there, however, but one book remained that was, at first, not familiar. A square blackened leather-bound book was pulled from the scarce pile. *Codex Univerza* it read, the book Zephyr had taken from Bixby as a gift for aiding him in securing his library. He thought given its' form that it may have been another storybook, since the longer reads were often smaller. Zephyr turned the solid cover and attempted to read a twirling text in the center of the papyrus. He turned the page in defeat, but found a faded hand-painted picture. It depicted a simple scene of a countryside, where at the west and east ends were small castles. There was a pale blue sky above and green hills below. Zephyr turned three pages until he met the first bout of literature. He began to read:

"*Lo! Say to the tale of two kings, The first was Summe Red, who bestowed upon his people Eternal life, that they might toil in the world And never diminish. No ruler had they, nor army to command, for the people were free and bright in their own wisdom throughout the land of Sunoa.*

Yet, another king there was, named Univerza, who deemed the world best measured with balance and bounds. He believed that all men must one day fall, for fate and destiny must govern the earth."

Another painting was made beside the story, this one depicting two ocher crowns atop two supposed kings. One was dressed in a navy smear and ruby details, whilst the other wore a black cape and white adornments. Both stood at ready to parry the other in a clear green field. Zephyr continued onto the next page:

How swords clashed, how battle rang! They were warriors whom bellowed, and blows fell heavy. Summe Red stood firm, his endless life giving him strength in war's embrace. There be no defeat for Summe Red by blood. But Univerza, with cunning thought, turned his own blade upon himself, and with that act, bound himself to the earth. With the pierce, he too bound all men, all fruit and beasts, to him.

Summe Red faltered then, for he knew not how to battle this fate. Thus, mortality was sealed upon the world, and the endless days of man were lost and turned over to the Born.

Before he could go on, the door of the cottage swung open in a gust. It was Willa, not at all surprised to see Zephyr. In the quick scare, Zephyr closed and tossed the book aside.

"What's got you pissed?" He asked the storming woman. She turned to him and threw up a fist clutching a tiny bag and waved.

"Lost five coin to those damned men from the Bard. Five! You know how much a dozen eggs they chargin' across the way?"

"Six?"

"Seven!" She said with a furious growl. In her bout of anger, Willa threw herself stomach-up over Tomas' flock-bed. "You've been busy?"

"It is difficult to stay still now."

"Organizing storybooks helpin' ya?" asked Willa.

"Well, many are destroyed. I owe it to him to at least take out the ugly," Zephyr explained, stacking the remaining books atop the codex. It was that moment Zephyr's left brow quivered.

"Go on to the Greyhound, get yourself a pint. Swear it'll better you than this," her tone softened and she rolled onto her belly and spoke with a smile, "just dodge the Bard-men."

"Ah, but it won't do me no good. I anticipate being restless 'till death." Zephyr rose to his calloused feet, "and I can count them days on these fingers. I ain't in the business of fending of death."

He withdrew himself from the cottage and entered the barrack where he lay atop the haystacks. The air was thick with the high-sun heat void of wind. Light beamed through the glass-less

113

window, and his eyes became tied to the tiny dust motes rolling through the air. His mind settled and began to ponder the story of the two kings. *Victory by sacrifice.* The thought unsettled him. *And bound all men. All became mortal.*

Zephyr returned to the cottage after some time and retrieved the books.

"Ye aren't finished with them? I think they're sorted Sir Solta," Willa laughed while sweeping dirt towards the fireplace.

"I figure they're safer by my side; we haven't much and I can't trust Leon to keep them out the brook."

As Zephyr made his way towards the door, Willa grabbed a hold of his shoulder, pulling him back. She thought he was strange in his effort, and couldn't let the lie be. Though, when she did he dropped the books, yet he was not quick to gather them up. Instead, Willa bent and took them. She saw the black book and knew it as different, yet still retrieved it.

"I'm sorry," said Willa as she presented them to Zephyr. "What good are the stories if not beside Leon? Is it not his liberty to have them beside his bed?"

"I will read to him in the barrack tonight," he struggled to say. "He prefers I read them, and I will do so until his final night." Zephyr was unimpressed as he spoke and took the stack. Despite the guilt he felt in his harshness, the father went on to the barrack.

Zephyr continued to read the codex in private:

Yet Univerza, wise in his deed, wrought a gift from deep wisdom, and granted men the power to wish.… a magic of great wonder. Yet he alone could grant such boons, and the people, longing, beseeched him. Some sought wealth, some sought children, others wished for power lost.

But the price was high, for King Univerza, seeing greed take hold, laid a sacrifice upon each wish. Loved ones must perish for dreams to take root.

Then the people wailed, stricken with sorrow, and cried, "Where is our salvation?" But Univerza spoke no more, bound forever to the foothills, to the depths of the earth, Imprisoned beneath rock and root. With each wish tainted, the people grew weary.

Few pages remained, though he did not read them. This book told was the sorcerer Sticks had described, and yet he still doubted it. This supposed land named Sunoa was one uttered in few other storybooks, and yet persists. He'd never heard of it beyond its' fantastical roots. The country-land in which the Four Kingdoms protruded was established Bethal, though the country's history prior to the Mor Empire's arrival is unknown. Foreign bodies were even lesser discussed, and what spattered around were bits and pieces of wartime.

Late that evening Zephyr had read a different storybook to Leon in the barrack.. He left the boy there once he'd fallen asleep and ventured quietly into the City. He sought to catch the professor leaving his final class at the Alchame Astra School in search of answers.

No different than a phantom, he roamed the streets under flickering lamps passing by drunk folk who wandered and laughed.

Once he approached the brick building, he stood at a distance from its entrance. He inspected the moss invading the grout, and the haze accumulating into droplets and into puddles by its' heavy doors. He could hear the commotion of young students' chatter as they were released, and then poured into the square. A sea of heads, bobbing and twirling into groups and then dispersing down separate alleyways and streets. Eventually an elder dressed in the cosmically adorned robes emerged from the amber-lit cavity of the school. He had a magnificent long, white beard which sharpened to a point. His eyes were obscured behind thick oval spectacles, and his hands held a single large book. Beneath the beak of his hood, Zephyr saw his face. Then, he approached the man.

"Aye," he began. "Are you a professor?" His voice somewhat empty and shaken.

"I suspect you are a parent; I promise each student is doing quite well and no, I will not discipline failures by warting their fingers." The professor quickly nodded and moved past Zephyr.

"No, no sir. I am not a parent. I assure you, and I don't care whether you… wart their fingers," Zephyr caught up to the elder. "I am from a kingdom unlike this, and academia is not ordinary; I would like to ask you simple questions."

"Lessons are not free, get on," the professor dismissed him, but Zephyr kept at it.

"Tell me of the land Sunoa. Is it real?" The elder finally stopped and turned to Zephyr.

"*Simple*, indeed. Why've you asked me this?"

"I… I've read it in many storybooks to my child, and I'd like to visit the ruins of such a place."

The professor fixed his spectacles to the bridge of his nose and contemplated. Then, he gestured for Zephyr to follow. The two went on into the school, which presented a lustrous and warm entryway with chandeliers dripping oil onto the stone floor. One hallway was lined with shelves of encased literature, leading into dark depths. A wooden bench was sat beside the entrance to a theater hall, the one in which Tomas and Zephyr listened from the street. He could look in, seeing how the levels of seats began lower than the floor his feet were planted on, with seats leading up into darkness. The professor gestured For Zephyr to sit on the bench, and then sat beside him.

"I less dabble in our makeup, more-so in the mystery of the arcane and its' biology. I will make a special case."

"Is this a true land? I've read of the two kings."

"Aye, yes it was. Partially the land in which we sit now, in fact. Before the Empire built upon this soil of Bethal, there was a long period of impoverished communities, a wild time of conquering and violent magic. There were no establishments. Of course, the Mor we live beneath today built us our Four Kingdoms, but we're but a splinter. The two kings you speak of, are you following?"

"Yes, please go on."

"The beginning times, and prior? Nothing. Sunoa was once this land, and whatever kingdoms it held are dust in the stone of these floors. But, I do entertain the idea that ruins may be preserved where King Summe and Univerza once lived. To visit such a place, one which was even disgraced long ago, I cannot claim as enticing."

"I know their story,"

"And it holds nothing for trade. The soil is no good for harvest, there are no settlements," the professor's voice turned raspy and low. "Once our Empire divided this country into its' four kingdoms, much of our people's past was widely constrained, and the shavings of it were burned." Then, the professor leaned towards Zephyr. "However, there are legends which I will not dare teach which tell of an ancient library, one from the First Days, the time of Univerza and Summe Red, which holds the knowledge of all sacred time. I believe it to be woven cosmically of the lost arcane."

"Do you believe him to be still bound there?" Zephyr had asked, and the professor grew a small smile.

"We never leave this place, no matter the sediment we dissolve to."

"Thank you, professor. I won't bother you with my troubles any longer."

"And you'll set out to find this land? Well, I do wish you luck," the professor told him as they walked out of the school and into the courtyard. "I hope to be the first to hear from you on your return." Zephyr shook the old man's hand, and the professor gestured locking his mouth, as to not speak of the journey to another soul.

Uncertain of his fate, he visited Ambrosia. Three children danced around her gravestone and on to several others as Zephyr approached, and in anger he picked up a fist-sized stone and threw it.

"You're rotten!" He called as they ran out and down the dirt road. "Get out, you bastard rats!" He then found her stone with a small crack in its' corner, and he fell onto his knees, moving to sit beside her. "What have I done? What have I done with you." He conjured potent tears as he faced the moonlight. "This world has failed us. You wouldn't want me to rot, would you Rose?" As the cool mountain air flooded in, Zephyr's fight had lessened, and his body calmed. Distant firelight in the windows of homes of the Ringards and behind him, the City, had been put out, and he remained. Silent but for the skeleton-chimes of tree canopies becoming brittle in the cooling. He hoped Ambrosia would tell him the answer, and as the world became quiet, he listened very closely.

9. Tales of Old

Zephyr returned to the Broadmere's and joined Leon in the barrack where he still lay asleep atop the beaten hay. The young boy's eyes twitched and his breath was slow. His health was dramatically better, but the father only saw a simmering pot boiling until it curled over its' rim.

Once it was extinguished, what good was he? To seek the sorcerer Sticks was of bad taste and greatly illegal, although there could be no worse punishment. The Queen's instruction was a misnomer which barely crossed his mind in these final days. But as the sun continued to rise, Zephyr's desire to contest to his fate strengthened.

The following evening he'd visit the Maiden tavern where Eldric welcomed him to a pint. Zephyr drank it with an exhausted chuckle. Pitter ran about the tavern chasing a spotted cat, and Willa badmouthed the old farmers. When Oswin raised a finger at her along with his voice, Eldric intervened and set them apart. She then joined Zephyr at his table.

"Some day, I reckon."

"Some day… nothing," Eldric warned her. "Let Oswin rot, and I assure you the coin will return. He hasn't as much time as you," he spoke low and softly, bringing Willa to growl. "She's always been the angriest of the drunkards."

"Yea, well when you're cheated a time too many, there ain't much to smile about," she said into her sweaty palm. Zephyr's knee was rocking in anticipation as he decided to ask her of a dire favor, which he began to whisper.

"I can't thank you and Tomas enough for helping us. I owe you far more than we can offer, and even if I could…"

"All the coin I've lost would be beautiful," she laughed. "You don't owe us anything, Zephyr." Her eyes were far more careful than his, and she noticed his hiding.

"Willa," Zephyr leaned in and looked up to her, "I've recently learned of an opportunity which may call upon you, another favor."

"Go on then," she said with immediate concern.

"Perhaps I can gamble, as you do but with far greater odds, to save my son from this untimely curse."

"Zephyr, you should let this be," she finally confessed that defeat should be called. Her nose crinkled and her head shook lightly. "I think you should let this be, now."

"But there is a chance I could save him, Willa. An ancient magic exists out there northward…"

"And what does this call for, Zephyr? What then… sacrifice a thousand chickens for some fragile Greenfolk trick? It's no good, Zephyr."

"I would travel for but a day and night, and if the journey proves too extreme.… "

"Then you will return, and do so with lost time."

"Willa, I ask of you not to carry my own grief, but to make use of this life Leon's been gifted," Zephyr pleaded, and Willa let her hand hold his as she plead her own.

"What other magic exists? It's all regulated, confined to law and court. Even the Greenfolk get their visits when they… turn pebbles to seed," she hysterically waved her hands and her brow caved inward. "What could it be that does not endanger this very land?"

"I will seek… a wish," he whispered, his words striking her like a bow. Willa then stormed through the tavern and out onto the grass where Zephyr followed quickly behind.

"You know it's enough that I lose all I earn each day here, right?" She partially joked, still fueled with disbelief. "Wish-granting is fable, Zephyr! It does not exist!"

"It does, and I know this to be true, Willa, and I will journey northward and I will save….my….son."

"Even if it were to be true as you so vigorously declare it to be, what will you sacrifice? Huh?" Her arms were then folded and her head tilted in wait. A pit then grew in her stomach as she saw his eyes wonder again. "You would not, you wouldn't."

"I ask you only to care for Leon until I return. Like I said, a day and a night. I will make no promise of being successful, but I will ensure my return," Zephyr spoke as if it were his last breath. He allowed no room for negotiations, and as ever, he was determined. Willa's face began to collapse as she ran to Zephyr and embraced him. Dust and sand kicked up into the gold light which broke into the shadows of nearby trees. She cried into his frail shoulder, and yet he wondered why. What was he and Leon but a forsaken family from a disgruntled land who should have died alone in their dampen alleyway.

"And you'll return."

"A day and a night."

The next morning passed slowly. A cool wind curled beneath the loose wooden slats of the Broadmere's old barrack, stirring the scent of old hay and damp canvas. Zephyr sat cross-legged near the hearth's embers, watching smoke coil gently from the last dry twig. The breeze whistled faintly through the cracked shutter overhead. Outside, birdsong returned hesitantly, scattered and thin like the world still remembered the storm.

Leon lay across the cot, his color healthier than it had been for weeks. His breath came slow but even, his lips parted slightly in sleep. Zephyr watched his son's chest rise and fall and felt his heart grip like a clenched fist. He ran a hand across his brow, pushing aside dark strands of his hair as his mind wandered.

He reached to a nearby pack and retrieved a cloth-bound bundle. Inside were a few charcoal sketches.… rough portraits of markets, coastal ridges, fleeting faces of folk who never knew they were seen. Among them, one was worn and heavily smudged: the likeness of a bearded man with sloping eyes and a crooked smile. Zephyr stared at it for a time before Leon stirred.

"Papa?" the boy rasped.

Zephyr folded the drawing back into the cloth and tucked it away. "I'm here," he said gently, moving to the cot.

Leon reached for him blindly, half-awake. "Did you leave?"

"Only to stir the fire. You're safe."

The boy blinked slowly. His voice was thin. "You looked sad in your sleep."

Zephyr offered a smile that failed to reach his eyes. "Did I?"

"Were you dreaming of mama?" Leon asked.

Zephyr nodded faintly. "And of someone else."

Leon watched him.

"There was a man," Zephyr said, after a pause. "His name was Jeffrey. He had long arms and a louder voice than most of the town. A baker once. Later, a man who painted fences beside me when work was thin. He used to tell stories better than any bard. Said he'd once danced with a witch and survived."

Leon blinked. "Was he your friend?"

"A good one. Maybe the last before we left. He defended me when others feared me. When Joab named me heretic."

"What happened to him?"

Zephyr looked away, his eyes glassing.

"He disappeared. Or… he was taken. The Council sent for him. Said he was a sympathizer. I'd already been exiled by then. I never got to say goodbye."

Leon turned his face toward the window and the light pouring through it. "Do you think he's okay?"

Zephyr swallowed. "I hope so, Leon. I hope he found a quiet place. Someplace better than what we left."

There was a long silence. Leon's hand found his father's, and Zephyr grasped it gently.

"Papa?"

"Yes?"

"I want to see all the people you've painted."

Zephyr smiled sadly. "Someday, when your strength's returned. I'll show you the faces of everyone I've met. Everyone who mattered."

Leon closed his eyes again, soothed by the warmth of the hearth and the scent of his father's old coat. Zephyr sat beside him, unmoving, staring into the flickering ember as though it might whisper the shape of things to come.

10. *A Nomadic Fellow*

The stars were blinking eyes which struggled to stay open. Sabbath and George had ridden for half the day and all of the night since they crossed the furthest fringe of Olderag's domain. Southward lay Taria, and beyond it, the cracked hills of the old borderlands where emissaries dared not linger, and where the smoke of the Mor Empire's signal pyres coiled endlessly in warning or welcome, depending on who bore the torch.

It was common knowledge among those of all four kingdoms that the Mor are an ancient governance, one which few have ever witnessed with their own eyes. There were seasonal scribes, often twice each year, that the Mor had delivered to each kingdom, reaffirming magic-law and granting coin to bolster and regulate economies and trade. Though, not a soul could tell of *where* they're settled north of Taria, and none could truly judge the potency of power over the land of Grasp.

Sabbath rode at the rear of the saddle while George continued guiding the horse its reigns, a restless knot of limbs and iron thoughts. Her cloak flared in the wind, revealing a jerkin stitched with mismatched patches and old scars from past disputes. Her hair had been cropped short prior to their leave, and the glint of the dagger she kept tucked into her boot was never far from her touch.

Behind her, George clung to the reins like an anchor to the past. His beard was hoarfrost-white and clung to him like lichen to a dying tree. He had once served under the great nobleman Gerrard Robin before the first uprisings of the eastern frontier, and though his bones creaked and cracked with every gallop, his eyes had not dulled. He had seen wizards burn libraries and kings pardon murderers in the same breath. And now the flames had closed in on them, and Jeffrey hadn't much time.

The horse, an old mare unnamed, seemed to know the path well. And it was she who led them to a hollow where a single cedar tree stood like a prophet atop a buried chapel. There, nestled between two stones that bore a runic glyph of long-dead nomads, they found a place to rest.

Sabbath slid off the saddle and landed hard, stretching legs that had grown stiff. She unstrapped her dagger and left it beside a trunk, then bent low to brush away moss and clear a dry patch beside a stone. The air was damp and smelled of wet bark and rust.

George eased himself down, his joints wincing. "Should be fine here," he muttered, removing a satchel of jerky and hard bread. "No signs of sigil-marks or Greenfolk. I think that marking there is from long ago. You can see millennia of rain has drawn over it. Must be our lucky spot… no one's come here to claim it theirs. Get on then, girl. Get a fire up!"

"No place near these woods is lucky," Sabbath replied, already setting stones for a small pit. "Not with Joab's fingers sewn throughout the place."

George grunted. "Aye. That cursed wizard's had too much time to bend the sky to his will. If we can rouse the Council, maybe we can put an end to him before he turns all the South into another shrine to his false divinity."

Sabbath struck a spark with a flintstone over shaved kindling, her lips grim. "The Council won't move for fear alone. They'll want proof. Stories. Names." She paused. "Blood, probably."

George sat heavily, chewing the dried meat without joy. "That we've plenty of. Too much, if you ask me."

The fire came alive slowly, coughing blue smoke into the treetops where it mingled with the stars. Sabbath leaned back, resting on her elbows. For a while, neither spoke.

Then, Sabbath broke the quiet. "Do you think he'll come after us?"

"Joab?" George asked. "No. Too proud. He won't stain his boots tracking us. But he'll send someone."

She nodded. "I'm ready."

"No, you're not," George said, not unkindly. "But you're brave. That'll carry you further than being prepared."

Beyond them, in the clearing, the trees whispered to one another in a language older than speech. A mist coursed throughout. The fire cracked. The horse, tethered near the grove, snorted softly in her sleep.

Sabbath laid back fully, staring at the stars. "I had a dream," she said, voice half-distant.

"Oh?" said George.

"There was a tower. Not Southern. Older. Made of red glass or ruby. Inside, every step I took echoed with voices.... some I knew, others not. And at the top... a throne made of roots. And someone was there. He didn't speak. Just watched me. His eyes were empty."

George looked toward her then. "You dream true? I never heard of such a place."

Sabbath didn't answer. Instead, she rolled onto her side. "I don't know. But it didn't feel familiar."

George sighed, weary in soul. "There's something stirring.... it's gotten to your head. Too many things left buried. Too many old debts unpaid."

They lay that way a while atop a raft of fell trees, the fire flickering low. Sabbath, eyes wide in the dark, listened to the hush of the woods and wondered how far Joab's breath could travel. She wondered if, even now, the Grand Wizard's hand stirred the strings that set the stars to twinkle.

Just as her eyes began to close, George whispered across the fire, "Tell me, what will you say to them once we reach Taria?"

Sabbath exhaled slowly. "I'll tell them the Southern Kingdom's wizards have broken pact. That Joab's enchantments are twisted. That magic's being used on the people, not for them. Something… miscreant. And that King Olderag allows it because it gives him control."

George nodded, shadows crawling along his cheeks. "And you believe they'll listen?"

"I don't know," she said. "But they have to."

Dawn bled slowly into the canopy. A pale gold light spilled between the needles and branches, making everything damp shimmer as though dusted with ghostlight. The fire from the night before had smoldered down to blackened wood and soft gray ash, the final curl of smoke rising like a whisper to the sunlit gods above.

George roused first. His joints protested, and his old bones cracked like thawing ice as he reached for his boots. Sabbath was already awake, sitting cross-legged with her chin resting on her knuckles, eyes watching the trees as if they might move.

"You don't sleep much," George said, voice rasping.

"Didn't feel like it," she replied. "Not with the forest that quiet."

George grunted. "You're right to feel it. Something's in the wind."

They packed their things quickly…. Sabbath laced her boots, fastened her tunic with leather ties, and slung her bow across her shoulder. George muttered a brief chant over a stone from his pocket and buried it near the embers. An old northern superstition to keep the dead from lingering where one has slept.

The mare groaned but stood willingly as Sabbath mounted first and helped George onto the saddle behind her. They set off toward the eastern ridge, following a sloping trail carved by degora and deer hooves and rain. The forest grew brighter as they climbed, the trees thinner, the air more open. When they reached the crest, Sabbath pulled the reins gently and stared ahead.

Below them, in the fold of the valley, was a strange and crooked scene. Rough wood and hide had been lashed together into a misshapen outpost of lean-tos, racks of meat, and cages filled with bones. The scent of bitterroot and burning pitch wafted upward. Around a large blackened cauldron squatted the Koba…. green-skinned goblins with too-long fingers and twitching ears.

There were eight of them, barefoot and shriveled in stature but feverish in motion. One poured oily water into the pot from a wineskin, another stirred it with a spearshaft. Their tongues lolled from their jaws as they chanted, the cadence fast and shrill like birdcalls in a thunderstorm.

"What in all gods' names…" George breathed.

"Koba," Sabbath whispered. "Has to be." She leaned forward, watching. Her eyes were narrowed, studying the way the goblins scurried…. organized but wild, frenzied but deliberate.

One of the Koba screeched something and waved a length of cloth…. tattered and stained purple, like it had been torn from a noble's garment. Another goblin snarled and dunked it into the cauldron, which hissed and billowed with a thick gray steam.

"They're brewing something," George muttered.

"Miscreancy," Sabbath replied, voice flat. "Smell that? Ironroot and ashcap. That's hex-brew. They're preparing for something. Something of *witches*."

George rubbed his beard, leaning forward in the saddle. "Too far from Cornlot. If they're here, they've moved beyond their usual haunts. And they don't travel without a reason."

Below, the goblins finished their brew. One gathered the potion into a horn flask bound in twine. Then…. without word or warning…. they scattered like insects, ducking into the trees, four to the north, three to the east, one climbing up the side of a fallen pine with uncanny speed.

"They're splitting up," Sabbath said.

"And leaving the outpost," George added.

"I want to know where they're going," Sabbath said, already nudging his mare into a quiet descent. "Keep low."

They rode down the far side of the crest, threading between bramble and fern, careful not to snap a twig. Sabbath led them on foot in a slow arc through the woods, trailing the eastern trio of goblins, their hunched shapes bounding ahead like shadows made real.

George clung tight, murmuring an old soldier's prayer in the back of his throat. "Whatever mission the Koba have undertaken, it is not random. They walk with purpose."

The short abominations carried poorly bound scribes of spells to be spoken in dark tongues and hidden vials. Sabbath's jaw clenched as she followed them deeper into the woods.

The trees had thinned where the bramble choked the path, and the forest bent to a low, fog-slick glade. Mist clung to the knees of the world. Sabbath and George crouched behind a fallen birch, its bark flaking like old parchment. Just beyond, in a shallow dip between two moss-wrapped hills, stood a crooked cart hitched to a weary gray horse.

A plume of steam rose from a copper bowl in the hands of the cart's owner.... an odd, portly creature who wore a muddied vest stitched from dried lily leaves. His legs were thin, banded, *froggish*, and he squatted atop an overturned bucket beside the fire. He hummed low to himself as he ate, scooping up broth with long, flat fingers. Sabbath blinked in disbelief.

"*Riverfolk*," she whispered. "Just one of them it seems. What's he doing here?"

George grunted softly. "He's from the Marsh-breed. But they aren't nomadic folk. Barely traders. Haven't seen one of them in forty-some seasons."

The frog-man muttered something guttural between slurps and flicked a beetle from his bowl. The horse behind him gave a sharp, shrill whinny.... its hooves stamping nervously. But the frog-man did not turn. "*Settle down, Plopnose, you dramatic slab of hide,*" he croaked lazily.

Beyond the pyre of smoke, crouching in the reed-thick shadows, the Koba moved.

Sabbath counted four then. They skittered close on all fours, bearing their bubbling concoction in the horn-flask. One goblin had already begun unscrewing its lid, holding it reverently like a holy relic. Their guttural tongue wove into the air in wet, hissed syllables…. miscreant chants.

"What are they doing?" George whispered.

Sabbath narrowed her eyes. The lead goblin raised the flask and poured its contents over the flank of the horse and the wheel-spokes of the cart. The wood groaned as though centuries passed in a second. The polished oak spokes blackened, split, and rotted. The horse let out a tortured scream, its knees buckling, its hair paling and molting in clumps. Even from their distance, the air curdled with the sharp stench of rusted age.

Still the frog-man did not stir. He smacked his lips loudly and leaned back on his elbows, wiping his green chin with a petal.

"I won't sit by and watch," Sabbath growled. She reached behind her shoulder and plucked an arrow from her quiver.

"Sabbath, wait," George hissed. "There's four of them…. "

She was already gone. Moving like a thrown blade through the trees, Sabbath loosed her first arrow. It sang through the fog and struck the shoulder of the goblin closest to the horse, spinning the creature backward with a shriek. The others shrieked in alarm, turning toward the trees just as Sabbath sprang from the brush.

She fired a second.... clean through a goblin's throat. It collapsed, limbs twitching. Another scrambled up the side of the cart but was caught in the shoulder by her dagger before it could leap. It fell with a crack, flailing.

The last goblin turned to run.... but George was already on it, his old reflexes sending a boot to its chest. It hit the ground and hissed a curse before George silenced it with the butt of his sword.

Sabbath stood heaving beside the horse. The aging curse still lingered.... the steed's legs were shaking, the cart beyond saving.... but she reached for the flask and kicked it into the coals, where it let out a shriek like a living thing.

The frog-man had only just stood up. He blinked slowly, turning to survey the chaos, his half-empty bowl still in hand. "Well," he said in a gravelly drawl. "That was unkind."

"You deaf?" Sabbath shouted. "They were cursing your damn horse!"

"I heard 'em, lass," he replied. "Been following me for some time. Figured Plopnose was just throwin' a hissy fit. If them bastards wanted to do something I'da think they'd done it days ago!."

She blinked. "You didn't...."

"Wait… Fumper," he said casually, sniffing the bowl. "Generally kind-folk greet one-another. Used to worse things than goblins and cranky young ladies. Least you came fast." He glanced at his horse. "Plopnose'll live, poor thing. I've got just the thing," he said while rummaging through a rucksack, then he peered up. "*Ugh, w*agon's gone to peat, though. Flippin' aged a hundred seasons now!"

George trudged up, eyeing the goblin corpses. "You're lucky we were nearby."

Fumper shrugged. "Luck's relative, or somethin'. Guess while you're here, soup's hot. Sit, if you want."

Sabbath lowered her bow, shaking her head. "You're insane."

"I'm a merchant," Fumper replied, sitting back down and sipping loudly. "Difference is slimmer than most know."

She and George exchanged glances. But thought it would be a good opportunity to rest. Their journey was not yet over, and Fumper offered food. They sat atop fell logs in the patted clearing. Below the sky's pale morning light, the glade returned to stillness.… save the faint wheezing of Plopnose and the crackle of cursed wood dying into ash. But Sabbath could feel it: the Koba weren't finished.

Fumper crouched beside Plopnose, his long fingers trembling as he splayed them over the mare's shaking legs. Red light pooled between his froggy digits, weaving like strands of lightning-thread through air.… delicate, pulsing, alive.

"*Hold, girl*," he said softly. "Ain't no poison stronger than old Craddle. Not while Fumper's breathin'."

The web of red light shimmered, its filaments tightening as he pressed it to the withered veins that coiled through her leg. The strands hissed softly, binding flesh and bone, drawing away the black rot that had begun to bloom beneath the skin.

Sabbath stood nearby, her arms crossed, watching with narrowed eyes. George knelt beside her, rubbing his temple.

"Didn't think Craddle magic was still practiced," she spat.

"Ah, the froggish tribes have used it heavily. Gives them solace; no king allots for it."

Fumper didn't look up. "That is true. Only by fools and frogs," he said, brow curled. "But even fools get tired of watching good creatures suffer."

The red light pulsed once more.... then dulled. The last thread vanished into Plopnose's hide like mist into morning, and she let out a soft, weary breath, her leg steadying beneath her.

Fumper patted her side. "There. Like sewing up a torn sail in the wind."

Plopnose nuzzled him weakly, her eyes gentle.

"Fumper," Sabbath said, stepping closer, "where did you learn that? Can I?"

Fumper stood, cracking his knees. "From a witch who owed me a bowl of soup. And paid it in magic. But much of my people learn it from elders. Only way we can treat such wounds. We've no protection from the Mor. As far as I'm concerned, these forests are lawless other than the laws *we* set." He smirked, his breath fogging. "Now then. Where were we headed?"

11. The Plague Strays

Leon was fast asleep and Tomas had returned to the cottage after many hours astray within the City. Willa once mentioned his wandering in passing, that he was a fool no better than her with his coin. He'd stumble drunkenly into taverns and not only lose whatever he'd have on his person, but he'd return home in debt. As Zephyr lie in his shack, Tomas stepped in just before he could snuff out his lantern.

"Ye must be a fool; you aren't journeying to your death early. Perhaps this curse of yours is just. What are you thinking?"

"Quiet yourself! I don't need the boy hearing you," Zephyr growled at him, then straightened upright. "I am not abandoning my boy, I am retrieving what I owe."

"An absolute fool-you would burn your time. I have given you the warmth of our home, and I have *burdened* myself to go to Sticks for you. Sir Solta, what could you possibly be leaving for?" Tomas spat at him. "Why would you think of leaving your boy in his last days? You've given up already, why do this to him?"

"I will return the next morning at the very worst. This is incredibly dire."

"What is more dire than to lose any more precious seconds? You are willing to throw that away?"

"The chance to reverse this, Tomas. I need to. If I fail, I'll die in this battle forced upon me. But I will not die without at least presenting a sword to the head of this devil," Zephyr could barely speak so quietly and yet as he did, he was so very clear. Tomas was speechless, his eyes wide and his body limp against the door frame of the shack.

"There is nothing else, Zephyr. We did all we could. The thousand books tied to you from Olderag is far too elaborate to unwind. Besides, you would die at the town square before you even saw his fortress. Zephyr, there's nothing left."

"An ancient story," Zephyr rebuked, "one I now know to be true. A land not far from this, I've learned, once housed a great battle. The victor of it still remains, and he grants *wishes*."

"Ha!" Tomas rubbed his eyes. "You've gone mad, is that part of the curse?"

"The land and its' battle are true. And I will travel there, and I will plead my case." Then, Tomas sat atop a mound of straw.

"Wish-granting is fiction, a childish tale."

"It may be, but I must see for myself. For, if it is true, the boy will be saved. Tomas, I sacrifice nothing, and I ask not for you to attend my funeral, but to give him a memory of joy."

"No matter what you bring with you on your return, you will return a fool," Tomas said finally, leaving the shack.

Zephyr sat atop the hay in deep regret. Exhaustion weighed on him, yet his eyes would not close. He let himself fall to the story, which he wondered about so aggressively still. If what he finds is true, Leon would one day become a man, and he would grow to learn of his father's efforts. And, if not, he would pass on knowing his father even chased storybooks to save him.

The following morning, Leon accompanied Zephyr on a walk along the brook. The sun was shattered before them, and bees and hoverflies floated all around. There were large reddish mushrooms sprouting from groves that the boy would kick stones at, occasionally striking one, sending a puff of spores into the air. Leon then walked through the water long the rocks.

"Tomas and I did not go much further. It gets deep!" He yelled while jumping forward, letting the current build up to his knees.

"And ye caught a few?"

"I got just one, a sunfish. Tomas got a couple bigger ones. Y'know he said he used to catch spearfish in the ocean. You ever seen the ocean when you were a boy?"

"I don't believe I ever did. You know, child, the ocean is far closer to here than the Southern Kingdom."

"Really? And I can catch spearfish too!" He cheered.

"I don't know about that, my boy. They are far heavier than you. They'll pull you in and make you one of them!"

"I hope I can see one some day. I hope I can see the ocean. Maybe that is where they'll take me."

"Who will take you?"

"The spirits, maybe they'll take me to the ocean."

Zephyr knew Leon understood that he would leave soon. Though, the boy still had life in his eyes and his voice. He spoke with joy and his eyes were bright.

"Maybe your mother will be there with hot spearfish waiting for you," He spoke as they reached where the brook became unruly, Zephyr sat beside his son atop a long-ago sawed stump. The life Leon smiled with, he could not bear for it to settle. He'd lost his mind the moment Ambrosia fell, and although he versed himself in patience, he could not dare see the day. "I will be leaving for but a night, this night. And I hope to return with a gift for you."

"A gift? What sort of gift?" Leon sprung to his feet. His smile and wonder were a sword through Zephyr's neck as he corrected himself.

"It is a surprise, my boy. And I will not promise that it will accompany me on my return, but, it would be such a magical thing. I want that for you." The boy embraced his father in excitement.

"Is it a fetchwillit?" He asked, citing a wooden toy he'd seen other children playing with at the festival. It was a mechanistic thing, whereas a spring would eject a wooden ball into the air, and would occasionally catch in the same small seat it shot from.

"It may be; you will see when the time comes. The Broadmere's will give you a day, just ignore the bunch if they mention coin."

"They couldn't hold on to a pricked froglamp," the boy spat out in a rolling giggle.

The pair continued on along the water, and as Leon continued to rummage through the stones, a crack of the brush came behind them. It sounded as though an animal tripped over a root, but Zephyr suspected something else. He went on towards a tree shrouded in greenery to confront whatever it was. Though, as he peered around its' bark, it was no furry thing. No, it was Pitter, and she was hunkered down in a mess of twigs and leaves. Zephyr extended his hand and pulled her into the air and into the daylight.

"Have you lost your way child? What're you sneaking around like a pest for?"

"I…I was sniffing for them seedless bettles I was. The smiths pay quite well for 'em," she stuttered, and the two could see the guilt in her eyes.

"Were you snooping, child?" He finally asked her.

"*Gah!* I was not! The bettles, I told you. I will get on now, I can't keep Eldric waiting for me," the little girl said, freeing herself from Zephyr's grip and turning away.

"You tell me why you were snooping.… what good is that to you? Were you going to try and rob us? Now, I know Eldric is no friend of thieves. Explain your deal."

"Miss Willa said you were going to the north, and I wanted to find out why," she said with a sharp confidence.

"It is no business of yours," said Zephyr, "but if you must know, I am searching for a special fungi, one that a professor in the City has commissioned me to find. How's that?"

"Boring," she said in a huff, scoffed, and skipped away downstream.

"Is it really fungi?" Leon asked quietly.

"No, of course not."

"Who is that girl?"

"Pitter," he said, guiding the boy back upstream.

"How do you know that girl?"

"She's an estranged child who roams the local tavern. She's a friend of Willa and Tomas. An orphan."

"Who is Eldric?"

"A blacksmith, my boy. He looks over Pitter and many other lost children. He is a kind soul, but you mustn't let me ever get in a tussle with him, his arms are bigger than you, my boy! He was once a knight, and I fear the day they request his return. He cares well for the orphans of Alexandria."

The continued on till they met elevation, and decided to turn back, and their commute was inscribed with memories of Ambrosia, and her words and lessons. Leon could recite her quite well, catching the curl of her voice and its' cadence.

"She was far more noble than her own mother," Zephyr told him. "A many times she'd travel on horseback through the dense swampland of the south and trade berries with hunters. They could have easily nabbed her, and she was just a girl at the time. Yet, she'd always return bearing hides and liver."

"How come she never brought liver home to me?"

"My boy, once you were born, we had two men in the hut. She could finally rest and tend to what else she likes, while you and I took care of her. I tell ya, she thought there were two of me."

"That made her happy?"

"Of course it did. Her palms were so calloused until you were born, and with you, we took the weight from her shoulders and turned it into a pit for cooking our dinner, and doors which did not swing at the gentlest of breezes. Come the day you can marry a woman, it is important you understand your duty, boy." Leon's face fell as Zephyr spoke. "It is the most dire of gifts we could bear; the relief from what life burdens us with. Should you smile and lie asleep before your wife, you are no man at all."

But the boy was not listening. His eyes were pinned to his bare feet, and his enthusiasm had gone.

"I won't find a wife," he murmured, then Zephyr understood. Leon fell into thought of his final days, how he truly will not live to experience the responsibilities of a man. Zephyr took his dirty hand and held it as they walked silently through the grass towards the first homes. It was clear to Zephyr that Leon could not know exactly *what* he was hoping to bring back for him.

The supposed "gift" was but lines of a storybook, and in his search, may find nothing at all. Perhaps he might try and purchase one of the fetchwillits Leon was so excited about, if the journey is fruitless.

The midday sun cast long fingers through the narrow windows of the Broadmere cottage, illuminating motes of dust that danced in the quiet air. Tomas stood by the hearth, binding a leather strap about the satchel laid upon the table. Willa's hands worked deftly at filling flasks and folding cloaks, her gaze flickering now and then to the pale figure lying near the window.… young Leon, his breath unnervingly slow and harsh, more so since the day the sorcerer Sticks brought life back into him.

Tomas brought a map to the table in which Zephyr sat. It was stored long ago, now its' edges flaked away and the dust which coated the scroll was thick.

"You'll not see him again," Tomas spoke, voice low but edged. His hands tightened around the leather strap of it, knuckles white. "He has but days, Zephyr. And you'd leave him so?" Tomas unraveled it before the man, though, reluctantly.

Zephyr did not look up, though the muscles in his jaw shifted. "If there is even a whisper of truth in the tales of the King, then I have no choice, Tomas. You'd see me sit idle while my son fades?" He said in a rumbling, fractured voice. Tomas's eyes darkened. He inspected the scroll, finding a faded painting of the Kingdom of Alexandria. Northwest of the high castle were ponds with the Greenfolk illustrated as tiny figures. Beyond their woodland were rolling hills with jagged boulders, close to the ocean. There, the marked paths ended.

"I'd see you beside him. He calls your name in his sleep. No king's magic will change what's writ."

Willa's voice, soft as falling leaves, broke between them. "Tomas, hush. Zephyr's heart is torn enough." She set a woolen cloak upon the pack and turned to the man. "If there is aught in the north that may grant a wish, it is yours by right to seek it. But promises are like snow.... beautiful, fleeting. You've assured him?"

Zephyr at last lifted his gaze to Willa, something hollow and burning behind his eyes. "Ruin or no, I cannot bear to count another day knowing I did not do all I could."

The silence between them thickened, broken only by a quiet cough from Leon. It seemed the spell was wearing thin, time was running out. Tomas's fists unclenched, though the shadow remained upon his face.

"Well," Tomas muttered, gathering the last of the provisions, "then best you travel swift and return swifter. If the gods still heed the prayers of men, mayhap they'll spare a mercy yet. Few ever travel beyond where the *stonemen* reside. Those who do, rarely return."

"Stonemen?"

"Cursed tribes, fists turned to stone, feet to earth. Harmless folk, they shouldn't cause you any worry," Tomas explained, but almost as though these tribes were truly dangerous. Willa stepped forward, laying a gentle hand upon Zephyr's arm.

"We'll watch over Leon. I will keep him by our side."

Zephyr's shoulders sagged, gratitude warring with grief. He nodded once, a man already half upon his journey. He went to his son, ruffling his auburn hair and trying to bring a smile to his face.

"I will return by midday tomorrow, this is a promise I will keep."

"I love you papa."

"I love you too, my boy. The Broadmere's will look after you 'till I return. Willa, would you read him his stories tonight?"

"Of course."

Zephyr kissed the forehead of his son, gave him a hopeful smile, and left the cottage. Outside, the sun dipped ever so slightly, casting long shadows toward the north. The damp smell of earth clung to the air as Zephyr stepped from the door, a battered pack slung across his shoulder. In his belt, only a rusty dagger sat sheathed, the hilt worn smooth with age.

Behind him, the residence was silent. Willa had pressed a kiss to his cheek before he stepped out, one Tomas saw and yet swallowed his regret and anger. She had whispered no words, only a look full of sorrow and unspoken prayers. Tomas said nothing as well, and only nodded at Zephyr once he left.

His feet crunched over the dirt road as he made his way beyond the village's edge. He scarcely noticed the bustle of traders and townsfolk setting up stalls, so lost was he in the weight of doubt. Each step northward felt like betrayal; each breath heavy with Leon's fading voice.

At the crossroads, a creak of wheels caught his ear. He turned to see a modest carriage, drawn by two shaggy horses, the driver a stout man clad in rough wool. A trader by the look.... pots and goods piled high in the back.

"Ho there!" Zephyr called, lifting a hand. The tradesman pulled the reins, eyeing Zephyr with mild suspicion. "Where bound, stranger?"

"As near of the Greenfolk as you let, if your path bends so," Zephyr replied with earnestness.

The man scratched at his beard. "I'll take ye as far. Metal, have you?"

Zephyr offered only the sheath of his dagger, which had copper embellishments at its' seams. The trader reluctantly nodded, jerking his chin toward the back. "Climb in, then. Best not tarry.... roads ain't so kind this season."

Zephyr settled onto the wooden bench beside the man, the horses lurching forward. As the village slipped into the dusty air behind him, his heart twisted, a thousand doubts gnawing his thoughts. Leon's pale face lingered in his mind's eye. Would the road north bear hope.... or only another sorrow?

The wind blew sharp as they rode, and Zephyr's hand rested lightly on the dagger whose blade was bare against his skin. Northward they went, toward legend, toward folly, and perhaps toward something more. At either side and of great distance, the trees loomed dark at their underbellies, and their canopies bright and shimmering. The vast kingdom, decorated in clouds at the castle's pillars, fell beyond the heat of the day, and Zephyr bid farewell to it.

The countryman let him off where the dirt struck into the forest, disappearing from there onward. He'd about fallen asleep until the carriage came to a halt, whereas the hours of a reverberating ride lulled him. The man left with his horses without hesitation, and he did not even take Zephyr's sheath as payment. He was alone then but for the breeze which ran along the treeline. His nerves quivered as he looked forward. He took one last glimpse at fields at his back, and begun on his journey.

The path was quite overgrown, bearing a many roots and boulders, fallen lumber and the dense buzz of occupied branches. There was little to see, as the canopy above let only pins of light through. There were, however, long decrepit stone walls hidden in the brush which would disappear into the earth and reemerge, like bones from a lost time, ancient farming settlements. After an hour, Zephyr rested against a fell tree and observed this place. The dirt of the path was becoming enveloped by moss, increasingly so, and increasingly narrower.

He went on for some time afterwards, only stopping when he'd reached a brook. There, he cleaned his hands and face, leaving only sap embedded beneath his nails and beard. The trip was not so treacherous until then, and he wondered if it would remain so. Zephyr crossed the brook, wetting only his ankles, and followed the path forward.

The brook met him again as he converged westerly, and it had widened and deepened. But there were signs of life, such as abandoned baskets, sewn material and even clay bowls. He picked up one bowl, finding broken pieces of it in the grass. Light finally glistened in this place, as the trees had opened up and brought Zephyr hope. Then, voices came. He wondered what he'd stumbled upon. At a far distance down the current, he saw figures moving through the water. He went to them with the idea they may know where he was, or if they knew of his destination. Though, as he approached them and they noticed, he quickly learned that he may not be welcome. It was the supposed *Greenfolk* who many in Alexandria have mentioned, and his unfamiliarity with their king was blatant as he was at a loss for words. It was what may have been two teenage children, whose faces were that of frogs, yet they wore woolen collared shirts and frayed overalls.

"A yeti!" One pointed at him and yelled. But the other laughed.

"A stranger, why are you here?" The other asked Zephyr, but his head only tilted in astonishment. "You're not allowed to be here, Papa said no strangers can be here."

"Yeah, you're not allowed here! I'll get Papa," the first said and rushed out of the brook and through the woods.

"Why are you here, stranger?" It asked again. Zephyr's eyes were wide as he watched its' giant mouth speak, and its' nearly black eyes blink in such a bizarre fashion.

"I am passing through, I mean no harm."

"All strangers mean harm, and Papa will be sure to send you back!" The frog-child left the water and approached Zephyr with pace. Suddenly, the frog-child struck him with a curled, wet fist in the stomach, sending the man back onto his bottom. "You stay put until Papa gets here, you hear all-right, Stranger?"

"*What in the Gods' name?*" Zephyr could only mutter as he tried crawling away from the kid. Rustling came from the woods and out appeared an older frog-man who was out of breath. He rushed to Zephyr and pulled him to his feet. His few long fingers nearly stuck to his forearm, and he was disgusted.

"Get on now boys, I will sort this out," the frog-man said in a low, smooth voice. "Now, tell me who you are.... if you've come to issue a warrant then I will deal with you how I've dealt with the last stranger who came this way!"

Zephyr thrashed and released himself from the frog's grip.

"A warrant? Sir, I've no clue who you are. I am passing through, like I told those children."

"Passing through?" The frog said was such surprise that even Zephyr's face lit up. "No one passes through our home, let alone a stranger. Now, you tell me the truth.... who are you?"

"Zephyr, that is I," he stuck out his hand in hopes that he could find trust and lessen the hostility. The frog-man and Zephyr did shake and he could feel the world quiet down. "I did not intend to barge into your home; this path is not very clear."

"Are you lost?"

"Well, I would not say so as I've stumbled across you… *kind*… folk. I am headed to a land not far from this, and I will do so if you let me pass through."

"Aye, there be no nature beyond this brook that harbors ordinary men," the frog-man rubbed his wide chin, "even the chicks will kill ye. You tell me the truth, or I will have the Grandfather of our village make a message out of you!"

"I am a cursed man, and I bear no magic. I bear no warrant either. Your unregulated magic is no business of mine, and nor is my business of any relevance to you."

"A curse? Have ye brought a plague with you?" The frog-man asked very quietly, tilting his massive head and inspecting him with one eye open.

"No, and if you just let me through, I will ensure the people of Alexandria of how kind you folk are. Sound like a deal?"

"Hah!" The frog-man took Zephyr to his side and began towards the woods. "I'm pulling your tail, there ain't no plague that could harm us."

Unwillingly yet with more comfort, Zephyr let the frog-man escort him through the woods until they reached a clearing.

The heat of the day settled in a dense haze over a bustling village of froggish children and adults tending to play and chores. There were mud huts and a larger mud-hall, and firepits and drying racks for fish. To the right and beyond some huts was a fenced-in area where strange and colorful livestock the size of goats shuffled together.

Caters are long bug-like creatures, the same genus of ordinary caterpillars, but far larger. The Greenfolk and many herdsmen within Grasp farmed them for their meat and silk. A pond was to the left of their enclosure, empty of children or canoes. Once the first frog-woman, who sat atop a stump while weaving a basket, noticed Zephyr, the village grew quiet. Some wandered close into a scarce crowd.

Then, from the largest mud building came a massive bull-frog elder. He wore only a cloth around his incredibly wide waist with his barrel-like green stomach fully exposed. The rest of him was dark emerald, and his pinpoint eyes were hidden behind lumps and warts.

"I mean no harm…. " Zephyr tried to utter, but the elder summoned a red bolt of light at him, sending him upwards and onto the dirt. The crowds chirped and laughed.

"Why is there a stranger? Who is this stranger Bulo?" He asked the same frog-man who brought Zephyr, who lay defeated.

"A passerby, father. He wishes to continue northward." The elder then slowly approached Zephyr, and each step shook the earth beneath them.

"What for, strange man? To see the Stonemen of the foothills? *Hm? Or…* to take the caters we so *notoriously* breed here in Kappa Grove? Now stranger, plead your case." His very voice was like thunder, and it seemed even the birds in the canopies were listening silently. But Zephyr was stunned, particularly by the elder's use of magic, knowing now he could die to those three damp fingers.

"I am venturing to the ruins of a long-wasted kingdom, and if you are so kind, I would like to continue."

"*Hm,*" the elder groaned. "And what awaits you of such importance? For, all treasure must be looted and there is no stone different to that of this very land you're seated upon." He chuckled with the village, and Zephyr brought himself to his own feet.

"The king still lies there, and I will retrieve a wish," he spoke with roughness and this sparked the incandescent frog.

"A Wish-Granter! And so this stranger is ready to strike such a deal, and does he know the consequences?"

The laughter of the villagers died down to a murmur as the elder took a step closer to Zephyr, his wide mouth twisting into a knowing grin. The elder's deep-set eyes gleamed like wet stones, and his massive hands flexed at his sides. The elder then flicked a finger and turned away, heading back into his mud-hall.

Bulo shifted uneasily. "Father, he claims to be cursed," he said, his voice lower now. "But bears no magic."

The elder turned back to them and let out a throaty croak, amused. "A cursed man with no magic, seeking a wish? Oh, how all fables meet the same epilogue." His webbed fingers traced the air before him, and faint tendrils of red light shimmered in their wake. "You believe this king will grant you a wish?"

Zephyr clenched his jaw, brushing dust from his tunic. "I do."

The elder tilted his head. "And what would you wish for, stranger?"

The question made Zephyr stiffen. He had expected resistance, perhaps mockery, but not this… an invitation to speak of his purpose. He glanced around; the villagers watched with quiet curiosity. Even the great cater-like beasts had ceased their shuffling.

Zephyr exhaled. "To lift the curse, one which has consumed my wife, and soon my son. Then, I will be no more."

The elder hummed again, rolling the words on his tongue as though savoring them. The elder's expression darkened, the light of his magic flickering out. "You seek a wish, yet you know nothing of the price." His voice, though quiet, carried weight. "The Wish-Granter is no *gift-bearer*, stranger. He is but *Death*, and for every boon, there is a burden… stay as long as you must. Come dawn, we will see you out."

"I need not that allotment. I will continue now."

The elder nodded slowly. "Provide nourishment to this man before his departure."

Bulo brought Zephyrs to the edge of the pond, where the water gleamed with the brightness of the sun. The air was thick with the scent of damp earth and reeds, and the only sounds were the occasional chirrup of unseen insects and the gentle lapping of water against the bank. Beneath the surface, enormous tadpoles, some nearly the size of Zephyr's head, glided in slow, lazy circles. Their translucent, jelly-like bodies rippled with movement, their tails undulating like ribbons in the current. A few surfaced briefly, their tiny, unformed limbs twitching before they dipped back into the murky depths.

Zephyr watched them, both fascinated and unsettled. "Your young are… large," he muttered.

Bulo let out a deep chuckle, draping his long arms over his knees. "Aye. When a Greenfolk-kid spawns, they do so in great numbers. But few make it to their second summer." He gestured to the water. "The strongest will grow legs and crawl upon the land. The weakest.… " He made a snapping motion with his fingers.

Zephyr frowned. "What takes them?"

"Ah, the world is full of hungry things," Bulo said. "Some with teeth, some with claws. Even the water is no safe place."

Zephyr glanced at him. "And that is why your people wield magic?"

Bulo's throat pulsed slightly as he considered the question. "Aye," he said, his voice quieter now. "It was given to us long ago, by a woman who did not belong to the land, nor to the rivers or mountains. A witch, with a heart black as iron and eyes like dying embers."

Zephyr's brow furrowed. "And yet she was not malevolent?"

Bulo nodded. "Many generations past, she came to our people in the deepest part of the swamp, not this. We migrated towards the coast of these lands from Krythia. She had been cast out of the world of men, hunted for the magic she carried. She was not old, for she was suspended at her age, not older than you or I. She told us that the world would never come to respect us for what we are, and so we must learn to be as we are, without the strange kingdoms who once governed us." He lifted a hand, and red light shimmered between his fingers, like blood catching fire. "She taught us this in order to keep us alive, for we may be no more than oxen, tending to their wetlands as the beasts do their fields."

Zephyr felt the warmth of the red orb, even from where he sat. The same energy that had struck him to the dirt mere hours ago now pulsed gently in Bulo's palm, alive yet contained.

"With it, we heal our sick, we strengthen our young, we drive away those who would see us as nothing but prey," Bulo said. "But the world beyond Kappa Grove calls it unlawful. Tainted. A magic that should not be. Though, this magic is far less threatening than it can be silly. The children can turn rocks to saplings, yet it is only my father, the Grandfather of Kappa, who has learned to kill a man with it."

Zephyr watched the flickering red light, uneasy. "And yet you still use it."

Bulo's eyes gleamed with something ancient, something that could not be swayed. "Aye," he said simply. "Because to live with it is no different than eating." The light in his green hand flickered out, and silence settled between them once more. Zephyr turned his gaze back to the water, watching as a tadpole surfaced, its tiny, rounded face and dots-for-eyes peering up at the sky before vanishing below. He wondered, then, what it truly meant to grow in a world that sought to take you before you had the chance. "Are you sure this king still waits in his place? And, if he does, are you prepared to uphold your end of his deal?"

"I am, and I will save my son from the dark that I have bestowed upon him."

Bulo couldn't provide Zephyr any further insight, and let him eat from a bowl of insects a smiling frog-woman left him with. Aside from what was still twitching and crawling, he gave the bowl to Bulo who sent him off on his journey.

12. The Ancient East

Three leagues north, the forest broke into rolling hills and scattered fields of stone. Among the boulders lived a people Zephyr had only heard of in whispers. They were named the *Stonemen*, and they never ventured even to nearby settlements. Unlike the Greenfolk, these people were cursed long ago, and still retained a human torso, head, and down to their elbows and knees. Though, their hands and feet were incredible stones, and the ones on their feet made each person far taller than any ordinary human. Their stone-bound legs made them tower above ordinary men, tall enough to peer across rooftops if they wished..

But the Stonemen and women lived in several caves scattered around the foothills, and although they could not hunt traditionally, they survived by baiting rodents, catching insects, and harvesting berries and vegetation of the area. Zephyr had no issue in approaching them, noting how slow they roamed around and their seemingly exhausted expressions. He even sat atop a boulder to rest and none of them approached him. But when one did, their knowledge and story had Zephyr leaning forward. The man's eyes wept as his great stone-bound hands rest in the dirt. The weight of them cracked the dry earth beneath him, and when he shifted, the sound was like boulders grinding together. His face, though weathered and lined with age, remained human.... scarred but expressive, his eyes deep wells of memory. His voice, when he finally spoke, was heavy as the mountain wind.

"We were men once, same as any in Alexandria." He lifted one of his stone hands, "merchants, craftsmen, we built the very halls in which they ruled us. We sought the north where we could reach distant villages, where trade could flourish beyond the reach of the king's greed. We wished only to carve a path through the wilds, to bring wealth to our people." The Stoneman sighed, his breath deep as the earth itself. "But the mountains are old, countryman. Older than kings, and yet the king himself made sure we could not do as we wished."

"What happened?"

The Stoneman let his great, burdened hands fall with a dull *thud.* "A curse he brought upon us, one to ensure the trade routes would never come to be." He flexed his fingers, or what remained of them... huge, jagged masses of stone fused where flesh once was. "It was the curse of this very earth, as if from the gods, some say. A punishment, nevertheless, sent by the king himself for daring to defy his borders."

"You survive, though."

A low chuckle rumbled from the Stoneman's throat. "Aye, we do. We break the earth with these hands. We carve shelter from the hills. The mountains gave all but our breath, and so long as we breathe, we endure." He met Zephyr's gaze then, his expression unreadable.

"This Wish-Granter...."

"Our people bid never to see Death as he lays, for the price is far too high. We will eventually be but the rocks you sit atop, and there is no undoing. Tell me, countryman, what do you bear that is so odious to seek this?"

"One in which time itself has been shot into me like an arrow. And... it is my time which has been plagued and eats away at me, from the inside out."

"A curse unseen is often the heaviest to bear." He shifted, the weight of his great stone limbs cracking the earth beneath him. "May the road ahead show you mercy, countryman."

Zephyr remained seated, dusting grit from his cloak, as another of the Stonemen approached from the shadows of a sun-warmed crag. This one was younger in bearing, though the curse had claimed him no less cruelly.... his forearms were banded in jagged granite, and his bare stone feet left deep impressions with each slow step. His voice was softer than the first, but carried that same buried weight, as though drawn from beneath layers of earth and memory.

"You speak of time, traveler," the second Stoneman said, lowering himself beside Zephyr with great care. "You are not the first cursed soul to wander near our caves. But you may be the first to speak plainly of your burden."

"I have no time for riddles anymore," Zephyr murmured.

The Stoneman nodded slowly. "Nor do we. What little time we have left is not counted in hours, but in the seasons that wear down our edges."

They sat in silence for a stretch, the breeze rustling through tall grasses, carrying with it the scent of wet rock and distant fire. Then Zephyr asked, "Have you seen others pass through here? Travelers… creatures, maybe?"

The Stoneman's gaze turned eastward, toward a ragged treeline. "We've seen much. Even in our silence, we watch. Goblins passed here not long ago…. the Koba, I believe your kind calls them. Mischief-ridden little crows, all teeth and poison. They skitter through the hills like whispers, but even they know better than to linger near us."

Zephyr furrowed his brow. "You don't fear them?"

"Fear?" The Stoneman gave a grinding chuckle. "Miscreancy flows off our stone like water over cliffs. Their poisons rot skin and bone, yes…. but we are already half-dead. The Koba cannot unmake what has already been made part of the earth. We'll outlast these hills."

"But others…" Zephyr leaned forward. "Have they harmed others?"

The Stoneman's eyes darkened. "Yes. Travelers, greenfolk, wanderers. We've seen their aftermath…. rotted wood, aged flesh, curses carved into the soil like wounds. But I've also seen those green-skinned healers stand their ground. The Greenfolk don't fight like men. They unravel things. Undo what's been done with light, not steel."

Zephyr exhaled deeply, a flicker of hope moving behind his wearied eyes. "You think they can fight Miscreancy?"

"I've seen them stem it. That is not the same as defeating it," the Stoneman said. "But where your kind burns a plague with fire, they burn it with patience."

"Do you think I'm a fool?" Zephyr asked.

"Only fools seek answers from men of stone," the Stoneman said, and smiled. "But only the wisest dare to listen when the stone speaks."

Zephyr stood slowly, brushing grit from his sleeves. "Thank you. If the hills swallow you one day, I hope they do so gently."

"And may they never remember my name," the Stoneman replied, then looked up toward the sky, where clouds crawled like old beasts across the sun.

Zephyr turned toward the north, where the edge of the foothills gave way to a great haze over distant forests. The hill where Zephyr rested sloped like a fallen shoulder beneath the midday sun, steep and wind-scoured. He lay upon his side, propped on one elbow, his back pressed against a patch of wild sage and thistle. His breath moved slow and steady, though not from calm…. but weariness, that heavy cloak of a man who has carried too much for too long.

Below, the Stonemen moved. At first, they seemed like the landscape itself come to life…. boulders that rose and trudged with aching slowness. One dragged a rounded slab larger than a wine cart across a flat of earth, digging trenches with its stone feet. Another heaved a moss-covered rock over his shoulder, its size absurd, yet the motion deliberate, like a memory he could not forget. Three others dug together in silence, shaping what Zephyr understood to be a den: not a home for comfort, but a hollow for rest, protection, and eventually, burial.

Beyond the stone-clearing, a sudden crack echoed. Zephyr shifted, peering through blades of tall grass. One of the younger Stonemen, perhaps not yet fully hardened, had struck a bounding creature…. field-born and swift. The mammal, like a hare but broader of back, twitched in death beside the weight of the Stoneman's fist. The stone limb dripped red, and the younger figure did not cheer, nor revel. He merely lifted the body, turned, and trudged back to the shaded caves.

Zephyr watched in stillness, his eyes like stone: distant, unreadable, dimmed by years of slow erosion.

They are not alive, not truly, he thought. They are echoes…. men who spoke once, laughed once, and now murmur only with their footprints. But still… they go on.

He laid his head back against the dirt, closing his eyes. "*What of me?*" he asked the silence. "What am I if not stone-bound myself, rooted by dread and hope alike? What is a father whose child will die unless the stars unbury an old King of death?"

He wanted to run…. but where would he go? He wanted to fight…. but with what sword does one strike time?

A sharp wind tousled his hair. In the shade of the hill, his shadow shrank beside him. He thought of Leon: his pale lips, his flickering breaths and the unrelenting spread of the miscreant curse. Time was winning.

He exhaled through his nose and watched a Stoneman set a boulder in place with a thundering *thunk*. Dust swirled around the edges of the den's new roof.

"They suffer, too. But slowly. Their doom is steady. Mine waits just over the next dusk."

He pressed his fingers into the grass. The petals bent like all things beneath fate. And in that moment, Zephyr realized, perhaps the stone envied him. To die fast, to burn up in desperation for one you love… was that not the kindest way to erode?

He said nothing aloud, though his chest tightened, and his thoughts rumbled heavy as falling rock. Even if death waited beside him in the next shadow, he would find Univerza, or the dusk begin its feast.

13. The King of Death

Zephyr rested for an hour before the weight of wasted time gnawed at him. The task at hand was urgent, he knew it all too well. His body protested, his legs stiff, his back sore from the long day's march; he did not want to continue. But he had no choice. What good was time if left unused? He would not spare even the bones of it.

From then on, he was unsure where exactly to go, or where to find King Univerza or the ruins of his castle. Would he and his fortress have been consumed by the earth after all this time? He did not lay much thought to it, that he would find nothing and roam aimlessly in these unnamed lands. Zephyr nearly gave in to the pain as he climbed another hill. Murky clouds infested the sky and although he had lost most of the day thus far, without the sun the world was much darker. But like several collapses before, Zephyr got to his feet and continued on.

The once-gentle slopes of the foothills grew jagged, the earth rising and falling in uneven steps of stone and dirt. The wind howled between the rocks, carrying with it the scent of salt from the distant sea hidden behind a curtain of light rain.

Zephyr pressed forward, the callouses of his feet now soft and ripping from the dampness. His breath came heavier with each step, his limbs burning with fatigue. The weight of life…. not just the miles, but the days, the years…. settled into his bones like lead.

His knees ached. His back screamed with each incline. He had walked far before, but the foothills were no even road. Here, the earth was cruel, demanding more than he had left to give. He wiped a grimy hand across his forehead. His skin was slick with sweat, but the wind had turned sharp, biting into the dampness of his clothes. He was slowing. Though, the clouds were parted in some areas across the vast land, and the rain would die and return in subtle waves.

The thought gnawed at him…. what if he could not go on? His breath shuddered as he climbed over a steep rocky hill, his arms trembling under his own weight. He dragged himself onto flatter ground, collapsing against a jutting stone. His legs throbbed. His lungs felt tight. He could not remember even the finest details about his life besides Leon and the folks he'd met this day. He looked westward. The sun had sunk low, bleeding gold across the horizon. The sky darkened at its edges, and with it came the creeping realization…. night would fall soon.

Zephyr swallowed hard, pushing himself up. He could not rest here. Not in the open, where the wind would steal the warmth from his body and the darkness might bring unseen dangers. He glanced ahead, scanning the uneven terrain. Eastward there were mountains barely visible through the haze, but just to left of them were large pale objects protruding from the earth atop a great hill. Gritting his teeth, he forced his legs to move, staggering toward the structures.

In but another hour, each step sent a dull, numbing pain through his joints. The shadows stretched long across the foothills, the last light of the sun fading. He was furiously close, panting hard and his heart quivering as he found civilization, or even the forsaken castle. Regardless of what it was, Zephyr knew he needed to reach it.

His muscles shook intensely as he came up upon the structures. Zephyr wanted to let the air out of his lungs and scream in victory… but there was little air left. What was true, however, was that he had found a crumbling, yet enormous, ancient temple whose structures he saw were sixteen monolithic columns of great grandeur, and tremendous decay. They stood atop an immense stone platform which long ago may have had thousands of folk stood atop it. But there was no sign of a king, nor a throne for him to sit.

There was no true castle, nor any true buildings either. Only the monstrous columns and their platform remained of this place, and in its' day would have been fit for a god. There were stone steps which led up to the platform and disappeared into the earth, and all Zephyr could conjure was to lay along them indefinitely until he'd fallen asleep. The light of day had fell, and not even a fire could be lit to warm him. In his exhaustion, Zephyr did not even wonder what Leon or the Broadmeres would think of him not returning this day, as the journey was far longer than he'd anticipated, and his old body slowed him down.

The morning came softly, bringing daylight of pinks and amber hue to the land. It was then Zephyr awoke and immediately noticed how close to the ocean he had made it. There were forests which sat at the foot of this hill, and the long grass brushed in a low breeze. He may have been energized, but his body ached intensely. Though, in his excitement he stood before the fallen kingdom and attempted to reach the platform.

At the top of the stairs he could make out the elaborate stone-cutting and geometric patterns, carvings in the monolithic columns. Long lines which stretched to the center. In the lines were flowers and vegetation which had been slowly breaking through the foundation. He wandered slowly atop the stone, marveling at its' scale.

Some skinny object stood at the center, equal to parallel columns. It was a sword, and its pommel pointed at the sky while the tip of its rusting blade was struck deep into the stone. Its guard and grip were of a torn leather, blackened with mold and the silver of it was well-worn. It was strange to him how it hadn't been looted, but he saw it as an omen that fortress would remain indefinitely, and this sword pinned it in its' place.

After inspecting one of the columns in awe, Zephyr went onward to the far end of the platform. The hill dipped downward there, and all he could see from his stance was the aching sky. He followed down another set of stone stairs and onto the grass where he could look below at a great wilderness. The hillside beneath him was blanketed in lavender and yellow flowers, swaying and dancing slowly. But an oddity sat below in the grass. A black figure, one which sent Zephyr's heart into a void. There was panic, but Zephyr decided to face what he'd travel all this way for.

He made his way downward, attempting not to fall and roll down to the foot of this great hill. As he reached the figure and stood below and before it, it was evident that this was King Univerza, *Death himself*. An obsidian black hood shrouded the skull within, and its' cape contained the rest of him. One knee was bent upward while the other leg had been partially enveloped by the earth. Weeds and flowers were sewn through the bones of his forearm, and little insects crawled in and out of his maw. He knelt before the dead king, chuckling to himself. Zephyr embraced his defeat, yet wept with chaotic joy at having reached his destination. He cried into his palms, and as he did, a pressure was put atop his fallen head. It was cold, shaking. When he looked up, the dead king's hand had risen from its' soil to him.

"*King?*" He whispered seemingly to himself, but the skeleton of the first king spoke back in a chillingly slow, deep, world-trembling voice.

"*You peasant, knelt before I, the ruler of this vast expanse, this land; you have knelt before I, King Univerza. Plead your case.*"

He was all but stunned, and his eyes twitched. Zephyr looked to the skeleton for an answer to is infinitely-tied knot, a key to unlock time stolen from him.

"I am Zephyr Solta of the Kingdom of Olderag; I have journeyed to you in this very land of Grasp, through Alexandria, and all of earths' bidding."

"You speak of false republics; you hail from lands unbeknownst to their ruler. Zephyr," the King said in a rolling thunder, *"have ye arrived to proclaim your failure… in exchange for relief?"*

"Aye," he frantically spoke. "You wield long-forgotten power, one which I find may realign the stars of this very disastrous sky."

King Univerza's jaw barely moved as words expelled from inside. His icy arm nearly shattered as it waved before Zephyr.

"I smell plague upon you. An infestation of your soul, bound by a thousand codices, woven… never to be undone. Fear, I smell from you. Frantic… as a fox. You are dying, and you have suffered from death before, and you have suffered from I."

"It is true, your royalty. A curse has been placed upon me, all but for a painting with false direction by Queen Zerk Olderag of my very kingdom. In the wake of their rule, I am without my Ambrosia, and soon without my Leon. Thereafter, I shall join you and them in this soil. And so, I request your hand, but I understand your terms. I request for Leon, a blameless child, free of this curse. I will bear death if only given time to return to him."

"And so you may, and as you wish, this can be put forth. A deal of scripture, I as Death will present. The conditions of it are not to be meddled or not followed, and in doing so, payment is still collected."

"To the clause and agreement, what pay shall I provide to you, King?"

"Of Zephyr Solta's endeavor to reach these lands, the source of his cause will be in blood. A princess of this Alexandria, one who wields Persuasion, will provide to you her eyes, and her eyes you will paint. No other will see, and no other will paint. To provide this painting to the King, her father, will grant Leon Solta indefinite relief from this spell-bound curse. The Mortal Sword you will possess will declare our deal as complete, inscribed into the earth with the blood…of Zephyr Solta."

Zephyr stood before the hillside, seeing it now as a throne, his breath shallow, his body trembling…. not from fear, but from the weight of what had been placed upon him.

King Univerza loomed above, a great skeletal figure bound to the earth itself, his bones entwined with roots, his skull crowned with jagged rock beneath the obsidian hood. Empty sockets stared into Zephyr's soul, but within them burned the remnants of something ancient, something beyond life and death.

"The deal is struck," Univerza intoned, his voice a whisper and a roar all at once. The wind carried his words like echoes from another age.

"Your son's curse will be lifted. He will walk this world free, unchained by a fate you brought upon him."

Zephyr's heart pounded. Leon. His son. Free. No longer shackled to death's creeping grasp. Zephyr said nothing, only staring at the great, lifeless skull. His lips were dry, his chest tight. He had known there was no other way and that his own life was well-settled in this end.

And yet, His hands were calloused and worn, twitching at his sides. His body had carried him through endless lands, through cursed places, through the very teeth of death itself. All for this moment. And still, the weight of the choice pressed down harder than any mountain.

Leon would live. He would laugh. He would see the sun rise a thousand times. But Zephyr… Zephyr would never see him grow. The thought made his throat close. He exhaled, steadying himself. His eyes flickered to the deal's final demand…. the painting.

Alexandria, the Princess of a kingdom she will someday rule, she whose eyes had never been seen by any man. The eyes that, if freed, could deconstruct the very republic she controls, or construct an end to the Mor Empire and all its' life. Of course, to paint her eyes would empower the name of *Solta* as being of immense greatness. If he agreed, Univerza's magic would force her to reveal them to him. For but a moment, the veiled mystery of her gaze would be his alone. And with his own hands, he would immortalize them in paint, stroke by stroke, with *true* color.

His fingers curled into a fist. He thought of Leon… his laughter as a child, his quiet, unshaken courage, the sickness that had withered him, stealing his future before it had truly begun.

Zephyr lifted his gaze. His voice, when it came, was rough, quiet. *There is no other way.* A cold wind swept across the land, rattling the bones of the king, stirring the dust beneath Zephyr's feet. He finally spoke, and his voice did not waiver.

"Then let it be done." As he spoke, a black flame expelled from King Univerza's hand, growing until it flooded the world. In a great impact, it burst, and the blackness dissipated across the hillside. The King's head slowly fell, and the shadow of his hood buried his skull.

Zephyr went up the hill to the ruins, and he saw at a distance the sword which the King deemed as the *Mortal Sword*, suspended above its' once permanent place, blazing in the same black flames. Once he reached it, he took the sword by his frayed hilt and watched as the flames dissipated into the air and faded until all that was left was a shimmering blade. Reserved... for him. While in shock, the blade then burst as well, firing black smoke into the air. It nearly scared him, and Zephyr realized it could not see any bloodshed other than his, and on the day, would appear again. He sighed in relief however, since it would be far easier to carry. Zephyr looked back across the stone plateau and across the column's shadows, and stepped forward to begin his return.

Then let it be done.

14. Flemeth the Punished

The chamber into which Jeffrey Flemeth was dragged reeked of sulfur and silence. Not the silence of reverence, but of repression.. It was hollowed from the old stone beneath Deletaria Castle, a keep long buried from maps and minds alike. Chains hung like threads of a dead spider's web, and the air shimmered faintly with residual magic… sour, stale.

Grand Wizard Joab stood before the altar-like dais at the far end, draped in crimson robes embroidered with thorns and serpent glyphs. The staff he bore pulsed with veins of green fire, its runes carved deep with the sharp end of truth withheld. The state watcher held Jeffrey fast, his wrists locked behind him, ankles raw from shackles.

"Jeffrey Flemeth," Joab said, his voice cavernous, almost amused. "You brokered trust to a man now cursed. A traitor, exiled. And worse… you sought to rally the ignorant and spark rebellion in my sanctified domain."

Jeffrey raised his chin. "Zephyr is no traitor. He painted what he was told. It was *you* who sealed his fate. Besides, is it not the *King's* domain?"

Joab gave a thin-lipped smile, the kind that turned warmth to winter. "One cannot hold a blade without a brain. I suppose *I* am the weapon. And yet, here you are. Still defiant. Still naive."

With a flick of Joab's staff, the watcher released Jeffrey and stepped back. Magic energy coiled through the air, thin emerald strands that pierced the shadows like fangs. Jeffrey stumbled forward.

"I will show you what your defiance costs." Joab raised his hand, fingers crackling with dark energy. The light struck Jeffrey's face, directly into his eyes. A searing white filled his mind. He screamed. Not from pain… at first, but from the loss of sight so instant it felt like falling into an abyss that had always been beneath him. Then, worse: they returned.

With equal violence, Joab conjured the eyes again. Identical, and yet Jeffrey could see too *much*. Threads of power danced around the room, things no mortal should see: memories of others, flickers of Joab's own wicked thoughts, pain born centuries ago. His sight had been altered to witness more than vision, it was now a torment.

"You will see truth now," Joab whispered. "Even when you close your eyes."

But the torture did not end. The Grand Wizard turned to a vial upon a pedestal. Its glass writhed, as though the black liquid within sought escape. Jeffrey knew what Joab possessed.

"Miscreancy… you are such a belligerent nonce… you will rot in hell!"

"You'll learn what it is to rot while breathing," Joab murmured, uncorking the vial which pulsed with swampish light. The liquid spiraled into the air and latched onto Jeffrey's skin like hungry leeches. His limbs trembled. Bone groaned beneath sinew. The aging began at his knuckles.... he could feel them swell, crack, twist. His back arched with pain. Muscles spasmed until the tissue began to decay. His very marrow was fire.

Joab circled him slowly. "This is what the Koba called a *slow bloom*. Not a death. A reminder. You will live, but every day will feel like your last. That... is justice."

Jeffrey collapsed to the ground, the light finally relinquishing him. His body was wracked with tremors. He could still see.... gods, he could see *everything*.... but no longer lift his arms. He was bound now by the pain of a thousand years caught in a single vessel.

Joab leaned down. "You are my message, Flemeth. The council has a strong suspicion of a vermin with the intention to fib to the great court of Taria. *She* will be caught eventually, and when Zephyr breathes, he will *feel* what his brotherhood cost. Defiance is quickly tended to under Olderag, haven't you learned?"

"*Taria?* Who are you talking about?" Jeffrey coughed. "Seeking the Wizard Council?" He thought once that maybe Ambrosia and Zephyr would journey to the temples of order, but he knew the Soltas had soft teeth. They would *never* seek to dispute. Then it came to him. "*Sabbath?*"

Joab had sat back onto a dark-damp royal seat. "This 'Sabbath' girl, I know little of but for lack of guidance. She does appear to be a rebellious kind. However, Taria sits beyond the great wilder, and the terrain is *very* treacherous and the webs of Olderag reach *very* far. Her and that old man will struggle."

"*Old man…*" Jeffrey bit his tongue. "George as well? How do you know all of this? Have you got watchers posted on every branch and rooftop? Sounds like you're terrified! I always knew you were *weak*, but cowardly, to be so paranoid…. you're quite fragile, Joab," Jeffrey pushed his luck further, enduring the pain and torture as if he'd felt it before.

"The *King* has taken a liking to whom the Yippire deem as *familiars*. They're assisting in our endeavor. I suspect we will be quite successful. All people beg for justice, but squeal once they've seen it. Little Sabbath is naive as such, no different than what lies before me here. You're not scared of the end, are you Mister Flemeth?"

Northward, the forest swallowed Sabbath and George. The wind carried no warmth, just silence which prowled like a hunter between roots. It prowled between the twisted roots and bare boughs like a thing hunting, cold-breathed and clawed with silence.

Sabbath sat hunched in the saddle behind George, her hands gripping the old man's belt of braided sinew, knuckles white. The morning light was thin, sickly, as though the sky had only half-bothered to rise. Mist clung to the undergrowth and hovered in low, unmoving sheets, neither smoke nor fog but something more deliberate, more watchful.

The forest had changed. Since leaving the glade where Fumper had seen them off with blessings and figroot poultices, the woods had taken on a bent shape, as though leaning inward, closing. Pines grew with their bark blistered and hanging, and the moss had turned a bruised grey-blue that neither of them recognized.

Sabbath looked over her shoulder. Again. "You feel it too," she muttered. "Don't lie and say it's just the wind."

George exhaled through his beard. "Aye. Been feelin' it since the stream. I fear we have a *stalker.*"

"Koba? Do you think they want revenge?" she asked sharply. Her voice struck the trees like a snapped bone.

George chuckled dryly, the sound like boots scraping frost. "If it were goblins, they'd have made a racket already. They don't stalk quietly often. They spring, cackle, throw vials unprovoked. Besides, they don't care for vengeance. Their dead are ash before they're mourned. Too many young to bury the old."

Sabbath clenched her jaw. "Then what is it?"

George tilted his head slightly, as though listening past the forest's hush. "Ghosts, maybe. Forest doesn't like travelers anymore. Could be it's grown old and tired of boots."

The trees suddenly swayed, though no wind stirred. Sabbath looked again and saw something. Not form. Not face. A ripple, like oil dragged across water. A streak of cold shimmer, low to the ground. Another to the left, tearing between the trunks too fast for shape.

Then came the whispers. They brushed against her ears in sounds too warped for speech: the creaking of doors unopened for centuries, the crack of wood splintering beneath their weight, the hush of parchment turning without hands. Sabbath's skin prickled.

She reached for her sickleblade, but George raised a hand.

"Don't," he warned. "These aren't foes we can cut. Keep still. Let them pass."

The air thickened. A draft of sour brine filled her nose, like stagnant ink left too long sealed. Her heart pounded but she stayed frozen, every breath held in her teeth.

Then… quiet. The tension uncoiled. The mist lightened. The forest breathed again. They waited. George shifted. "They're gone. I think."

Sabbath stepped down from the horse and wandered off the trail. A clearing of bare roots and stone stretched before her, and amid the debris lay a single book, its cover untouched by dew or dirt. It sat perfectly centered atop a stump split long ago by lightning.

She knelt and examined it. The leather was soft, a deep ink-black. The title was pressed in silver, faint but readable: *Urald, The Librarian*. There was no author's name.

"Don't read it," George said behind her, his voice suddenly iron. "Not here."

"I wasn't going to," Sabbath muttered, sliding the strange book into her rucksack. She stood and gave one last glance to the forest's deeper paths. "Let's keep moving."

As they mounted again and rode on, Sabbath swore she heard the faintest turning of a page far off behind them, where no living thing should be.

15. The Conclusion Ceremony

Willa and Tomas stood with Leon in the dirt road outside their cottage, both adults aching in the frustration of his lateness. Zephyr returned that afternoon, carried home by a passing tradesman whose horses had found him in rough shape just beyond the treeline.

Willa and the boy rushed to his side, and Zephyr embraced his son tightly, and her thereafter. Tomas watched them as they cried and scolded him for not staying by his word. Zephyr was not malnourished, as he'd only been gone for but a night. Willa scurried inside to fix him an early supper. Zephyr then met Tomas; their handshake was firm but cold. With Leon beneath his arm, they joined Willa inside.

"You said you would arrive before supper… *yesterday,*" the child groaned as they stepped through the door.

"I never said before supper, and I did believe I would return. The paths I followed… they were much further than I'd hoped."

Zephyr stopped to take a look at Leon, whose eyes were slightly darker than when he'd left. Though, he still held a bright smile in his father's return. Zephyr took a moment to inspect the child, and saw that his fire was still lit. He grabbed a hold of Leon's face and smiled wide, then embraced him.

"Did you find what you were searching for?" Willa asked from behind a bubbling pot. Zephyr had nothing but dirt and a vacant hilt, one which he thought not to display to anyone. He also did *not* acquire the children's toy that Leon was so excited for. He thought quick.

"Come 'morrow I will show you, my boy."

Over supper, Tomas cleared his throat. "The Kingdom hosts the *Conclusion* Ceremony," Tomas spoke quietly. "The end of Morgenmete."

"Yes! Papa, the Broadmere's told me all about it! There will be sweets and pudding, oh how sweet it will be! There will be bears and they will fight! Can we go?" The boy was swinging his arms around as he spoke, and Zephyr's head nodded to him and Tomas.

"Of course, my boy. But, bears?"

"*Mhm,* and they pierce one another not with claws, but with mallets and daggers," Tomas's words carried a sharpened edge, and Zephyr caught on: Tomas wanted his dagger. He reached beneath the cloth ripped and wrapped around his waist and presented Tomas with a very dirty, weapon. "No blood, very king of you Sir Solta."

"The wilder was very king to me. And, thank you."

Later into the night, Willa stood near the low-burning hearth, her fingers splayed over the rising warmth as if drawing strength from the flickering glow. Leon sat cross-legged on the floor, absentmindedly tracing the grooves in the wooden boards while Zephyr leaned against the stone archway, arms crossed, watching her with the wary eyes of a man who may soon save this boy. Tomas expected him to have gone asleep by this hour, and approached him.

"While you're here, I should say Willa will bring your linens to the brook for a wash some time tomorrow. I shan't hold this coldness, and you'll grow roots out of that tunic."

Zephyr leaned in and whispered to Tomas, "I will show you the very treasure you doubted, after the Conclusion Ceremony." He spoke with a growl, leaving Tomas to hideaway in another room. Zephyr joined Leon in listening to Willa, letting the boy drift quietly into wanderlust.

"You've both come so far without knowing the roots of the world you're standing in, and for it to be scarce and in bad use where you hail from, I should tell a kinder story," Willa said softly, almost to herself. Her eyes lifted to meet Zephyr's. "But if you're going to survive naively here, you need to understand more than what toads and the governance teach; I will teach you of the stems."

She turned, brushing the bronze-like curls from her face, her voice steadying. "There are six *stems*. Six paths from which all magic in our world is drawn. Some noble, some corrupt, but none without consequence."

Leon looked up, brow furrowed. "Stems? Like a tree?"

Willa smiled faintly. "Our scholars have long believed all magic to *stem* from life itself. That all fantastical things you see come from within each of us. Let me tell of how deep they go." She knelt beside him, drawing six interwoven lines into the soot-covered stone with the tip of her finger. "The first," she said, "is Invetia.... or Governing magic. It's the domain of wizard councils and law-casters. They uphold order through enchantments that bind, judge, or reward. When a bounty is posted or a punishment handed down through spell, it's their doing." She paused, eyes flickering to Zephyr. "The second is Regulated. Harmless, on paper. Common folk can use it, so long as they're licensed. Think parlor tricks, games of light, maybe illusions for tavern shows. It's magic designed for safety. Containment."

Zephyr admired her as she spoke, but maintained a firm stare into the shadows of the space. When he'd first met her, she seemed far rougher, wilder, yet similarly just as sweet as treated Leon.

"You don't have to stay," she noticed him. "He's easy enough to carry once he's fallen asleep. You on the other hand..."

"No... no. I'll get on in a moment." He felt order in her voice, and wanted to hear her out. The night seemed to soften the longer he stayed.

"Persuasion." Her voice grew quieter. "It's increasingly scarce. Optical, they say. One's eyes change if they bear it. Those with Persuasion can bend the will of others with nothing more than a glance and a word. Make them believe anything. Do anything. It's not taught. It's... *born.*"

Leon shivered. "The Princess..."

"Yes," she rose her finger to him "and many before her were forsaken or... removed. Few live long enough to cause harm to a great people, but the Princess is she, royalty."

She moved on, her finger carving another vein into the soot. "The fourth stem is Red-Bog, or 'Cradle' magic. Tribal. Earthy. Web-like in the way bolts of light stretch from fingers. The Greenfolk and their other communes wield it.... though they're disregarded by governance for it, as it *could* harm others, but it has lost its' potency. This magic shifts reality in favor of the caster. One could strengthen a harvest, or turn one to rot. Although it is not so harmful now, it is still deemed dangerous by our Kingdom and many others."

Zephyr let out a breath. "No worse than a wizard turning the floor beneath you to ice."

Willa gave him a long look. "Or a mage healing frostbite," she said with a bite. She drew the fifth stem.

"Disquisition," she continued. "Spell-casting magic tied to writing and language. It's the most common in our city, the easiest to learn. Recipes, healing incantations, practical uses. Most every town has someone who practices it and are permitted, scribe-healers, cooks, alchemists. While not necessarily claimed by the Kingdom, there is no trouble of it, or little talk of it."

Finally, her finger rested over the sixth line, the soot now smudging her skin and fading against the wood.

"And the last: Miscreancy. It too is bound to books and scrolls. But where Disquisition brings healing, Miscreant brings rot. Poison. Decay. It's the language of goblins. ... those that remain, anyway. It's ancient and cruel, but no less powerful."

Willa sat back on her heels, looking at the web she'd drawn.

"These are the six stems," she said, her voice hollow now. "The branches may differ, but they all drink from the same roots. No good, no bad."

"And perhaps, the source is no less mysterious, my boy," Zephyr spoke for Willa. "And it is all nature, and it is no less beautiful than the brook or hills. So, treat it as such."

Willa smiled to the man, who tipped his brow and turned to his son. Leon had fallen asleep once she'd spoken of the fifth stem, yet he'd dream of the sixth until daylight. Zephyr lifted the child and rested him in his hay-filled chest at the foot of Tomas' bed. Before he could step out the door, he felt the stare of the Broadmere girl. He first sensed her disapproval of him perhaps for his tendency to falsify the future. But, it was not, and he glimpsed at her eyes during his goodnight 'farewell'. It was riddled with sorrow, a deep sadness that whatever he wasted time searching for, was truly a *waste* after all. Though, he still gave her a smile, and tended to his makeshift room in the hay-shed.

The following morning, the Broadmere's joined Zephyr and Leon in the courtyard just outside the castle's tall gates. They were but bugs among a sea of bobbing heads, all of whom spoke with full mouths and berry-stained garments courtesy of the King's own carts. There may have been four or five scattered through the crowds, each with their many baskets becoming empty.

The people of Alexandria awaited for Princess and her parents to present themselves to announce the end of Morgenmete. The folk, who gathered from their villages, within the kingdom's walls and from its' outskirts, celebrated no differently than any other festival. Leon had scurried off with other children and Willa gathered redberries and whatever else she could fit within her waist bundle. Then, the gates opened wide and as the bridge descended across the moat. The chatter grew quiet, and all the kingdom's folk watched in anticipation.

In her majestic beauty, her glimmering blonde curls, jewels embedded in her robes and gold handwork within her silver crown, Princess Alexandria walked between the Queen and King. The King, whose fists were dense and tense, stood behind his daughter with a heavy brow. A star of light shot from Alexandria's fixed mask, asserting to her watchers that what restrained her was red-hot. Her feet were bare, sat naked atop the wood planks of the bridge. Knights were filed at either side, then she began.

190

"Morgenmete, a festival in which we celebrate the gift of our survived harvest… ends in bright eyes, young who jump about these very streets, and guardians who bear the strength to once turn dead soil into road, and into walls, and into shelter."

Her announcement began to fade from Zephyr's ears as he glanced through the people in search of his boy. He did not notice the Princesses' sudden halt in her speech. Her head scanned slowly across the crowd, and her nose twitched as she appeared to have smelt something odd. The wait for her to continue grew, and the King's right heel struck the wood beneath them.

"I… yes… I see this season as a successful one, as were each cycle prior, and I anticipate another, come the next. In the heat of today, go on with your children, indulge in the fruit of this land we have cultivated, for it provides us with 'morrow. Morgenmete has concluded."

Hazah! The knights barked with their swords raised. The Kingdom's folk repeated, and the chatter exploded. And once their still bodies began twirl and dance throughout the square, the Princess seemed fixed upon the crowd. Although her eyes were hidden behind the fortified mask, one would think she was searching. It may have been that her nose was still twitching, still tracking. Before one could notice, the King and Queen retreated with her back towards the castle, and the bridge lifted and the gates were pressed and locked together.

Tomas grabbed a hold of Zephyr's tunic before he could go off and find his boy.

"Now, go on about your venture. I saw no *fetchwillit*, now go on."

"There are conditions to this deal, and it is no easy feat," Zephyr explained beneath the cheerful commotion. "A portrait, one of her. The *Princess*, without her confinements."

"A painting? And her eyes? Zephyr, now tell me what color they be?"

"Tomas, I don't... "

"No one knows, Zephyr. Nor will you. That is, not without having your head splayed atop a guillotine. So now tell me, what will you do with this painting?"

"I... I gift it to the King."

"The King? And you think he'll accept it? His council will see it as insult, Zephyr. They'll brand you a fool, maybe even a traitor. Have you learned nothing from Olderag?" Tomas scolded him with redness, nearly spitting upon him. Zephyr's head grew heavy, but he knew what was true.

"A portrait, yes. But I believe this to be the only way, Tomas."

"What an appropriate ending for you, Sir Solta. How will you even do it? To be so close as to illustrate even the imperfections, to paint each strand of hair, to see her *eyes*?"

"I... I am not certain," Zephyr began to turn away, and Tomas did the same.

"Likewise," said Tomas, departing from the festival.

Willa returned to Zephyr, who had just scooped Leon up from a group of village children near the bakery. His cheeks were flushed from laughter and the remains of a sticky honey-apple clung to his fingers. They continued with the day's activities, sharing warm bread, browsing vibrant stalls of dyed fabrics and glimmering trinkets, letting the slow gravity of full stomachs and long shadows pull them toward home. But before they could slip away, Leon tugged at Zephyr's hand and pointed, eyes wide.

"There! Look, there's a crowd!" he said breathlessly. "The bears!"

Zephyr and Willa exchanged a glance. He was tired. They all were. But there was something rare in Leon's voice, some brightness that hadn't been there in days, though it was so integral to who he was.

They followed him through the crowd which thickened as they neared the massive stone-ringed arena, half buried in the red earth. Its towering arches groaned under the weight of spectators clinging to every rung and wall. Roars of anticipation spilled into the sky, carried on wind and sun.

Inside, the arena was a wide bowl of packed dirt and dust, churned by the weight of creatures who had fought there before. Already in the ring stood two towering beasts.... bear-warriors, as they were called in the these eastern dialects.... massive brown brutes clad in ornate armor that shimmered silver against the afternoon light. Teardrop-shaped helms gleamed atop their heads, and plated armor hugged their forearms, knees, and chests. Their claws, thick and black as obsidian, were tipped in fitted gauntlets of forged steel that clicked like teeth when they flexed their paws.

They faced each other in stillness, hulking and slow-breathing. Then, with a sudden thunderous *thump*, one lunged.

The crowd exploded as claws clashed. The bears roared.... deep, guttural bellows that shook the walls and the seats where spectators stood. Dust bloomed up from beneath their feet as they grappled, each strike a heaving effort of muscle and mass. One swung wide, catching the other's plated shoulder with a ringing *clang*. The second retaliated with a powerful shove, sending his opponent skidding back across the earth, clawed heels gouging twin lines through the dirt.

Zephyr felt the force in his own chest. Even knowing it was exhibition, choreographed, restrained, there was a primal intensity in the way the beasts collided. The crowd roared with every grapple, every evasive twist of the massive forms. It was both brutal and beautiful, like watching living statues war.

Despite the bloodless nature of the match, every blow landed with punishing intent. Occasionally a spark would shoot from the armor where claws struck, and the sound was deafening. Metal clanged. Roars echoed. And beneath it all, the rhythmic stomp of bear-like footfalls against the ground created a pulse that infected the crowd.

Leon was fixated. He stood, arms flailing with every movement, his voice lost in the cacophony but his face glowing with awe. He threw invisible punches into the air, mimicking the warriors' movements with the wild excitement only a child could conjure. His thin frame bounced on the balls of his feet.

"Oh! Did you see that one? That one was *so close*. Did you see?!"

Zephyr watched him, his own lips parting in a quiet smile. He could never grow tired of his excitement, the boy's eyes were not glazed with exhaustion. For this moment, the weight of his fading time had nearly lifted. Here, in the chaos and cheering, in the violent poetry of two armored beasts clashing, his son had come alive again.

In the arena, the stronger of the two warriors threw his opponent with a ground-shaking slam that drew gasps and whistles from the crowd. The fallen bear groaned, rolling onto its side, defeated but unharmed. The victor rose, towering and regal in his dented armor, and beat one paw against his plated chest once, twice, three times, letting loose a triumphant roar that echoed into the crowds. Leon threw both arms into the air, beaming. "*He won! Ha! He really won!*"

Zephyr looked down at his son, whose skin was pale and whose breaths were still shallow with each day, but whose spirit, for this fleeting second, glowed brighter than the sun overhead.

Willa said nothing, but her hand found Zephyr's, and held it with a pulsing grip.

16. Death Herself

The air inside the Broadmere's hay-shed was thick with the musk of old straw and lantern oil, but Zephyr barely noticed. He sat on the edge of the makeshift cot they'd made for Leon, just three planks laid across barrels, cushioned with flattened burlap and a woolen blanket and stared at the only vacant wall rid of mold or dust. Leon lay beside him, staring at the auburn sky through the glassless window. The light of the evening peered through slits in the wall. There was a gaze Zephyr felt watching him from the shadowed doorway behind him.

"You've upset him, you know," whispered a voice in the dark. It took only the cadence of it for Zephyr to recognize that it was Willa.

"What's done is done; I can at least tell him I tried," Zephyr said, standing upright and facing her, or the faint figure of her.

"What exactly *did* you do?" She asked, but Zephyr was abrupt in his ushering her outside. Instead of standing where the boy could still hear them, the pair walked quietly down the street.

"I only pursued a story he loves, to find if it was true. I could tell him his father was *mighty*, that fairy-tales were real."

"There's little in the north," Willa tried him. "Nothing but them frog-folk and wilder. Maybe the Mor, too. But… wait. Did you travel to the empire? I doubt that you could in but a night.… "

"No, Willa. The Mor may pull our strings, but they're no fairy tale. I only wanted answers."

Their walk went off the right-hand side, away from the distant kingdom and the farmlands. Willa led him along to where a field opened up, one he hadn't explored yet.

"So, if you cannot tell me *what* his fairy-tale was, could you tell me if it was true?" She asked, but it was then that Zephyr could finally see her face illuminated in a low glow from at their feet. Zephyr had never seen such a thing, and his brow curled when he looked beyond her. *Millions* beyond *millions* of radiant sparkles dotted the field.

"What are these?" He asked, tightening his fist as though he was threatened.

"Corubugs," she whispered. "Though, I've never seen so many here."

"Do they sting?"

"No," Willa chuckled softly. "They don't."

Her gaze lifted to his eyes, and the look implied she still awaited an answer to her earlier question. But Zephyr, knowing the truth of wish-granting and Univerza, could only let his head fall in sorrow. *But*, Willa embraced him tightly, a warmth he slowly forgot was possible. They swayed in the sea of starry insects and darkness. When his head lifted from her collar, her hands found the base of his neck, and she put herself forth for a kiss. In the momentum of their sway, he accepted it.

The two journeyed back to her cottage where Willa went inside for the night, and bid Zephyr a goodnight of rest. The weight of the ancient King's decree was heavy on his bones when he lay down. The echo of Univerza's voice still ringing beneath his skin like a curse of its own. He dragged a hand down his face, smearing sweat and the residual of berry-sap and dried saliva, then stared at his fingers as if they might hold the answer. "*Princess Alexandria, for she is Death herself,*" he muttered, then exhaled deeply. "*A mask forged by the Grand Enchanters themselves, a hall of sorcerers,*" he whispered to himself, once mentioned by Willa.

The Grand Enchanters were a group far greater than the Grand Wizard Council of Taria but most thought they were myth. They were tightly knit with the unknown legion of Mor in a land no one knew of. The mask itself was sealed with a rune-lock and blessed with sunstone and blacksteel and silver. No one had seen her eyes. Not her handmaidens. Not even her the dogs which roamed the castle halls, if rumors held true. "*Her gaze holds the power to cause men to walk into flame, betray empires, drown with a smile.*" Zephyr leaned forward, elbows on his knees, the straw rustling underfoot. A thousand questions clouded his vision. "*How do I see what I'm not meant to? And if I do… how do I not lose myself in her command? Her desire to remove herself.*"

Persuasion could hollow out the will like rot. A blacksmith who forged blades for the Alexandrian knights had once slit his own throat after a girl suspect of the magic whispered something to him at a banquet table. Just a murmur. Though Willa assured Zephyr that this occurred long ago and was but a tavern-tale.

A flicker of fear lit behind Zephyr's ribs. He thought of Leon…. his son…. laying still in his arms, his breaths heavy, yet slower, the time between them stretched like drawn wire. Zephyr… could not… fail him. At some point in the night, Zephyr retrieved Leon from inside the Broadmere's cottage, just so he could be in his presence a moment longer.

Could he trick Alexandria? No… fools thought they could outwit a Persuader. Could he mirror her eyes as to avoid staring directly? What if that didn't work? Maybe in some flickering lantern light, her mask removed only briefly, he could glimpse just enough without letting her see *him*. But even that was plagued in uncertainty. He would need shielding. A spell? No, not just that. He needed someone who could weave a charm of resistance, something worn close to the heart. Red-bog witches could be of aid. Or one of the old clerics from the Bard.

He would find them. He had to. Though, he could simply present the King with the proposition, one where they could commission him just as King Olderag did. Leon, his only son, hung on the thin thread of a brushstroke, and the secrets behind a mask no one dared touch. Zephyr carried Leon to his makeshift bed back inside the cottage, where he would dream of the bears close to the hearth.

Before he allowed himself to sleep, Zephyr wondered what might happen to him if he did not *sign* the deal if the day came. If he handed the portrait to King Jean St. Auclaire and the Mortal Sword's blade materialized out of black flame, if he refused to embed it into himself. Would Leon remain ill and meet his end, or could he vanish with the gift of Univerza? Come the next sun, he would seek Tomas' help in devising a plan.

Zephyr drifted in silence, unbothered by weight or wind. The space he entered had no walls, only the illusion of containment, pillars of light spiraled into nowhere. Above him stretched no ceiling, no sky, only velvet darkness pierced by glinting stars. He floated, or perhaps he walked, though the floor was not solid. Beneath his feet was a translucent sheet of crystal, smooth as still water and clear as air. Through it, galaxies twisted in solemn rhythm. He could see the shape of his own silhouette mirrored endlessly into the abyss.

The library.... if such a name could hold its vastness.... was infinite. Vast shelves stretched into spiraling rows in all directions, their architecture not built but grown, branching upward like frozen lightning. Each shelf was formed from an iridescent crystal, faintly glowing, humming with imperceptible magic. Every book within them pulsed with its own internal light.... some dim as dying embers, others bright as comet trails. The spines bore no titles, only runes that shimmered and rearranged themselves when glanced at, as though each volume was aware of being seen.

Zephyr reached a hand toward one of the books. It rose at his thought before his fingers could reach it, floating gently into the air like a leaf in reverse autumn. The cover unfolded like wings, and the pages turned themselves. No words. Only images.

He saw Ambrosia smiling through the window of their flat in Tuopo, combing Leon's hair. He saw his boy splashing in a stream near Cuepo, mud clinging to his heels. Then, a darker page. He saw Joab's eyes glinting green with fury. The Queen's painted lips. The hand that pointed at him. The black sack over his head.

He tried to touch the memory… tried to hold Ambrosia's face within it, but as soon as his fingers brushed the image, the pages shattered like stained glass, and the shards dissolved into drifting motes of star-dust at his feet. The book re-materialized and returned to the shelf, humming gently, as if amused by his longing.

Another shelf floated near. Another book opened. More memories. But these were not his. An old man weeping at a desk. A woman in a tower folding a letter she'd never send. A child screaming as flames rose behind him. Each page flickered with the same softness, the same fragility of breath caught between past and prayer.

Zephyr turned, but the library did not. Instead, the rows turned with him, morphing, reshaping. A new corridor. Another. He realized then: it was not a place at all. It was a memory palace of the soul… his own, or perhaps every soul who had passed through death's door.

Far ahead, a great bell tolled. It did not echo, it reverberated through bone and thought, felt more than heard. The star-lights dimmed slightly, as though bracing themselves.

Then he saw them. Figures. Tall, draped in robes woven from fog. They moved between shelves, not walking, but gliding, their faces obscured by veils of starlight. Not spirits. Perhaps the leaders of the Mor, he may have thought. They did not look at him. They never spoke. But wherever they passed, books opened in reverence.

Zephyr tried to approach one, calling out, though no sound came from his mouth. One figure paused as if hearing something. It turned. There was no face beneath the hood.

In its reflection, Zephyr saw not himself… but Leon, asleep and pale in the hay. The reflection shifted: Ambrosia, sickly and still, whispering something he couldn't hear. Then, the image warped… another version of himself, older, gaunter, dragging a burned canvas through ash. That Zephyr turned toward the real one. Their eyes met. His reflection whispered something, and the library shattered.

"The wish is written."

Zephyr staggered, windless. The dream had turned cold. He turned… an instinct, nothing more. Suddenly he was standing on solid ground. A stone floor, ancient and dusty. The crystal shelves were now dark and brittle, and he suddenly fell.

He woke up abruptly, finding that it was all a sickening dream. It was deep into the dark hours, when the world was still and silent but for fireflies and rodents rummaging through the fields outside, the sound of footsteps caught Zephyr sleeping. He did not hear them come closer, and he did not hear the floor of his hay-shed creak as one small… light… foot stepped through the doorway.

17. The Grand Escape

A small, bare foot pressed delicately onto the hay-shed floor, caked in mud. The wood did not creak. Zephyr froze, dread curdling in him. *Some lawless child, or worse, a thief.* But when red, jewel-stitched cloth appeared at the knee, dirt dulling its opalescence, his fear faltered.

But jewel-adorned red cloth met at their knee, and each tiny opalescent stone was hidden beneath dry dirt. Then, as quietly and with the slowness of a creeping fox, the robber's head presented itself. Their approach into the barrack was careful. Zephyr made no sound as they continued in, their nose sniffing, then pausing to listen. Then the person stopped a few feet away from Zephyr, and it was clear to him that they knew he was there. The dark posed no curtain for him as he thought, and swallowed in nervousness and confusion. He saw their silhouette correct its posture as they faced him. From the moonlight cast through the empty window, details of their face began to show. Across their face, silver details began to show as diamonds and gold began to glisten. Brighter than the stones and metal, a slight smile grew, for it was no night-bound thief, but instead *Princess Alexandria herself* showed. Zephyr could not speak, nor could he make an escape as she blocked the doorway. He quivered on the inside thinking of how she might remove the mask and turn him into some slave for the Kingdom's Wizard Council to experiment on. But she did not speak, and instead the Princess threw herself forward and embraced him. Only then did she mutter a whisper.

"I feel I have been searching for you since the beginning of time."

Zephyr could not grasp her intent, and failed to remove himself from her arms. Her head turned to face him as if she could look into his eyes and cast a dark spell. Though, her wide mask which encapsulated the bridge of her nose, eyes, and the entirety of her forehead, seemed so sincere.

"Dear Princess, I am certain you are not where you believe to be. I believe I am not who you are seeking," Zephyr tried to explain. *"Surely I am not.... "*

"And yet, you are. There was no telling of what's come of me, but I've become aware of your soul. A sweetness I smell of you, an intrigue I ought not to let die."

"What is it? I… Princess Alexandria, I proudly accept this… visit… but I best not keep you from the King. I… I can bring you to the nearest guard and they will bring you back," said Zephyr as he shook his head in disbelief.

He managed to direct her out onto the grass. The world was much brighter beneath the low night sky, and the Princess's dress glistened. A blood red with constellations of gems. She flailed her arms in a fight.

"I cannot leave you, we are so tightly woven. I knew it at first embrace."

There was a ruffling just outside a distant cottage, and a small lit flame flickered. Out of fear one might misconstrue this bizarre rendezvous, Zephyr ushered her beyond the barrack and through dense brush.

"We need to get you back, I cannot be seen with you," he finally asserted. "If a guard or any of these folk see you, the King himself will have my head rolling in the town-square. Kindly, allow me to bring you home."

"*Blasphemy*! I *kindly* say no. I cannot, for there is all but what I desire. I *desire* to stay."

Zephyr was dumbfounded at her fierce refusal. In a swift motion he grabbed her waist and attempted to guide her through the brush once more.

"*I can't die… no… not yet.*"

She rustled from his grasp and stood before him, blind and yet so sharply aware.

"*Die? No, you can't die,*" the Princess spoke frantically. "You can't die, please."

"I… no… no I cannot. If you will not let me escort you home, please tell me why you are here."

But the Princess had no words as she stood in a daze. Her guarded head faced him stubbornly, as if her brows were heavy,

"*Let me stay but for the night. Please.*"

Zephyr could not bear raising his voice any further. Instead, he let her follow him back inside. He pondered whether to leave and at least notify the Broadmere two. But his thought fell faint as the Princess sat atop the hay where he slept. He saw her mask once more and determined his fate would be an early end if he betrayed what she sought. Still, he awaited the moment she revealed her eyes and made him no different than a well-mannered dog.

"So then… might I understand the reason for this? I mean no harm to you, and I would prefer we bring you to the castle safely."

"I will not return to those… cold walls. I instead wish to be here, and so I will be."

"I understand your… wanting to perhaps be free of… expectations of you. But Princess Alexandria, I am not of your benefit, and I bear nothing of use to you."

But she only sat there facing him with a wide smile. Zephyr remained baffled, nearly agitated. Never in the past did he wish to disturb any folk. Not by speaking loudly at night, or being determined by a king as having *kidnapped* his kin.

Zephyr thought he may be dreaming, feeling as though he could trip over his own feet at the sheer absurdity of it all.

"Then I will get on to bed. I… here." He took down from the tall stack of hay and organized a rectangular platform for her to rest on the other side of the barrack. She seemed defeated, letting her shoulders fall as she slowly made her way. Zephyr did not look at her again, and he laid facing the cold wall. It wasn't long after many regurgitation of the same thought that he fell asleep. All the while, Princess Alexandria did not move, and she did not speak.

Come morning, his weary eyes wandered across the barrack, now glowing in the early heat. She of course, was no longer there. Though, the imprinted straw remained. It was then the smallish weight pressed against him, near the wall, that he found the Princess coiled up beneath his limp arm. In a frantic spasm he ejected himself from where he lay and found her to be truly there. Remnants of hay were scattered through her light golden hair and mud still coated her feet and dress. He watched her for a moment, still under an exhausted spell, trying to make sense of her.

The sound of a low breeze rolling through dry grass outside caught the air, and Zephyr sat atop another stack as he pondered what lie before him. It was evident, he soon understood, that King Univerza's deal might have enchanted her in such a way. He thought he would have to develop a plan, and Tomas would aid him, to get so close to the Princess as to paint her. To convince her to reveal her eyes.

To avoid her Persuasion if she felt so inclined. But alas, she lay before him and beneath an odd spell of obsession and affection. It would be easy enough, however, to convince her to sit for a portrait while she remained under such unwilling control. It was nearly as if the ancient King of Death sought to help Zephyr, but he knew better than to trust such a happening. There would be some caveat, he anticipated.

When she awoke, Zephyr knew not to confront her any further. He thought to play along carefully. He was far closer to saving Leon than he could have hoped for, and the key to unlocking his future lay daintily in a muddied dress. Cautiously and in terror, Zephyr lowered himself back onto the stack and let her conform to him once again.

She slept with her mask still, he had observed. Never seeing light or true dark… Zephyr understood that well, for Olderag once stole it from him. The silver and jewels caught what little light filtered through the empty window, casting an amber aura across her cheeks. Her breathing was slow, but not shallow. As if sleep came easy to her now, as if there were no world to fear when she was beside *him*.

Zephyr did not move. He only watched. A part of him wanted to curse the Mortal King for this…. whatever enchantment had been woven into her heart was not of her choosing. And yet, here she was. Not in a tower or marble chamber, but in the dirt beside a cursed man.

She snorted and slowly sat up, brushing the frost-kissed grass from her shoulder. She stirred, her lips parting just slightly as she turned her head as if to look down to Zephyr.

"You breathe like someone trying not to be watched," she whispered. Her voice was velvet…. warmed by sleep and intimacy. "But I hear you very clearly."

"You're real then," he said, eyes narrowing on the mask, trying not to imagine the power that lay hidden behind it.

"But a ghost, is that what you anticipated?" She questioned him, stretching with feline grace. Her fingers toyed with the edges of the silver mask and then she spoke softly almost to herself, "I am no ghost. You might ask again, and I could say I don't know," she murmured, pulling her knees to her chest, her voice softening. "I could say it's the stars. Or fate. Or madness."

"Madness, surely," Zephyr joked, letting them chuckle together. "What is incredibly urgent is our understanding that no other can know you are here. If I am caught in your presence they'll…"

"Town-square, I know. But it'd be by no stone. It would be *far* worse. A flame so bright, the peasants will crowd around just to feel the heat of it, and my father will leave you as ashes."

Zephyr's head shook in horror at the thought, and he was mortified of the truth in her tone. But she cracked a slight smile and pressed her forefinger to her lips and *shushed* him.

Zephyr! A woman's voice came from the cottage outside. *Zephyr, I've come with clean clothing. Tomas spared you these; your tunic is still quite damp.*

Willa Broadmere appeared in the doorway holding a folded tunic and breeches. Though, they fell to the dirt and wood as she gasped and covered her own mouth.

"No… no… no, Willa. This is not as it seems! See… see, she wandered through the night just outside this very barrack. No better than Pitter does, and I offered her a dry hostel," he pleaded, but Willa was far too astonished.

"The… Princess? Why have you… Tomas!" She yelled once, but not again as Zephyr took a hold of her arm and pulled her further into the barrack..

"You speak not a word to Tomas or the boy, and Alexandria will explain this mess."

Willa was not impressed, and she was visibly dumbfounded as Princess Alexandria told of her sudden endeavor to find Zephyr. Intrigue and the *sense of soul*, she reiterated. A *love* she'd never experienced prior. Alexandria told of when she first found Zephyr, which occurred at the Conclusion Ceremony of Morgenmete.

"You smelt of rich earth, dry blood. I heard your voice, and you called for a child. Though I cannot see, I believe I could from the moat."

But Willa's eyes smoked in disbelief, and her sharp gaze at Zephyr hinted of her suspicion that whatever he'd venture northward for had somehow played a role in Alexandria's enlightenment.

Just as Willa began towards the doorway with a headache, Zephyr joined her outside and spoke privately without the Princess.

"What are you doing? Why is she here?" Willa whispered fiercely.

"I cannot explain that now, but I was not told this would happen."

"Told what would happen? Zephyr, do you understand how dangerous this is? Knights are probably scouring the City now, and they *will* find her. I will not be an accomplice in this."

Then, Zephyr reluctantly threw his arms at his side and explained, "I was told that I must paint a portrait of her, and the curse would be lifted. But of course, it cannot be so great if not to present her eyes, but I thought she would remove her mask at, say, a festival or the arena. I didn't think she would have done this."

"And yet, there she lay, and you've brought home with you a terrible hand, Zephyr. I cannot believe you. Perhaps this curse of yours is but the plague after all," she said in anger, leaving him abruptly.

When she entered the cottage, Leon threw himself out past her followed by Tomas. Anxious to avoid letting either learn of the Princess, he met them in the grass.

"Tomas wants to take us to the City again to find a fetchwillit, come Papa!" Leon jumped with excitement. Zephyr hunched down to him and ran his rough palm atop the boys' head.

"You and Tomas go on, I will get on to the brook and have fish ready for the fire when you return. Come noon, I will take you on an adventure. How's that, Leon?"

The boy nodded and Tomas took him under his arm. A quivering smile nearly broke from Zephyr.

"Oh, Tomas. Could you source a sheet of linen and thin board of poplar? I would like to create a gift as my thanks for….your kindness."

Tomas agreed, and left with the jumping boy down the dirt towards the Kingdom. When Zephyr spoke, it was as if he did so with little breath. He had doom in his breath. Not relief, but defeat. His sacrifice, whether Leon would understand or not, was certain. The portrait must be complete.

The earth was damp along the brook, and each of Zephyr's bare feet pressed deep into the moss. After some time he had determined the thick heat of the barrack was rude to keep her in, and he brought her through the forest.

The Princess who now wore Tomas' clean tunic and trousers looked nearly as the local folk do, albeit her hair was still remarkably smooth and her… infamous mask. From her side, Zephyr could see how thick its silver was, and how each garnet jewel was that of great weight. Her head tilted ever so slightly downward at her feet, telling of its density.

The sun crowned above in a sky stripped of clouds, casting dappled shadows through the canopy of elm and poplar. The brook ran quiet and low, its cool waters parting around stones worn smooth by time. Here, between the whispering trees and the babbling current, Zephyr felt he walked in the presence of a creature spun from myth.

His steps were hesitant. Every crackle of a twig beneath his heel seemed too loud. He kept looking over his shoulder, as if he expected a knight's blade to gleam behind every tree. The weight of her presence was heavier than armor, for it was not just her status that burdened him…. but the strange gravity of her gaze which was haunting, even behind the mask.

Alexandria walked with a kind of ease and lightness that mocked him. She moved through the underbrush like she'd known this path since her infancy, and yet she could not see. Zephyr, on the other hand, felt clumsy and exposed. He kicked a rock by accident, winced, then cursed himself silently.

"Your heartbeat," she said suddenly. "It's loud enough to scare the warmbellies and sibbers."

Zephyr nearly tripped once more as he spoke, "you… what?"

She smiled, her chin tilted with resistance toward the sunlight. "You must be terrified. I don't blame you. But you needn't be." Her hand brushed across tall reeds, fingertips barely grazing the golden heads. "This land… my land… it knows me."

"The brook?" Zephyr asked, recovering his composure as best he could. "There's little to be impressed by."

"The brook, the moss, the stones. The breath of the trees. The Kingdom is more than walls and thrones. It is rhythm and silence, sir. If I am to rule it, I must know its music." She paused at the edge of the bank and knelt to trail her fingers through the water. "You should too."

Zephyr stood a pace behind, unsure of what she meant. "I'm afraid I know only the music of fleeing," he said, squinting at the play of light through the branches. "And warmbellies, on occasion."

Alexandria let out a soft laugh and glanced back, her masked face unreadable but her voice laced with warmth. "Then I'll teach you something more." She motioned him forward, and when he hesitated, she added gently, "you mustn't always brace for the arrow. There is no monster of it. Once a munition, yet prior, kindling. Here, the vest we protect my castle with, yet prior, a home for the fish."

He crouched beside her, the cold water wrapping around his fingers. She was right, it had a song to it. It burbled and whispered secrets only the earth could hear.

"This brook widens and splits the southern forest lands from the hills," she began, her voice now shaped by something regal, practiced. "To the east, past the groves, are the traders' routes. You'd know them by the stone stacks they leave: tall, smooth pyramids built by hand as tokens of safe passage. No man or woman may touch them without permission from the lead merchant. It's a sign of deep respect."

Zephyr listened, his brow knit with interest despite himself.

"To the north, there's the Veilar Forests. Hunters never return from it, but our scholars say it's where the old temples rest, buried beneath vines and silence. And somewhere beyond… I've yet to learn."

"The brook tells you more than I could ever learn." Zephyr said, his voice barely above the water's hush.

Alexandria turned her head toward him, as if she could see his awe. "And lately, it is very loud."

"And yet it will be yours, all the noise of it. What will you do with all of it? Once the crown is yours?"

She did not answer at first. Instead, she dipped both hands into the brook and let water slide between her fingers, cupping a small silver fish before setting it free again.

"Father asserts I will look down across the kingdom blindly, that he and the council will hold my hand. They will not place their trust in me, not with my *ailments*," she said at last. It was clear to Zephyr that she believed her Persuasion and disease were indifferent.

He stared at her, and for a moment forgot the danger, the curse, even the portrait. "You believe that's possible? You are not sick… no… you hold a very special and powerful gift. They are only scared you will not do their bidding, that you will light a greater path for your people."

"I cannot," she whispered. "I will bring great peril to these people, and so I will stay blind to them. I could not bear harming them, and I could not bear seeing their faces as I do so."

Zephyr's lips parted, but no words came. The wind stirred between them, soft as breath on skin. The water sang a little louder, as if it too were urging him to speak. But before he could, her hand reached for his. Not as royalty. Not as fate-bound enchantment. Just her fingers, cold and clean from the brook, seeking his warmth. His heart calmed and he let her hold it.

She truly believed that with her eyes revealed, she could not help but deconstruct whomever and whatever came across her.

"Have you worn this… mask… since birth?"

"No! There was no telling, I was only an infant! I was but a child, prancing near the moat on days no brighter than this; I refused to return to the cover of the castle when a storm approached. It was of no threat, and all children should live loudly no matter the rain or sun. It was our elder Page Bentley who I struck, and when I returned to father in drenched velvet, Page was swiftly… *swiftly*… executed. But it was only when I banished father from our halls, that he and mother arranged my first visard. Mother said it took a witch to get him to return from the courtyard. He… wanted me to marry, yet I hadn't lived but fifty seasons!"

"And from then on, you were bound. All because they were terrified of choices you hadn't made yet," Zephyr said as he unbent his knees and stood before her. "And yet, you've made the choice to arrive here."

She joined him at his chest, granting a subtle smile. He was beguiled by her sweetness, the settled tone of her voice. It was then with a rare confidence in Zephyr that he slowly reached for her mask. But, as his fingers met its cold, dense silver, that Alexandria pulled backward.

"No…why would you?" She cried. In a fit of disbelief in him, she turned and stormed back towards the village.

Zephyr sped after her, knowing that if she caught the attention of a tradesman or other folk, it would be an early end to him.

"Alexandria… Alexandria, you wait!" He announced, getting to the front of her. Then, he realized what King Univerza had set for him… the deal they made. "I would like to paint a portrait of you," he said in another defeat. "One which the Kingdom and the lands of Grasp will treasure until the end of time… one of your beauty, your smile which crescents, your hands which rule, and your eyes which cast hope. Might you sit with me so that I may forge this treasure?"

Her fingers reached for his and her head tilted ever so slightly leftward.

"A painting?" She asked delicately yet still tinging with anger. "And fill you with regret once my shield is removed?"

"What you bring is solely your decision, Alexandria. Peasants, merchants, all of your people will come to know the true *you* through this painting. The very oils illustrating your eyes will bring them to trust in you. Would you?" Zephyr asked softly, and he offered his palm. Reluctantly, though, with an ecstatic smile, she agreed.

18. The Forest of Centurion

Sabbath and George had ventured far beyond the foothills and realm of Olderag. They'd eaten a prickled notch George had found hillside, then continued.

"Eastward are swampish lands, damp, difficult to navigate. Known to Tarians and Southern folk as *Spearland.*" George spoke above the wind. "The region harbors the Swampfolk and all their farms. Despite thriving in greater numbers than the Greenfolk or Riverfolk, the Swampfolk are *far* more brutal, even produced great warriors who once aided Taria in battle. Or so the story goes."

George convinced Sabbath that a westerly route would be quicker, leading them through the forestlands to clearer paths, while Spearland, notorious for its dead, dagger-like trees, would derail their endeavor.

"Over this hill," he told her. "We'll have a clear view of where we must go."

They had traveled to great elevation on their journey, and George assured her that at this crest, their path would ease. But once his mare had trudged up the moss and onto the iced-over hump of earth, the view made Sabbath question what they'd gotten into.

"The world's frozen over here?" She asked. "We lack the pelts for this, George. I knew we should have gone east."

"No… no, dearest. It *is* quite cold here, and will be as we continue on. But the valley you see there is that of Centurion. It's sheerness is not of ice, but of *time*. The pine of this forest secrete a silvery sap. Over thousands of seasons, the sap builds and coats each tree, the pollen coating the moss, and all becomes a twisting mirrored column. I've known very few who have dabbled in these woods, but rumors tell of futures and other lives you can see within the sap. It'll be a joyous trip, c'mon now Sabbath!"

George let his horse descend the hill, while Sabbath walked on foot behind. She shook her head, irritated that this *fantastical* forest was the most convenient route, where Spearland offered momentary refuge and food.

"What awaits us there, George? Laggards with underwhelming threats or maybe even the Koba?" She asked rhetorically.

"No, I doubt those beasts would traverse there. The forest is far too pristine to harbor anything rotten. I *would* however advise against staring blankly into any clump of sap."

"You truly believe you can see through them… at other lives?" She scoffed. But George's voice fell from his jubilant tone.

"Oh *yes,* I would simply play it safe, Miss Sabbath. Ya wouldn't like to find out the hardest way, I assure you. The futures and other lives could poison ye brain, make you feel guilt like you've never felt, or show you horrid things."

"*Horrid things*," she mocked his words quietly, and followed at a distance behind him.

It took but an hour to reach the cusp of the Forest of Centurion, and Sabbath grew weary as they approached it. The first trees were ordinary, dark and damp. But their hidden sides were thinly glassy, rough and glittering. The moss and stone harbored a veiled frost.

The night had come upon them as they traveled, but the moonlight through the glassed canopies above made the forest hold a silvery mist, and all was faintly visible through a light sheet. The bark of the pine was several inches beneath the icy glaze, though the air which coursed the forest was humid and comfortable. There, Sabbath understood how one may get lost staring at a tree. Though she refrained from staring, her peripheral caught glimpses of herself walking along. Reflections of George and the mare passing infinitely at all sides. Sabbath ducked beneath a low-bending branch, its weight bowed under the ancient glaze of silver-sap. Her hand brushed the bark, and it was warm.... not with fire, but with memory. Like something long buried beneath snow, still faintly breathing.

George sat astride the mare, still humming a tune older than even the trees around them. The hooves padded silently on the mossy ground, muffled as though they walked through a painting.

"You say you've known few to pass through this place," Sabbath muttered, her voice quieter than she intended. "So what of those who did? What did they see in the sap?"

George's tune faltered. "I knew a woodsman once," he said slowly, "back when I was half the coward I am now. He wandered into Centurion chasing a snow lynx for its hide. When he returned, he said he'd seen himself cradling a daughter he never had. Named her Tansy. Said she had freckles and cried whenever the wind howled through windows. The man had never so much as courted a woman before then."

"What happened to him?"

George was quiet. "He built a cradle out of pine. It still sits under the eaves of his old shed. Never used."

Sabbath rubbed her arms. "So the sap lies?"

"No," George said. "It shows *truths*. But not all truths come to pass. Some are choices you didn't make, others that never belonged to you at all. Lives you *could* have lived, or do in another time. It's like touching a river's surface and seeing the ripples stream, yet you could never follow each."

She paused by one of the trees. Beneath its curved, glimmering coat, she could just make out her own silhouette, walking alone, no pack on her back, no George ahead. Her shoulders were broader, scarred. Older. She turned away quickly before she could study the reflection's eyes.

"And yet," she muttered, "this is the *convenient* route."

"More convenient than Koba blade-fangs in the dark," George said. "They're more apt to mess with the Swampfolk."

Sabbath snorted. "I feel they aren't too picky."

"Although they are foul-smelling, poison-fanged, twitchy little rat-bastards," he said without pause. "Aside from messin' with folk, they keep to their hollows and nests. They won't dare this place. Miscreancy doesn't like being watched."

Sabbath raised an eyebrow. "You think the forest watches?"

George's eyes gleamed in the low light. "I *know* it does. You'll hear it before long. Don't be scared when you do."

Silence folded over them for a time. The trees groaned softly, and Sabbath thought she heard a sigh on the wind.... too soft for a human voice, but shaped like one.

She tried to shift the mood. "When we reach Taria," she said, "do you think the Council will even *believe* us?"

George grunted. "Depends who's left in it. The Great Wizards aren't kings, Sabbath. But they've teeth like kings do. If Joab's reach has grown into Taria, they may already be puppets."

"And if not?"

"Then you'll have your reckoning. A real one."

"I don't want a reckoning," she said, bitterness crawling into her throat. "I want justice. I want Joab to suffer. I want

Olderag's courts undone. I want those twisted laws burned and buried in the Sea of Cinders."

George nodded, not looking back. "Aye. Then speak carefully. Show the truth. Not your anger."

She looked at his back for a long moment. "Why did you come with me, George?"

His voice was quiet, nearly lost in the shifting saplight. "Because I've lived too long doing nothing."

They pressed on beneath the dreaming trees, shadows curling and unspooling beside them, every surface catching their breath and reflecting it back. The forest was beautiful, yes, but it was also full of grief. As Sabbath adjusted the weight of her rucksack, something shifted inside it. She paused. Unbuckled the flap. *The book, Urald, The Librarian.* She didn't remember it being that warm. She ran her hand over the cover. It pulsed faintly, as though remembering too. Just as quickly as she retrieved it, she stuffed it back into the rut-sack.

George had walked at a distance while guiding the horse, and Sabbath trailed behind with her dagger prepared for any blood. Though, George had continuously suggested she leave it sheathed.

Despite that he had advised her to keep her eyes forward, the temptation of staring directly at one of the trees was all too potent. She did so, once he had disappeared beyond the brush, and found a thick, millennia-old pine tree. Just at the head of a cove, it called to her. Echoing voices whispered like distant bells. She rushed to it before George could see her. Carefully she lay her palms upon the marble-like coating, looked at herself against the silvery sheen. Then, just as he told her, the image of her melted in coils as a scene began to play. It was peculiar, she thought. She saw through someone else's eyes; a bright day, a courtyard, pink blotches of flowers. A middle-aged man's head leaned into the picture, one with braided hair and a magnificent beard.

"You need to stop running off, young Sabbath," the ghostly man said within the sap. Sabbath's eyes squinted as she wondered who he was. Then a woman appeared at a distance, approaching her in a clean and pearly gown.

"Our daughter is quite the traveler, isn't she?" The woman said. *"You haven't gone far, I'm glad you're alright."*

Sabbath had realized that in whatever reality she saw in the sap, her *parents* accompanied her. Her nails dug into the tree, barely piercing the mirrored bark.

"Mother?" Her voice waved and shivered. But the apparition she saw, whoever she was in that reality, did not speak. Her illusion of a mother embraced the *false* Sabbath, and the hand of her father fell behind her shoulders as well. She couldn't feel it, the warmth of guidance, but imagined she could.

"A life I haven't lived, or one I've yet to find," she bravely told herself. The hole it left within her was great and hollow, it nearly made her sick. George had gone quite far, and she convinced herself to leave the tree and find him.

George had strayed far as well, for Sabbath couldn't find him. But even *he* could not stay true to his requests and greedily turned to a slightly younger tree at his west. He licked his lips in anticipation, believing he might find himself dressed in a king's attire, or sat among busty women in a tavern. But he found neither. Instead, the image of a cold cavernous place darkened the sap, and what he had seen horrified him. So much so that he left with his horse and began retracing the path to locate Sabbath.

What he'd seen made him tremble, and once he found her, he could barely mutter a word. But when he saw her, she too was distraught. Her eyes were red and sore, her arms curled up close to her chest. George took her under his arm, understanding that she'd seen something terrible as well.

"And now you understand," he reconciled. "We should keep on."

They continued on for some time, but the stain of her potential parents not giving her up remained in her eyelids. She had fallen behind him once more, but this time he took notice.

"Sabbath, let's go."

"I've got private matter, old man. I'll be but a moment."

George sighed, and remained in his spot while she scurried off the trail. Unbeknownst to him, she had stumbled through dense brush until she found another great pine. Sabbath was desperate to see the same scene, thinking she would. This pine was rooted in the pit of a grove, where weeds struck high and flowers were frozen in time at its base. Frantically she grabbed hold of it and waited anxiously for the sheen to churn.

"Come on, come on!"

When the view finally began to build, it was just as dark as whatever George saw. It was an odd scene; through her own perspective, she saw a vast great-hall of a castle, and she stood at where a throne might sit. The hall was dim but for light beaming through mosaic windows. Goblets of burning emerald fire were situated down the way, with silhouettes of warriors stood in formation away from her. The *false* her turned slightly to her right, and the sight was vivid yet baffling. A taller woman stood, cloaked in a black gown and black hair. Her face was strange as well, donning a wildly fluid but metal mask over her eyes with long wisps of spikes striking off like monstrous eyelashes. Beyond this woman, a third female stood. Similar in shortness as Sabbath, but with phantom hair blooming from beneath a witch's hat. Sabbath's eye twitched with disbelief, that she was of some dark royalty in this tree's universe.

When she rejoined George, she had to hide the fact that she was shaking. The wretched feeling that burned her insides had shed into a different one. She could be *royalty*, for the trees may show one's current future just as they could other realities. If this were to come to fruition, who would dismiss her as a loud orphan? Who would brush off her words, or pay her no mind? She could yell orders and *all* would have no choice but to listen to her. The idea made her itch, and the hollowed core of her began to burn with anticipation.

19. The Yippire Coven

The path led Sabbath and George further through the Forest of Centurion to the foot of a hill obscured beneath crystallized brush. Fireflies still thrived here, for water must have been nearby. George determined that they should climb the hill to their right for a greater view. The horse remained strong, but George instructed it to remain at the bottom.

Before they could ascend the hill, Sabbath hushed him and hunkered down abruptly to the sound of numerous voices in the distance. They were whiny, feminine, mumbling wicked things she couldn't make out. George followed her up carefully, laying with their stomachs against the hardened moss. Sabbath slapped the back of his head and pointed at the group below.

"Witches," she muttered. *"What are they doing here?"*

"I haven't a clue. Look," he nodded forward. *"Three of them."*

The two watched as one witch, an elderly one with a hunchback and cane, weakly struck the bark of a tree over and over again. The solidified sap shattered into a small dust cloud as she went on, and the witch then lowered to the earth and began to collect what had accumulated in a pile.

"The sap must hold magical properties. I've never seen such a thing. They're harvesting it."

"But what good could it do?"

"I'm not sure, young Sabbath.

Neither Sabbath nor George had much experience with witches, mostly tales or wars from long ago. George knew of witches being fashioned as useful adversaries to Olderag or other governments, providing hexes and advice in enchanting weapons, though few ever saw the application in real life.

The three witches had moved closer, all three smashing stones against the trees, and their voices became clearer.

"Yerrib, are you sure this concoction will do it? We've nearly wasted our harvest in the pot. I think this damned tree-dust is worthless!" One had given up, seating themselves in the glittering dirt.

"Oh Margy, you're helpless. Our last brew just needed a bit more *potency.* Make yourself useful!" The eldest one said. Though, all three were equally as decrepit. Each had the figure akin to an old goblin, with curled spines and plump bellies.

"What if the vision you saw was merely of another life? We've spent too many moons here, I vote we… we leave and grab our pipes and make good of what we have," said the third with a wavering voice.

"Enough Merich! It is not about the *vision*… it is about time! With enough of this century-dust, we can see far more than all the realities and futures. Pick up your stones and get on with it!" The eldest Yerrib demanded, brandishing her palm to reveal an orb of fire. The two others did as she said, and tirelessly struck the stone.

George had glanced down behind him and saw that his horse had wandered off. Quietly, he descended the incline to search while Sabbath stayed put.

His search proved not too difficult, for the prints of hooves were but impressions in the sap-frost over the earth. It was nearby that he found her stood idly and shaking her head beside a shallow grove and indent within the ground. Her broad muzzle was wet and sniffling.

"Why've you strayed, love? You mustn't be trouble."

As he pressed against her neck to guide her away, he peered into the grove in which she had marked. He decided to step into it, entering a small cavernous place. In all but ten steps with his body morphed to fit, he encountered the end of the dwelling. It was there he saw a smallish figure sat before a glorious but harrowing sight. The network of roots of a tree on the surface was frozen and wild before him and this figure, its flesh retaining a shimmering silver finish. An aurora of color and light emanated from the silhouette of this figure, which he believed to be a girl. She knelt down and faced this light as if it were an iridescent fire, though it was in fact an illusion playing just as they did on the bark above. The girl's hair was that of the sun's corona but whiter. Then, he spotted the black, pointed hat laid atop a stone. "*A witch…"* he spoke beneath his breath. Swiftly he left the grove without making a sound and ushered the mare away and went on to find Sabbath.

When he and the horse returned to the hill, he saw no sign of her at the top. He thought she may have been tempted to find another tree. But as he crept around, she was nowhere. *"Sabbath?"* He quietly called around, but no answer. It was when he peered around the hill where the witches were, that he found her laying on the ground while the three eldest witches stood over her.

"Well, what will we do with this *rodent?"* One asked with a cackle.

"Rodent? I fear that may be you, Merich!" The second said and struck the first with a tiny flash of lightning to her long nose.

"Enough you two! We mustn't treat our guest with insults. *However*, she may prove quite useful to us. Tell me, young woman, are you a mercenary of the *King?* I thought he bestowed trust in our coven by now. Speak then!" Their leader ordered Sabbath, who rolled to her side to face them.

"I live by no rule, less that of a *King!"*

'But you *must* hail from some place. Perhaps Taria?" The witch asked. "Surely you're not just some wild-thing!"

"Unbind me, and you can determine that for yourself," Sabbath declared, leading the witches to laugh hysterically over her.

"Feisty, all right!" The third pointed. "Let's take her to the pot, I'm certain we've got a recipe suited for the *spice*."

The three had lifted her up, zapping her periodically as she fought.

"Unhand me!" She called out, but George could not help. He was far too frail to put up a fight against a trio of witches, no matter how much *older* they were.

"Where is the young-one? Miss Ella!" The one by the name of Yerrib yelled out. At a distance, they waited for a smallish girl, the same one George had seen in the grove. She held her witches hat tight to her head as she ran. The coven then scurried off deep into the woods.

"*No… no.. not good at all!*" George muttered to himself as he climbed atop his horse and began to trail the coven at a safe distance.

The air grew thick with the sharp perfume of broken pine and spent magic as George led his horse forward, silent as wind over glass. Through the sap-coated trunks he followed, far enough to avoid the crackle of arcane murmurs. He was close enough to see the glitter of spellfire at the witches' heels as they exited the Forest of Centurion and began to levitate. They had left no footprints in the loamy forest floor, only streaks of scorched moss and drifting motes of amber dust.

Sabbath hung limp between them, suspended in a cradle of reddish light that shimmered like boiling silk. Her boots dragged now and then across the ground, leaving faint lines through the frost-hardened thistle. Every time she stirred, one of the witches would wave a withered hand and mutter a binding word, and her limbs would slacken once more.

George clenched his fists around the reins. His joints ached. His breath steamed before him in the silver night, and his old bones begged him to stop. But he pressed on.

They broke through the outer glade of the forest and into the open field beyond, where the glassed pines gave way to an ancient prairie that rolled down in brambled knolls and lonely stones. In the pale moonlight, the witches flew.

George's horse halted in terror, snorting and bucking its head. But George leaned close, whispering into its ear, "go, now… go!" He kicked its flanks gently, and the mare shot forward, hooves pounding the field. The witches moved faster, their silhouettes gleaming like dark lanterns against the moonlit sky. George's cloak snapped behind him, and frost kicked up behind the charging steed. He could not see where the witches were headed, but the air grew heavier with each league, and a pulse of magic quivered in the earth like a sleeping heartbeat.

Then he saw it. A hollow in the hillside…. more a wound than an entrance. It gaped wide, ribbed with roots and shrouded in hanging moss, a natural cavern most would not suspect as being a residence. The witches veered low and glided directly into it, the red net curling Sabbath into the dark like a silk cocoon. George pulled the reins and slid from the saddle before the horse could protest.

George left his mare tethered to a gnarled root, brushing his hand over her snout with final affection. "Be still now," he whispered. "You'll know when to run."

Then he turned, his old boots whispering across the moss-slick stone, and slipped into the cavern. He crept to the entrance, pressing himself against the stone. The cave mouth pulsed with unseen wards…. glimmers of runes etched in languages long dead shimmered when touched by moonlight. A whispering wind exhaled from within, smelling of copper and old, burned flowers.

Footsteps scuffled. Sabbath grunted…. a deep, hoarse noise of resistance. George leaned back, breath shallow. He needed a plan. He needed time. But the darkness before him offered neither.

Inside, the world transformed. It was not a mere tunnel…. it was a kingdom buried beneath the skin of the earth. A sprawling dungeon spiraled before him, a cathedral of stone and fire. The air seethed with sulfur and smoke, echoing with clangs, chants, and a low rumble from the river of molten lava that cut the massive cavern in two. Spidery bridges of bone and timber arced over the glowing chasm, connecting the two halves of this subterranean world like stitches in a wound.

Hundreds… no, *thousands* of goblins bustled throughout. Some were Koba, the rot-eyed miscreants he had seen before, with their hunched backs and dripping hands. Others were stranger still: pale-skinned, with golden jewelry looped through their ears and nostrils; some walked on all fours with stretched limbs and crimson eyes. They churned enormous monolithic gears, their grotesque muscles bulging with the strain. The sound of turning stone echoed like drums in a forge. Others gathered around black cauldrons bubbling with emerald potions, stirring with femurs or carving runes into mushrooms the size of pigs.

Above them, in a ledge-carved alcove that overlooked the ruinous splendor, the witches readied the pot. George dared not cross the threshold yet. But he listened.

"*Bind her at the three-candled basin!*" hissed Yerrib from inside.

"Aye," crackled another, "then we'll stir her mind 'til it sings us the truth!"

Yerrib, Merich, and Margaret.... gnarled as tree stumps and just as stubborn.... chanted over a great iron cauldron whose contents sloshed with purple mist. Sabbath was suspended above it, curled within the threads of scarlet light, her limbs bound and eyes wide with fury and disbelief.

"We'll rip the truth from her soul!" Merich cackled. "Let the brew reach its rolling rage!"

Margaret, ever clumsy, fumbled her satchel.... and the century dust, shimmering like powdered moonlight, spilled across the stone.

"Blast it all!" she screeched.

"You vile goat!" Yerrib barked. "That took us two seasons to gather!"

The elder two rushed to help her scoop the glittering powder, bickering like hens in a storm.

George crouched behind a jutting slab of basalt, watching, counting the heartbeats between each motion. This might be the only chance. He slid along the shadows, keeping low, preparing to spring. But someone was watching him. A soft presence, a hush in the chaos. He turned to see the fourth witch… the youngest. He recognized her, for her hair shimmered like ghost-light, falling down her back in ethereal threads. Her face was not cruel like the others', but calm. Thoughtful. Her hands were clasped before her, and she tilted her head gently, as if she'd expected him.

"You followed us," she said quietly.

George stiffened, unsure if spell or trick would follow. "She's a girl. Brave. Angry. Honest. Your elders… they'll kill her for it."

The young witch looked toward Sabbath, her violet eyes dimming. "I know." She turned back to him, voice soft as moss. "They think they can see every future. But they only believe the ones that feed their greed."

She reached into the air and tugged. The spell-thread unraveling Sabbath snapped, and the red light fizzled into mist. Sabbath dropped onto the ledge, rolling to her knees. She looked at the young witch in disbelief.

"Go," the witch said. "Run before they notice. This place is no fate for you."

George helped Sabbath to her feet and together they sprinted down the steps cut into the rock. But the moment their boots struck the cavern floor, a shrill cry ripped through the chaos.

"Yerrib! I see a roach!" roared Merich as she spotted Goerge and pointed her long, crooked finger. Then, Yerrib raised her knotted staff and lightning cracked from its tip. The bolt hit George square in the back instantaneously. He flew forward, crashing into the stone with a heavy grunt, his limbs splayed unnaturally.

"No!" Sabbath shrieked, turning back. But when she fell to his side, the grumbling of nearby goblins reverberated in the stone beneath her. One Koba atop a bridge above them snickered and hurled a gourd-shaped vial of green liquid. It shattered across George's chest, spilling a hissing cloud of rot.

He looked up at Sabbath as his skin began to flake and pull. Bones showed through, glistening white and blackened at the joints. His breath rattled, shallow and final.

"Dearest Sabbath," he said, voice like wind in a hollow. "Long ago…in the sap. I seen but darkness. An emerald sear."

Sabbath let her head fall beside him. She cried in terror, *"no George, no!"*

"I thought… I thought it was someone else's future." And then his eyes, still human, closed for the last time as his body bubbled and evaporated. Only bone remained then.

The dungeon burned brighter now. Sabbath rose, trembling, and turned toward the howling coven and the advancing goblins. She did not cry. She could not find her dagger, for the coven had taken it once they found her in the forest. She could only run, unable to put up a fight against the horde of goblins and the wretched powers of the coven.

20. Even the Shadow Leaves

Leon swung a wooden cradle upwards into the air, carefully stepping as his eyes met its descent. He did not catch it on the first, third, or fifth go, but eventually the ball would land in the cupped contraption leading to an electric cheer. Two other boys of the City joined him, and the three would attempt to catch what the others tossed.

Zephyr had convinced Alexandria to remain hidden within the hay barrack until his return that evening. Tomas had gone to the tavern with Willa, so Zephyr could finally focus on his time with Leon. But the late day and all of its blue and amber light could not numb the dread which burrowed deep inside. The father was frantically excited, however, knowing the boy would go on and do so in good health.

Joab's curse had become somewhat of a debt for Zephyr, understanding that there *was* a cure to it. But the price was deathly high. There was a fleeting awareness in the boy as he pranced through sparse crowd with other children. Days ago he showed conviction in his eventual fate, and though artificially, he seemed to have forgotten.

Once the sky above grew violets and deep auburn waves, Zephyr and Leon walked the cobble streets out of the City. They'd fed upon hot pies, and were no match for a boil Willa prepared. The boy's eyes grew weary as he lay beside the hearth, and Willa retrieved a fraying storybook from the boy's basket.

"In the quiet vale of Caernhollow, where the winds hummed lullabies and the stars blinked like sleepy eyes, there lived a very small tree. She was not strong like the oaks nor tall like the pines. Her leaves were soft and silvery, and her bark smelled of honey when warmed by sun.

The birds rarely built nests in her branches, and the deer did not sleep beneath her shade. She was too small, they said, too still and strange.

"Why don't you grow taller?" asked the wind.

"I'm not sure I'm meant to," said the little tree.

Every spring, the trees around her grew higher and thicker, casting their shadows over her. They reached for the clouds, and some even touched them.

Summer passed, and then autumn, and then many more. Still, she did not stretch herself like the others. She watched the world instead. . . . how the ants made their tiny towns, how the moths told secrets to the moon, how the brook changed its song after the rain.

One year, a great storm came to Caernhollow. It howled like a wild thing, and the big trees swayed and snapped. Their height made them brave, but also brittle.

When morning came, the vale was quiet once more, but many of the tallest trees had fallen. Their roots torn from the earth, their canopies broken.

The little tree stood, untouched. Her roots, though small, ran deep. Deeper than the others ever guessed."

The boy had fallen asleep and limp before the ants dug their homes. But Willa had continued, and Zephyr listened silently. As she concluded the story, her words grew firm and her eyes became daggers. She was unhappy with him, with whatever dark spell he might have brought upon the Princess, with the *danger* which trailed along with it. Zephyr could not help but notice unheralded emotion from her, that the royal girl, who was her own burden, had induced a deep sadness. He gave Willa no closure, for the time they spent together was short, and his endeavors were far too frantic to give cadence or empathy.

Zephyr had joined the Princess in the barrack by a dim-flickering oil lamp. Both lay adjacent from one another atop the stacks, her mask staring at him ominously over a thin smile. The powder of her cheeks was well-dirtied and smeared. Zephyr was removing his frayed tunic when Alexandria questioned him.

"The boy… tell me about him. Is he an orphan?"

"The boy? He is not, he is my son," he said, but did so with hesitation. The Princess grew quiet.

"Why have you hidden me from him?"

"Children.. .nothing is safe with them. They go on and tell whoever they find first. Regardless of what they would do to me, they've already taken your soul away from you. I fear they are no strangers to strict punishment."

"I am certain of it too. Though, is that woman his mother? You're… wed?"

"*Hah!*" He chuckled in disbelief, growing nearly exhausted of Alexandria's reaches. "She is the 'great' Willa Broadmere, an ordinary drunk. But… she has allowed my son and I refuge here. Far better than the damp nooks of the Bard. No…my love passed on. She was *very* ill; it caught her very quickly."

"I… I am terribly sorry," she consoled him, letting her palm fall over his knuckles. "A great woman she must have been, and I trust that she possessed a generational luck to have spent her life with you."

To Zephyr, the story had long burnt out, and he could share little of the true events. For, if he had, her enchantment might shatter. It was as delicate as glass, this endeavor. Even with her sweet magnanimity and how she would fall into his arms if he allotted, she was not Ambrosia, and Leon would meet her soon if he was not diligent.

In the silence of the night, still by the dying flame, Zephyr retrieved the poplar board and unraveled the linen Tomas had provided after supper. He presented it before Alexandria, letting her hands drift over each.

"And what if I say the wrong thing? Though unintentional, my words will carry far more than the weight of the earth beneath us." Her hand grabbed a hold of his forearm. "I can't hurt you."

"Eyes cannot bring the pain of a blade, and although yours could, I trust that you are an *incredibly* responsible wielder," he assured her. Despite the stories he's heard from local folk, even how she made her father unconsciously banish himself from their castle, Zephyr did not believe she could truly cause any harm. She would have to do so with intent, he naively thought.

"And the people will build trust in me, if they can witness my eyes?"

"The mask obscures *Alexandria,* as all men can see their beginnings and ends just from the color," Zephyr attempted to concoct the perfect design of words, but even he had little faith in his voice. From a small satchel, one provided from Willa, he retrieved an egg and an assortment of berries, fruit, and dried plants. He left them atop the linen sheet, and let Alexandria decide for herself. Her fist suddenly presented the egg to Zephyr, tightly and yet not cracking it.

"Incorporate my red bliaut; a thin tunic does not incite *trust* in my mind."

Zephyr smiled and took the egg. He went on to sort out broken clay vases and bowls, directing each ingredient into their place. He pestled garnet flowers he'd gathered, stripped seeds from vanipar, and beat the yolk. Over his shoulder, he heard the hay adjust as Alexandria began to move. She removed her heavy silver mask, and his heart began delve deeper into the cavity of his chest. He turned to face her, finding an implausibly prepossessing complexion. The bridge of her nose was slight, her brow was subtle and blonde, and her eyes were of an oracular amber. They were not of the sea, nor forests, nor the sky. They were neither reminiscent of lake-beds or bronze. No, they were of the sun, opalescent as its rays just before dusk. Her pupils were obsidian marbles as they gave into the dim light, which to her must have been far too bright.

Although captivated, he managed to orient the canvas, readying it with pins. Hey lay dusty bowls before him atop a bundle of straw. Alexandria was cautious not to speak, fearing that just one sentence might order him to his doom.

Though, this wasn't quite the case when he began questioning her, a mechanism in which to capture her head move as she answered. He would note how the shadows ran and disappeared behind her smallish jaw, how the light of the flame would cascade through the very fibers of her corneas.

"How vital is my birthplace to your sprawling domain? Are all of those beneath Olderag as sooty and unkempt as we feel? Tell me, how does Jean view the southern Kingdom?"

"Sooty is the first word that comes to mind," she fell into a giggle. "He is incredibly vital to our exports. And I believe a great abundance of our spring harvest flows downward to the southern people."

"The good soil is very scarce along the boundary. Now… rest your chin atop your palm, and look *very*… very serious."

She did so naturally.

"However our merchants are solely reliant on your fisherman. The lakes west of the Hides are extremely overburdened."

"My, you may be more knowledge about the southern land than I. How might that be?"

"I accompany father plenty in his talks of trade and war."

"War? Is Alexandria still under threat of the sea-bound men? I had assumed your walls were high enough to keep them out."

"The Batesmen posts are very well fortified now, we've little concern of their kind. No, I speak of Krythia," Alexandria's eyes rose as she relaxed her wrist from its placement. "A tradesman from the east who was directed to bring with him chickpeas, but instead gave only a harrowed announcement. One of an occupation, and our mercenaries on their travel."

"And yet the eastern folk are always so soft-spoken and proud. What could have stirred them?" Zephyr continued on, pressing beads of vanipar oil against the linen. "Desensitized I would assume?"

"The party is not of their own people," her hands fell to the dress. "A *coven.*"

Almost humorously, Zephyr contested. For witches were widely believed to be secluded to far from establishments, while sorcerers were often the commissioned. "And how's that? Wouldn't they much prefer to sneak potions of… rot and poison into citygoers water? I cannot fathom what they might do with a stronghold like Krythia."

"There is no telling, but the tradesman was famished and weak. But I believe in our mercenaries will return with answers, and a liberated kingdom."

Crickets and hoverflies whipped outside through the grass. The small lamp only remained lit from the settled air, though on most nights Zephyr would blanket himself in straw to ward of the cold.

Zephyr's thoughts dribbled out of his head and dissipated as they fell, realizing that he may complete the portrait in one session, as Alexandria showed no exhaustion, and he showed no letting up.

"I've yet to hear the horses, they are not looking for me," she asserted, almost brazenly.

"And yet, you're here. Why hasn't the King sent his knights?"

"To not scare the people," Alexandria spoke in a stable, quiet voice. "He'll flood the streets with peasant-dressed watchers. Merchants, minstrels, butchers. Come the next dusk, militias will raid homes without announcement."

"Even to be at the bay of panic, would this not make people lose faith and trust?" Zephyr had stopped painting. He looked far into the amber amulets of her eyes.

"The kingdom will have time to react. You mustn't question my father, for he is the cleverest of governers. He knows the outcome well before his fist has struck his knee. Or… he *believes* he does. I anticipate my return will be my houppelande's sleeves withdrew and your hand in mine, and you would be my *king*."

Zephyr was nearly starstruck by her enthusiasm. Just as such, he felt his heart wilt as her love for him was evidently robust and potent. She did not envision the world continuing without Zephyr alongside her.

He debated in his mind if, once the painting was exchanged and the curse transferred, if her love would remain indefinitely. Then… her future would be tainted with the infinitely recurring memory of her lover's death. Just as… he might, through, with the promise that he would someday rejoice with Ambrosia in another place.

The two turned quiet while Zephyr's eyes became pins which navigated Alexandria's hair.

"Olderag kept us uneducated, and I know little of these lands, even from story. How has Alexandria come to bear your very name?"

"The roots are not very elaborate," she said with a smoking glare. "The very first queen of this kingdom was the

Great Alexandria, and you should know she ruled beside Trein the *Bastard*." Her head turned sharply as she spoke of the long-dead king and queen.

"What made him a *bastard?*"

"I believe for his never-ending obsession with wartime. He thought his people would admire him, but their rebellions only grew stronger and more potent. Those who remained in his support were but slaves to the bastions protecting our City and villages."

"I cannot blame him," Zephyr uttered. "Integrity is not lost once conceited, but it *is* fortified in success."

The hours went on until the sky grew no darker. The canvas would shake time to time as Zephyr grew weary of his ability. What was once a well respected gift then killed his wife, and now he teased with the idea that he may not be able to produce as strikingly beautiful portraits as he once had. However, he knew that if King Jean St. Auclaire did not accept the painting of his daughter, that whatever punishment he granted could not be as cruel as his current suffering. Just as a wick could be blown out with pursed lips, Zephyr would wish the King's response was just as swift.

A breeze crept through the slats in the barrack walls, brushing the surface of the linen like a breath from the gods themselves. Alexandria had shifted her weight and now rested her elbows atop the bundled straw, chin tilted just so. Her gaze, once playful, now brimmed with something older.... some understanding deeper than her one-hundred-some seasons should permit. Zephyr paused his strokes. The pigment in the bowl had dulled, as though it too feared marring her likeness.

"You do not sleep," he remarked softly, not as a question, but as a notice.... an admittance of her presence lingering too long in his spirit.

"Not tonight," she replied, "I fear dreams might paint me somewhere I no longer belong."

Zephyr lowered his brush and reluctantly spoke, "you belong here."

"No," she said, not coldly, but with precision. "I was carved from opulence and duty. I don't belong among these stacks of straw. I only *remain* here."

Outside, the moon crested above the ridge, its light so pale it seemed afraid to touch the earth. In its ghostly shimmer, Zephyr could see the unfinished canvas, the portrait, just near realized, half-hoped-for. He saw her amber eyes staring out from the cloth and was struck by how alive they looked… how *sentient*, as if she had passed her spirit into the very weave of the paint.

Alexandria stood in ache, letting the folds of her red bliaut settle about her ankles like river water. "Will he know it's me?" she asked, nodding toward the painting and with wit.

Zephyr's mouth opened, then shut once he inserted question into the matter. He hadn't considered the possibility that Jean would see through it, that he might gaze into the painted eyes and feel the unmistakable pull of his daughter's life, the way Zephyr himself had moments ago. He wanted to lie, but lies no longer obeyed him.

"If he *knows*…" Alexandria started.

"Then he'll send his fists before his spit," Zephyr finished.

"And the boy?"

Zephyr flinched. "He's already gone, in some ways. Not yet in body, but… his fate is closer now. He bears a curse which hastens in the presence of truth."

Alexandria turned from the painting, wrapping her arms across her chest. "Then we lie in our place and we… banish ourselves from rule and we'll….save your boy, too."

"*Ah*," Zephyr groaned. "He is saved. Whether it be in the soil of this kingdom or I make my final painting in blood."

Her eyes widened, then narrowed. "I won't let you die," she whispered.

And somewhere, beyond the hills and the expiring night, the first of King Jean's shadowed militants entered the City in silence. Their footsteps were but drips of rainfall onto clay shingles. Zephyr's mind was infested with the thought, knowing that his arrival to the Kingdom was not taken kindly. Many thought he and Leon brought with them a new plague, while others much like the decrepit folk at the Greyhound just simply didn't take kindly to the exiled.

There was an unbeknownst hour near to dawn in which Alexandria had given way to the weight of the moon, and Zephyr concluded the portrait with few stray hairs arching atop her shoulder. He was relieved, chuckling to himself silently. His head fell to his palms; he *knew* he was near the end. Zephyr thought to award himself with a tale. Something lighthearted in its story that he could lay his soul against to rest. He searched in a bundle of straw where he hid *The Quire of the Collector*. Though, he could not recall if it was actually *The Collector's Quire*. Nevertheless, he could not find it. In a subtle panic, Zephyr dug his fists into the bulk of the straw with no luck. He exhaled, and believed it to be a sign that he should *actually* rest. In the absence of the lamp-light, he joined her in the nest of hay.

His final thoughts were chaotic and his breath wouldn't settle. Though he did not love her, her presence substituted that which was absent, warmth and weight. Though her words were quickly discarded, her head would tilt and her lips would part in a world he knew was entirely theirs. Before he joined her in dreams, the corroding truth came again, that she would soon be without him and the spell would fade. To bring this upon Alexandria, the realization brought frost upon his heart.

21. The Watchers & Commissions

The morning smelled of ink and glue, a city's breath, stretched thin across the countryside.

Zephyr stood in the doorway of the Broadmere's cottage, sleeves rolled to his elbows, drying his hands with a linen rag mottled with paint. His eyes squinted against the dust-kicked sun, watching Tomas return up the hill, something crumpled in his hand, his face unusually pale.

Tomas approached, the paper clenched like a snake's skin, and presented it to Zephyr. Upon examining it, he read from the poster. The parchment was thick, ridged with seal wax in the corner. Black script bled into the fibers like a wound.

◆

DECLARATION FROM THE CROWN OF ALEXANDRIA

◆

Let it be known that Her Royal Highness, *Alexandria of House St. Auclaire*, has been taken from the High Keep under unauthorized escort and is considered a figure of compromised will.

Any man, woman, or child who harbors the Princess is committing high treason and shall be put to death without trial. A bounty of seven-thousand gold lions is offered to any who provide information that leads to her return, unharmed and unaltered.

Be advised: The Princess carries with her a maleficious trait. A rare enchantment deemed a threat to civil order if persuaded otherwise. Her likeness may not be known by face, but her silver mask and red bliaut shall betray her.

The Crown grieves her absence. Let her be found.

…. King Jean St. Auclaire & Lady St. Auclaire

◆

Zephyr's fingers grew numb at the edges. Not from cold, but from something worse… *recognition.* The weight of inevitability.

He swallowed hard, then turned slowly toward the barn, leaving Tomas to his shaking head.

Inside the hay barrack, the air was still, thick with sleep and straw. Alexandria lay with her knees to her elbows. She wore the infamous red bliaut across her waist, though its hem had gathered soot and nettle from their last night fire. The mask sat nearby on a stack, its expressionless sheen turned toward the ceiling.

When Zephyr entered, she looked up in a daze, then rested her head again.

"There's no need to speak," she said softly.

"They've posted notices."

He assumed that at each market, square, and cart, her obscured face and red ink was plastered.

Her hands folded slowly. "So, their hunt begins. He means to reclaim me before the people see my face. Before the kingdom can wonder why the girl behind the mask would ever want to run."

There was a long pause. She stood then, stepping over loose straw to meet him. Her bare feet made no sound. The morning light slanted across her cheeks, softening her skin in the absence of powder. The two joined together again in the straw. Some comfort came to Zephyr as the idea that she *might* be willing to sway a curious knight or watcher if they were to happen upon her.

Come forenoon, a commotion broke out from the Broadmere's cottage. Willa had arrived home shortly after she departed for her typical tending of the tavern. An astonished Tomas ejected from inside the structure, and Leon followed as well. Frantic steps turned into a sprint, and faded into the distance. Zephyr awoke disgruntled as the smallish boy ran into the barrack. He believed the ruckus to be a matter of Alexandria's absence from the castle, but it was anything but.

"Papa, Eldric's left! Papa!" The boy yelled for his father, and the man quickly asserted that he did not care very much.

"What is it boy?"

"He's gone to Cornlot, Willa said they found...." but the child stopped abruptly. His pupils widened as he looked beyond Zephyr at red fabric strewn across his abdomen. It was then in their silence that Alexandria awoke as well, lifting her head to see Leon stood in awe. Before he could berate his father for blatantly disavowing his mother with some local woman, he saw the familiar silver mask lying on the floor. Zephyr made quick work to grab the boy and bring him further into the barrack.

"You're... the Princess?" He said in a gasp and immediately covered his eyes with one palm and one ear with the other.

"She won't hurt you, boy. Get your hands off your face!" Zephyr assured him, then inhaled deeply as the charades were over at last. "Leon, you must understand this well. Alexandria has...

banished… herself, and I have hidden her here to keep her safe. Do you understand that, boy?"

He nodded yet it was evident by his eyes that he was not listening.

"Are you going to make me croak like a frog? No… are you going to make me… "

"She will not make you do anything," Zephyr groaned. "As long as you do not speak a word of her escape to any person; not Tomas, Pitter, or any child you meet in the City. Say that is understood."

"Understood Papa. But… but why? Are you under a spell? Did you put my Papa under a spell lady?" The boy hysterically grabbed his father's forearm.

"I did not," she said softly and quietly. "Your father has simply offered me refuge. Now, you won't tell a soul, will you?"

Leon shook his head. Zephyr let himself fall backward into the straw. His plan was becoming riddled with knots and each step forward was onto a knife's edge. To heighten matters, Willa rushed into the barrack in search of the boy. Still riddled with disgust, she found the trio huddled at the furthest wall.

Alexandria was subject to burning questions from the boy, accompanied by Willa's kvetching disapproval. Once he settled, Leon finally broke the news of Eldric's leave, and Willa told what she'd heard.

"Cornure was overtaken by a goblin tribe, the Koba kind."

"He's of the militia, then?" The Princess asked. "I've not heard his name."

"He's a smith now but was once of the acting forces, yes. I'm sure he'll return in the coming days. It has just been a many seasons since he last left."

"And it is Eldric you say? Might he be a Blackmere?" Alexandria questioned her with an ascending curiosity. "I *do* recall an elder who once stood with the courtyard line. He was a Blackmere. He died of the… "

Willa nodded with her eyes pressed until they were slits.

"The Green Blight. That was his father, it was."

"My dearest, he was a drunkard. I suspect his son be of little stray?"

The princess spoke condescendingly, which surprised Zephyr to the point of readjusting himself upright. A smallish grin came of the Princess, one potently mischievous. He ushered Leon out of the barrack to avoid the argument.

"Get on, find Pitter and let her know. Make sure the other children know not to wait for him come supper," he directed his son who reluctantly ran off.

"Eldric is one of the warmest hearts of the Bard and he is the father of all the lost children who roam these villages. Now tell me, your holiness, *Alexandria*. Why *do* these children be without their parents? Could it be that they had all died on these assignments?"

"We care for our knights and guards and treat them as royal as the body they protect. The rewards are *substantial* for our men, only a small few turn their coin to pints."

Willa had enough of her contest, waving a dull nail at the Princess.

"You speak of falsehoods on matters you have little say in! Get on with it then, *Princess*. I doubt they've ever raised a knee and planted a foot to your order."

"Enough Willa!" Zephyr announced. His dissolving voice turned the world silent. The two women looked fiercely at one another. Before she could turn and storm out into the day, Alexandria's eyes began to illuminate in reddish iridescence.

"You may excuse yourself, miss Broadmere, *indefinitely* from the premises of this estate."

Silently and with wide eyes, Willa did not blink. She did not offer a rebuttal, nor did she exchange worse words. Then her eyes fell, and she slowly turned and exited the Barrack. Her use of Persuasion betrayed Zephyr's beliefs, that she was terrified of her own magic. Naively he thought she was innocent and would forever refuse to bewitch another person. Her anger was quickly built-up and perhaps cause for it, Zephyr thought. Though, he was haunted nonetheless, and whatever words he muttered in affirmation were faint and delicately placed.

"I… I haven't much more to go. Just some imperfections," Zephyr struggled to say as he sat back atop a stack. The Princess sat upright without a word, then flashed her glittering eyes and an unashamed smile. He went on to decorate her dress with its appropriate jewels. Struck with the recurring anxiety that he was no longer safe, the portrait emanated an inauthentic light that only he could see was a subdued madness.

The Kingdom's apothecaries, storefronts, and town-squares might have become occupied with King St. Auclaire's watchers, just as Alexandria spoke about. But Zephyr envisioned they might be preoccupied with the conflicts north of the Kingdom, where Eldric would meet the Koba tribe. A sort of distraction, he thought.

The painting was soon complete and the Princess joined Zephyr in examining it, finding that it perfectly demonstrated the very power in her stature, the essence of her true self. Her dainty hand held firm to his left shoulder, and each nail pressed hard into his skin, nearly with intent to puncture.

"A gift to the Kingdom, *your* Alexandria," he stated. Hoping her grasp would ease, he stood before the painting and lifted it to the light cast from walls' slits.

The completed portrait meant the final leap was near. There was little time left for Leon, and he needed to act diligently.

The very thought twisted something inside him. Her use of the gift… *that* gift… betrayed what he believed to be true of her. That she feared it. That she kept it buried like a bad root. That it only ever shimmered behind her tongue but never took breath. The portrait no longer seemed to sit on canvas, but to stand among them… alive. She was luminous. Commanding. Not merely

Alexandria, but her *Highness*, unveiled, unleashed. The power of her stature had been captured with such brutal honesty that Zephyr felt, for the first time, he had painted something *dangerous*.

The gold flared. The whites of her eyes gleamed like opals beneath smoke. Her mouth curled ever so slightly, just as her real one did now, as if the two had become one and the same. Evidently, one would bear the curse of another Kingdom soon.

22. A Gift of Remembrance For Thee

Leon joined his father at the entryway of the barrack, exhausted from his morning scurry to alert the children. Much of those who roamed the Bard and even those of the neighboring villages remained together in Yippire, and he told his father and Alexandria that Pitter would stay with them under the care of a spice merchant.

Zephyr brushed his son's wild hair with his palm and let the boy catch his breath. The boy blinked up at him, fingers sticky from blackberry preserves, a smudge of syrup reminiscent of mud, and Zephyr could not tell of the difference. Alexandria sat beside him, folded neatly with the tunic heavily pricked with straw and trousers cinched high on her waist. A new golden braid fell loosely over her shoulder.

She had removed her mask earlier, and though her gaze remained turned downward, she no longer flinched when Leon stared.

The portrait was removed from its poplar board and rolled into a scroll, well before Leon had returned.

"I won't be gone long," Zephyr said, crouching beside the boy. "Stay inside. Don't open the door for anyone. You're on guard; you're her *protector*."

Leon tilted his head. "Where are you going, Papa?"

"To gather a feast for Eldric's return."

His fingers brushed his son's shoulder… too briefly… and he stood. Alexandria met his eyes. No words passed between them, only a nod. A quiet pact.

Zephyr left through the narrow door and into the day. Away from the aperture of the barrack, he retrieved the painting from inside his shirt and withdrew an object from the sleeve it made. A bladeless hilt… a quill to soon sign his name.

The Princess and Leon shifted to the floor and the boy's eyes were fixed with a wide, unblinking stare. "You won't take control of me, will you?"

She chuckled and shook her head. "No, Leon. I have no desire to; you're a child. What good could you serve me?"

"I don't know. Maybe you'll make me…"

"No, Leon. I will not make you do anything. I've told you once before, even I am scared to speak without my mask," she softly lied to the boy, and Zephyr would never know it.

"I never get to sit with anyone but Papa or Miss Willa. Miss Willa says I talk too much."

"You do not," Alexandria replied. "You speak with *purpose*. That is something even kings forget."

He grinned and tucked his knees beneath him, eyes shining. "Can you tell me a story?"

She considered him for a moment, then adjusted her posture. "Yes. I'll tell you one most children are forbidden to hear. But you must listen closely, and not interrupt. I will tell you of the goblins, have you met one before?"

"Never, no! Papa says they live far yonder and are too dumb to mess with people."

"I can tell you more, if you might."

Leon nodded, his hands clutched into fists of excitement.

Alexandria withdrew a deep breath and she began to speak deliberately slow.

"There are tribes hidden beneath the hills.... beneath the very roots of the world. In caves and marshes. You may have never seen them, but they are always near to all villages."

Leon's gaze grew as she spoke, the world around him softening to a blur.

"Their skin is green as jade and rough like bark, their ears long, and their teeth sharp and crooked. Though there are a many tribes and communes, the ones occupying Cornlot are of the Koba tribe. While they aren't necessarily fierce as men, they can cause great harm to ordinary folk. They have lived in these lands for more millennia than you have toes," she continued. "Before even the earliest kings of Alexandria were born. Before castles. Before language. Back then, they did not wear rough garments or leather boots... they were *animals*. They built tunnels like ants, cities beneath the stone, dark and winding as spiderwebs."

"But they are mean?" Leon whispered.

"Rarely," she said. "Only when they feel the land has wronged them. Or when something sacred is taken. Then, they rise in compact groups. Much of what father has said is their fascination with meddling. Potions of poison, trickery. Their eyes burn like coal and their mouths carry chants older than written speech."

Leon gulped. "Can they read?"

Alexandria shook her head slowly. "No. Reading is a human gift. But they remember. Every word, every mark, every chant…. they pass it through voices and paintings made with bone and soot. The vibration of life is easily digestible to them, just as it is to me. Their scrolls are inked in blood and berry-wine, but we've only known of very few across thousands of seasons to ever recite what they collect."

Leon pressed his hands to his cheeks. "Willa said they poisoned the wells in Cornlot."

"They very well could have," she admitted. "They crush foreign flowers and steal venom from frogs, and cast small red bolts, akin to how them froggish Greenfolk go about it. They harvest fungus from beneath the dead and can brew a tincture that can slow your heart until you cannot even grasp a hilt."

"And Eldric will kill them?"

She softened her tone, brushing back a loose strand of hair. "I do not think so. To attack, I do not believe in those beasts.

He and his group will brandish their steel and the Koba will scurry back into the shadows of the canopies in which they spawn. They've always seemed to remind us of their presence whenever we grow too proud of ourselves. But your friend Eldric has gone with the knights. He's strong. Capable. And if he so chooses not to be, another will take his place."

Leon exhaled in relief. "I like Eldric. He's a father to the lost children, they truly need it."

Alexandria chuckled, though there was shadow of unease in her tone. "Then we'll hope he returns quickly, and that you'll see him again."

Leon turned thoughtful, fiddling with strands of straw.

"Do you think the goblins ever feel lonely? That they wish to live with people?" he asked suddenly.

She paused, caught off guard. "What makes you ask that?"

"They hide all the time. They live in the dark. I think I would be lonely."

Alexandria looked at the boy intensively. His hair tousled, cheeks flushed from the warmth of the day, eyes filled with a kind of innocence that even kingdoms could not extinguish.

"I think they do," she whispered. "But they know nothing else. Some creatures are born in shadow and learn to love it. Others are born into light… but must hide, all the same. They cannot live as we do."

Leon leaned into her arm without speaking. And in that quiet moment, Alexandria realized something she hadn't expected: she *wanted* to protect him. Not for Zephyr's sake, nor for the spell that clung to her soul to which she was unaware, but for the boy himself. For, without Ambrosia, she felt he was in need of a mother's warmth.

She knew not of the curse which plagued the boy and his father, neither did she understand that her affection for Zephyr was simply of the King of Death's deal. Her desire to care for the boy and experience life with his father was all too natural, yet odd in its electricity.

During their time together, Leon reared a nasty cough. Alexandria thought it was odd, the season was ripe with heat and the cold had left the Kingdom's mind. *How's he gotten sick,* she thought. But something strange began to stretch from his eyes. In his painfully content face, his veins began to show, and they were black.

Miscreancy? She thought. Blackened blood was common of the arcane poison. But he hadn't met the Koba, and she'd known of few cases of the magic ever being used even near the Kingdom.

He giggled once from another story, but it was interrupted by another cough…. dry at first, then harsher, deeper. It pulled from his chest like something buried, and when it ended, his small hand hovered near his mouth, uncertain. Although she was unaware, the hourglass's foot grew heavier than its head.

Alexandria stilled. Another cough followed. Then a third. She turned to him, brows knitting. "Leon?"

He blinked up at her, cheeks suddenly flushed, but not from warmth or joy. His eyes looked glassy now, rimmed faintly with red. The black veins of his face stretched further.

"The damp, I get sick often from it," he croaked, but the rasp in his throat betrayed the words.

"We're in a hay barrack, Leon. It is not damp here," she said with kind reason. She laid the back of her hand to his forehead. It was warm. Too warm. "This is no illness, child."

Frowning and slightly frantic, she disobeyed Zephyr's direction and left the barrack.

Alexandria went out and into the Broadmere's cottage unannounced, luckily doing so in the absence of Tomas and Willa. In the dust-blanket which layered the floor, she found and reached for a cloth. She drenched it in a basin near the buttery and returned to Leon, assuming not a soul saw her.

Against his forehead she dabbed it a few times, then against his neck. Her fingers hovered over his pulse. It beat fast, uneven.

"A sickness? In this heat?" She stood abruptly, gathering a dirty linen Zephyr had left against the floor, bringing it to drape around Leon's shoulders. "You need water," she murmured. "And rest."

Leon nodded, suddenly docile while Alexandria's mind stirred with quiet dread.

How has he gone Miscreant? she thought. *The winds are dry. The wells are clean. The cold has long left this kingdom's bones. This is a forbidden magic.* She thought the Koba or another tribe could have infiltrated her own walls. Though, she dismissed the idea as the goblins could never organize such a feat.

She glanced toward the window, where the light cut sharp lines through the dust in the air. The stillness outside suddenly felt unnatural. As though something had settled over the land that did not belong. Willa may be able to aid in bringing the boy to physician. She dismissed the thought in spite of the Broadmere woman.

"I… I will get your father, he cannot be far," she told him. "Stay as you are, I will return with him."

With little attention to her cadence, the Princess rushed out of the barrack and into the world. Onward down the road and towards the crowded Bard, all was so bright, and not nearly as alive as she thought while blinded. She saw people in the distance, and their garments were muddied and stained. They walked with dragging feet. Alexandria bit her bottom lip and her eyes fell beneath her brow, and she set on to find Zephyr.

The most threatening of folk were not the occasional guard which stood before the entryways of diplomatic halls and the republic buildings. They were the bakers and millers, carvers and even minstrels. He could not help but feel their cold gazes and heavy brows, as if each was assigned to find him, and only him.

The idea that his head might be removed or his body burned outside the monolithic gates of the castle was not one he wished to linger on. However, he felt it was increasingly more likely that King Jean would find the portrait insulting, even suspicious. But maybe Zephyr painted the Princess as an omen of her return to him, which he might find to be highly respectable and empathetic. His fate remained unchanged along either course, yet Leon's was not.

The greater portion of the day he spent navigating the residential regions, walking quickly but unsuspectingly through tight alleyways and busy streets. While most folk went on about their day, some crowded at lampposts conversing around a familiar posting. Zephyr could only don a concerned countenance if one of them met his eyes.

Near the amphitheater and sumptuous bakeries and markets, Zephyr climbed the thousand or so steps leading to the greater plaza at the perimeter of the castle's moat. He did not stop to rest or admire the farmland from above and how the squares receded to the forests.

In time, he met the final set of granite steps where a mob of ordinarily affluent City-folk at his right thrashed around a guard, pleading questions and doubt in their council.

What have you done with her? One man asked with his fist waving.

The King has killed his own kin!

The mask hasn't met their agenda. We rebuke the King!

Their energy was unmatched and tireless. But by their garments, none of the folk appeared to have traveled from the lower villages and territories as these residents were well adorned in jewelry and wore turnshoes.

Enough! One guard yelled over the chatter. *We are in search of her, and I advise you all do the same and stop wasting light waving nails!*

Zephyr stepped without offering too much attention to the crowds. He kept to his endeavor and approached a lone guard stood to the right of the gates. The castle-guard's metal chest-plate and armor were untouched, and entirely that of a mirror. His face was hidden behind a dense helmet in which his eyes were but black slits. His halberd was planted to the stone ground with its blade readied above his head. As Zephyr drew closer, the guard came to him.

"Have you come with information on the Princess?" He said sternly, almost as though it was not a question.

Zephyr stuttered as he spoke, "I… I've come with a gift, perhaps an omen for her return."

Zephyr retrieved the portrait from the belly of his tunic, to which the guard immediately seized it. The statue of a man did not directly inspect the item, but instead whistled towards another castle-guard from across the plaza. A far bigger knight, Zephyr thought him to be nearly eighteen-stone. His footsteps were heavy clomps against the earth below. This guard took the scroll and unraveled it halfway. In but a moment of uncertainty, his shielded fists rolled the painting again and nodded to the initial guard. In a hesitant move, he pulled a pulley to first lower the draw-bridge.

23. The Exchange

The crowds took notice and flocked to flood the gate. Once it settled and its mechanisms clunking gears locked and its chains quieted, the two guards pushed the gate inward. The larger guard took the painting and trudged onward towards the castle. Then, in the same cadence as he opened it, the first guard closed the gate and left the bridge at level.

While many folk demanded answers on the Princess's whereabouts, Zephyr remained silent as he was unsure exactly if his deed had been completed.

In the mess of loud merchants, nervous children, screeching women, Zephyr turned among them and began his slow departure. It was on the other side of the hordes where he broke into a conservative chuckle. He was unsure if he should cry, pray to Leon, or embrace what awaited him. His hand met the base of the hilt, which he withdrew from his waist. He anticipated the blade to materialize in a fit of black vapor.

But it… did not.

Zephyr shook his head and presented the unfinished sword before his face, nearly bringing all the blood in his body to his eyes.

It can't be, he thought, as though the ancient King Univerza, that of death, had made a fool of him. The Sword of Mortality remained as a skeleton and its blade remained a fable only seen atop the plateau of Univerza's ruin.

The loud creaks and metal-scraping of the gate emerged above the crowd's voices. The large castle-guard along with a trio of highly decorated and lesser-armored knights stood at his side. Zephyr broke from his hysterical fit when the large guard raised a heavy finger.

"That man, there!" He announced in a thunderous voice.

Zephyr did not put up a fight, and instead made their work easy as he walked towards the trio, meeting them among the crowd. They took him by each arm and escorted him towards the draw-bridge.

The initial guard closed the gate as they passed through, and Zephyr's head hung low in anticipation for the King or his council to berate him before an incredible punishment. But before they three knights and he could enter the impenetrable oak gate to the castle, the gates themselves opened to reveal the godly silhouette of King Jean St. Auclaire himself.

"State yourself," the tall yet elderly King spoke. Zephyr forced himself to look up.

"Zephyr Solta, of the Kingdom of Olderag."

The King's gaze was that of a thousand suns, and the weight of his black velvet gown and intricately embroidered doublet were evidence of his might. A silver fur rolled over at his neck, and his crown was that of mountain peaks dipped in molten gold and pressed with emeralds and opalescent Alexandrite.

"This painting of yours; castle-guard Lethar has informed me… that which you believe it to be an omen of my daughters imminent return. In dire times such as this, I will allow you to plead your case before the court in lieu of verdict. Come," the great man said slowly. He and his company of men who most will never hear of departed into the shadows of the castle, to which without a choice, Zephyr followed.

Through long, straight halls silent but for the many steps of knights and he, Zephyr watched as paintings in golden borders passed him by. The floor was of a slate with marbling, and the ceiling was far above where light could reach. Fires burned in their chalice-like decoration between each portrait, and Zephyr came to learn that each person was a previous king accompanied by his queen on the adjacent wall.

He could only glimpse into the few rooms they passed, but each was vastly different from one another. One had a great score of empty knight's armor while another was heavily blanketed in exotic pelts and with busts of beasts he'd never seen.

They brought him into an echo-ridden court in which sky-colored banners hung from the highest mosaic windows. A long inky-blue carpet ran straight between staggered benches on either side, and it led to the elevated throne of the King himself. The Queen was already sat next to the colossal throne in her own state seat. Her own crown sparkled in the little light of which cast from above. Stones of garnet and sapphire, entirely gold.

The knights left Zephyr at some distance from the throne while the many council members, wizards, state guards, and loyalists took to their own seats and stances. Their presence fell beneath dusted shadows where only the gold and silver adornments of their robes made themselves known. Unlike Olderag's chamber of determination, Jean St. Auclaire's boasted a vastness which could only be overlooked if one were to stumble across King Univerza's Great Hall in its' original stature. Though, Zephyr could feel a pool of blood at his feet, and he imagined himself keeled over within it, attempting to understand the thunderous words of a dull-witted king.

"State your business," a dark figure stated from the leftmost seats. At the forefront of the rows was a wilted-hat-wearing elder whose cloak and jewelry were that of a Grand Wizard, with stars embedded in the fabric. This man's attire was far more prodigal than Joab wore, and of a pale ocher color. His beard was no different, and similar in length and volume. He was smaller than Joab, and remained seated. Zephyr felt he was less of a threat, perhaps less likely to bring emerald fire from his palms.

"Bearing the weight of… Princess Alexandria's untimely leave," Zephyr began with a quiver to his voice, "I, Zephyr Solta, have brought it upon myself to create a portrait of her. I aim to incite a religious hope among the Alexandrian people."

The unfamiliar Grand Wizard flipped a heavy page of a codex which lay before him. His eyes hidden behind the circular lenses which sat atop the bridge of his long nose.

"Gatehouse Keeper, Lethar Odeman has analyzed the *gift* in which you've presented our castle-guards. Is it true, Mister Solta, that the portrait which depicts Alexandria St. Auclaire, also depicts her without her bridle?"

Zephyr felt the tension relieve from his posture, understanding the formality the Kingdom of Alexandria held, which Olderag governance lacked. He peered across the many rows on either side, and did so slowly.

"This is true," he spoke. As he did, disgruntled movement came from the shadows, and the official's disapproval was a potent stench. Zephyr felt his case slipping through his hands. The polished marble floor became blood-red once more.

"Do you believe you did so accurately, Mister Solta?"

"I believed her eyes were best represented as that of the sun in its birth, of a motherly warmth… and promise of a new day. Though there is no telling, and I possess no say different from what the Alexandrian people deserve to believe."

The Grand Wizard turned another page. Then his skinny neck extended over the book and his stinging voice cracked. Yet he did not give a verdict.

"Mister Solta, it is the council's cooperative understanding that the Kingdom accepts the portrait as the gift which you proclaim it is. The authenticity of its design, however, can only be confirmed by the maker, of whom is not you, Mister Solta. It is King St. Auclaire himself. I bid my analysis in lieu of your Majesty, King St. Auclaire."

The room shifted forward, and the great King of this pristine land sat with an unpropitious expression with a raised hand. The pool of blood Zephyr once imagined beneath him had dried up. With the King's rise, the council and all officials stood from their seats and faced him and the Queen, and lowered themselves with its descent. The Queen's wicked crown and heavy garments made sure she was of little threat. Then, the room grew quiet once more, and the King began to speak.

"You are a mysterious figure, Mister Solta. I heard of your arrival within our walls prior to the commencement of Morgenmete, and that *many* were concerned of a plague you were thought to have carried. Alas, I've yet to grace your burial, and no other has died. Might you speak of this?"

"It is true, I confess, that my late wife has since passed from an… illness. It took her very quickly, and our child was feared to have suffered from the same. Though I have not gone cold or green, and our child has lost his fever. We brought no plague, and if we were a threat to the populous, we would not have chosen to be so nomadic."

The King peered towards the Grand Wizard, and their eyes still seemed uncertain. The Great Hall became one he knew, and felt the tortured cast upon him.

"You are from a foreign land, one which harbors a potent need, of which our Kingdom satisfies. There is little you may have learned during your stay. Now tell me, why have I and Lady St. Auclaire bound our daughter behind the confines of her bridle?"

He did not expect an answer, it was evident in his tone. Zephyr knew not to tell of what he knew, and instead lied under oath. For his demise was certain no matter his words. Yet, he still chose to lace his voice in integrity.

"I've given little thought to the matter. But rumors tell me of a power she possesses. Many are fearful of that power."

"Fearful?" The King questioned, almost surprised.

"Whispers of it, but from a great many. As I understood, she is kept as a rabid dog; once a bright familial body, and ever a violent demon constrained to a cage."

The King did not respond as his words fell without air. His weight of his frown was both heavy and visceral. But Zephyr did not wish to annoy him or the council, and although he did not fear being dismembered or burnt in a pit, he remained noble and with dignity he stated his claim. To his own amazement, the King did not refute.

"And for her own good, and the good of our people," he began and faced his officials. "For if untamed and freely wild, there would be no governance. No *willing* governance. I should pronounce to you that your portrait is strikingly familiar, and grossly true. Have you any idea of how *true* it is?"

"I do not, your Majesty. But I feel as though a greater fate was bestowed upon me once I first made my markings of it. Whether it be of the Gods or intuition, nevertheless I see only hope in its presentation."

The castle fell dead, and all of its constituents were uncertain of Zephyr. His words, though true, were questioned by some, but mildly so. The King, however, was impressed by the cursed man.

The King did not rise from his throne at first. Instead, he stared at the great marble slab before him, hands folded over his lap, thick fingers twitching slightly with thought. His crown caught a stripe of light through the stained mosaics overhead, casting rust-colored streaks across his cheekbones. When he did speak again, it was low and jagged, like the creaking of an ancient gate.

"Join me on a walk, Mister Solta."

The knighted guards thrust from their cold places, but the King was quick to raise his hand.

"*Unattended.*"

The guards planted their feet once more. The Queen remained as well, and her head did not even turn. One may have thought she was a mere skeleton sat there. The council remained bowed as Zephyr stepped forward across the polished stone, heart steady only by force of will. Even with the King's word, an assigned servant woman scurried in their trail.

Through a shallow arched passage, a great corridor had been carved on the other side, once hidden by tapestry, now drawn back to reveal a densely decorated hall and a sparse scattering of sconces.

The King moved slowly, as if gravity clung heavier to his limbs than to other men, and Zephyr followed, wary of each echoing step. A hundred spaces to the end of it, they turned rightward.

Through another arched passage, they entered a long chamber.... one unfinished. The servant woman remained behind in the hall. The scent of fresh plaster and dust of stone was sharp to Zephyr's nose. The walls had not yet been painted fully, though elegant designs had been etched into the bones of each wall, waiting for a coat. The furthest wall which was free of clutter was the largest and was of a ruby-blood color. Massive windows without glass opened onto the blinding daylight, and scaffolding clung to the walls like spider legs.

At the heart of the room stood a raised dais. Atop it, no throne. No altar. Just a wide, empty table of redwood, gleaming with lacquer.

"Here," the King said, pausing at its edge, "will be my war table. And beneath it.... just beneath.... there shall be a vault carved deep into the bedrock, sealed in iron. A chamber of divine record. A library of blood."

Zephyr glanced toward him, then scanned the dusty place. He did find a book seemingly out of place sat on the table, and there were no others nor a shelf to harbor it. When he saw its cover with a glance, it was grossly familiar. *"The quire…"* he whispered to himself.

"What is it?" Asked the King. Zephyr had to think quickly, for any indication that his intentions were rooted in ancient folklore and blood could spell an early end to his mission.

"A war room? Have you encountered a stalemate in the advancement of your Kingdom?"

"A crimson nave," he spoke. "A sanctuary of sovereignty. It is here, our future will be written before it occurs. A marvelous idea my Queen has drafted and ordered."

The King moved a hand over the redwood, almost gently. "We are beset by wild tribes, as you know. And zealots. And liars. Disease. My daughter, who I love beyond reason, grew quickly, and her power was unrelenting. She may not have known it," he added with the faintest tilt of his brow, "but the arcane of her blood was formidable, and that which she saw and spoke was written before she was even birthed."

"What is it you mean, your Majesty? Do you truly believe she is so threatening?"

The King turned to him fully now, the full might of his shadow cast across Zephyr's feet. It was evident that the answer existed in the stillness of the air, and the King would not reiterate it.

"This portrait of yours, I find it courteous, and I do accept it as a gift. The Queen and I will fix it above the mantle here." The King's gaze directed to the structure between two towering mosaic windows. "She and her eyes will bless each rite made here, and every future we dismiss will be beneath her. I believe it to be customary for the artist to witness where his art will remain."

The King presented the linen as a scroll from beneath his arm. Zephyr accepted it, and unraveled it to see her once again. He turned and held it before himself, right between the gleaming daylight, and imagined it bolstered above where a hearth would eventually be lit. The King was unsure of Zephyr's uneasy expression, believing that it may not be what Zephyr had hoped for. He was quick to interrupt Zephyr's imagination.

"I will ensure that Treasurer Collette will have payment delivered."

Zephyr could not remove his eyes from Alexandria's portrait, nor the motes of dust which hung in the light beams beside it. He nodded to the King, giving a glimpse of acceptance, to which the crowned great smiled.

"I relieve you of my grasp, and you shall remain here as you wish. As you depart, Miss Toule will escort you beyond these walls," his voice left in a whisper, one with a distant annoyance that the servant ensured her presence.

The painting would become emblem for global conquest, as if for her to grant approval while remaining silent and deaf to the talks. Likewise, if Zephyr understood that to leave her portrait in the possession of the Kingdom meant she would undoubtedly return and remain masked indefinitely. Perhaps she would never sport the same crown as her mother or the distant First Alexandria. The implications were monumental, as a great population may never know of the Princess for who she truly is, the motherly spirit she emanated.

He took the book from the table, which the King had ignored. It *was The Collector's Quire*, a second copy of that of which he took from Sticks' yard. The King may not even know he'd taken it, and this time he *would* read it. But not here. There was little time and space to mess about, and Zephyr's focus turned back to the painting. Though, to reclaim the portrait and withdraw it as a gift would prevent Univerza's deal from dissolving Leon's curse.

He could not envision either on their own, and instead he saw her with the boy curled as he would with his mother as she read a storybook beside a low flame. There was no blood-pool, and no screaming. No obsidian. Only a flickering amber.

A jagged and bladeless hilt remained at his waist, heating up and prepared to sign.

24. The Mortal Quill

Alexandria St. Auclaire, who of which was the subject of a strenuous search, hid in alleyways and in the cover of sculptured shrubbery. She knew better than to get caught, to be noticed by hysterical city-folk and dragged by state watchers or knights. Though she had never seen the newer regions herself, each cobbled road still led inward toward the great staircase.

Each town she passed through seemed surprisingly unaware of her escape, with wizards in the midst of crowds showing off contained instances of regulated magic. Music threaded through the tame chatter as well, with strings plucked beneath birdsong.

The only recognizable feature of Alexandria was that of her hair, but it too was well-tangled and no longer braided from the night of her escape. Though, its scuffled curls and bright blondness were far cleaner than the Bard folk or those of Kapt and the Ringards. She sported Tomas' tunic and nettled trousers. Though, he was still unaware of her ever hiding away in their barrack. Her borrowed garments and muddied feet made her look even rougher than the crowds, yet she still knew she was out of place.

Across storefronts, she managed to go unseen, and those who *did* notice her, did not recognize her. She remained kept to quiet corners when she could.

She quietly scurried down between two brick flats, and at the end she peered to the right. There she witnessed a bustling market of alchemists and tradesmen of Taria selling their herbs and medicinal goods. It was there she witnessed the first guard. He was a watcher, sporting a pale gray cloak and ashen stockings and wielded a long wooden staff. His eyes hid beneath the shadow of his hood, though his head scanned slowly across the plaza. She decided to go leftward away from him. However before she could leave the alleyway, a small voice rang from behind her.

"Are ye a mugger?" A thin girl asked. The lavender fabric of her dress was clenched in her small fists. "Are ye looking to mug someone?"

Awestruck that she was found, she knew the child did not recognize her right away.

"I am not, dearest child," said she, and crouched to meet the girl's gaze.

"You are quite pretty, Miss. Why are you stood here all strange?"

"I am searching for someone."

"Who?"

Alexandria grew a smile, and told the girl that she was in search of the Princess, though of course she spoke of herself.

"You should look for her too, and pray she returns to the castle unharmed."

The sweetness of their exchange warmed her heart, but the child's bright eyes settled and stared into nothing, and her own smile fell. Suddenly, the girl collapsed to her knees and her palms pressed together. She began to mutter a prayer under her voice in rapid succession.

Alexandria realized what she had done, and she was all too panicked to correct the little girl. Her Persuasion knew no boundaries. Even if she tried to undo it, the command would hold… the child would pray without end, unless another witch intervened. One would find her later, and only a witch might be able to dissolve the spell.

Frantic, Alexandria ran from the alleyway westward until she met another storefront. However in her leap into the daylight, the voice of a burly man called after her. He'd seen her run suspiciously from the alley.

Miss! Slow down, Miss!

Another shout.

Halt, woman!

She could get a glance of the two watchers barreling from across the plaza. Few of the village folk took notice, as many would be chased by the officials on any given day.

Her lungs burned as she jolted through the back-ends of the marketplace, her bare feet slipping over wet stone and decaying plaster.

The sounds of the market grew fainter behind her, strings, chatter, the low thump of footsteps over brick until only the pounding of her own blood filled her ears. She found herself in horror of what she'd done; she did not dare look back. Her mind clung to the image of the girl kneeling in the dirt, palms pressed together, lips quivering with endless prayer.

I didn't mean it, Alexandria thought, wild with guilt. *I never meant to.* Her own palm struck her temple as her eyelids were tightly shut. *I knew I would, I knew I would!* But meaning had no purchase against Persuasion. Yet her voice would always order.

She finally peered into another road where a less populated storefront loomed, a crooked apothecary wedged between a weaver's shop and a smithy. Its sign swung low, a rusted plaque bearing a green sigil: a coiled root. The door hung ajar, the smell of crushed herbs and acrid smoke curling out into the street. A low breeze carried leaves, dust, and her own poster, disappearing down the way. The store at her left was vacant and unmanned. Alexandria ducked inside.

The interior was dim and narrow, cluttered with shelves heavy with clouded jars. Dried mosses dangled from the rafters. The air was thick, almost syrupy, and for a moment she had to lean against the door frame to steady herself. She fell to her bottom as a much greater group of watchers and guards ran across the road.

On to the Guardant walls, we'll get on eastward. She mustn't have gone far!

A noise came from the deep within the building, and an elderly woman yielding but a wooden rod showed herself.

"Are ye lost? You cretinous bunch have stolen all I have; there is nothing left for you." the woman rasped in a preexisting defeat. "Why can't ye leave me alone?"

Alexandria's tongue caught in her mouth. Her heart still hammered violently.

"I… I have not come to cause you harm, and I am no baron. I apologize, I believed this place to be abandoned. I seek refuge," she said, low, her voice trembling at the edges. She dared not say more…. dared not *accidentally* command.

The old woman watched her a moment longer, then jerked her chin toward a narrow hallway behind the counter. She must have seen the terror in Alexandria's face. "Back room. Keep your fingers tame."

Alexandria bobbed her head in thanks and slipped through the cramped passage. She found herself in a small room, empty but for a cracked wooden chair and a thin window peering out into overgrown back-gardens, where bentberry vine and shadewort grew wild. A place forgotten by the world.

She collapsed into a lopsided wooden seat. For the first time since Zephyr had left that day, she let her hands shake.

What have I done? she thought. *What if they find the little one before they find me? Will they see her muttering prayers to the stones and think her cursed? Think her... witch-born? Or will they suspect... me?*

She pressed the heels of her hands to her eyes. She could almost hear Willa's voice scolding her, Tomas' quiet judgment. Even Zephyr, who had trusted her with Leon, would look at her differently if he knew how easily a slip of her tongue could shatter a life.

A new fear slithered into her chest... *If I cannot even speak without consequence, how can I ever go back? How could I ever be queen, or wife, or even mother?*

The door creaked and Alexandria stiffened, hands darting instinctively to cover her eyes. Though it was only the ancient woman, her hands remained.

She shuffled into the room, setting down a cup of something steaming and sharp-smelling onto the floor beside Alexandria's chair. Her milky gaze flickered over her once more.

"You've escaped a man, haven't ye?" the woman said, not unkindly. "I can see it thick as honey on your skin."

Alexandria said nothing, but offered a reluctant shake of the head.

The old woman gave a grunt and straightened. "Don't matter to me. Seen worse things in prettier girls. Stay a while. Leave before dusk."

"I can't," she finally spoke. "They'll find me if I am too confident."

"And who, young lady? Have you killed a person? You seem far too dainty." Her wrinkled face tilted, then exploded with an idea. "Ye have put Miscreancy on another! How novel, a doll as yourself riddled with the rotting arcane. *Ooh,* you're something!"

"*Persuasion,*" Alexandria scoffed. "And you're no less vulnerable."

"Persuasion? Just as the Princess…" the elder woman paused and her eyes widened. She scanned over Alexandria with speed and took a step backward. She seemed to sense no danger, yet her lungs had gone hollow.

"You mustn't worry; I need to keep going. If you speak a word of this, I cannot guarantee your next actions will be yours."

Alexandria went through the clutter towards the storefront, peering down the street through the dusty windows.

"My goodness, *I am harboring the blind royal herself!*" The elder whispered, nearly excited. She followed behind Alexandria.

"Look at that end, would you? I cannot let the watchers see me, if they do.…" but she abruptly went quiet. She looked over at the old woman, her body fixed facing east down the road. Alexandria's head tilted as she approached the woman. "Do you… do you see anyone?"

The woman did not speak, nor did she turn to face the Princess. She was frozen in her place, as if her feet melted to the floor. Alexandria's eyes fell as her heart shuddered. The poor elder had lost much of her business to thieves and robbers, and now too the remainder of her life.

"Face me," Alexandria instructed quietly under her breath. The woman did, her eyes staring blankly at her. "You will roam the City until you find a watcher, and you will request assistance from the *first* witch you find. They will help you."

Though expressionless, the elder's right eye turned glassy, and a tear began to grow from its corner. She shuffled out into the day while the Princess cautiously ran out and straight into another alleyway.

The elder did not have to travel as far as Alexandria had hoped, and found a watcher posted at the far end of the road in front of an apothecary merchant. And although he believed the woman to be ill or deranged, he peered beyond her and saw Alexandria bolting from one store to another.

It wasn't long after that a horde of armored men were rushing after her again, taking to various nooks. In her sprint, she thought she'd gotten away. Alexandria caught her breath behind a sprawling brick wall with little room at either side to navigate. But as she finally felt safe, one watcher, a castle-guard, found her at her left.

"Missy, you're a bit more troubled than the King pronounced! He'll knight me once I've passed you on…"

Before she could turn to her right, a second guard fell into the scene. Both had bright, ecstatic eyes and drooling mouths.

They crept towards her, space turning thin. In her spree of unraveling rules, she thought to speak.

"You!" A skinny finger pointed, "go on and tell the others you saw me by the Guardant Walls, and you'll check there indefinitely."

The guard at her right quickly ran off down the alleyway. The first at her left had turned pale, cold. Before he could think to run off, she caught his gaze.

"And you… you will not speak of this. You will remain here, unable to speak. And if any state watcher pushes you to answer, you will fight them. Bloodily. Until either you or they can no longer see, or your teeth meet the leather of your boots."

Her command darkened his gaze, and he did remain there as she ran off. She did not look back, and he did not move, not even twitch. She'd turn onto a deserted street, where she soon heard the clash of fists and metal as the watchers fell upon the guard she had cursed.

She thought once that she was becoming a plague to her own Kingdom, and that even a Heightened State Witch would be at wit's end trying to undo the spells placed upon these folk. That the concoctions needed would soon be no match to her wrath. And… it was her wrath which brought her muddied and bloodied feet to bend and spring as she searched for Zephyr; she sought only to save Leon from his fever.

Alexandria made her way to the towering staircase which led towards the castle. Although there were many city-folk traversing the area, she paid little mind to them. She took a deep breath and began her climb to the clouds.

Why is she running?

Is that a robber? Someone, stop that woman!

I see her! Get her!

The numerous calls were not unique, fading far into the wind and crowds. She kept forth unknowing to the gathering stampede at her back.

She neared the plateau above before her feet had given way to their wounds, her bloody footprints leading to where she collapsed. The bunch of officials, state watchers, guards, knights, and ordinary folk all gathered below her.

The King has been worried sick; you need to come with us.

Leave her!

Don't look in her eyes, she'll curse you!

Get on with it, I'll get her by the arms.

I'll grab her legs!

The voices built to a thunderous chaos. Few officials turned to fight one another, all anticipating *they* would be the ones to earn the King's blessing, and get their reward.

But Alexandria, depleted of spirit and with her fists clenched after making a mess of her people, faced them. She looked at the furious, joyful, and fearful many, and without the heart to fall limp to the thousand grasps, she began her order.

"Each of you will stop as you are, and lower your fists. You will not look at one another as a foe, and you will not curse your neighbor. You will fall silent until our next dawn. You… do not… see me. You will make your descent to the lower villages and Bard, and you will tend to your ordinary duties without memory of this evening. You will do so now."

And in the quiet breeze where leaves crumbled in the corners of the steps, the many people slowly turned away from her. They went on down to the lower levels of the Kingdom silently and without ever turning back.

They grew gray in the mist of the cloud they had reached, and in time she could no longer see them. In their absence, Alexandria wept into her palms. She could not lead, nor could she govern. Her voice could only order, and make puppets out of militants, elders, and children. Her fear spilled from her lips, and what she'd done could not be reverted. Like a tree fallen in death, its rings forever ended.

25. *A Twisted Fork*

Sabbath found herself deep within the woodland north of the Forest of Centurion, where she finally felt safe enough to collect herself. The wretched coven *killed* George, and she could barely hold herself together once her breath caught. She saw death in many forms prior, but never as gruesome or horrifying. She could have found comfort in talking aloud, to hear from *herself* that things would be okay. But her hands shook relentlessly and she curled against a monolithic stone. Her cries eventually quieted and harmonized to a lullaby, and in the dampness of the grove, she slept.

It was only morning when she could look across the sunlit earth and stare at the frost without tears forming. It was this hour that she found George's mare grazing in a vast clearing. She was golden in her place, and when Sabbath approached her, she embraced her softly around her neck.

"I'm so sorry… I'm so… so sorry. Come now."

She guided the horse into the woods to figure out what to do next. Without her dagger she was far more vulnerable, and the thought of running into the Koba or coven made her stomp in a fit.

"Damn it all… " Sabbath muttered to herself. *"Damn it all!"*

Before long she decided to continue northward despite being far from their original path. Only George knew these lands, albeit from long ago. She could only keep on rightward of where the sun headed. George's mare even knelt before her so that she could saddle-up with ease.

She halted their progress, pulling the reigns abruptly. They had only made it deeper into the forest aimlessly until Sabbath met a fork in the road. But there was no road, nor a path that confused her. It was what she *felt* which troubled her. Less George's death, it was what she saw in the Forest of Centurion that made her eyes fall to her hands. *A future,* one of royalty and power. A future with a *voice.* Though, it may not be and the illusion she saw could be just that: an illusion. Perhaps in another life she became some sort of dark queen. She thought of who she saw there. A taller woman who's hair was scorched to charcoal, with her face obscured by a viciously ornate and spiked mask. Her mind began to fill slowly with suspicions. She only knew of one figure who sported a similar bridal.

"Alexandria!" She said aloud, finally. Sabbath began to speak to the horse as if it would respond. *"That must be who she was! Maybe we'll cross paths, maybe she'll see me and… maybe she'll hear me. You… "* she looked down at the mane of her. *"You need a name. Miss…Dorothy. How's that sound?"*

But the horse knocked her head back and refused to carry on.

"What is it?" Sabbath asked her, and Dorothy remained frozen. "You don't like it?" Sabbath tried to understand her, and ran her palm through her bronze fur. It was then that her jagged nail caught against something. She felt around and thought it could be an old scar. But the line had shape, and when she looked, she saw the letter 'A' branded against her right shoulder. "What's it stand for?" But no answer. "Then *A* you shall be."

Though she never heard George call her by any sort of name, *A* seemed happy, for she finally lifted her hooves and began through the woods.

The woods parted just enough to let in the morning sun, spears of gold piercing the mist like fingers of fate. Sabbath sat astride A, her fingers wrapped loosely in the reins, the weight of her thoughts heavier than any saddlebag.

The silence gnawed at her. Even the wind through the trees seemed to whisper of what she had seen… of the woman in the sap, regal and wreathed in shadow, and standing beside the mask-burdened Princess Alexandria. The image had seared itself into her mind, vivid as the moment George died. A future unclaimed. A throne in ruin. And her, Sabbath, at the heart of it.

Her fingers twitched, remembering the feel of the magical bindings, the cold gaze of the coven. They had wanted to use her. They saw something in her. And now… perhaps she did too. "I could bring him back," she whispered. "Him, and Jeffrey. If I had the power…"

A low wind answered, brushing past her ears like a voice not quite formed. Not speech… no… but presence. A knowing. She rubbed her arms, as if her skin had grown suddenly too thin.

She shook her head. "Just keep riding," she told A. "Keep moving. We'll make it to Taria. We'll tell the Council. They'll listen. They have to."
But even as she said it, doubt crept in like a vine around her throat.

They followed a ridge where the trees thinned to old, moss-cloaked stumps, their bark peeling like skin. A clearing opened ahead, and there in the midst of it stood a lone figure, a skeleton, hunched and wandering, its bones held together by some unseen tether of old magic. A taggard. Its eye sockets were empty, but it turned its skull as she approached, as if it could feel the warmth of her living breath.

They instinctively slowed to a halt. Sabbath dismounted carefully, her boots sinking into the wet moss. The taggard stepped back, almost shyly, its bony hands raised in gentle defense.

"It's okay," Sabbath said softly, stepping closer. "I'm not going to hurt you." She crouched before it, her voice warm, maternal almost. "You've probably been here a long time, haven't you?"

The skeleton made no noise, but its head tilted slightly. "You didn't ask to be left behind. You didn't ask to become… this. People pass by and mock you, I'll bet. Throw stones. I won't. You deserve more than that." Sabbath reached into her pouch and took out a tiny strip of cloth from her old rucksack. It was nothing, a rag from George's pack, used to tie herbs. She gently wrapped it around the skeleton's finger. "There. A little dignity," she whispered. "Even if no one else sees you."

The taggard bowed its head. Sabbath smiled… tired, small… but real. Then she stood and climbed back onto A's back. The forest felt quieter now. Or perhaps… it listened.

As they left the clearing, Sabbath dared to glance back once. The skeleton remained where it stood, but it had turned to watch her go, its head raised like a sentry.

For the first time since George's death, Sabbath felt something bloom within her. Resolve.

Not vengeance. Not yet. But the shape of a voice, perhaps the one she'd seen in the sap. A voice that might command fate rather than be broken by it.

"Alexandria," she said under her breath, "You better be ready." And onward they rode.

26. A Mess of Many

In time and with her body weak, Alexandria met the plateau outside of the castle. She carelessly redirected a regular fruit-merchant who only suggested she looked familiar. He and three children would tirelessly throw redberries and pink beaufruit at one another until the cart ran dry or the tendons of their arms snapped.

A knight was ordered to remove his helmet and bash it with his sword until the sword's edge bent dull. A doctor who had aided an elderly man in a walk was sent to descend the thousands of steps. Her ruin had only begun, and her inability to reason in the face of question was pronounced.

Alexandria met the monolithic gate of the castle, which was in the process of opening once the bridge had locked into place. However, she did not order the lonely castle-guard at its dial to do so. Once the sections turned inward, it was Zephyr himself who walked slowly across. He was aided by Miss Toule who saw his leave.

"Princess?" The guard approached her once he'd caught a glimpse of her frayed hair and torn garments. She went towards him with her arms before her as if to embrace the man, but instead ordered him to sleep.

Miss Toule galloped past Zephyr and got the Princess's arms in her grip.

"Alexandria, what has come of you? What has happened? We need a physician, oh my lord!"

But the Princess removed herself from the smallish girl, leaving her dumbfounded. Alexandria went to Zephyr, who was baffled by her presence.

"What are you doing? Why've you come here? I was just heading back to you. The King accepted your portrait," he muttered. Zephyr inspected her, finding that she was in dire shape.

"It's Leon, he's fallen ill! It's Miscreancy, I could see it in his face, Zephyr." She grabbed his arm and turned. "We need to get a sorcerer at his side now!"

But Zephyr stopped in his tracks as he witnessed the scale of disorder which befell the plaza. There were fights, knights thrashing their own skulls, children sat in their place as fruit and broken sections of carts flew overhead.

"What's happened, Alexandria? Did you… did you do this?"

Her frown grew and her eyes glossed over with tears. Her body fell limp while her hands met her temples.

"They wouldn't stop," she cried. "They wouldn't stop, I had to make them stop. *I didn't mean to, I didn't.*"

He stood in a daze at what lay before him: the Kingdom had fallen into a strewn-apart spool of turmoil. There were unbound guards shoving ordinary folk to the dirt, legumes and stones being pelted into walls. He only thought to embrace her tightly, discerning the disorder from what she'd caused, bones collapsing atop bones.

He parted her head from his shoulder, finding the dried dirt of her cheeks ran in streams to her chin. Alexandria wept as he ran his fingers through her knotted hair, untangling it. Between their embrace remained the hilt, and against the skin of his waist he felt it begin to burn. He let the Princess regain her posture and wipe her eyes while he withdrew the hilt, to which her quivering brow grew heavy. The King of Death, Univerza, was awaiting his *signature*.

"What is this?" She asked, her voice muffled beneath a mess of preoccupied screaming and chants. Zephyr was reluctant to elaborate, and yet still whispered.

"A quill, to mark a deal once made, complete."

He presented the hilt before him, and in its radiant heat, a burst of red fire and black smoke unsheathed the missing blade. The sound it made was that of a roaring bear, to which many guards and knights turned toward in fear. Alexandria fell a step backwards as her eyes widened.

"The *Mortal Sword?*" She sputtered. Even after frail clouds parted, the blade's light cast an orb against the ground. "What… what have you done? You… found him?"

But Zephyr was wildly timorous himself, as if the leather-bound grip itself was red-hot. Beyond its steaming steel, he saw her with her head tilted, a look of realization washed over her.

"Is… that why we are here… together? You found the Dead King and you've made a deal with him? You've… you've used me?"

Just then as he refused to answer her, the Kingdom's people and officials began to approach. When he turned to face the crowd in fear they may overwhelm him, many flinched at the blade's embers.

Levereter!

He's born of Hell, set him aflame!

Jail him, guards!

The many voices were but chatters of treetops to him, as they were of no use. The sword itself would soon impale his stomach, leaving them with their hate, and the Princess alone to fight the herd. One knight approached swiftly with two others at his back. Though, Zephyr waved the sword and the trio retreated some paces back.

"I had to save my boy, Alexandria. I cannot allow him to fade into the night as Ambrosia had. *This* was the only way."

"There are!" She cried, "no spell is without a key, you have to believe me! *We can find the key.*"

Whilst he was distracted by her cry, a knight took a heavy step forward, leading Zephyr to point the flaming blade at him. Many in the plaza heaved and murmurs flooded the air.

He'll kill the Princess!

He's the baron!

Grab him!

"I've nothing but a story unwritten, and its author my boy. For he's under a different blade which I've burdened him with. He… he's yet to find all his days, both rotten and new," Zephyr turned to Alexandria, his own palms shaking. "A masterpiece you are, undoubtedly so. For only the color of your eyes could have saved me from the blackness of hell I've drawn. Alexandria, this blade will mark my name in the earth beneath us, but in my blood will be the unraveling of confinement for him, to extend his stay. I hope it unravels yours."

Atop the clouds and folk and guards and light, and beneath the castle's pillars and arrow slits, Zephyr turned the sword over and pierced his eyes in wait for darkness. All the guards who'd exited the castle flooded the drawbridge, and all watched. But… it did not come, and the world did not quiet. Before his arms could thrust downward, a knight had run up the steps and grabbed one of his wrists. The plaza erupted in screams while some cheered. Zephyr was knocked to the ground and the Mortal Sword spun in a fiery display.

"*The sword!*" He cried, while guards began to close in and assist the first.

His fists and feet were pinned beneath heavy shins. Alexandria thought quick, knowing that he would likely be punished to death by her father. She would be tortured as well, she knew it. An official servant of the King made his way across the bridge with a cloth sack in hand. She feared for her lover and herself, knowing that a future together was all she would settle for. She barely hesitated in her reach for the sword, and as she brought it before her eyes, the wrestling atop of Zephyr came to a halt.

"Off of him!" She declared, "get on across the bridge!"

One would never know if their scramble to an orderly march away from the beaten man was out of fear of the sword, or the persuasive essence of her eyes. To them, death was death, and although the archaic blade would only make promises to Zephyr, most shuddered and recoiled at the sight of it, thinking it could do worse than kill. But as the ordinary folk remained still in their wreckage and the knights and guards looked blankly from the bridge, she saw her father, King Jean, stood corpulent beneath the shadow of his castle. His glare was that of a crow's wings, and his wizard council were his arms. It was evident to Alexandria, among the mess of the plaza and the sheer displeasure in her father's eyes, that she must *truly* escape. She faced Zephyr and pulled him upright, and as she traded him the sword for his life, the blade reignited.

"Come now, we must tend to Leon." Alexandria thrashed forward but Zephyr remained. "What are you doing? He hasn't much time!"

"I know he hasn't, and it is my doing. But… there is no means of preserving his life without the tip of this blade meeting my skin."

Alexandria went to him once more, and saw that he did not understand, for the curse which burdened him was *not* one invetia, but miscreant, verboten and of an unknown source.

"The black of his blood, he is not bound by a thousand scriptures. He was infected, and I suspect Ambrosia too. His fate is not doctored by Olderag; we need to get to him."

"But that can't be, Alexandria. I'm a cursed man, a curse of a *Grand Wizard*. There is no saving unless I conclude my deal."

There was little space between them, but even as the Princess placed her hands at his jaw, he did not stray from his cause. Before she could insist on their flight once more, the ping of an arrow struck the stone floor at their feet. Tens of more arrows came, all intended for him yet carelessly close to her. King Jean St. Auclaire's orders were evident, that Zephyr was a traitor and had kidnapped her. Though, he understood she had weaponized her magic as he always feared, and kept his knights at bay hidden from her sight.

"You need to trust me, you do not need this deal," she pleaded, but he did not need the persuasion.

The two ran off down through the terrified crowd and down the thousands of steps. In their wake, guards and militants would slowly raid the streets at a safe distance, and archers plucked at their strings and fired down through the mist of the clouds. King Jean stomped his foot as his men did not call any contact.

"She must return safely, Jean. We must ensure her life," the Queen approached him at his side. But his anger grew rapidly.

"Call a retreat of the archers. I want watchers at every corner of the City. Have Lethar and my council tend to the Red Room. Send a mercenary to Cornlot to order a retreat. Alexandria will *not* depart these lands. Alert the Guardant Keepers, and bolster the southern ends. Fleschire,"

The old Grand Wizard from the Great Hall answered him with a shake to his voice.

"Yes, your Majesty?"

"Send for the Yippire Coven," the King snarled. "We've many knots to undo."

"Of course, your Majesty," the wizard said and scurried into the shadows of the castle.

The Kingdom of New Alexandria had never looked so manic. The cobbled veins of the City, once golden in evening light and filled with the song of bells and markets, now twisted in disarray beneath the weight of shouting men and spell-drunk wanderers. Through its alleys and towering stone streets, two figures pressed onward, one in torn linens that reeked of salt and straw, the other limping upon two bloodied feet, heat and embers blazing from the Mortal Sword.

The City, the great belly of New Alexandria, was becoming infected as unknowing officials shouted at the Princess and Zephyr along their escape. The people had not fallen to plague or famine in times prior, but now to enchantment. The chaos had bloomed from whispers alone, like mold at the feet of a cathedral. Somewhere between Zephyr's awaiting sacrifice and the Princess's Persuasion, a crack had torn through the latticework of balance. Now, knights turned their spears in confusion, priests muttered contradictions into smoke, and children ran unsupervised, tossing stones at merchant doors. Many of which were not enchanted at all, and simply fell to the hysteria.

From the far end of the market alleys, a fire had broken out as a cook knocked a wooden rack into an open flame while he watched the two sprint by. This fire met at the wooden beams of the Billmon Nitana's Grocer, and several young, new alchemists at surrounding stores had abandoned their stalls entirely.... glass vials shattered in rivulets of blue smoke, oils running like blood across the stone.

Alexandria, dirt smearing the hem of Tomas' trousers, had outpaced Zephyr during their descent down the thousands of steps. But with her bare feet, she eventually slowed. Her hands scratched from sneaking through alleyways, bones aching from shouldering past panicked townspeople. She moved not like royalty but like prey, hounded by the very kingdom meant to adore her, and how she poisoned it.

Zephyr followed, barely steady on his limbs after the knight's blow. The failed fulfillment of his pact had left something gnawing in him.... some unseen debt in his bones. His breath was ragged, and yet he pushed forward, for each moment counted against his son's failing breath.

They passed the brick and stone outpost of Alchame Astra, where students, once poised in parchment and sorcery, were practicing in a courtyard as they hurled fire sigils and wind pulses in uncontrolled bursts. One boy had begun levitating a lone brick above the building's pillars, circling madly with chalk eyes and dripping palms. Their freshly inexperienced tricks collapsed when the pair hurdled through, leaving the students wildly dazed. Beneath a vine-strewn canopy at the school's entrance, professors scribbled runes over their chests like blessings, struggling to contain the aftershocks of all the broken magic.

27. The Thousand Steps

The gates to the Guardant Walls loomed like open jaws to the east. The fort was unmanned…. its soldiers redirected to the City's center, attempting to recapture the heir who had vanished from their grasp. Those who remained, refreshed with new bodies, cleaned their eyes of dust on the lookout for the Princess, save Zephyr. Many feared if they *did* encounter her, they would live indefinitely without aim, eyes glossed over, trapped in invisible webs of Persuasion, cast without intention by the very woman who would then rule them.

The Princess's magic had long been contained… bridled like a stallion too proud to kneel. The bridle was gone for some time, collected dust in the barrack. Her eyes, exposed, could not undo the spellbound, but could the loyal, the weak-willed, the devout. And even now, she tried not to look too long at any one face, lest her words or her gaze pull the strings of yet another mind. Though, the weapon she had become was fully ready.

The two fled across the Hallofields, near the Greyhound which still beamed with chatter from Bolin and the other drunken farmers, and the cemetery beside it oddly peaceful. Perhaps the dead were the only ones who remained unchanged, them and the drunkards. They climbed the back ridge away from the Bard and fields, where at last the scent of churned soil carried reminders of a life quieter.

Kapt, the most distant of Ringard villages, showed no sign of the kingdom's fracture. Even from a distance, Alexandria saw folks going about the late day as they would any, leaned against carts and roaming slowly across the dirt road. An ox wandered freely between hedgerows while a small boy followed behind. A single guard leaned against the post, chewing a root and staring blankly at the setting sun, unaware to the uproar descending from the castle's hill.

The village shimmered faintly in the ascending evening mist. Lights burned low behind windows, and smoke curled in slow drifts from chimneys. A village so healthy. Whilst Zephyr and Alexandria reached the cottage and barrack, word had gotten back to the King from the mercenary who accompanied them on their departure, and as the second mercenary was going to retrieve it, that Elric and the armored militants had driven the Koba back into the hills, but whispers of poisoned wells and haunted shrines remained in Cornlot. The King grew more concerned of it in the moment, sat with twitching fists pressed with weight against the arms of his throne. Fleschire, the Grand Wizard of the Kingdom, orchestrated relief to the enchanted people with help of the Yippire Coven, who were the King's choice for aid for such storms. For it was they who the Queen and a younger Fleschire commissioned to unbind him when Alexandria used her magic as a child.

The pair stumbled across the yard of the Broadmere's just as Tomas was bringing kindling into the cottage. He took notice of Alexandria, but could not determine who she was. By then, the Mortal Sword had gone dark, and its blade remained.

"Zephyr, I believe we are at our maximum of guests. Why are you running? Have ye pissed off a merchant? I told you, you needn't steal, we can get you what you need."

"Thank you!" Zephyr yelled as he continued behind the Princess.

"And who is this? I believe we've pushed the limits of our guest-arrangement, Sir Solta!"

But they entered the barrack and left Tomas confused. It was in the dying light that they fell to knees beside a coughing Leon. *He hadn't died,* not yet. His face was webbed in black and his skin was dripping in sweat.

"Come now boy, your father is here. Take my hand, please boy," Zephyr shook Leon's limp hand until it gained strength to grip his thumb. Alexandria nearly smiled as a tear broke from her eye. *"I'm here, my boy."*

As they coddled the dying child, Alexandria was quick to thrust herself to his other side. Her eyelids pierced and her hands slowly turned in circular patterns.

"What are you doing?" Zephyr asked, "you bear only Persuasion, it's no use. I... I must fulfill the deal."

Alexandria cried, "no! This curse is miscreant, I told you before! I may be no sorcerer, but I've studied Fleschire and the council." She began to whisper, "I need to, *I need to.*"

But as she attempted an odd amalgamation of Disquisition and Cradle magic, a practice she was not well versed in but had seen many times within the castle, Tomas burst in. "I'm not sure if you've seen Willa, I haven't seen her since yester. . . . " his head flew back as he saw her hovering over Leon. "What… is going on here? Who are you?"

Zephyr was quick to jump to him, grabbing his shoulders and assuring him that she was of no threat. "Tomas… Tomas you mustn't worry, allow her to treat him."

"The… The Princess? You cannot be here! Are *you* the reason I cannot find my sister? What have you done! Sir Solta, what has she done?" Tomas yelled in anger, his arms breaking from Zephyr's constrained hold. "I forbid you from these premises! You tell me where she is, now!"

But Alexandria ignored him. She continued until her eyes began to emit an amber glow. Zephyr peered back to see Leon's black veins retreated from across his cheeks. Tomas had enough, and shoved Zephyr aside to confront her. In his momentum, his extended arms thrashed Alexandria backward into the straw.

"You will tell me what you've done to Willa? Where can I find her, you forbidden bastard!"

Terrified and yet unwilling to persuade him, she told him of her order, to which she did not know where Willa had gone, but that she had been told to leave. "She was insulting me, antagonizing me."

Tomas took a pace back and shook his head. "*You!* You truly are the monster the King proclaims." Then his waving fist met Zephyr's chest. "A demon *you* are. I expect you, the child, *and* the storybooks off our property by dusk. Good day, heathens." He stomped off with a fury. Zephyr felt ashamed and guilty of misusing their trust, and bringing forth this mess to the Kingdom. But Leon's complexion had improved, yet the blackened veins crept slowly back.

"We haven't much time," she insisted. "Miscreancy can be reversed, but only by a hermetic hex of the coven. Drawn from the air, anyone can learn. It just takes practice."

But no matter how far she could push back the infection, it continued to grow. Alexandria could only manage to deter it long enough before another exit strategy could take shape. Zephyr was unwilling to listen to her hysteric hope, and found himself dragging the Mortal Sword out of the barrack and into the dying day. As the steel engraved the wood floor, it reignited, leaving a small trail of flames until it met the mud outside. He saw no other way, and no other future of his. Alexandria rushed after him, flailing her arms out to stop him. Swiftly, Zephyr collapsed to his knees and turned on himself.

"*No!*" She cried, collapsing in horror. She threw her arms up as if to stop him with magic. With his eyelids pinched and his lips quivering, his fists tight around the hilt, the sword... fell...

limp. It clanged and sparked over few stones and died in the damp grass. His arms fell at his sides and his head hung.

"*I… I can't… I can't. To see my boy live, I cannot bear the darkness of it.*" The Princess scrambled to his side, embracing him tightly. "The coven, they can fix this?"

"They can, but they're commissioned by my father, they'll be of no use to us. I could attempt to persuade one from their coterie, we just need to be quick. They'll turn us to ash if we're caught."

As weak as a skeleton, Zephyr slowly got to his feet, his head shaking in reluctance. He failed to save Leon, and betrayed the King of Death. The wish would no longer be granted, but he trusted Alexandria to source a cure. For, if the curse truly *is* miscreant, then it holds no labyrinth of conditions, only a persistent and arcane plague bound only to the Soltas. The few tears he had left managed to shed as he rustled the ill boy over his shoulder. Alexandria grabbed linen sheets to cover hers and Zephyr's head. She vowed to him there that she would only use her Persuasion under dire circumstances, but in their effort, they'd journey back towards the castle as ordinary folk.

They moved as ghosts through the early dusk, veiled by the linen and pandemonium which expanded from the castle's plateau. The road that once led them away from the castle, away from ceremony and fate and the laws of men, now wound beneath their feet once more, only reversed, and far crueler in spirit. Where before they had fled through cobbled corridors and whispering fields, they now stalked back with the heavy shadow of a child dying between them.

Leon clung weakly to Zephyr's back, his weight featherlight and unnatural. His arms dangled like rope, and every so often, a wheeze escaped him. The rot had returned, curling in black webs beneath the skin of his chest and throat. Alexandria had pressed the curse back like a rising tide with her makeshift spells, but already it pulsed again… relentless, returning.

They had no time left. Alexandria walked beside them, her head down, her silver mask tucked deep in the folds of her cloak. Her hair had been tied with bundled straw, and her voice, so powerful, so dangerous, remained buried in her throat like a blade kept sheathed. She had seen the fear in Tomas's eyes, of which she'd banished Willa unknowingly. She had tasted the revulsion in his words. Still, she kept her head low when she could, for both their sake.

Through the familiar fields of the Ringards, they moved unnoticed. The village of Kapt glowed behind them, its people still unaware of the fevered heart of the Kingdom. In the distance, firelight still clung to the Billmon Nitana Grocer, smoke rising in quiet plumes as ash began to settle on alchemist stalls abandoned by frightened apprentices. The fire from the market's alleyways had reached the City's western wall, but the people still danced on rooftops, mistaking spell-drunk stupor for festival.

In their diligent steps, a thunder through the ground as if the heart of the world quaked. They hadn't made it too far through the Bard before needing to peer backward. While Zephyr expected to see a nightly curtain of rain, the truth was far more menacing. He was baffled in what he saw, and Alexandria paid no mind to it. It was only when Zephyr did not continue on beside her that she glanced back.

"We need to keep going," she muttered, but her expression fell once she'd witnessed it too. A gargantuan black *feline*, or so it seemed, stood at a far distance at the edge of the village. In the dying light, it was a storm in and of itself. This *feline* was much lesser so, and each of its four limbs were entirely straight and pierced the earth with pointed ends. It had no tail, and no mouth either. It *may* have had fur, but no details were made clear as it was as pitch as obsidian. The eyes were but glowing red orbs, and what terrified Zephyr the most was its lack of mouth, nose and ears. The beast did not possess anything that made a living thing a thing. While it was not evident to either of them if the *cat* was a threat, Zephyr turned away with petrified eyes.

"The Collector," he could only whisper beneath his breath.

28. Crystal Eyes to Brew

Elladanty's fingers stung with cold as she scraped the century dust into a cracked ceramic basin. The glittering powder shimmered faintly in the torchlight of the dungeon cavern, delicate as frost but heavier than guilt. The elder witches had been careless again. Merich, or perhaps Margy, had spilled a bowl's worth of the precious substance when cackling over some half-boiled miscreant potion. The floor beneath the cauldron sparkled now like the stars of an extinguished sky, and it was Elladanty, sent to gather the remnants like a scolded rodent.

The youngest of the Yippire Coven knelt among the ruin of the spillage, her dark skirts dragging through the grime. Her long hair, the color of ghostlight, silver and stuck to her cheek in sweaty threads. She brushed it away and muttered under her breath.

"Fools. They wouldn't know a true future from a frog's breath."

She dipped her fingers again into the edges of the powder, careful not to let it cloud too far into the cracks. The sap was dangerously potent… harvested in slivers from the bark of the ancient Centurion pines and ground over days with crystal pestles. Drinking it was forbidden outside the rituals. Forbidden, unless you were one of the *witches*, as Elladanty had come to think of them… Yerrib, Merich, and Margaret.

Not witches, no. *Parasites.* Gnarled fingers wrapped around power they didn't understand. Whispering promises to kings and dukes, stitching themselves to thrones like ticks behind the ears of hounds.

"They think they guide fate," she hissed. "But they only drink it like it's wine. Drunk on what could be."'

Her anger was bitter as the metallic scent of the sap. When the spill had first happened…. before the three old crones shrieked and stormed away to squabble about measurements… Elladanty had knelt beside the thickest pool of dust. She'd touched it. Not enough to be noticed. Just the tip of her finger, pressed against the bark-flour, and brought to her lips. And there… *there…* she had seen it again. The vision. Not a dream. Not a trick of light.

Three figures stood in a cathedral of glass and ash, where the sky wept smoke and stars. One was taller than her, and cloaked in a robe dark as extinguished flame. That was the one with the mask… silver and spined like a crown of thorns. The other was younger, not quite a girl, not yet a queen, with a sword of black fire and eyes like mirrors.

And *she…* Elladanty… stood among them. Crowned. Smiling. A queen of rot. She had seen herself… whispering to cities, unraveling whole courts with a word. The faces of the dead hung in her shadow like lanterns. And she had *hated* it, recoiling from the thought.

She had felt her blood *scream* with disgust. The destiny promised to her by the sap. The same sap the coven wasted trying to guess the right horse to back, the right king to manipulate. A dozen kings they had worked with… St. Auclaire… Olderag, whoever held the highest purse. But what had it earned them? A dusty cave and rotted dignity.

"They use magic like men wield swords," she muttered as she stood, *"blindly and always against themselves."*

Elladanty gazed into the dust as if it might speak to her again, but no visions came this time. Only her reflection in the iron basin… young, tired, and furious.

She thought of *Sabbath,* the girl she had freed. George had spoken gently to her. He hadn't begged. He hadn't threatened. He had looked at her as though she *mattered.* And Sabbath… Sabbath had fire. Sabbath had looked at the witches like she already knew what they were… *relics.*

Maybe *she* was one of the three in the vision. Maybe Princess Alexandria, too. That meant she wasn't alone in it. That this future, if it was real, could be shared. She did not want to be reshaped, however. For the world her superiors envisioned was far bleaker than she ought to ponder.

Elladanty closed the lid on the basin and whispered, *"If I'm meant to rule… it won't be at their side."*

She dusted her hands and turned toward the rear tunnels of the dungeon. Let them cackle over cauldrons and chase down goblins with their potions and prattle. *She* had a different path to find. And when next she met Sabbath, if they met again, perhaps they wouldn't be enemies, but allies of circumstance.

"Miss Ella, have you seen my crook? I could have sworn I left it by this shelf," Merich asked her in a whine.

Elladanty's fist heated up as an amber light began to build within it. "Don't call me that!" She yelled with rare bravery. Then the light extinguished with her anger. "I saw two of them nitwits toying with it earlier," she said finally.

"*Hm*," said Merich. "These pestering imps may be more trouble than they're worth!" Merich waddled off with one hand on her hip in search of the goblin responsible.

Elladanty had wandered off to her own abode through the cavernous dungeon. Though, she did like this new home, for their residence was but a commune of cottages where she had easier access to the fields and forests. Here, and with the grimy and growing cabal of Koba and other tribes of goblins, she was restrained to only the molten glow of the ravine's river of lava. It was there that the goblins, who Yerrib had pulled from their own hives, specialized in concocting and hoarding miscreant potions. Some were fairly decent blacksmiths who prepared an arsenal of blades. Despite their lack of tongue, their grunts and snickers were enough to communicate with each other, but the noise made Elladanty furious and she'd often escape to her dwelling.

She found her room through torch-lit and damp paths where a scrap board of wood lay against the aperture like a door. She struggled to move it enough to enter. Once inside, she fell over her bed of goose feathers which Merich had conjured in abundance one day. Their softness was no match for the ache blooming behind her temples. Elladanty groaned and turned her face into the bedding, trying to block out the distant clang of goblin smiths and the shrieking laughter of her elders from deeper in the caverns. The air in her chamber was thick with the scent of ash and mildew, and the single crystal bulb, lit by a flame, glimmered faintly overhead like a dying star.

With a grunt, she sat up and reached beneath her pillow. From beneath it, she drew a thin sheaf of papers bound together with twine. The pages were worn at the corners, edges crinkled from many times being hidden and handled. She unfolded the top page carefully.

There she was, *herself*, sketched in soot. *Elladanty*. But not as she was now: not the girl with dirt on her skirts and crystalized sap on her sleeves, not the wide-eyed witchling scraping century-dust from the floor. In the drawing, she wore a flowing gown the color of lavender moonlight, her hair soft and brushed, her eyes luminous, warm. A subtle, elegant diadem rested upon her brow. Around her were scenes of peace: children playing in flowered courtyards, Greenfolk harvesting side by side with men, a Great Hall of glass and song.

She flipped to another: herself standing beside a masked woman, both cloaked in deep plum robes, but not laughing wickedly as the coven would have. They were weeping together in front of a broken throne, hands clasped. Another showed her kneeling beside an old man in chains, healing his wounds with red cradle-light spun from her fingers.

"A princess," she quietly spoke. *"No… more than that. A queen who listens. Who chooses."*

A voice stirred the cavern wall beyond her room. "Ella?" came the honeyed tone, one Elladanty knew too well. She gasped and scrambled to shove the pages beneath the bed feathers. Her hands trembled. The crystal above her flickered.

The wooden board at her door creaked as a figure pushed through it. Sophie Spirally, her mother, ducked beneath the crooked threshold with her signature grace, a movement rehearsed and ribboned in falsehood. Her dress was freshly charmed, the hem rippling with small silver runes, and her hair coiled like serpents drugged with perfume.

"There you are, darling," Sophie said sweetly, stepping fully inside. "You've gone and hidden yourself again."

"I needed quiet," Elladanty murmured, back already turned toward the bed. Her hands clenched the edge of her cot.

"Quiet is overrated," her mother said, brushing her hands together like she'd just done something worthwhile. "In a stronghold such as this, there's *no* time for quiet. There is power to be claimed, Ella. Yerrib's vision is coming to fruition."

Elladanty remained silent. Sophie tutted and wandered the room with sharp eyes. "You've made it so cozy in here. Much better than those rotting cottages we used to call home, don't you think?" She laid her hand lightly on the wall. "The goblins are useful. Tireless workers. Faithful, in their own revolting way. And Yerrib is right, we *must* honor her guidance. She's led us to a greater vision."

"Well, rock can't rot. But it still stinks of mildew." Elladanty said sharply before she could help it. Her voice echoed slightly in the cramped stone. "Do you even *know* what she saw?"

Sophie's smile tightened. "Does it matter?" she asked, tilting her head like a doll. "She is the oldest. The wisest. We trust the river knows where it flows, even if we cannot see its mouth."

"*That's not trust,*" Elladanty muttered. "That's blindness."

Sophie's gaze sharpened like a blade unsheathed. She either misunderstood her daughter, or refused to listen. "You're bored, child. I know that. *You are a flame waiting for a breeze.* But this coven is your family, and Yerrib's magic, however strange, *works.* The kingdoms rise and fall on the backs of women like her. Like *us.*"

Elladanty wanted to scream. Instead, she turned away. "What if she's wrong?"

Sophie stepped closer, her hand brushing her daughter's shoulder. "She *isn't.* And you'll see that soon enough, dear Ella. You *must.*"

Elladanty swallowed hard, her throat dry as ember-dust. Beneath the feathers, her fingers curled against the hidden pages, the drawn face of the gentle queen pressed to her palm.

She didn't believe Yerrib. She didn't trust her. And deep in her heart, she knew whatever vision the old crone had seen, it was not *hers* to claim.

29. The Collector

There was little one could prepare before facing the Collector. Even at a great distance, it was a void torn in reality, infinitely black, staring ominously and incapable of making a sound. It was feline, yet monolithic in stature, and its limbs which sharpened to singular points did not disturb the earth, nor did they sink into soft mud. *The Collector's Quiresh* was minimally written, and difficult for Zephyr to digest once he'd happen upon it. Even Pitter, who Zephyr thought to be sneaking eerily nearby, could not decipher the blotted ink.

The Collector did not exist elsewhere in literature, barely spoken of in fireside tales. What was evident, however, was that it was an agent of King Univerza, and as the dead King was stripped to bone and bound to a hillside, had created The Collector to retrieve debts. The *Quiresh* mentioned it so in the barely legible ink that the hellish creature was simply a condition within each *wish* the dead King would coordinate. Though, it had been a many thousands of cycles since The Collector was needed. The Quiresh offered no method of which the beast would fulfill his role, but Zephyr understood that it would ensure a conclusion to the deal.

The Princess stood famished at the corridor of the arcane school. Zephyr had laid Leon atop a stone half-wall so that

Alexandria could retreat the miscreant infection once more. Although behind the cover of dense ferns and away from folk, the Collector's presence riddled their hearts with terror. Zephyr rested his shoulders as Alexandria waved her arms slowly over the boy's head.

"It won't be long before it's caught up to us, Alexandria. We've no use but to face it."

"Face it? That *thing* is a spawn of hell. We will be no supper to whatever abomination it is. If it will follow us, then the knights and archers can tend to it." She stood up and inspected Leon's complexion, nodding to it's sterilization. "We've got to keep on. Death waits."

Zephyr was unwilling, having already accepted defeat long ago when he sat in his lake of blood, blind. His head fell back in anguish, his body aching. Frustration built as the Princess naivety was potent, despite all paths leading to the same fate. The Collector was not a beast to be slain, nor one to outrun. In the Quiresh, the conditions of a deal were immovable. *For you promise the sky death as it promises you night.*

Zephyr closed his eyes, listening. There were no footfalls, no rustle of trees, yet he knew it moved closer. The air tasted thinner. "The old texts lie," he muttered. "Or they forget. Or they dare not remember."

"What do you mean?" Alexandria paused, wary. He stared forward, expression unreadable.

"I mean that the Collector existed before Univerza ever raised his single tower. Before his lips shaped curses into contracts. There are mountains older than the Kingdom… there are *things* older still. The Quiresh didn't invent it. It merely *named* it."

Alexandria shivered, brushing a leaf from Leon's brow. "Then what is it?"

Zephyr's hand hovered midair, his fingers twitching like they remembered the strokes of a brush he could no longer hold. "There's a tale from the western caverns, the Oracles of Drun, a story my father gathered from the Mor's takeover of the Old Southern Kingdom," he said. "They spoke of the *Null One*, the Breathless Cat, that stalks the edge of time and memory. A servant, yes, but not to kings. To *balance*. To consequence."

She frowned. "A myth? Then why do I feel its gaze behind my spine, even here?" Her voice cracked. "The Collector is not a warden of pacts… it is the shape of debt itself. An echo given form which the Dead King tamed. The King is only a guide for it."

They stood still for a moment, wind brushing through narrow alleyways and through the brush, like whispers too ancient to decipher.

Zephyr continued, speaking like one possessed by his failure. "No roar. No blood. Just… reclamation."

Her voice lowered to a tremble. "And what was owed? Your life? You sought to exchange it for Leon? You would leave me here… in the imprisonment of the mask… what future is there if you don't see it with me? I can't believe the coward you are… had I known you would betray me.… "

"Less betrayal," he muttered. "Our future is promised no different than birth, and we'll meet in the everlasting day indifferent to the night which came prior. I never thought to leave you in pain, my dear Alexandria, only to undo the end I've made for *him*." Zephyr had laid his palm over Leon's chest. His breath had gone low and quiet, his eyes wandering through his exhausted eyelids. "Olderag's portrait was faulty by the Queen herself, I never could have known. It was meant to be a gift for him from her, but she did not know the color of his eyes. Of course, I was punished. But my dear Princess… you've come softly to save me from this curse, for you've nurtured him and have given me hope that my boy will live. The Dead King's wish was tempting, of course I sought him out."

"You hadn't known the curse was of Miscreancy… otherwise you'd seek a witch like we are. So… the wizard council beneath Olderag had fooled you. *Peasantry*," she cursed. "I fear he has adopted a corrupt ruling, and if so, my kingdom is under a dire threat. Wizards can't practice Miscreancy, for their scriptures and blood are bound to a parallel creation. Once we can relieve Leon of this curse… I… I must tell my father."

"You'll return to him? But they'll keep you confined…"

"But if the goblins have learned to organize and making dealings with the Southern Kingdom, that is an army the empire would fail to diminish. Their tribes repopulate far too quickly. To be organized and cooperate with man…."

Alexandria's hysterical rambling fell short once the Collector had come over them. Through the distant chatter of townsfolk nearby, it had silently approached them. It's head lingered over theirs with orb-like red eyes void of corneas staring downward. Alexandria fell beside Leon as Zephyr stood up from his place to face the beast.

"You get back! My boy's curse is faulty and not as promised in our deal. Be gone at once!" Zephyr announced, his fists clenched. But the Collector did not move, nor did its head tilt in the slightest. It would not speak, as Zephyr was expected to know why it had arrived. He thought to brandish the Mortal Sword as a threat to the beast, and in doing so the blade reignited. *"Let the dead King Univerza come and assess this knowledge, for it is tainted in lies. I will plead my case to him, get on now you demon!"*

The beasts's eyes only flickered, its head tilted. There was no use to speak lowly of it, let alone threaten it as it simply awaits a signature. Zephyr thought as much, stepping back. He thought it may be harmless, only a menacing figure without fangs, without any sort of weapon. Though, the Collector was prompt to show the cursed man that the deal held no negotiation. It's long spider-like appendage slowly raised over manicured hedges and struck the earth before them with a speed and weight that cracked the air. Soil and broken stone rose and rained atop the trio and left Alexandria dirtier than she was ever conditioned to be. Zephyr hurried without much reason other than a brutish response. He brought the Mortal Sword from his hip and with speed, slashed at the stygian limb. The slice produced no blood, no tissue. Though it *did* appear to momentarily displace the inky matter, leaving the Collector to stumble. There, Zephyr saw his chance to hurry the Princess and his boy away.

Further through the City in the labyrinth of the market alleys, Zephyr kept refuge within a stall. Along their staggered sprint, the Collector followed behind at a slow pace. They would lose sight of it as they weaved through buildings and storefronts, believing they were outrunning it. Behind a half-wall where delicate glass capsules and trinkets sat atop, Zephyr cleaned Leon's face of soil. The boy's face was still infested with black veins, but his eyes had opened slightly.

"Papa?" He murmured, his hands raising slightly.

"Not a word, boy. You've fallen quite ill, but you're a strong boy, you hear me? *You're strong.* You aren't going now, you're staying here….you're staying with me. We're… we're going to fix this. You hear me?" Zephyr's words shivered as his eyes turned glassy. He did not believe himself. Leon's mouth gasped as the distant thump of the beasts' limbs struck the ground. He began to panic.

"*Sleep,*" Alexandria said. As she did, the boy's head fell back and his eyelids pierced. Zephyr was taken aback, astonished that she would use her magic on his son. "Once we can get to the castle and revert this curse, they will wake him up. There isn't a need for panic, nor to terrify him."

Zephyr bit his lip in anger, unable to speak. His trust in her had turned sour, but there was little time to fuss. But before they could move to another stall or further down the road, the canopy above them crashed, and the entire wooden structure around the trio had deconstructed in a blaze of debris. *The Collector had found them*. In the smoke and mess, Zephyr was displaced against the stone embankment beneath a higher plaza. The Princess, behind a curtain the curtain of it, was knocked onto her hip. He rushed over to her aid, finding that her thigh had torn from a jagged wooden post. Blood smeared onto her knee and began to pool beneath it.

"Alexandria… there's little I can do. You mustn't go on," he said. "I… I…."

"You will live to see him… *please… please!*" She cried. She could not bear the thought of a life without him, nor one in which his boy left him. "*Don't be a coward, meet the day. Life will not wait, but death will.*"

The air shifted upward as the Collector raised its sharpened limb once more, having now reached them. The soot on Zephyr's cheek parted as a teardrop rolled down. The Mortal Sword lay at his right, and surprisingly, the blade ignited. He thought her blood might have had some adverse affects if the pool had reached it, but it was blood from his brow that had met his hand, and smeared across it. Zephyr hastily swung the sword as he turned, removing a segment of the beasts' limb once more. The dark matter poured as black mist, and the Collector haltingly collapsed onto its right side. The world shook when it met the ground, the sheer weight of it sending dust-clouds flurrying away. But its left limb battered the stone floor as it attempted to raise itself again. Zephyr ran around it, weaving between collapsed carts. The beast turned its head and focused in on him, beginning to crawl with weight.

"Get on to the boy! It seeks only I, and I will draw it away!" He yelled past it.

"*Stop it!* You'll get yourself killed!" Alexandria cried. She could not walk with her wound, and her grasp only caught air. She managed to crawl across mounds of rubble towards where Leon lay. He remained sheltered within the nook of the torn stall, sleeping until she would command otherwise. The Collector had turned aggressive, struggling to pin Zephyr with its limb, or even get upright. Behind him she saw the stone embankment, and despite her cries, he lifted himself onto it and ascended the castle's stacked buildings beyond her sight.

Hordes of town folk fled their homes and away down the roads. She hadn't seen anyone she'd persuaded already, nor did she think of it. Their stampede coursed through the intricate steaming jungle of the Kingdom. None paid any mind to her laying beside the boy, their eyes pacing frantically as not a soul understood what this beast was, or the danger it was to them. It did not, and would not, fix its eyes to any other but Zephyr, but its rampaging hunt left roads turned over, brick buildings deconstructed, and apothecaries in flames.

The distant screams traveled far and speeding carriages had gone towards the Greyhound where Tomas had drunkenly pressed his temple to a supporting beam. He slurred as a tradesman called out to anyone who could hear.

The Kingdom's been overrun! A great catastrophe is upon us, gather the young and get on!

A local woman named Barbara Leftower, who he called 'the fairest lady' strung to his arm, whispering a question.

"What is it Tomas? What has gone awry?"

Tomas' eyes were barely open when he turned to face her, "I haven't a clue, but it may just be the *Princess*. That coarse woman made a fool of us Broadmere's, shacking up in our *barrack*, forbidding my own sister! I'd set a coin or two that she's finally making a plague of herself, I always knew it. That mask was medicine, now look!"

Plumes of black smoke curled upward in the distance, making pitch pillars stretch from the fog-lain Kingdom.

"Shouldn't you go on to help? Eldric and the others haven't returned, and a *strong* man like you could save their fragile lives," Barbara spoke in a soft tone, leaving her hand against Tomas' chest. But he broke from her seductive hold.

"*Ay*, what good would I be? Hah! I'd turn into a slave the minute she sees me… surprised she hadn't when I caught her. This great dynasty is due for a revision. Say, *we should go to Taria*. Leave this rot in the dust. I think a great life awaits us there!" He spat out, and Barbara Leftower scolded him for the thought. She and her tightly balanced and buoyant brown hair sought heroism from him, to which he was nothing but a drunken, cowardly young man. She left him and went into the tavern without a word. Tomas chuckled in his lonesome and stared back out across the dampened fields, squinting. Little crossed his mind, but the adventure of saving a *different* woman in need tickled his brain. He spat out at his boot and set on towards the Kingdom, stumbling in his canter.

King St. Auclaire sat in his tall, golden-pillared throne as the Queen pressed her frail palms against the velvet fabric of her gown. The castle's Great Hall was silent but for muffled chatter outside the entryway doors. They opened for a moment, and Miss Toule came walking with speed straight ahead. Her heels clacked against the marble floor and occasional wooden planks. She sought not to distress the King any further, but the matter was urgent. Then, once she reached him some fifteen paces away, she awaited her order to speak.

"Go on, Miss Toule," he said lowly.

"A… A guard of the south courtyard has caught a terrible sight. Your holiness, I plead not to spoil this already-rotten day, but significant damage has been done below the first plateau. The… the Market Alleys are hidden in fire and smoke," she scarcely uttered. But the King was naive as he did not understand.

"Then the extent of Alexandria's damage has gone much further than the plaza. She hasn't been struck with an arrow, caught from behind with a blindfold, what good are these men?

Have they even caught a sight of her?" His voice erupted then and his fist slammed against his quilted armrest. "She is a *disease* and must be stomped out…. "

"But… it is your daughter, your Holiness."

"*My* daughter has gone rogue, just as we always knew she was capable of. That… is why… she dons… a mask! Have you gotten word from Binsop? The coven must be close. We may need more resources."

"Your….holiness, not a soul has found her I fear. But the destruction we've seen could not be from *just* her," she finally managed to say. "Myself and Lethar feel something has invaded the first grounds, something powerful."

The King's head tilted in disbelief. He rose from his seat and slowly stepped away from his throne. The fur of his cape dragged across the floor as he approached Miss Toule. "The Koba? They were put out by the Blackmere man, or did they lie to our mercenary?" He asked quietly, then grunted, "perhaps the mercenary himself lied. Tupin will need to wash the dust off the guillotine, he's about to be a *very* engrossed drudge." The small girl's eyes were wide and terrified.

"We're unsure at this moment. Lethar and Binsop deny that she'd cause such wreckage to create such plumes. I digress. Your Holiness, I will fetch Binsop."

"Alert our watchmen, and send Lethar here. Fleschire!" The King yelled into the catacombs of the castle, echoing indefinitely through the hundreds of halls and cavities, almost indefinitely.

Binsop the Noble was a distant and quiet man, sporting no hair atop his scarred cranium, and a frosted beard sheltering a dry mouth. He had coordinated many defenses in his younger years at the Guardant Walls where the men of the sea had attempted to infiltrate through. Though, those hundred-some years ago hadn't changed his tactics, and organized invasions were less frequent to the point of rarely happening for most of their reign. With the Mor Empire dictating a fortified leadership long ago and solidifying the four Kingdoms and all of the counties which composed them, Binsop had little to do. As he crept towards death, he and Lady Binsop found purpose in the King's newfound Red Room, anticipating a war they'd yet to learn of.

He sat at the cold hearth where a fire would someday be lit, analyzing the dust particles which descended from the mosaic windows behind him and onto the vacant sand table. The echo of the King's call for Fleschire did not even make his fingers twitch. It was only the arrival of Miss Toule that he accompanied her to the Great Hall in lieu of the Grand Wizard Sir Fleschire.

"Alexandria is near," the King ruled. "She's yet to leave the City, but Miss Toule has informed me of a unheralded disturbance. Before we lose men to whatever it is, get your eyes and report back."

The tall Binsop nodded without a word, leaving through the distant doors with loud, weighty stomps. Miss Toule could not turn back towards the King, out of fear that he may have gone mad in this turmoil, ready to sever the heads of anyone who utters even a *word* he disliked. For, she was not greatly respected, but relied on frequently. She'd do the bidding of conversation for him, but she was only a small, dispensable girl whom he may carry no guilt in discarding. She could only nod and await an order of dismissal.

The Grand Wizard Fleschire did not ever hear the King's call, as he stood at the eastern courtyard's manicured entrance, which most common folk were unaware of as it was strictly for state officials to transfer goods in and out of the premises. He stood in silence beside Lethar the Gatehouse Keeper in wait for the Yippire Coven. Hoverflies and butellbugs danced around the wizard's constellation-embroidered robes and landed in his long, white beard.

"I'm jealous of the reward for undoing this mayhem, I can't imagine he lets her live once they've dragged her back," the Gatehouse Keeper muttered. "Paying five women my weight in coin just to help some peasants snap out of delusions.… " Lethar scoffed. But Fleschire did not bat an eye. A bearded grin began to show, and the gallop of horses down the narrow forested road caught his ear.

"What good is coin to a witch?" Fleschire asked rhetorically. The carriage came into their shadowed sight. "*The King pays in blood,*" he uttered just before the two black horses reached them. "Good day! Ah… well… a day nonetheless. Please, please, we welcome your return to Alexandria. It has been a great while, but your qualifications are of great value in dire times."

The first two witches crept out from carriage, while three more fell out the opposite side. Three were of great age, one with missing eyes, two with canes. They were of course, Margaret Thistle, the sweetest of the bunch in her pale blue vest. Then Merich Biddlephi, the oldest and blind. Some say she lost her eyes to a squabble with King Olderag some time ago. Then Yerrib, a silent elder with her pointed fingers wrapped around the head of a cane. The other two were Miss Sophie Spirally, the voice of the coven, notoriously donned in black robes and younger than the prior three. Lastly, Elladanty, the young daughter and a witch who has never accompanied the coven any time before.

"A young one," Fleschire spoke. He faced her with a warm smile and presented his hand. "This?"

"Elladanty, my only. She is due for learning. When your hireling-boy delivered the King's message, I thought it would be the perfect opportunity for little miss Elladanty," Sophie said calmly. Her hand met the obsidian-straight hair of her daughter, her eyes adoring her so. Lethar groaned to himself.

"We haven't time to waste; the King asserts urgency. Come on then," said the Gatekeeper Lethar, starting his march back towards the castle. Fleschire rolled his deep eyes.

"Okay, hurry along."

The shadows had grown longer in that hour than any sundial could measure. The Kingdom of Alexandria shook in the battle held at the knees of their realm. As Zephyr fled through shattered streets made by the Collector, and the dying boy was cradled by the once-bright heir, the very stones of the Kingdom seemed to groan under the weight of the beast's judgment. The Collector crawled behind him still, not with the haste of wolves, but the cruelty of war-horses. Towers and pillars collapsed without acknowledgment. If Leon was awake, he would be in awe of it, as if it were a dragon from the fairy tales he knew.

In the ruined Market Alleys, steam hissed from broken glass which once held potions. The alchemists' stalls were all undone, their tinctures mingling into foul-smelling streams that pooled near the gutters. All the while, the great beast clambered onward and upward. And deep within his bones, Zephyr knew: it would follow him across mountains, through oceans, beneath even the roots of the world if it must. Yet the Mortal Sword had struck it. That, too, was not forgotten.

Binsop had arrived near the halfway of the thousand steps with a newfound army of knights at his back. They'd only step when he did, and halted as such. Peasants screamed as they fled up past them towards regions of the Kingdom they'd not known their whole lives, all in fear. It was then that Binsop caught a glimpse of the Collector, which he nor even the King or his ancestors had ever seen. It was evident to the Noble that he could not relay this sight himself, as his long-sword and twenty-some men could not let this terror continue. He called back to a young emissary by the name of Guy Liefly, who anxiously awaited his task.

"Liefly! Hither!" Binsop yelled. The boy struggled to get through the armored bodies but managed to reach the Noble. "Tell the King… an ancient threat has arrived!" The emissary was swift to nod and battle his way back. "Men, I cannot promise your lives! *Save the King!*"

Save the King! The knights chanted in unison as their voices became a roaring fire in their charge down to the market plaza.

Once Guy Liefly carried the word to the first castle-guard, he made his way with speed into the castle where the Yippire Coven stood together before the King. They had just constructed their method in which to go about their unraveling of Alexandria's Persuasion. Only Margaret Thistle could properly recite when the Princess had forbid her father many years ago. But even then, Margaret had taught Yerrib and Miss Sophie of the hex she had to construct. Elladanty stood to question her.

"Is it no less bound to the scriptures as invetia, or the nature of cradle? Surely Persuasion cannot be so dangerous," the young lady announced in a bout of confidence. Then, Merich told of her only encounter with Persuasion.

"You ask as if it's it can be measured like a flame, or a thread to be pulled and resewn. It is not. No… it is a *presence*, not a power. And I'll tell you now, I've felt it only once… and that was enough. I was younger than you, though I hadn't the softness you still wear on your cheeks. I resided near the Tarnish Cliffs, in the days before Olderag could snatch my eyes from their sockets and boil them no different than eggs! It was early summer when I wandered down to the bluefruit stalls… beaufruit, they call it now. *Hmph.* As if renaming sweetness makes it any sweeter!"

"Merich…" Sophie tried to shut her up, but there was no stopping the old witch.

"Stop it now! Perhaps Elladanty could learn to listen better than you! Now, there was a merchant there, tall and bent like a shepherd's cane, and he prized his beaufruit like rubies. Folk could barely afford a single rind, let alone a cluster. Then she came… this girl, all silk bronze hair and star-bright skin. Dirt on her knees, but her feet moved like moonlight. And her voice… *ah, gods*, her voice. She asked the merchant for fruit. He scoffed, said she hadn't coin enough for a taste. She tilted her head just *so*. Said, 'Are you sure?' That's all it was. *Are you sure?* The man blinked. Dropped his coin box on the ground. Then… gave her *every last piece*. I remember the smell… it was as if summer itself had cracked open. She smiled, curtsied, and disappeared down the path with more fruit than any child should carry. I went to him. Asked what had come over him. And do you know what he said? *'She was right. I wasn't sure'*. That's all. As if it had always been his idea. He sat down and wept, not for his loss, but because he could not understand what he had lost. That's what Persuasion *does*. Not a curse. Not a charm. A re-writing of life. A bending of truth so perfect, it leaves no seam to stitch shut. That was my first taste. And my last. And I'll tell you this, little Elladanty… the Princess bears it unbound now; you don't meet her eyes unless you're prepared to forget who you were."

Emissary Liefly later reached the castle and was rushed with urgency by Tupin the Lawful and guards. The King let him speak few words of the beast ravaging the lower sects of the Kingdom. Within the deep chambers of the castle, where moonlight pooled across the floor like the memory of rivers long dried, King Jean St. Auclaire stood at the far end of the Great Hall before the steps leading to his throne. Faded tapestries rustled behind him in the hush, bearing heraldic beasts that had not stirred since the war of the Four Shores when the Guardant Walls were constructed. Before him many paces away, the Guy Liefly knelt, weary from the long trek back, a scroll clutched in his dust-covered hand.

"Binsop sent me to retreat and provide your Holiness with the message, of which I have… made into scribe."

The King read slowly, his eyes narrowing as though to press the meaning from the parchment. At last, he lowered the page, and in a voice deep with weariness and rising thunder, he spoke, "it is not by my daughter's hand that the lower cities burn. Yet the *infection* she's brought has turned our elite plateau into a plate of mania. Did you see the beast yourself, Liefly?"

The silence that followed was not merely stillness but the echo of something ancient being remembered.

Liefly's voice trembled as he rose, presenting his twitching palms. "Your Grace… Noble Binsop has sent word, but I *did* see the destruction of it, and I *did* witness the beast itself. The ruin wrought upon the Market Alleys, the tremors beneath the first plateau, the fires licking the grocer's towers, the demon is a greater doom. It was nearly body-less in its blackness, I suspect *she* has brought it here."

The Grand Wizard Fleschire, who had lingered in the dimness beyond the throne's dais, stepped forth. His beard swept the stone, and his eyes, pale as starlight, were heavy with old knowledge.

"It walks, then," said he. "Bound no longer to pact nor parchment. A warden of forgotten debts… a herald of the Dead King's will. I feared the hour would come, that some *fool* would be cowardice enough to light its kindling once more. King St. Auclaire, only he who summoned the demon can make waste of it, for it will not leave without concluding a *deal* with the Dead King. For, the beast is *the Collector*, and we cannot be foolish in its presence."

The King did not look at him. Instead, his voice rose like a blade drawn in haste. "Summon Tupin the Lawful. Let him not delay. And bring before me Lethar Odeman, Keeper of the Gate, for his eyes are sharp and his memory long."

The court moved with haste, as bells tolled faintly in distant towers. Soon they came: Tupin, cloaked in mail and bearing the golden band of justice upon his brow; and Lethar, sober as a watchman at winter's gate. Before the throne they stood, and the King addressed them with the authority of a mountain storm.

"Jean, no blade will draw the Collector's blood, for it hasn't any. Sending more bodies will only endanger them! If it were *her* who embarked on this deal, Alexandria will have to uphold her end."

"*It is not her,*" the King snarled low. "The traitorous foreigner, Sir Solta. He came here, sought precious reward for finding her, it must be him who found the Dead King!" His shaking palm and heavy brow turned to the officials. "Tupin, son of Renwald of Early Cuepo, I charge you to gather the Pale Order. Let no faint-hearted men march beside you. Seek those who withstood the brine-curse and the siege of the southern bluffs. You shall go to Noble Binsop and join him. This beast… this *Collector*… must be cast down"

"I told you, Jean, you cannot defeat it!" Fleschire barked with his long beard furiously waving. But King rose his palm to him. Then, the echoing voice of the Queen rang in his ear, "*ensure her life.*"

"Enough! I want the head of the southern man, Sir Solta. Once it faces me in this court, I understand this *Collector* will retreat." He and the Grand Wizard faced each other in anger, with the King grinning as Fleschire swiftly left.

Tupin bowed low, and said only, "As you command, sire."

The King turned then to Lethar, and his tone grew colder still. "As for those touched by my daughter's gaze, those whose minds now waver like reeds in a storm, you shall find them. Detain them, not in cruelty but in care. They are not enemies, yet they are not themselves. They are to be gathered, and their enchantments lifted.

The coven will tend to them within a guarded ring outside the gates."

Lethar's hand fell to the hilt at his side, not in threat, but in solemn vow. "So it shall be."

The King gave a final command to the distant bodies within the shadows of the hall, and pressed to the back walls, the coven. "The Yippire witches are to be given honor and space for their craft. The enchantment must be unraveled… *thread by thread.*"

30. Hunt for the Signatory

The aching twilight gave way to a cool and dark night, and the Yippire Coven had just emerged from the castle after the Pale Order of knights did their duty in gathering Persuaded folk.

Five they were, in raiment strange and ancient. Margaret Thistle, who walked with a cane of willow and spoke softly to the wind. Merich Biddlephi, blind, her yellow robes dragging over stone as her hollow gaze turned to forgotten things. Yerrib the Staunch, grey of hair and voice, who leaned upon a cane as gnarled as maple roots. Miss Sophie Spirally, dark-robed and sharp-eyed, who led them with the quiet gravity of nightfall. And Elladanty, youngest of their number, red-cloaked and wide-eyed, stepping softly in the wake of her mother. Fleschire met them by the Eastern Wing, where ivy clung to columns older than the crown itself. It was there that the Pale Order wrangled manic elitists, children, and elders into a herd, and the massive knights circled around them. The Persuaded people were screaming, sleeping, fighting one another.

"It be a dark hour," said he. "Not to read stars, nor call rain, but to mend minds bent by a power older than we guessed, one I do not possess. The King bids you enter the ring here and tend to our poor community."

Sophie Spirally inclined her head. "We shall do what may be done. The mind, once broken, may not be whole again… but perhaps it may be *steady*. The *moon* sheds unknowing divination, but I promise order will be restored."

Behind them, the wind rose. And far away, in the burning light of the lower sects, the *Collector* crept through flame and ruin, its limbs as long as shadow, its purpose unwavering. And in the north hall of the castle, King Jean looked not to his daughter's return, but to the *reckoning* that must follow it and the forsaken Zephyr Solta.

The five witches went among the corrupted many, tending to the loudest and bloodiest ones. A baker had his eyes hidden beneath his thick hands, flour and herb still flakes stuck to his knuckles. A man wearing only thin garments was found to be one of the guards, redirected by Alexandria and left without his armor. The eldest of the coven brought calming tangerine-flame from the air and let the sparkling embers fizzle into faces of the disoriented folk. And in their exhaustion, the silent knights of the Pale Order carried them to a nearby courtyard where physicians commissioned by the King and Queen would tend to wounds. Elladanty found a little girl wearing a lavender imitation of a princess dress. The child's face was buried into pressed-together hands and she murmured prayers. Elladanty fell beside her, bringing the little girl beneath her arm. She softly and slowly brought the child's hands from their face, revealing pierced eyes and a running mouth.

"Now now… you've better days waiting for you," she whispered. Elladanty's palms faced the night sky, her fingers like the trident-spikes of a crown. She summoned the amber aura from the air, guiding its glimmer down to the child. It burned and simmered across her eyes before dissipating into tracing specks of light, cooling to nothingness. The little girl's eyes opened, but danced in exhaustion. She fell limp into Elladanty's arms. *"And better days await no longer!"* She said to herself. She smiled and turned to a Pale Order knight, who approached her and lifted the child. Before he left, he stared blankly at her, as if to confirm her goodness of which isn't a familiar attribute of the coven. He left towards the Eastern Courtyard, and Elladanty went on to aid Yerrib in a fighting bunch.

The moon in its' crescent neared the apex of the sky, and many distant shouts of agony and defeat rang in the distance. The only Persuaded people were three sleeping castle-guards. Yerrib, Elladanty, and Sophia sat atop a short stone wall to rest. They watched as Margaret and Merich brought flames to their hands as they tended to the final Persuaded. Yerrib, however, was twitching as she delved into her own grave concerns.

"The Collector is among us," she said. *"You understand its purpose, don't you?"* Her scaly hands gripped onto Sophie's wrists, but her head shook.

"That it's some ancient monster… get your hands off me!" She declared. "It'll be slain before we even depart, what do you want with it?"

"*Oh!* I do not *want* it, deary. But if the Collector is here, it seeks the one who made the deal! The one who signs his life…."

"Bears the Mortal Sword…" Elladanty said quietly. "But what is it?"

"The Mortal Sword maintains this cyclical *suffering*," Yerrib breathed into her bumpy lip. "It is no good to anybody, but the absence of it would allow the Sword of Summe Red to return and bring eternity back to Grasp. Only one may exist, and I declare we rid ourselves of the King's bid in search of it!" The three witches looked out across the plaza, as if to see through the many walls and buildings.

"And we'd be…." Sophia started.

"*Immortal?*" Elladanty said. "But is that what we want? Shouldn't the world recycle itself, and make way for new beautiful things?"

Fleschire appeared over Yerrib's shoulder before she could speak, startling her and putting an end to her ramblings.

"The King requests that you all remain on our grounds until he can be assured that order is reclaimed. I anticipate no opposition, might I be correct?"

The decrepit witch nodded with a false grin. Margaret and Merich joined them shortly after, their heads barely hanging on to their necks. Yerrib only furrowed her brow at Sophie and Elladanty and remained silent as the last two women arrived, as if to make a pact to keep their early plan a secret. But not even Elladanty gave an approving glare; she wanted *nothing* to do with it.

Once the coven had departed, only a handful of Pale Order knights alongside physicians to aid the recovering folk in the Eastern Courtyard. There, and through the night, each would awake as if they were haunted by a nightmare, their bodies aching as if they fell in the midst of battle. A party of three knights and a watcher, by the order of Jean, took control over a local inn to house the effected until dawn.

The night had bled into a feverish fit. Zephyr had managed to evade the Collector as its limbs shed blackness across unsuspected boroughs and neighborhoods. In doing so, the King's stampede of armored and weaponized men prevented it further. Whilst he hid among dense alleyways, the beast made slow work of powering through them. Although it could not die as foretold in the *Collector's Quire,* it could not kill them. Binsop boasted plenty of slashes near the murky hip of it, leaving an oily charcoal gash.

I've got the head! One had yelled with his blade stood at the ready.

Cripple it! The legs are nearly done in!

Though, their war-cries were muffled behind the crash of stone pillars. The Collector had trudged into an amphitheater. Some men had their pauldron plates bent inward by falling stone, while others were directly flattened beneath colonnades while their cuirasses spat out. Binsop saw the never-ending hell in its ruby eyes, that it would not be defeated even if they managed to separate its head. He saw the smoking pieces of it stretching through rubble, how sections melted together as if ink fell down stairs in reverse. Binsop did not feel guilt as he finally caught a glimpse of the thousands of stairs to his east and swiftly made his way there. He sought to inform the king of this battle, that he did not *truly* understand the magnificence of the beast, its infinite determination, its *wrath*. As he climbed upward, a fresh new band of knights came stomping down, meeting him.

"Report of it?" A metal helmet requested. It was free of dust and blood, slashes and dents.

"Dismember it! Keep it at bay!" Binsop ordered. The knight nodded and led his twenty-some men into the smoking wreckage. He looked back at their armor, how it scattered fires spun off their plates, leaving them to face it.

Binsop sought refuge in the castle, far from where the Collector and its maelstrom of terror. Binsop had traveled through the Eastern Courtyard where he lay witness to the tireless Pale Order and the Princess' victims. Onward through the long halls he entered, his footsteps echoing as they returned to him. It was in the east-ward near the entryway of the storage cellar that he stopped abruptly; a noise came from the planetarium at his right. A blue hue radiated from the desks at the foot of a dust-blanketed astronomical clock. Binsop was unfamiliar with the room, and rarely ever ventured through the densely constructed chambers for it was not necessary to his duties. Though, the glow which pushed through the stone archway invited him in. It was there that he saw the Grand Wizard sat with his chest over the desktop and white fingers fiddling with a metal-toothed ring. The greater component of it was elaborate yet no larger than a porcelain plate. The glass center of it was what emanated the light, fading and illuminating as Fleschire adjusted the ring.

"Have you word of the King's whereabouts? The City is in dire shape; there's crushed bone beneath pillars...."

"He's gone to rest... until dawn," Fleschire spoke. "You've come to terms with the truth of *it*?"

Binsop snarled at the wizard, and with anger he ripped the ring from Fleschire's grasp. "That it cannot die... I'm so very aware. Even without limbs it continues on. I must alert the King. The coven must deal with this." Binsop paced behind Fleschire. The magnitude of destruction, if it met the foot of the castle, would surely bring devastation to the Kingdom. "We haven't much time, yet you sit here and the King's done to rest his eyes! Have ye given up? What good are you, the highest praise of wizardry in all the Mor Empire, tinkering while men battle a shadowed abomination?" Before Binsop could continue scolding him, Fleschire forced the nobleman to the ground with a great force of emerald light. He stood from the desk and looked down at Binsop.

"The Collector seeks nothing but closure of a deal we know nothing of. It may leave a trail of terror behind it, but it only seeks the sacrifice of whomever summoned it. You cannot *kill* it," he said fiercely. Then, the wizard took a step backward. "We can only let it chase until he who it chases comes to terms. Only then will it retreat." Binsop, still on his back, shook his head.

"Then we must find the signatory, and force them to uphold their deal." Binsop got to his feet, knowing that he was of little threat to the Grand Wizard who could simply seat him again. But Binsop's mind whirred at the idea of who the signatory was. Perhaps a peasant of the lower sects who wished for gold, or a mother wishing for health. Then, he sided with the King's earlier declaration. "Sir Zephyr, the man of Olderag's rule. *He* sought to take her, make a name for himself! We need to find him," the nobleman stated. "We cannot let this destruction continue."

"I believe it's a perilous endeavor; the signatory will give in. Will you strangle him until he believes he may as well be dead, or will you press your sword to his neck and achieve the same result? He cannot die by any means other than his own."

Binsop left the Grand Wizard out of anger. He believed Fleschire to be naive of the power of sharpened steel, that he *could* convince Zephyr to bring an end to the Collector's ruin. And if not, he sought to kill Zephyr himself no matter of the result it brought.

He entered another hallway on his quest to disturb the King, but the torches mounted against the wall to his left had gone out with a sudden breeze. The only light which remained was that of the Great Hall's torches at the far end of the hall. Binsop thought Fleschire had come to spook him, or that the coven may be wandering the castle. When he turned back, he saw no one. But sat on the stone floor, strangely enough, was a book he hadn't seen when he first walked. He went slowly to pick it up, brushing its floury cover until he revealed the title of it. *The Littlest Squire* written by B. Whelmfelt, an author which he'd never heard of. Reluctantly, he opened the loosely sewn book to read it.

In the kingdom of Grumblewood, where dragons occasionally snored smoke and turnips were considered currency by those who couldn't count, there lived a boy named Pit. Pit was of fifty seasons, scrawny, and rather small for his age.... which is why, when he declared his intent to become a squire to his sweet, warm mother, his confident declaration met the entire village, and where his father brought a frothing mug to his nose, the tavern erupted into wheezing laughter and one man even choked on a pickled egg.

Still, Pip was determined. He marched right up to the keep of Lord Percival Thatchington III, a decorated duke of the Kingdom, known more for his own loud mouth than any heroic deed.

Lord Thatchington, or "Percy the Proud" as the peasants whispered, was a portly fellow who wore armor polished so bright it often blinded people at court. He once tried to joust while facing backwards on his steed because he thought it "more charismatic." When the horse bolted and he speared a cabbage cart, he called it a tactical retreat.

Binsop threw the book to his feet. The outrage it brought led him astray from his mission to alert the King. Instead of traversing upward to the solars, Binsop with no haste went on in search of trustworthy militants who had once served beneath him. He whispered through his teeth, *"I am no fool... you're a dead man Sir Solta!"*

Before the sun had risen, the Collector *did* find Zephyr hid within the many piles of fabrics of a tailor's workshop some seven-hundred steps above the lower precincts of the City. Even with the Mortal Sword blazing when it happened upon him, Zephyr did not budge, nor did he threaten the beast with any sort of protest.

The ancient thing was just a head, and its limbs were slowly reforming from the scattered black shards. It stood in silence outside the building in which he hid, its shadowed face void of any features staring blankly in. Zephyr knew the beast to not cause any direct harm, whether it be to him or any other living thing despite its thrashing leading to many deaths. The Collector could only monitor him indefinitely until he sacrificed himself. Though, the wind was cold inside the tailor's workshop and where a hearth once blazed. Its embers had long since crumbled into pale ghosts, and only the scent of scorched cotton and dye remained.

Spools of golden thread and violet cloth lay toppled in the corners, like forgotten ornaments of a celebration never held. Zephyr felt comfort in the watchful gaze of the Collector. Knights had since retreated, with some remaining in towers and at a distance.

They were tired, and they too sought refuge in the Collector's tameness. the Mortal Sword rested against his thigh, its edge gleaming faintly. Though, there was no fire to feed it, for it needed no flame to burn.

Zephyr knew what the dawn would require. He placed his hand flat against the wooden floorboards, feeling the coldness rise through his palm like water up through root. The room was still. Even the city below, so often riddled with bells and shouting, had fallen into that peculiar hush that comes only before endings. He suspect most of the folk of this sect had departed soon after the pillars of the school collapsed. *"And so peace has arrived, and yet it is so loud"* he whispered, though no one answered. *"So very still, yet my hands tremble still."* He closed his eyes, remembering the barrack. The smell of straw, the boy's laugh as he swung his wooden cradle toy.

Leon, cheeks smudged with ash, eyes wide at the tales of goblins and talking trees and witches of fire and salt. How light had seemed to return to him, even as the blackened veins crept along his chest. How Alexandria had tried, again and again, to hold back death with trembling fingers and whispered hexes.

How her voice had become the only sound he could sleep to, that the Collector's red eyes had turned amber and mirrored those of Alexandria. But all of that had been bought with deception. He had *wished* for her love despite not knowing it was sewn into the deal. *He* had made it so. And now, all things born of that desire must be paid for. He pulled the sword into his lap. Its warmth pulsed against his skin like that of stones deep beneath the earth. Not kind but simply… owed. *"The wish had always been a simple one, hadn't it? Enchant her, make her love me. Let me paint her as she truly is. Let my son live"* He had painted her. Oh, how he had painted her. Her face, maskless and radiant, still lived upon the canvas hung within the great palace, the very breath of the Kingdom frozen in oil and egg. Her eyes, which had never looked at the world unbound, now stared forever forward, amber and unguarded, shielding the boy..

Outside, the light began to pale. Dawn had not yet broken, but the air changed. It grew colder, thinner, as if the stars themselves had stopped watching. The Collector's shadow reached through the window now, brushing the hem of Zephyr's bruised and bloody foot. A reminder. A summons. Yet, he did not weep. Not for himself. Perhaps he had already died, in some smaller way, the day he made the deal with a king of bone and silence.

Zephyr took the blade in both hands and placed it gently before him. His reflection in the metal was distorted, not by the steel's shape but by the uncertainty of memory. Would Leon remember him? Would Alexandria? Zephyr had looked with exhausted eyes at the building around him.   Beyond one pile of disorganized fabric was a shelf beneath a desk. There were trinkets and small woven containers. But beneath one container appeared to be a book. *"Perhaps a last one… for myself,"* he muttered as he stretched and crawled to it. He retrieved a small but dense ledger. In its first three pages, there were lines of chickenscratch and digits, quantities and measurements. But on the fourth page, a scribble of writing began. It continued onto the fifth and so on. Zephyr began to whisper to himself, as if Leon were beside him.

"When stars yet sang and the moon bore witness to the deeds of beasts and men alike, there dwelt in the shadow of the elder wood a small grey mouse by the name of Thistlewhisk.

Now Thistlewhisk was no common barn scuttler, nay…. for he walked upright, wore a cloak of mossy green, and read the language of birds. He dwelt beneath a tree stump carved with ancient runes and ate his bread with honey from the hives of the glade. But lo! Though clever of speech and quick of paw, Thistlewhisk did believe himself lowly, and of little worth in the song of the world.

'I am but a speck,' quoth he oft, 'smaller than the kings of beetles and weaker than a hare's sneeze. Let me scurry and hide; 'tis safer so.'

Yet as fate would will it, the peace of the glade was broken. From the black cliffs came a shadow.... a serpent of smoke and scale, called Malgore the Hollow-Eyed, who sought to feast on all things bright and tender. The beasts of the glade quivered. The badger barons sealed their doors. The squirrel archers fled to the high pines. And in the hush that followed, none did stand but the mouse in the moss-cloak.

Though his heart did thrum like a war drum, Thistlewhisk stepped forth. 'If none shall face the beast, then let it be me,' quoth he, and took up a needle-blade once used to mend the Queen of Swans' veil. He journeyed up the thorn-path, through fog and fern, until he stood before the serpent.

'Little one,' hissed Malgore, scales clinking like coins. 'Art thou a meal, or a mockery?'

'I am neither,' quoth Thistlewhisk. 'I am a knight of the Glade, and I name thee foe.'

Then sprang he upon the serpent's snout, striking thrice: once for the birds, once for the roots, and once for all meek things that dwell in peace. The serpent shrieked and fled into the dark earth, its pride wounded deeper than its flesh. And thus was the glade freed.

When the sun rose, the creatures of field and tree gathered 'round. They crowned the mouse with a petal of gold and named him Sir Thistlewhisk the Mighty, protector of the green and gentle. And from that day forth, whenever a small one doubted their worth, they would speak the old saying, 'even the smallest candle may set the shadows fleeing.'"

These stories arrived before him in unsuspecting places, at times of weakness and peril. He welcomed their teachings, no matter how vague or palpable. Zephyr wondered, particularly once he read the ledger, if these writings were left for him by a greater being. Perhaps the Collector had somehow provided each one, but it could not explain the codex of Univerza which he discovered long before the Solta family have migrated to the Kingdom of Alexandria. Maybe the Dead King knew what would come, and his phantom voice and being hid childish scriptures for him to follow. *He knew all along… might he know of all wandering paths and cursed men?* Then, Zephyr let his head rest against a stack of hoard of linens. *"A mountebank awaiting an easy catch, but he may just know all ends."* He whispered as if to confess, and yet he did not know what to believe.

Come the early dawn, before any peons or countrymen or peasants traipsed cautiously back towards the lower market squares or flats, the thinned coven began their quiet walk down from the inn in which the King had reserved for them. Sophie Spirally, Yerrib, and Elladanty coursed through vacant passageways and through hollowed plazas. Once Yerrib had spotted a watcher before a flowing fountain, she hushed the mother and daughter and directed them to hide behind a sizable trellis.

"If they catch us, we simply tell them we're exploring the deconstruction. You hear, little one?" The eldest witch said. Elladanty

nodded, still uncertain of her plan. *"The beast lies where the wisher hides cowardly. We need to continue down."*

"And what if the wisher concluded the deal?" Sophie questioned her.

"What… in the dead of night? Hah! A cowardly man may still be of great stature, and a man of great stature would leave the world beneath the sun. Let the village ponder his leave when they're well-rested."

Though, her spiel held no merit, and Elladanty and her mother rolled their eyes. A small stone archway shielded by vines of pothos led to the storefront of an apothecary, and the three witches shuffled their way once the watcher had turned north. There, the alley was narrow, lined with stone walls. A wooden plank revealed one door led to the Guidhall of Honest Trades, and another the Baker's Round.

Northward down the lane eventually opened up to a crossroad-space, and a marble statue which once depicted the delicate figure of a glasscaller lady. Yerrib knew some of the King's appreciation for such women, celebrating their heritage through said statues and many seasons of commissions, which are boasted in the castle's mosaics. Though, this statue was topped into fist-sized crumbs, and spinwool carts were but deconstructed mounds of wood. Yerrib giggled at the sight, knowing they were close. Her long bumpy nose twitched with her smile. Despite the Collector not emanating any smell, the witch declared she could smell it.

At the same hour, Binsop had pulled four of the Pale Order from the Eastern Courtyard and assigned them a *new* directive. They were without names, not slaves of the King but powerless to leave their posts. Though, Binsop was a Nobleman of Jean St. Auclaire, and his word held similar power. He informed them of the Collector's destruction in the lower sects of the west-end of the Kingdom, and how it pursued the officially-proclaimed traitor named Zephyr Solta. In finding him, they would force him to make good of his pledge, or they would kill him.

"Once this Solta man is pinned to the earth, the Collector will withdraw. The beast, whatever hell it hailed from, will no longer stalk our domain. There will be songs made of this morning, and you, each of you, shall be sung as its end." He turned then, facing the four stood before the flowery terrace of a wainwright stall. His eyes were shadowed by years, but keen as any blade in the armory. "Once the King is made known of the beast's retreat, *your* names will not be lost to time. You will be hailed as champions of the Empire, protectors of the Crown, guardians of Alexandria herself and *her* Kingdom. Statues carved and runes etched. Your grandchildren will speak your names like prayers. You will not be bound to the title of the Pale, but the Greats of it." The knights gave no reply, but their helms dipped in unison. "Onward then."

And Binsop, once again alone in his command, turned forward where ash still drifted like snow from the night. Though, in the brightness of dawn, the smell of burnt leather and the coolness of the air, he felt confident that he would return to the King later with a head in his fist and a future embroidered in golden twine.

"The bells of morning will not ring," he informed the knights once they'd happen upon the mess of an alleyway. The Collector and Zephyr hadn't reached these sects, but the mania which trailed behind the Princess in her initial escape had left the City in a mess. That in itself was unsettling. For even in times of war, siege, or poor harvest, the Crescent Bells of the Alexandrian turrets above the clouds tolled with unwavering precision. But on this day, they were silent, and the rising sun filtered through a sky marbled with soot and a red pallor that did not belong to dawn. Binsop, draped in his black-and-ochre cloak, descended the cobbled terraces of the High Hall with the slow cadence of judgment itself. He bore his sword of magnificent sheen, which struck the stone with each measured step. Behind him followed those with violet crests, furnished leather sewn around their steel. Their names were seldom spoken aloud. They were the last recourse, and in their company, silence was law.

The Market Alleys, once teeming with early merchants setting bolts of silk and cart-stacked herbs, now lay crooked and burned. Awnings were collapsed under the weight of charred debris. Glass from apothecary stalls crunched beneath the heel of Binsop's black jackboots. Beneath each crushed vial, bluish smoke still curled upward, whispering of ruined potions, failed enchantments, and alchemy spoiled by heat and fright.

They passed a fountain where children once played. Now the waters ran black, poisoned from something not poured, but *believed*. The hysteria of the night before had turned men into beasts, and beasts into rumor. Rumor into curse. They saw it carved into the faces of the few townsfolk who remained: those crouched in corners, eyes blank, mumbling the names of the dead. They scurried back to their nooks as the five men trudged on.

The knights moved on like phantoms: one to either flank, two behind and never speaking, but glancing often to the rooftops where shadows still clung, and where the shape of some dark memory might have passed hours earlier.

A woman, cradling her daughter in her lap, looked up as the five passed. Her mouth opened, cracked and gray, and only a whisper left it: *"Is it gone? Is it gone?"*

They did not answer. By the time they reached the second tier, a collapsed front of an Oil Chandler had formed a crooked hill of stone and wood. One of the Pale Knights strayed from their march and climbed to its peak. He surveyed the wreckage and offered a slight nod to Binsop, who followed suit without breaking pace.

Further and at the half-wall of a community terrace, Binsop looked out at the Hallofields, smoke still drifted lazily from the cottages of those who knew little of the nightmare. Even plumes still accumulated from the Ringards where folk were readying their hearths. He imagined chickens pecking at embers in the lowest villages if he could not accomplish his mission.

The stink of old magic, not foul, but sweet and strange, lingered in the air like lilacs of rot. A cart had overturned here, and inside it, dozens of crude drawings of the Princess, her face half-covered, eyes exaggerated in yellow ink, fluttered loose like dead leaves. Binsop caught one under his boot and ground it into the earth.

"*Fools…* " he muttered. "Let the witches bind their minds anew. We're nearly there."

As they passed beneath the arch of the south-eastern watch where they caught a glimpse of the Guardant Walls through the few remaining hedges, Binsop drew his cloak closer to his ribs. Not from cold but from a feeling older than dread. An awareness that, somewhere in the miles of ruins and misremembered alleys, something had been invited, and now refused to leave. The knights said nothing. But even they, armored and sealed, turned their helms more often than was their custom.

They moved lower down hundreds of the primary steps toward the roots of the Kingdom, where the Collector had last been seen. Though its body had not been found, the *mark* of its limbs was clear. Roads cracked like eggshells. Archways sagged where no weight should have been. Time itself seemed to stutter in some corners where candles flickered opposite the wind, or where children's toys lay untouched in rubble. At a broken tailor's shop, the third in their descent paused as if he'd heard a noise. A thin curtain fluttered from a shattered window. Threads the color of the sea lay strewn across the floor like veins from some slain god. And upon the wall: a single palm print, black and bleeding with soot.

"Here," said Binsop in agreement to the knight. "He was *right here.*"

31. The Devil & The Drunkard

The pale breath of daybreak sifted through a kingdom ruined in the dark, and over the bent hills and fractured stone streets of the lower sects of Alexandria, the air smelled of soot, iron, and old lavender, once pleasant, now rank with ash.

There, beneath the shadow of a crumbled millhouse, half-covered in the remnants of barley sacks and torn muslin sheets, Tomas Broadmere stirred from sleep. He awoke with a groan upon his lips, the sound lost beneath the groaning wind in which blackened banners still danced between stone gables. His limbs, crooked from the cold, ached with the weight of too much drink and too many regrets.

For a long time he did not rise, but blinked into the ruddy haze of morning with eyes dry and swollen, as if sleep had offered no real comfort, only silence. His coat, once a good woolen thing from the Ringards, was soaked through at the hem and stiff with dried wine. He reeked of elder spirits and a night walked poorly, and his stomach, offended by the sunrise, turned upon itself in protest. "Damn the sky," he muttered hoarsely, pressing a hand to his brow. "And damn the road that brought me here."

He sat upright with difficulty, one boot still on, one bare foot scraped and blistered from stones. Around him, the village was in ruin, not wholly destroyed but unsettled, as though the land itself had a fever in its sleep and shifted all that was once certain. Awnings sagged. Window shutters hung like broken limbs. The signs of merchants and innkeepers painted lovingly in years long gone, were snapped in half, lying in the gutters.

He blinked again, rubbing grit from his eyes. Before him, the crooked lane sloped downward toward the City's belly, where the market once bloomed like a tapestry of voices and smells. Now it was hushed but not with peace, but with the aftermath of madness. Here and there, townsfolk wandered as though waking from some enchanted sleep. A man in a cobbler's apron sat cross-legged in the dirt, staring into his own cupped hands as though they might hold the moon. A child clutched a doll with its eyes torn out, rocking gently. Smoke curled from a collapsed apothecary like incense from a funeral rite.

Tomas stood slowly, bracing himself against a lamppost whose iron had been twisted into a spiral, as if by some giant's hand. His tongue felt twice its size, and his throat burned. His thoughts came slowly, like oxen through mud. But one remained ever present, cutting through the fog like a lantern in storm, *"Willa."*

His sister. His blood. Driven out and banished by the amber-eyed heir who had wormed her way into their home, slinking in behind poor Leon like a shadow seeking warmth. The Princess. So pristine in title, so vile by her words. What spell she'd cast over Zephyr, Tomas could not name. What power she used upon Willa, he did not understand. Only that she had ordered

Willa to go and she, his proud, loud, unshakable sister, had obeyed. And now she was gone into this ruined city, he believed, amid fire and strange beast-lore, among smoke and whispers of cursed men and witches called from the hollows. And Tomas, drunken and furious, had left the Greyhound under moonlight to find her, vowing revenge and rescue in equal measure.

He remembered little of the journey down the high roads, only the taste of regret and the slow lurching of his own feet. He pulled his coat tighter and stumbled toward the alley's edge, stepping over broken crates and what might once have been silk.

Everywhere he looked, the Kingdom bore the marks of unseen claws… not of beasts, perhaps, but of magic, and fear, and something darker that had not yet been named. It seemed far too serious for even the Princess to have cause all of it. A flag of Alexandria, sunbleached bunches of beaufruit on violet, had been half-burned, half-slid down its pole. It fluttered like a sigh. "If she's dead," Tomas murmured, voice ragged, "then may all this fall. Let the walls split. Let the crown crumble." He kicked aside a crate, only to find beneath it a pair of shoes, unworn, never claimed by the merchant who sold them. He paused, something old and small aching in his chest. "Willa, where in all have you gone?" And so Tomas Broadmere, hungover and half-heartedly brave, made his way down into the deeper alleys, hand upon his belt dagger, rage in his chest like kindling. He was no knight. He was no scholar. But he would tear this Kingdom apart stone by stone if it meant finding his sister, and casting out the heir who turned his home into a shrine of lies.

Tomas had eventually stumbled upon an even greater mess, a bazaar entirely deconstructed, fruits and goods squashed between massive sections of foundation. There, he saw a tradesmen wandering around a chard cart, and Tomas understood that the Kingdom was under siege, that perhaps the Koba had defeated Eldric and the other militants. But the goblins weren't so rabid as to cause this, nor had he seen one in many years. He went on to question the tradesman, asking if he'd seen a cloaked blonde woman, or a brunette. Though, he could only shake his head.

The Alcheme school, as it was a brick fortress, remained untouched but its hedge-bordered courtyard and its pillars were collapsed. A gray professor used a silvery spell, that of an unbound Regulated magic, in order to lift the monolithic stones in mid-air and stack them into a small mountain in the grass. He couldn't believe the sight of it. But the lack of bodies led him astray, and he went on to a higher terrace.

In the crossroads of a market square is where Tomas *finally* unraveled what had occurred. A storefront built into a vast lane of interconnected homes was heavily occupied by the City residents. They stood in a quiet circle around something. Once he'd break through a few cautious folks, he saw an otherwise disconcerting scene. *The Princess* laid within a crushed-in brick embankment clutching a small boy.

Get a physician! One scraggly man called out.

Is that her? My Gods, look at her leg.

We need to get this boy to a dry place!

A squat-elderly woman reached for the boy, and Tomas intervened.

"Leave him," he said. "He's the son of my friend." Tomas lifted Leon from the unconscious Princess, and his head titled as her tunic and trousers seemed awfully similar. Then, his face turned furious. "She's responsible for all this! She's banished my own blood. Now, I'm left to search for her in these *ruins*. How could she *ever* govern us?"

Many agreed in chaotic chaotic chants, and Tomas grew a smile in validation. But as the many discontent folk declared their fresh fight against the Kingdom, a soft voice murmured in the wreckage. When he'd turned, he saw the Princess with her hand holding the fingers of a fat old man. "*Face this monstrous assemblage; I bid you a protector over me,*" she said, and the squinting elder turned to face the others with a rabid smile.

"And so what, you'll turn us all to slaves? Are you just a villain of your people? What good does this serve you?" Tomas approached her. "I fear you are just a rotting disease. And you've endangered this boy!" Some gasped while others agreed in disgruntled blather. Even as a mob, the poor folk were scarce in their steps towards her. "What will it be then, Miss Alexandria? Will you turn us to your dark army, or will you make good of this *ruin*?" His question brought silence among the crowd, and left the Princess painting and upset. Her head fell as she understood what a monster she'd become. That her Persuasion truly was a contagious infection, and the words in which she spoke, no matter how little or soft, plagued which ever man she faced. But this was not her demise, and the Princess rung her fingers delicately through the air like a ballroom dance to summon a fiery ring. That mystical band expelled rapidly into a fine mist. She whispered, "*sleep*", leaving all but Tomas collapsed onto the ground.

"A small… dark army… then?" He asked, entirely vulnerable. The Princess, though wounded, carefully stepped over the fallen man she'd once Persuaded. "What is this, part of your book of tricks?"

Alexandria began towards the central hub where the thousands of steps remained. She did not look back, but invited him. "We need to find Zephyr, for he's grown too eager for my remedies."

"Eager for what? What had you promised him?" Tomas angrily shouted. Leon remained ill and asleep slung over his shoulder. "Tell me now. Why did you put them all to sleep?"

She finally gave in and faced him. "We're meant to see the coven, because they are the only beings capable of undoing my wreckage as they are his! Is that good enough for you? I apologize for sending your sibling away; I only wished for an end to her barking. But now, Tomas, if we cannot get the witches to come to his aid, either that boy will fall to Miscreancy, or Zephyr will…."

"Will what? What other end to this is there?"

"He'll sacrifice himself as part of a deal… a deal with the Dead King."

"*And so he truly did find him*… hah! I thought he was bluffing the whole time! And if he does fulfill the deal…"

"Leon will survive," Alexandria said at the edge of her breath. "But he will do so without a father. Not unless we can save him *and* Leon, and the coven I believe can help. The Collector will continue its trailing until the deal is satisfied, but if there is no curse to lift, there is no wish to grant." She held little spirit in her words and yet the weight was evident; Zephyr had given up long ago and despite fighting his demise in order to cheat his way out, the time had come.

"The *Collector?*" Tomas hastily asked as Alexandria turned again and began towards the City center. He ran after her with the sleeping boy.

Along their trek through the caved-in infrastructure of the Kingdom, she explained in better detail of *what* the Collector was: an enforcer of the Dead King, a hermetical deity assigned to the signatory. That it was incapable of killing, but its sheer size and thrashing limbs and terror were what caused this destruction. After several hundred steps, Tomas came to a halt and let Leon down atop a surprisingly intact cart of straw.

"I cannot carry him further if we wish to reach the top," he panted. Although he was a fit young man, Tomas' habits and saturation were crippling him. But at the next terrace above them, a middle-aged peasant woman was beginning her descent. Alexandria was quick to rush to her, and with her first words, ordered the woman to carry Leon all the way down to the Greyhound.

"Care for him until I arrive there," she whispered. The woman swiftly went over to the boy without a thought and lifted him like an infant before beginning her rushed journey. Alexandria turned to Tomas. "I cannot push the Miscreancy back now, we must hurry!"

While following closely behind, Tomas yelled up to her, "as a man, why can't we let Zephyr do as he must? It'll save Leon! We don't need the coven, just let him!"

The Princess stopped for a moment to face her mind. "Because I love him!"

Tomas and Alexandria found themselves then upon the twenty-eighth landing of the ascending tiers, where the streets narrowed and arched with green-laced ivy and long shadows. Even here, amid cracked marble steps and shattered torch-brackets, the path retained some sacredness, as though the stones refused to fall to the ancient beast.

Alexandria did not speak further. Her cheeks burned with the confession, and her breath came sharp. Her trousers, once ill-fitted, were ragged at the cuffs and bloodied at her thigh. She fell and tripped many times, wanting to let herself succumb to the pain. Though, she knew if she did, the throbbing convulsion of her leg muscle would send her into a haunted daze. Tomas followed, slower now, caught in the drag of that final admission. *I love him.* Those words echoed louder than any bell within his addled mind. He knew not whether it was love she'd conjured or love she'd been cursed to feel, and in truth, he wondered whether she knew herself. But still, she moved with purpose, her eyes scouring the veiled and pillared skyline above, where the spires of the castle stretched above the settled steam of the Kingdom.

Beneath their feet, the City still smoldered. Along the terraces and rain-slick walls, the scent of brine and alchemical dust lingered in every shadow. Here, the damage was more measured: glass had turned to powder, a gate sundered, a cobblestone path heaved from its roots. The Collector had passed this way shortly before dawn, surely, but not in fury. It had climbed like a thing long taught how to stalk cathedrals.

From time to time, Alexandria would reach the edge of a railing, casting her eyes down the ledges and battlements of the Kingdom below. Smoke still rose from the merchant quarter until it reached the Guardant Walls.

"He must have found a place to rest till morning," she finally said, her voice low and distant. "There was still black in Leon's blood, I've no doubt that Zephyr never found the coven."

Tomas spat at the ground. *"C'mon you lying bastard. Where have you gone?* He is the *worst* guest I've ever let stay in my home."

She almost smiled. "He's a good father, just bound to snaking his way to keep Leon alive."

They reached a narrowing stair of stone, carved long ago into a spiral that wound through a keep of thorns and hanging roots. The hallway ahead lay between what remained of the Royal

Conservatory, long overtaken by ivy and magpies. And the north chapel, where sun broke upon the stained glass of old saints and soldier-kings. Here, a strange silence met them. Not the stillness of peace, but the waiting hush of things left unsaid. Tomas drew his dagger, more for comfort than use. Alexandria stepped forward and placed her palm upon the mossy stone. Before she could continue, a mess of voices began to build behind her as footsteps drew near. Then, they turned the corner and Alexandria could not believe her eyes.

"*Yerrib?*" She exclaimed as the elderly witch threw her cane in excitement. "Yerrib, what are you doing here?" The witch hobbled over as Sophie and Elladanty stumbled beyond the wall. The Princess embraced Yerrib, believing that she could finally convince Zephyr that Leon could be saved without the deal.

"Oh deary! I am so overjoyed to have found you!" Yerrib cried in their embrace. "Oh, what a tragedy this is! We were so worried you'd be hurt, all lost here. Oh… oh my!" The elderly witch had spotted the open gash in Alexandria's thigh. "You're not fit for these streets my dear. You must see your father now!"

Alexandria took a step away from Yerrib, watching her excitement deconstruct into worry. "I… I will seek help elsewhere. Has… *um*… has he commissioned you? And… you?" She looked past Yerrib at the mother and daughter stood cautiously at a distance.

"Ah, this is Miss Sophie Spirally! And here, oh come here! This is little Elladanty, Sophie's beautiful young girl. Now, you must tell me Princess, what's gotten ahold of you to draw you into this? Are you sick?" Yerrib began turning her head every which way looking for sores. She seemed to trust the unmasked Princess for the time being, but still saw a corrupted future. She wondered how it would go, if Alexandria would request some devious deed, to aid her in making a greater mess of the Kingdom. But the Princess was far too shaken and horrified, pale in the face, to seem proud of what she'd done so far. Elladanty watched her closely.

"No, no. I've just… I've come to find that I cannot fulfill the tradition of this Kingdom, nor can I continue the legacy of my lineage." Alexandria turned to look down the alleyway where one baker and another tailor slowly came upon their destroyed workshops. "My very people do not trust in me, and I do not see a future settled without fear of… of my eyes… my voice."

"And so… you've Persuaded a great many, out of anger?" Elladanty asked with bravery, for it was her first meeting of Princess Alexandria. "Why've you done this?"

"Now now, child. You mustn't speak before your own mother!" Yerrib interrupted her. But Alexandria calmed them.

"This wasn't me, I haven't done this!" She fought.

Elladanty walked in front of Yerrib and faced Alexandria herself and voiced her skepticism. "Then what has?" But Alexandria could only look to Tomas, who stood with his dagger drawn still uncertain about the witch's intentions, despite Alexandria's ordinary squabble.

"Then it *is* true," Yerrib whispered like a snake. "The *Collector* has arrived here… following the deal in which it has come to conclude!" She turned to Sophie and smelt the air. "It must be near, and *you* must be in search of it!"

"Perhaps she's come to Persuade it," Sophie suggested. "Is that possible?"

"Surely it is, and it would make you the savior of this land. Then, the Alexandrian people will not only place their trust in you, but they will erect statues, chant your name! *Oh*, you have your mother's mind, I always knew it!"

Alexandria could only nod to Yerrib's discourse, knowing the truth was far more complicated and entangled in love and Miscreancy. She did not dare elaborate on why she was rummaging through the destroyed streets, or why she'd even left to begin with. She could only offer a thinly veiled excuse, that she could did not believe in herself. Which, although fair, left her remaining as mysterious, rebelling against her father.

Alexandria refused to return to the King, and Yerrib did not force her. She did however allow the three Yippire witches to accompany her and Tomas as they continued eastward. The Princess grew frustrated in their walk, knowing that if she'd let Tomas keep Leon, that Yerrib could have helped push back the infestation. Though, she was not yet ready to explain that stem of this turmoil. She did not even pause to question the three witches, believing that they were simply still on the hunt for disturbed folk.

Alexandria led them further through settled wrecked, following the blackened tiles which she believed to have been from the sword, less the crushed rock where the Collector followed at a distance behind him. She followed a wall and went around the corner of it to where a watchtower overlooked the eastern farmlands, and a cluster of storefronts remained in shambles, including what remained of a tailor's shop.

It was there that Alexandria saw it once more. "*The Collector*," she said to herself, and Elladanty repeated with wide eyes. It sat just as any feline would, with its front limbs extended to the ground with its back limbs bent and its bottom seated. It faced the distant fields below the scattered clouds. The beast had recollected the shattered remains of its body overnight, with each piece creeping as black smoke until it reunited with it. "Why's it so tame?" Alexandria asked Tomas as if he had the answer. Though, Tomas was cowered behind the corner of the wall. His dagger was drawn but once he'd seen the colossal thing, he no longer wanted any part.

"*It has found its commissioner,*" Yerrib whispered to the other two witches. "*Look child.*" The old witch was rubbing her palms together knowing that the sword was near. Alexandria stepped forth, careful not to disturb the ancient deity, who did not even glance its glowing red eyes at her. She met the terrace's edge beside it, and saw Zephyr to the Collector's left within the entryway of the open-air tower, staring out at the land. She did not approach him, but watched him carefully. He held the Mortal Sword still, letting the flames of it bleed upward over his forearm,

"Zephyr?" She asked softly. She saw that he remained fixated on the world. "We… we don't have much time. The curse will take hold. I… I've found the Yippire witches. They can help us!" But no matter how delicate her words were, Zephyr wouldn't face her.

Zephyr spoke without turning. His voice was steady, but hollow, like wind through a ruined nave. "You speak of time, Alexandria, as though I hadn't turned it to oil and spread it across a canvas. There is no time… no… not for me, for I will exchange it for him." The Mortal Sword's glow licked along his wrist, casting flickers of gold and infernal red across the shattered tower wall. "I have listened to your every word. Your faith. This *coven.* Your desperate belief that the Yippire witches might undo what was written in the blood-ink of Joab. But you do not understand the shape of the curse. It was not drawn by witches, nor by scholars or wizards. It is older, rawer… *Miscreant* by name, and Miscreant by will. I've wasted my time but the crumbs I'm left with I wish to ensure what was promised to me." He finally turned to her then, and though his face was calm, his eyes burned with something deeper than fire. "A coward, perhaps. But I have seen what comes of uncertain mercy. I saw it in Ambrosia's eyes when her lungs drowned in silence. I saw it too in Leon's breaths…shallow… stitched together by chance and your trembling hands." He took one step forward, the sword trailing a line of molten light at his heel. "There is no cure in their chants. No salvation in hexes bound to the law of earth and time, by the court of it. Univerza's magic does not answer to women of the wood or stars drawn in ash. It is *divine* in its cruelty. *Final* in its cost. And I.... " Zephyr stopped for a moment. He observed his hand caked in soot and soil, his other nearly molded to the blazing sword. "I made a deal."

"But our love… our love is no less a reality. We're bound together," the Princess insisted. "Even the air settled the day we discovered one another, as if the world itself knew it was ready for resolve. You… you were meant to save me from this *insufferable* cage so that we could build anew. This was promised."

Zephyr spoke quietly and slowly beneath his breath, "it was never promised, Alexandria. I've done all I could to scrape together accommodations to this *curse*. My boy deserves purity, not a… a mess of torn pages from different stories forged together. With this sword, I assure him that he is mortal yet healthy, and that without potions or hexes, he is unburdened." The Collector remained facing out over the eastern fields, unbothered by either testimony. It was silent, as if it were a reaper who knew to just wait, and let the dead die. The Princess approached the entryway of the tower and sought to draw Zephyr to her.

"A beautiful life, couldn't we have it? We… we just let them burn this vex. Please Zephyr. We could cater to this, and he will forgive you," Alexandria spoke under tears. The tangerine hue of her eyes shimmered, and yet they did not glow. For she could not convince herself to Persuade him, as if her love knew better. Zephyr, however, could not withdraw from his own enchantment. He came from the cover of the tower and approached her. Though, her quivering smile awaited an embrace which never came.

"Tell the boy… I've gone to promise the dawn that it will await him each morning," he spoke softly. Then with the force of his entire being, brought the pommel of the Mortal Sword to eclipse the early sun. Before the blade could swing towards his stomach, a mighty howl came from above them. All gasped as it was *Binsop* who leaped from the tower's balcony down onto Zephyr, knocking the blazing sword across the ground. The nobleman stood over the fallen man brandishing his own sword. There came a thunder of leather and mail, and from behind the tower came his select band of Pale Order Knights.

"The King shall have your head, not your ashes!" His boots crashed upon the platform's flagstones with a noise like shattering bone, and the trail of fire remained leading to the Mortal Sword. Zephyr turned, breath driven from him, pain flowering across his side… but his eyes flared with disbelief, not at Binsop's presence, but at the desperation in the warrior's face. The Pale Order's vaunted knight, the King's long-trusted wall of steel, now hunted not for honor, but for claim. For glory not earned, but seized.

"You would stop this?" Zephyr said, rising with trembling limbs. "You would risk the Kingdom's ruin for a tale in the court halls?"

Binsop straightened, his blade gleaming like cold justice in his fist. "No more riddles, cursed painter. I've seen the destruction wrought beneath your cowardice. The Princess, bewitched and *stolen*. The City, in ruin. The beast… your shadow, made flesh. The

King will not see you die by your own hand. He will see your blood spilled by *his law*, and I will be the blade that bears it."

Zephyr cast a glance toward the fallen Mortal Sword, its fire now low, flickering, waiting for a wielder. His thoughts tore through each second which passed. Leon's eyes fluttering with breath barely clinging, Alexandria's hands trembling as she stilled his pain. But Binsop raised his blade. "Your tale ends by the King's word, and I... I am the one who speaks it," said Binsop before raising his sword. But... it did not fall. Not before the sharp *thwick* of steel meeting flesh. Zephyr's eyes were pierced shut, his neck still intact. Binsop's arms fell before him, but his own sword remained at the ready. Both men turned, and the high-flame of the Mortal Sword was beaming beside the spine of Alexandria herself, who fell to her knees.

Zephyr shifted himself away from Binsop's stance and hastily got to his feet. He rushed to her side and fell to face her. The nobleman remained frozen and dumbfounded by what he'd seen, for the legacy he wished to solidify meant nothing if the Princess was not protected. Even Yerrib's hands spasmed as she stood in horror, and Tomas's mouth gaped at the sight.

"Alexandria! Alexandria, why've you done this? Oh... my love Alexandria!" Zephyr cried. Blood began to pour like a waterfall onto the ground, and the blade's fire brightened.

"I will not see a new dawn... not without you. But perhaps, in another life?" The Princess struggled to mutter. The flames grew so great that they turned different hues and the

Mortal Sword itself rung with a roaring hum. The light became white, turning from flame to something indistinguishable from the sun. Before Zephyr could intertwine his fingers with hers, static stemmed from the exposed blade protruding from her back and in a deafening barrage, lightning struck it in a million branches of blue light. The ground quaked to it, and all were blinded by it. Once it eventually ended, the Princess of Alexandria fell to her side, her tunic torched to leavings and as smoke curled from her body, the once-blonde hair which always remained perfect and shining, was now burnt to a sunless black. The sword had vanished, and yet the bloody aperture it made remained. The Collector too had gone without a trace, other than the wreckage of its' fight. Zephyr got to his feet and stumbled backward as Binsop and the Pale Order Knights rushed to her. He realized in its absence, that the Collector was satisfied, and the deal was signed. Not by him, but by her.

"Princess!" The great warrior cried, "Oh the Great Princess! She's dead!"

Even Yerrib and Sophie who wanted only but the sword, cried before her. In their skirmish, the cursed painter saw the world turn slowly. Elladanty stood in amazement and terror, her fingers trembling, seeing that the future she saw in the Forest of Centurion was but a fable, a life she did not live and relief washed over her. Despite this, Yerrib and the coven's future also fell, whatever the elder had planned.

From a distant rooftop, a shadowed figure, one of unruly hair and a nearby mare, watched as well. It was Sabbath who had rushed into the Kingdom of Alexandria within that hour and followed the destruction of the Collector, not far from where Zephyr had found rest. But Sabbath, unlike Elladanty, cried for a different cause. Her ruling beside Alexandria would be no longer, and the dark court she sought to lead was now petrified atop the terrace below.

"*The… the wish. It is… it's granted,*" he whispered to himself. Even still, the dread he felt poisoned his tongue. "*Alexandria… oh… my Alexandria.*" In his terrified daze, he thought of nothing else… but to run. Not only find Leon, but to flee the monstrosity of the moment, to perhaps save himself or misremember the morning.

He ran without reason other than to distance himself from the Kingdom, and Tomas followed quickly behind. None of the knights nor Binsop went after him as they could not even pull their eyes from the dead Princess. The City folk had soon come in droves to witness her end and the fall of the Kingdom.

Sweet Alexandria… oh sweet Alexandria

Her eyes… she truly is so beautiful

How has this happened? What had come of her?

Many voices rang in the hoard, but none could decipher how she'd come to this. As Binsop held her scorched arm, he cried into the air. "*Death to Zephyr Solta! Your head will be mine! Your blood will become paint, and the Kingdom of Alexandria will feast on the sight of it!*"

Yerrib had laid beside the Princess too, and cried not for her, but for the sword had vanished. Her hallowed words were entangled with dark magic, for she *could* have leaped for the sword when Binsop pounced upon Zephyr. Though, she knew she wouldn't have been able to make a run for it, and perhaps her plan was flawed from the very beginning. As her bent and skewed fingers caressed the now-black hair of the Princess, she realized one thing to be true; the Mortal Sword returned to its place, and she needed to find it.

Once the Kingdom recovered, and new streets were laid and columns resurrected, the King would seek it as well. If word spread through the varied sects of the Kingdom, many would seek King Univerza in hopes for a wish to be granted. If the Alexandrian House could contain it before anyone else, they could protect all from misconstrued and thorny desires. However he *wouldn't* seek the help of the Mor Empire, for they might utilize the Dead King's power for an even greater rule and withdraw from the shadows in which they are veiled. But King Jean St. Auclaire was no less devious, and the Mortal Sword was no less a weapon belonging to Death himself.

Several physicians, Fleschire, castle-guards, and all officials beneath the King had traveled to where the Princess lay. Order was swiftly made as knights pushed back the crying and screaming folk of the City, allowing the King's own physician Sir Cedric had lifted her body onto the lush bed and concealed her beneath a black velvet blanket. The Pale Order lifted the litter to their shoulders and made their march to the castle where the King would find his daughter turned to a dead root in the bloodline which carried the responsibility of providing prosperity to the Kingdom.

The banners above the city gates were lowered that day, their golden embroidery dulled beneath a sky that wept not with rain, but with silence. A hush deeper than the western sea's stillness fell over the Kingdom of Alexandria, for even the name brought weight upon the shoulders of all. Not since the days of the sea-fared war or skirmishes with the Koba had the cobbled streets and shining halls echoed so little. The Princess was gone. And the Kingdom mourned.

She, who once moved with the grace of ancient queens, her voice masked by bridle and duty alike, had become more than the blood that bore her. She'd fallen beneath the old Alexandria, the first Queen. Her death did not ring like that of a royal, but like that of the end. The very sun, which had lit her blade in its final blaze, seemed dulled now, dimmed by grief. Many questioned the brightness of which she was deemed so odious, and yet so inspiring.

King Jean St. Auclaire did not descend the marble stairs of the throne for a full day. His eyes stared into nothing, lips pursed as if cursed with silence. When at last he approached the velvet-shrouded bier where his daughter's remains lay entombed in oils and incense, he did not speak… not until even the Queen had been ushered away in hysterical tears. Then, with a trembling hand, he lifted the cloth that covered her face. The hair that had once shone like a summer field was blackened, crisped by the lightning of the Mortal Sword. Her brow, unburdened by the mask she wore all her life, looked delicate and sad. Her lips, pale as petals drained of dew, were parted, perhaps caught in the last word she tried to speak. The King gazed upon her uncovered eyes for the first time, and in them saw no enchantment. No curse. No Persuasion. His fist clenched, and his heart radiated anger. He wept not loudly, not in anguish, but like a man who had watched his entire kingdom fall to ash. And then, without request or decree, he knelt beside her. Long did he remain there, until dusk threatened to swallow the palace whole.

In the days that followed, Alexandria's name was sung in reverence. The Coven remained on the castle's grounds with less the task of unbinding folks to her enchantments, but to await the great funeral. The King ordered that her chamber never again be entered. Her mask, the silver bridle she wore since childhood, was not found but a sealed black-marble tomb beneath the palace, locked with arcane sigils by Fleschire himself, awaited it. The wizard's hands trembled as he constructed the magical bind, for he had once held the girl in his arms when she was but a child, unknowing then of what great burden she would carry.

The Yippire Coven was in shock while Yerrib was cloaked in her envy, swore beneath her breath that the Mortal Sword had not vanished, but merely returned to its slumber. She alone knew that one day, another would find it… one who dared wish upon the bones of the First King, the Dead King, Univerza.

Meanwhile, Binsop, once noble in name alone, took to silence. He did not eat, nor speak, nor ride. He had sought glory and found ruin. The tale would not sing his name, but hers… and in every retelling, he would be the shadow that tried to steal her light. He questioned whether he should remain or flee, anticipating that the King would have *his* head once he and the Queen caught their breath and could declare their war against Zephyr.

32. The Forsaken

Crowds wept deep into the night with candles flickering and damp cloth pressed to their nostrils. The garrison of Alexandria guarded the drawbridge tirelessly whilst shoemakers, accountants, and City-librarians led chants for answers of the Princess's death. Miss Toule had tried to reason with the horde, but was whisked away by Fleschire who saw the Kingdom's people grow too chaotic.

None could reach King Jean, not Binsop or any other servant. The King, in his fatness adorned in heavy robes and exotic pelts, kept to a chamber deep within his castle where the most obedient of the Pale Order had brought the Princess to. A funeral guild consisting of just three black-masked elders gathered in the deep chamber to assess Alexandria, along with the Royal Priest and the Royal Physician. They found her wounds, cleaning and fixing her abdomen where the Mortal Sword once was buried. The soot of its lightning washed away and stained the dressings in blood and ash. It was only when she was clean that the King knelt beside her and ordered all servants to vacate.

His heavy fist beat the rail of her coffin, sat atop a marble pedestal. Spit caked his white beard and his less-bruised hand squeezed her lifeless forearm.

"Traitorous fool. You came in solace and leave me here with nothing but this… this blackness. Traitorous," his words softened from a vicious growl to a cry. *"And for it, I will gather the might of all steel and disassemble you until you can but only watch your shins be carried away to a pit of fire. Your eyes, last we carry. The Gods look over you, my dear child Alexandria. Let them. Watch over your father as he embarks on Hell, for the spears and traps of it will all be trampled, and I will need your voice as sedative."*

The King knelt beside Alexandria for some time as the evening spoiled and the light which radiated from the mosaic windows turned cobalt. It was silent in the chamber, less his weeping and the drip of oil from a mounted sconce. The Princess lay in a cushioned bed, wearing the same dress she did when she died. Fleschire felt it was time to approach the King, pull him away from his daughter in order to tend to supper.

"Jean, there's little daylight left. Shall we arrange dinner?" The Grand Wizard asked, walking slowly toward the King with his hands calmly clasped, his violet cloak sweeping the cobblestone behind him.

"If the Queen is inquiring, then feed her. I'm not leaving her, just to cool and *rot*. I relieve you of your evening duties," said the King. His heavy voice echoed and Fleschire turned back to the archway. Before his departure, he walked back to the King and placed his hand atop his wide shoulder.

"We'll find him," he said lowly. "That Solta-man. Do you still wish him dead on sight?"

The King was silent but for a moment, never looking at the wizard.

"Bring him before me, and he will face the council."

"Of course. And… her? Will you present her tomorrow? Her skin is… scorched. Her dress, hair. All but perfect."

The King growled and thrashed away from Fleschire.

"She is the daughter of I, and thus she *is* perfect. Our people will see my daughter and memorialize her. Get on with it…. get out of here!"

Fleschire did as he demanded, and went up the coiled stairwell to relay orders for supper for the Queen.

Three veil-faced undertakers were swift to prepare her coffin when the King had finally left her side. While he was escorted by his tired Queen to bed, the undertakers lifted Alexandria into her new bed, one of polished marble and gold adornments. Per the King's request, she remained with soot on her skin and dress. The blonde of her hair had only kept to the curly ends, while the bulk of her head was blackened, her face smudged with ash. Her dress had a similar gradient, whereas the end was blood-red but turned dark as the fabric reached her abdomen. Her limbs were remarkable but for the stitched wound at her thigh and the black-soot of her hands.

The castle's lower halls breathed with mildew and silence, where torchlight seemed to cling reluctantly to the stone, leaving whole portions of the corridor steeped in shadow. Grand Wizard

Fleschire walked with his hands folded behind his back, the velvet hems of his robe dragging damp trails upon the floor. Beside him shuffled Lord Anselm, one of the king's quieter advisors, a man better suited for quill and scroll than for the midnight wanderings of wizards.

Their path was one seldom walked, a service corridor connecting the king's eastern quarters to the bowels of the keep. The air was heavy here, cool as a crypt. Yet the wizard's sharp eyes caught the anomaly at once.

"Still your step," Fleschire commanded, raising his palm. His voice echoed, more a command to the corridor itself than to Anselm. There it lay: an unassuming book, splayed on the flagstones as though dropped from careless fingers. But Fleschire knew at once: *nothing in these halls was careless.*

He stooped, his long white fingers brushing the leather cover. Its spine was unmarked, but the front bore a title stamped in gold leaf, worn and dulled by time:

"The Boy Who Painted Kings Too Poorly."

Anselm chuckled nervously. "A child's toy, no doubt. Perhaps one of the servants'...."

"Silence." Fleschire's voice cut like flint. His eyes narrowed, his nostrils flaring as he turned the weight of his wizard's senses upon the book. The air around it shimmered faintly, as if the torchlight itself bent unnaturally over its cover. He felt it in his marrow: the book was *not of this plane.*

"This is no servant's relic," Fleschire whispered, more to himself. "This was left. Deliberately." He flipped the cover, only to find the pages blank save for faint indentations, like words had been erased or devoured. He closed it quickly, his jaw tightening. "Not even the erasures of our world's ink behave so."

Anselm swallowed, pale in the dim light. "What does it mean, sir?"

"It *means*," Fleschire said, straightening, the book now in his grasp, "that something… or *someone*… has pierced the seam of this reality, and seeks to leave me a message. The specificity of its jab, the mocking of artistry and royalty alike… no, Anselm, this was no accident." His voice deepened, gaining that eerie resonance wizards spoke with when arcane certainty guided their thought. "This is a lure. A mirror, or perhaps… a prophecy."

The advisor's lips trembled. "What shall you do with it?"

Fleschire turned the book in his hand, as if it burned him to hold it. His eyes glimmered beneath the hood of his brow. "Deliver it to the Yippire Coven," he said firmly. "They are crass and revolting, but their hex-power might unravel its tether, might trace the shadow that planted this little jest in the king's very bones of stone."

"You will not study it yourself?"

Fleschire's laugh was hollow, without humor. "Study it? No, Anselm. I am not fool enough to stare too long into something that *stares back*." He thrust the book into the lord's hands. The leather was damp, unnaturally cold, and Anselm flinched.

"Go," Fleschire ordered, his tone heavy with arcane weight. "And see it reaches Yerrib's hand before dawn. If there is rot beneath the foundation of this castle, I intend to smell it before it spreads."

As Anselm hurried off with the cursed storybook pressed to his chest, Fleschire lingered in the shadows of the corridor. His eyes traced the stones where it had lain, and for the briefest moment, he thought he saw a shimmer, a child's scrawl etched into the stone, faint as breath on glass:

He will paint you poorly, too. The wizard clenched his staff until it cracked.

"Not while I draw breath," he muttered, and turned sharply into the dark.

Within the guest quarters of the castle, a hearth had burned a low flame, its red tongue now a whisper along the logs. Shadows danced across the tapestried walls of the *Hexward* hall, a distant limb of the castle where the Yippire witches were told to stay. Their plump bodies cast long and twisted silhouettes which seemed to dance while each of them laid across beds and cushions, just a form of their archaic-hex abilities. But after but a few moments, even their shadows fell to mourn.

Yerrib the elder sat hunched in the center of the chamber, her cane forgotten at her side. Her thick, gnarled fingers were pressed into the folds of her black gown, clutching it like a drowning woman might cling to driftwood. Her eyes, pale as rotted pearl, stared blankly into the embers.

"This is horrid," she whispered at last, her voice broken like frostbitten bark, "horrid, horrid, horrid! I cannot believe the audacity of the young woman. The future was so *vast,* so beautiful! Had my dear Alexandria just kept her eyes shut, we… I mean, *she* could have made such a wonderful queen."

Merich Biddlephi, who had seldom looked up since her death, merely rocked in place. The blindness in her sockets seemed haunted, like the darkness had spread deeper than flesh, into her soul. Margaret Thistle sat quietly at her feet, combing her fingers anxiously through a length of twine, her mouth thin with worry.

Miss Sophie Spirally poured herself a cup of black wine from the carafe. Her jaw twitched when she drank, though she masked it behind one of her pleasant, porcelain smiles. "We don't know that what you saw was *the only* future, Yerrib," she offered gently. "The Centurion sap… it reveals all manner of lives. Perhaps it was but a dream in the… in the broth."

Yerrib let out a single, sharp breath and maybe *accidentally* explained herself. "It was *our* future! All three of us. I saw it so clear, like the sky before storm! A kingdom *wreathed* in bloodroot and shade, ruled by those we birth, moon-wane and curse. *We were to inherit what men had spoiled.* And now," she added with venom, "the one who would've bound it all together has flung herself into Death's arms like a lovesick girl."

Yerrib's arms fell to her side and she collapsed in a pout. Miss Sophie and Margaret tended to her, wiping her poisoned tears. Across the chamber, seated on a stool beneath the narrow lancet window, Elladanty said nothing. Her fingers, folded neatly in her lap, trembled not with grief.... but relief.

In her own silence, she remembered what *she* had seen in the Centurion sap: a masked Alexandria, crown glowing like a seared wound, seated upon a throne of twisted bones and thorny stems. And beside her... *herself*, no longer meek, no longer afraid, but cloaked in silver and garnet, her voice a song that bent cities. And in that life... in that cursed, future kingdom, her eyes had not been her own.

"I think," Elladanty said suddenly, her voice quiet but steady, "that what we saw was not fate. It may be for the best."

All heads turned. The hearth gave a soft crackle. Yerrib's jaw stiffened.

"You dare speak like that, girl?" she rasped. "Do you not *mourn* her? That princess bore the eyes of destiny. *She was meant to lead us to immortality.*"

Elladanty met her gaze coolly. "She was meant to break us all. Perhaps all who remain below her. Now that she's gone, we may all be better off."

Miss Sophie shifted in her seat. "Ella, not now...."

"No," Elladanty stood, the sleeves of her pale-pink robe sliding down her wrists as she waved a finger. "I saw it too! The same vision as Yerrib. And I saw what it made me. *What it made her.* That throne? It came at the cost of thousands. The mask, the crown, the bleeding sky… *none of it was noble.* It was ruin wrapped in silk. Immortality shall only arrive after you've scorched the earth and there's no one left!"

Yerrib's lip curled. "You… are a child."

"I am your future," Elladanty replied, her voice darkening. "Or I was. But Alexandria made her choice. She undid that future by her death. And I…. I'm glad for it."

A silence fell so dense even the castle stones seemed to hush.

"Blasphemy," muttered Merich, though her tone held no weight.

Margaret stopped twisting her twine.

Yerrib stared at Elladanty, as if seeing her for the first time.

"No one," Elladanty said softly, stepping forward now, "asked what *our* place would have been in that vision. You saw power. I saw prison. I did *not* see liberty."

She looked to Sophie, her mother, whose eyes now shimmered with a thousand unreadable thoughts.

"You always told me the tree shows truth," Elladanty whispered. "But truth doesn't mean right. And now, we're better for it," she concluded. Then she turned, walking calmly to the door, letting her bare feet whisper against the stone.

Fury and anger filled the room, and as Yerrib stood upright, though wobbly, she let an amber force build in her palm. It was quick, but before she could strike the young witch, Elladanty could sense the heat. She turned with but a moment's notice and threw a silvery-cold bolt from her own palm. The force and speed of it knocked the old Yerrib to the floor. The other witches, including her own mother, rushed beside the elder and scolded Elladanty. Then, Miss Sophie stood before her.

"I don't know what's gotten into you, Ella. But you've done far too much. I am *very* disappointed in you," she said to her daughter in a low admonishing voice.

"Then so be it! You're no better than Yerrib, you insufferable hag!"

Her mother gasped and her eyes shot open, astonished that her daughter, the otherwise quiet and dainty Elladanty, could be so vicious. The elder witches were silent and frozen in place. But Sophie had to respond, and Yerrib anticipated she would. Her rotted teeth nearly broke from the pressure of grinding together. When Elladanty turned in a huff to make her dramatic exit, Sophie's anger had finally turned red-hot. She threw her arms forward and in the same motion, sent a violent rush of red-energy toward her daughter. For Elladanty, the world around her launched, relocating her to the middle of a field, far from the inn. Surrounded by the cool of night, with no firelight or structure but for hills and distant forest, she screamed at the top of her lungs. While she cursed her mother, she struck the ground repeatedly with fiery bolts.

In the same vein of anguish and vex, the nobleman Binsop hurried to his quarters not far from the Alexandrian castle. Once the King would gather himself come dawn, Binsop knew his head would be placed over straw. He gathered shining swords fixed above a fireplace. The boar's head in the center mocked him. His lady came into the hall and watched as he frantically packed.

"What is it, Binsop? I told ye to spend less time on the pint; who do you owe now?" She pointed a finger. Her blouse glowed in the firelight, a woolen shawl cocooning her other arm.

Binsop took a short blade to his beard, which was braided down to his collar. He tore off the dangling bit, tossing it into the flames. "Perhaps I'm too old in my age, my love. I do not deserve this title bestowed upon me."

"What is it?" She approached him.

"I've failed once more, and now I see no greater path here. A peasant man, a bastard, he's *bested* me, murdered the Princess." The cadence in his voice swung, "and because I failed to protect her, I believe that my life is in danger. We must be swift."

"The *Princess* is *dead*?" Her voice rung. "But… but what does this mean, Binsop? They'll capture you! They'll capture *us*! What have you done?"

Binsop took a heavy step toward her, but stopped himself. "Take this," he presented a decorative dagger which had never seen blood, much less an argument. "We'll… make do."

Binsop arranged a carriage that night, fleeing with his wife away from Alexandria northward to the great lands of Taria.

"What good will that serve us?" His wife asked, her faced hidden in the dark of night.

"The council will protect us. I can't let anything happen to us, you understand?" Binsop told her in a hush. She sighed, her anxiety flourishing. The late journey would be silent from then on, for not even the once-great warrior could entertain her.

Epilogue

Tomas tramped the broken avenues like a ghost in his own skin, his boots blackened, his eyes sunken. He had searched for Willa among the rubble and the wailing survivors, called her name until his throat was raw, until the knights and watchers told him to move on, calling him the drunk he was normally. He combed the fields outside the Guardant Wall, through woods where herds of fat caters waddled ahead of nomadic Greenfolk. They watched him with suspicion, over hills silvered with frost. Every farmhouse and cottage he passed he inquired after her, his voice weary but desperate, the answer always the same: *no one had seen such a girl.*

Three days passed and the world had gone dry. His hope, once stubborn as stone, crumbled to dust with every fruitless step. At length he stumbled back into the countryside's darker fringes, back to the places where his grief could be drowned. The stumpy man Sticks was bothered on two occasions, offering nothing but hypnotic bog-spells and tiny literature which Tomas stomped into the dirt.

Once he found himself back at the tavern where he once frequented, but now less her, even Eldric, who had not since returned from his task of clearing a northward village of Koba. Smoke clung to the rafters, ale sloshed from cracked mugs, laughter rose from filthy tables where games of dice played on. Tomas pushed through the crowd like a man already heavy in drink though his throat had not yet tasted the sour brew. He found his corner, ordered heavy, and let the ale burn its way down, mug after mug until he was loose enough to speak words he didn't mean to farmers he couldn't recall if he knew or not.

By the hour's turn he had found himself leaning on two women, sturdy, broad-hipped maidens who looked half his age. His eyes were dull, his grin foolish. He spoke with bravado that reeked of desperation, of a man performing for his own denial.

"Two beauties in one night," he slurred, his breath ripe with drink. "Fate has finally smiled on old Tomas Broadmere."

The maidens looked at him with disgust, shifting their shoulders away. "You stink of grief and sweat," one said sharply, dabbing her bodice where his hand had strayed. "Find your solace elsewhere, *fool.*"

Their scorn bit sharper than he wished, though he only laughed to disguise the wound. The laughter cracked at its edges, and beneath it his voice shook. His anger for Alexandria returned in the drunken haunting. "You've no idea what I've lost. *My sister...* gone! The best of me... vanished like smoke. Forbidden from this land by that wretched porcelain mutt! " He lifted the mug again, spilling half of it down his shirt as he drank.

The tavern's door groaned open then, a draft pulling across the floor. Tomas barely turned his head, thinking it some farmer or retired guard seeking warmth. But the sound was not of boots, but far softer and barely creaked the floor. His bleary eyes widened when he saw her. *Willa.*

She stood in the doorway, framed by lamplight and shadows. Her once shining curly hair, tangled from days of wandering in hot noon and freezing nights, fell across her shoulders in knotted bronze waves. Her face was pale but no longer vacant, no longer bound by that unnatural calm Persuasion wrought. Her eyes… her own eyes… were exhausted from fear.

The mug slipped from Tomas's hand and clattered to the floor. "Willa?" he whispered as spit ran down his chin, then louder, almost shouting, "*Willa!*"

The tavern grew quiet around him, all eyes turning. She moved toward him, unsteady but certain, her gaze never leaving his. For days he had pictured her broken, lost to enchantment or worse. Now she was here, flesh and breath before him. "How?" Tomas demanded, rising to his feet so quickly the table overturned. "By the gods, how? Persuasion… it can't be undone save by hex. Everyone knows it!" He reached for her arms, holding her as though she might vanish again. To his dismay, she was frail and her hands light.

Willa's voice was quiet but steady. "I don't know," she confessed. "I walked. And walked. Through fields, through rain. Every step farther from her. Then… I could stop." Her eyes flicked around the tavern, at the gaping faces, the spilled ale, her brother's drunken ruin. "Zephyr… Leon. Where are they?"

Tomas staggered back a step, half laughing, half weeping. "Alive" he repeated, tasting the word like a miracle. His drunkenness seemed to drain from him in that moment, sobered by her presence. He clutched her hand, rough and calloused from her wandering, as though it anchored him to the world again. He did not need to explain the rest there. He brought her to a seat to rest.

The tavern stirred once more, mugs lifted, dice rolling, laughter resuming. But at that table, beneath the dim lanternlight, Tomas and Willa remained fixed, staring at one another across the gulf of days lost. Once she'd gotten a half-loaf of bread and water, Tomas escorted her to their cottage where she'd finally sleep.

Not all who lay cold that night remained asleep, however. Although the castle was finally quiet, subtly riddled with the reverberating snore of King Jean, a creaking sound echoed through the deep chambers. A patrolling guard had just stepped into the courtyard after many hours of wandering the cavernous bellows when the sound came. Not a soul heard it, so it went unattended. The creaking came from a vaulted room, the sound of someone *waking* up. The wooden container from which they slept bent and groaned as they slowly sat upright, their silhouette burning behind two mounted torches. Then… a worried panting, a sobbing, heavy breaths. Hands elevated and trembling, the awoken figure crept out of their cushioned containment, standing in the glow, further inspecting their… their *burnt* body. Blackened hands and forearms, scorched feet, a cold and damp core. Their hair…

perfectly blonde and curled at the ends but… black as soot thereafter leading to the scalp. Though terrified of her own condition, the silhouette graced their white gown with delicate icy fingers.

She was not happy, not with the shivers, not with the empty room, not in her gown. She turned away from the light and towards the heavy door, finding a familiar body hoisted upon a wooden cross. A red dress, or lack-thereof. The bottom was a clean garnet color, but faded to a blasted-black abdomen with holes and tears. Angrily, she marched to the dress and exchanged her gown for it, relieved once its tattered satin fell over her body.

Upon a small wooden table beside the cross sat something that she thought to be a part of her. *The Mask…* she grabbed it, unaware of how it was found. Though, she was also unaware of how she'd arrived in this place. The memories were stab-wounds, and she pondered little before pulling the heavy door inward and crept into the castles organ.

The once-dead Princess was burning from inside as she stumbled into the unattended gardens behind the northwest corner of the castle. The world was dim, edges of tree canopies an illuminated silver from the moonlight. Alexandria began to cry uncontrollably, believing herself to be a laggard, or in hell. Perhaps she was a ghost, but few in Grasp believed in such an afterlife.

She thought of what to do, where to go. But only one destination filled her crystallizing mind. *Zephyr.* His name fell cold from her lips when she whispered it, and heat finally began to build in her core and her scorched palms. Alexandria had left him on the terrace with the Collector and knights, the coven too. She did not stop to think what would come of him if she sacrificed herself with the Mortal Sword, unaware if it would spare him.

In a frail yet determined mutter,

I must find him.

A Word from the Author

The Princess & The Painter is an immense project of mine, one I spent many years developing, scrapping, rebuilding. But in the end I found the original story, the one I would tell young campers in remote excursions in Manitoba, to only require an explanation of the world. The tale I would tell was derived from one of many dreams I've documented over the years, a simple story of a man's quest to save his dying son by making a deal with a mythical figure with conditions and caveats not disclosed. The story was special to me only because of its uniqueness, telling of one's adventure with love as a byproduct of the task at hand. Even then, the romance is twisted.

I would like to acknowledge all of those who took time out of their busy schedules to read through this story, providing incredible feedback which improved many sections. I would also like to acknowledge my fiance, my father, my friends, for dealing with my nonstop barrage of conceptual artwork to identify what fit the book best. One important lesson I learned was to stick with what felt like *me*, and not settle for anything less.

I anticipate *The Princess & The Painter* to be the first of three installments within the **A Vow of Time Again** series, and I say that with confidence knowing that well before completion of this story, I already had a blueprint and narrative planned out to finish the story. No stretching, no reaching.

I've written stories dating back to… well… elementary school where I (unsuccessfully) participated in the Auburn Book Project with picture-books under titles like: *The Highaway Mountain* and *Salt & Pepper*. Of course they were goofy and indifferent from any other ten-year-old's book, but to me they were highly visualized and in that sense, it was as though I was creating my own movies. Go on to Edward Little High School, I wrote *Dogwood* entirely derived from real experiences from many trips in the Canadian wilderness. I self-published that title with high confidence in the narrative, but little confidence in the editing and physical quality as I lacked any and all resources at seventeen. I do wish to update that book along with the sequel, *The Blonde Rapids*, and inevitably write the final installment, *Camp Summit*. But for now, I'm crossing off what is most relevant in my head. *Sisters of Krythia*, and *The Sky Gardener*. Though, I am increasingly excited for a future series that deals in horror, but I will keep that under-wraps for now.

Thank you all again, my family, friends, strangers who gave the rough copies a shot, thank you.